WINGS OF FIRE

THE DRAGONET PROPHECY
THE GRAPHIC NOVEL

For Jonah, my little bigwings.
—T.T.S.

This book is dedicated, as always and forever,
to Meredith, and to our pets, Heidi the dog and
Ella the cat, whose personalities and poses can
be found all throughout this book.
—M.H.

Story and text copyright © 2018 by Tui T. Sutherland
Adaptation by Barry Deutsch
Map and border design © 2012 by Mike Schley
Art by Mike Holmes © 2018 by Scholastic Inc.

Library of Congress Control Number Available

ISBN 978-0-545-94216-4 (hardcover)
ISBN 978-0-545-94215-7 (paperback)

10 9 8 7 6 5 4   19 20 21 22

Printed in China   62
First edition, January 2018
Edited by Amanda Maciel
Lettering by John Green
Book design by Phil Falco
Creative Director: David Saylor

WINGS OF FIRE

THE DRAGONET PROPHECY
THE GRAPHIC NOVEL

BY **TUI T. SUTHERLAND**

ADAPTED BY **BARRY DEUTSCH**
ART BY **MIKE HOLMES**
COLOR BY **MAARTA LAIHO**

graphix
AN IMPRINT OF
SCHOLASTIC

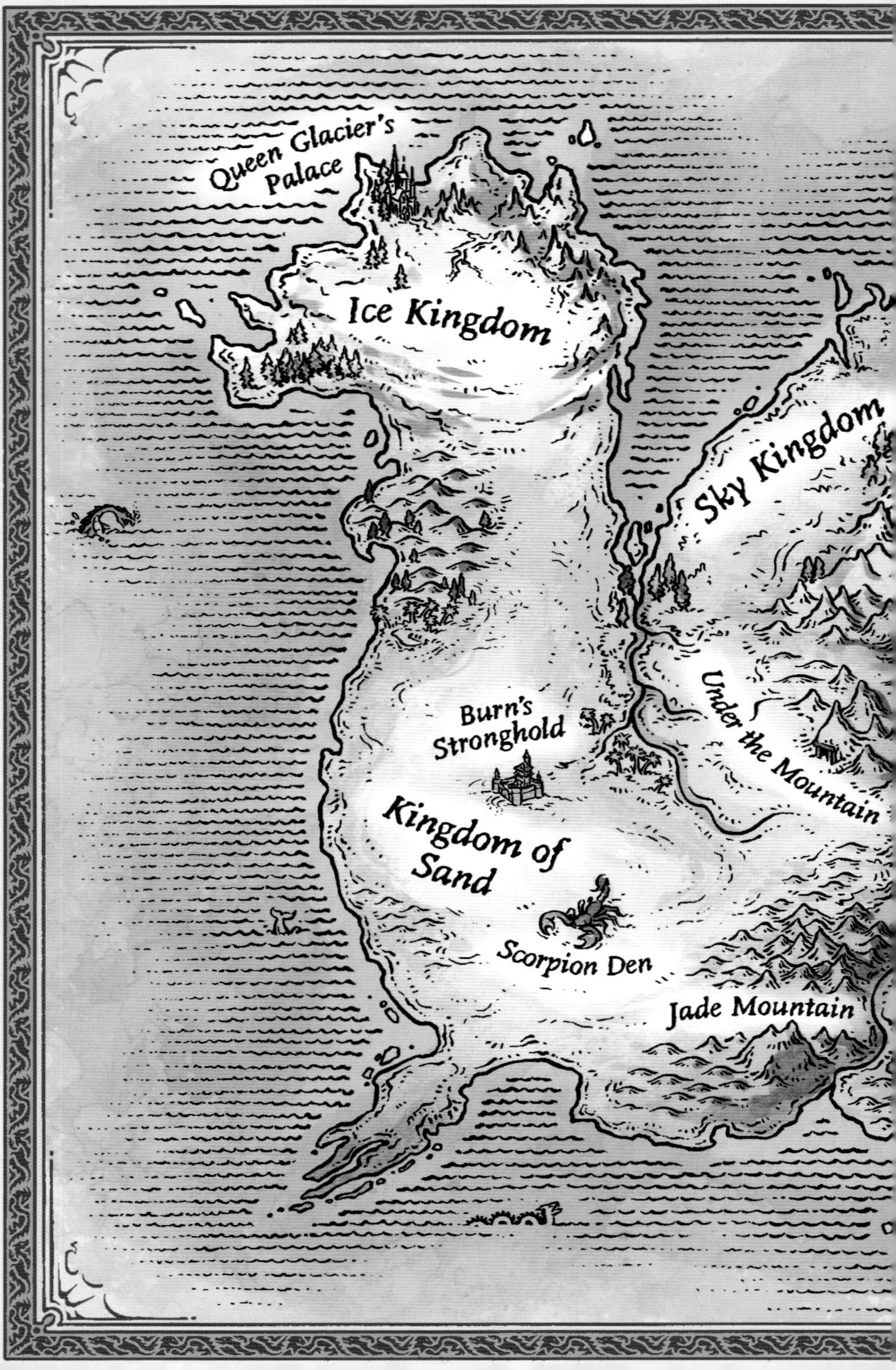

Queen Glacier's Palace
Ice Kingdom
Sky Kingdom
Burn's Stronghold
Under the Mountain
Kingdom of Sand
Scorpion Den
Jade Mountain

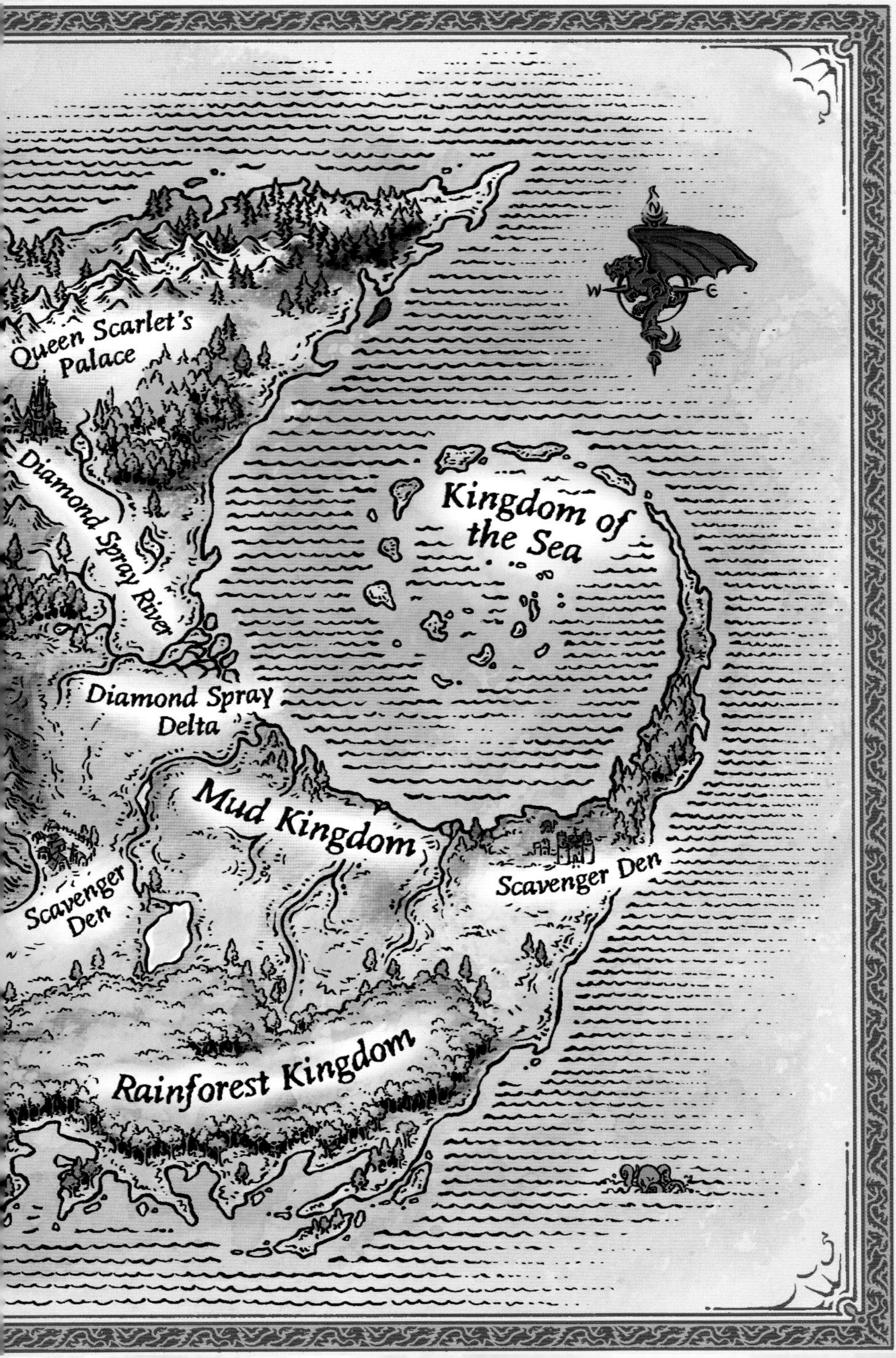
Queen Scarlet's Palace
Diamond Spray River
Diamond Spray Delta
Kingdom of the Sea
Mud Kingdom
Scavenger Den
Scavenger Den
Rainforest Kingdom
W
E
N

Queen Glacier's
Palace

Ice Kingdom

Sky Kingdom

Under the Mountain

Burn's
Stronghold

Kingdom of
Sand

Scorpion Den

Jade Mountain

THE DRAGONET
PROPHECY

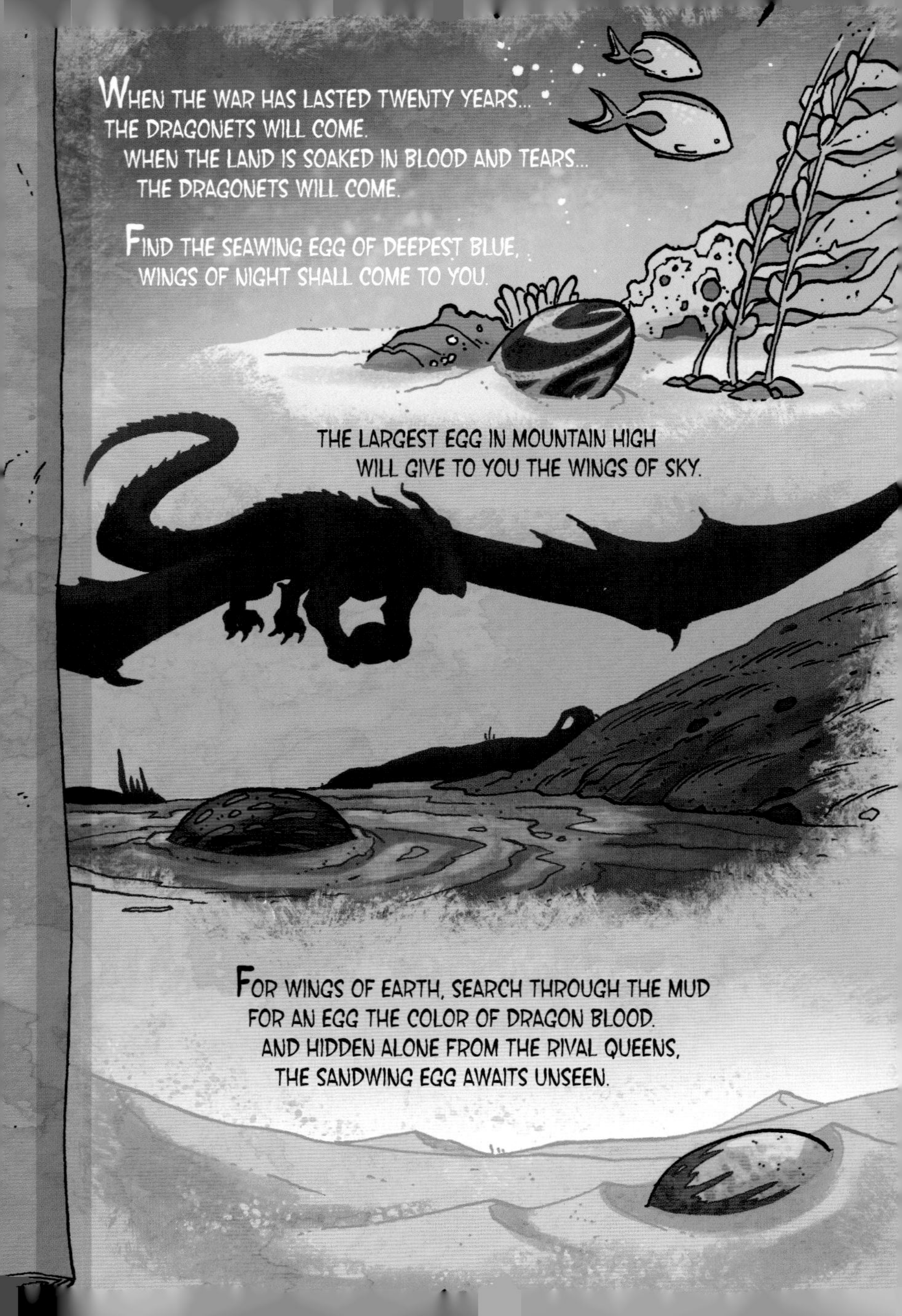
WHEN THE WAR HAS LASTED TWENTY YEARS...
THE DRAGONETS WILL COME.
WHEN THE LAND IS SOAKED IN BLOOD AND TEARS...
THE DRAGONETS WILL COME.
FIND THE SEAWING EGG OF DEEPEST BLUE,
WINGS OF NIGHT SHALL COME TO YOU.
THE LARGEST EGG IN MOUNTAIN HIGH
WILL GIVE TO YOU THE WINGS OF SKY.
FOR WINGS OF EARTH, SEARCH THROUGH THE MUD
FOR AN EGG THE COLOR OF DRAGON BLOOD.
AND HIDDEN ALONE FROM THE RIVAL QUEENS,
THE SANDWING EGG AWAITS UNSEEN.

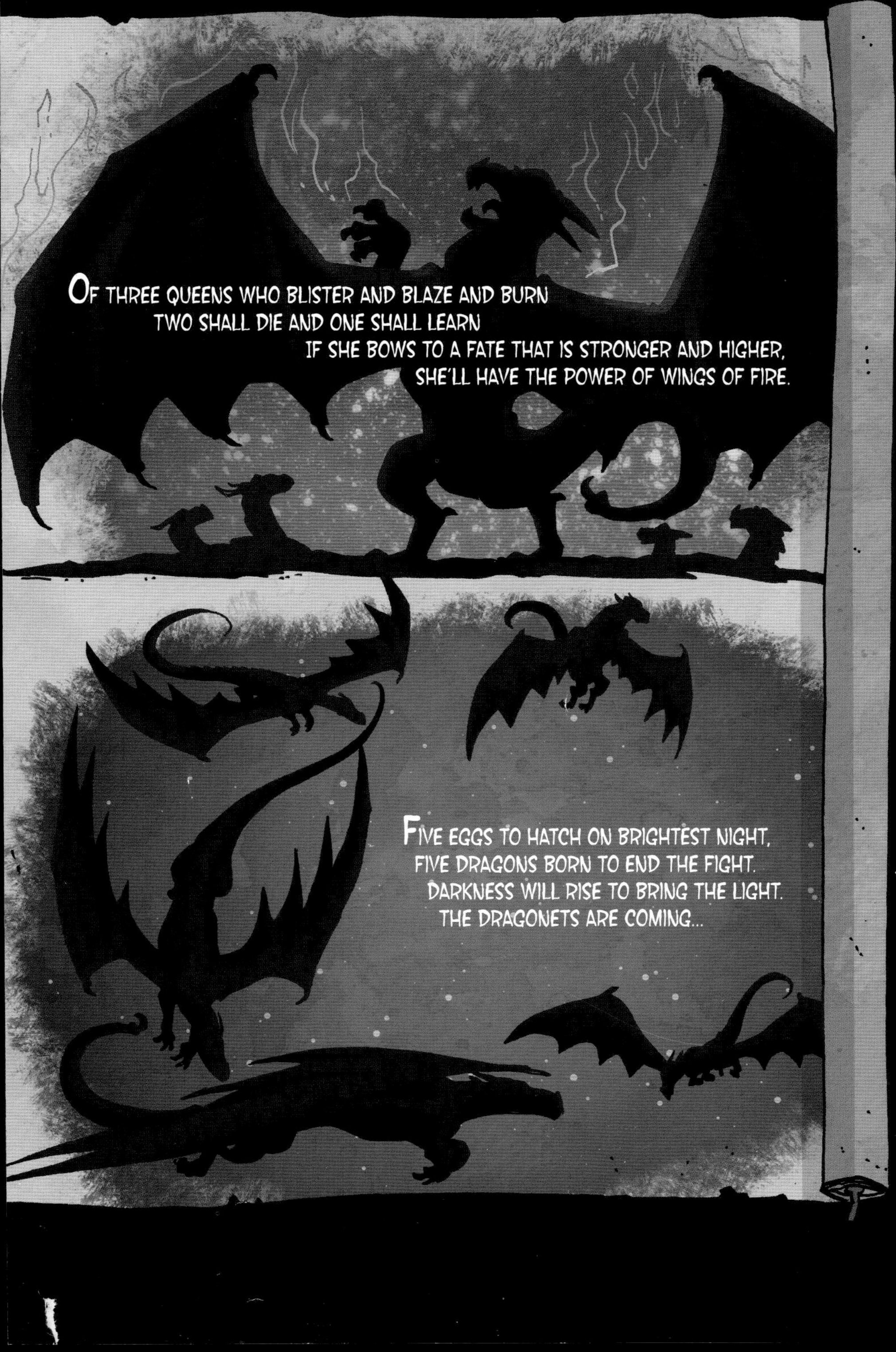
OF THREE QUEENS WHO BLISTER AND BLAZE AND BURN
TWO SHALL DIE AND ONE SHALL LEARN
IF SHE BOWS TO A FATE THAT IS STRONGER AND HIGHER,
SHE'LL HAVE THE POWER OF WINGS OF FIRE.
FIVE EGGS TO HATCH ON BRIGHTEST NIGHT,
FIVE DRAGONS BORN TO END THE FIGHT.
DARKNESS WILL RISE TO BRING THE LIGHT.
THE DRAGONETS ARE COMING...

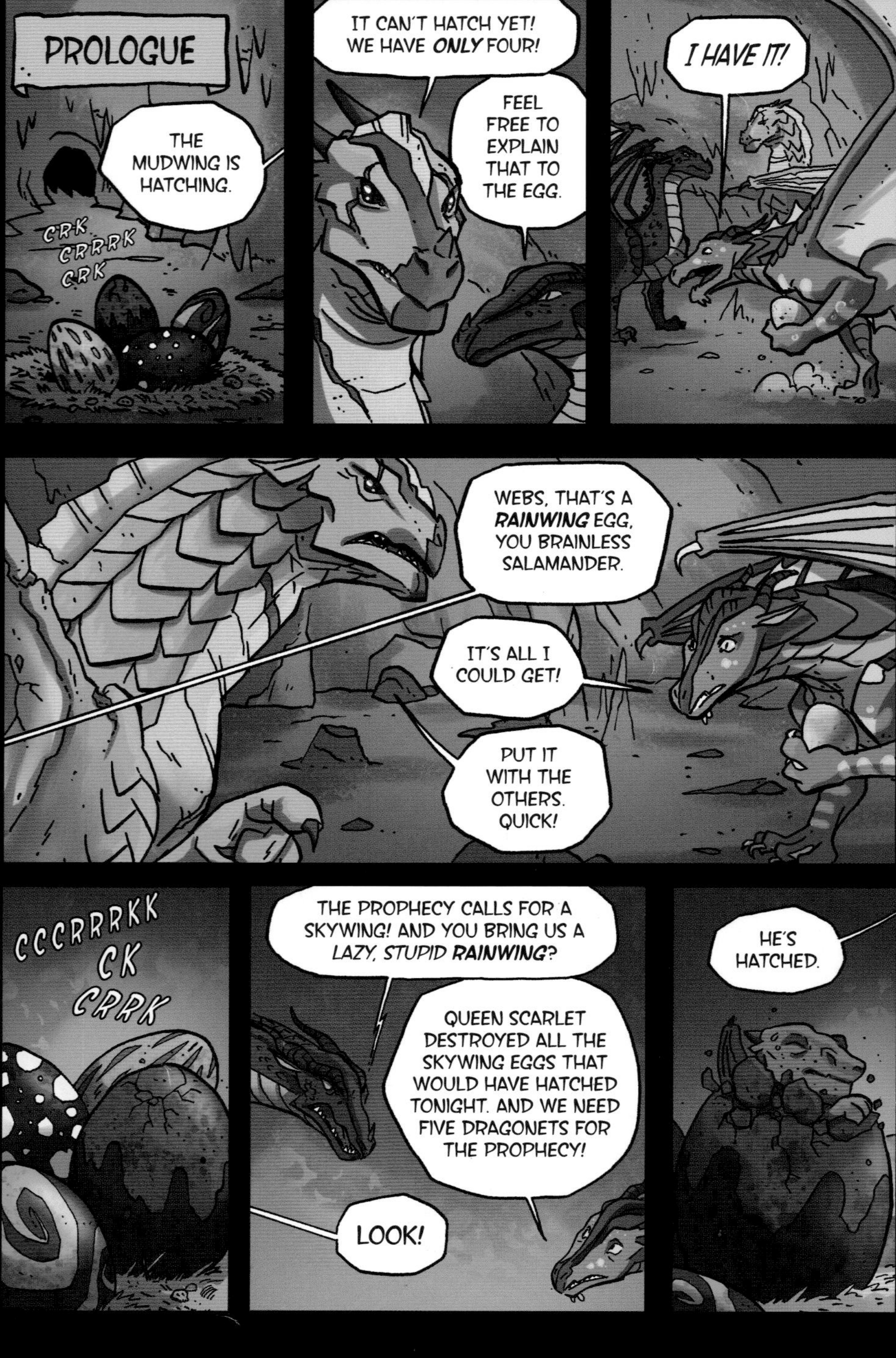
PROLOGUE
THE MUDWING IS HATCHING.
CRK CRRRK CRK
IT CAN'T HATCH YET! WE HAVE ONLY FOUR!
FEEL FREE TO EXPLAIN THAT TO THE EGG.
I HAVE IT!
WEBS, THAT'S A RAINWING EGG, YOU BRAINLESS SALAMANDER.
IT'S ALL I COULD GET!
PUT IT WITH THE OTHERS. QUICK!
CCCRRRKK CK CRRK
THE PROPHECY CALLS FOR A SKYWING! AND YOU BRING US A LAZY, STUPID RAINWING?
QUEEN SCARLET DESTROYED ALL THE SKYWING EGGS THAT WOULD HAVE HATCHED TONIGHT. AND WE NEED FIVE DRAGONETS FOR THE PROPHECY!
LOOK!
HE'S HATCHED.

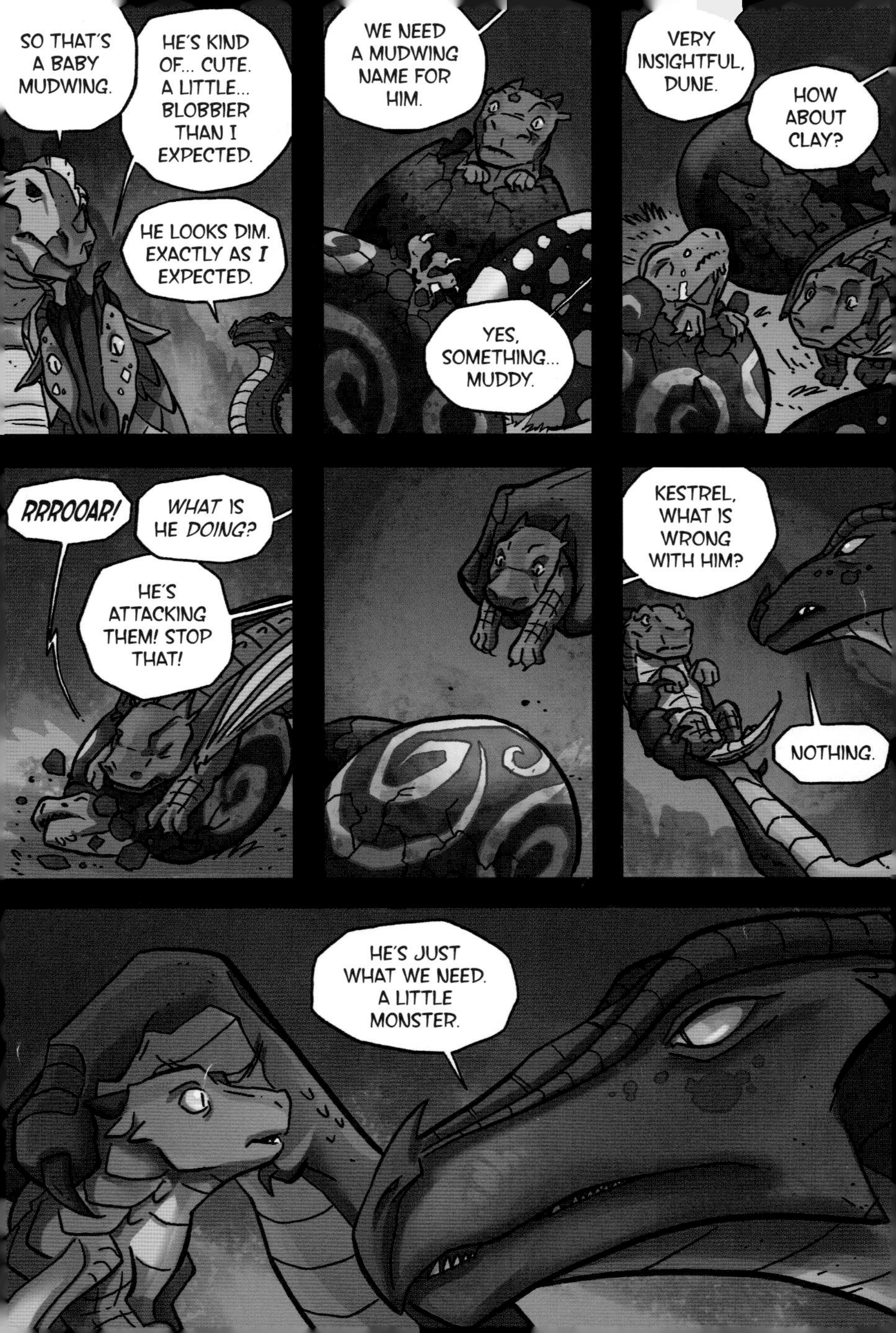
SO THAT'S A BABY MUDWING.
HE'S KIND OF... CUTE. A LITTLE... BLOBBIER THAN I EXPECTED.
HE LOOKS DIM. EXACTLY AS *I* EXPECTED.
WE NEED A MUDWING NAME FOR HIM.
YES, SOMETHING... MUDDY.
VERY INSIGHTFUL, DUNE.
HOW ABOUT CLAY?
RRRROOAR!
WHAT IS HE *DOING?*
HE'S ATTACKING THEM! STOP THAT!
KESTREL, WHAT IS WRONG WITH HIM?
NOTHING.
HE'S JUST WHAT WE NEED. A LITTLE MONSTER.

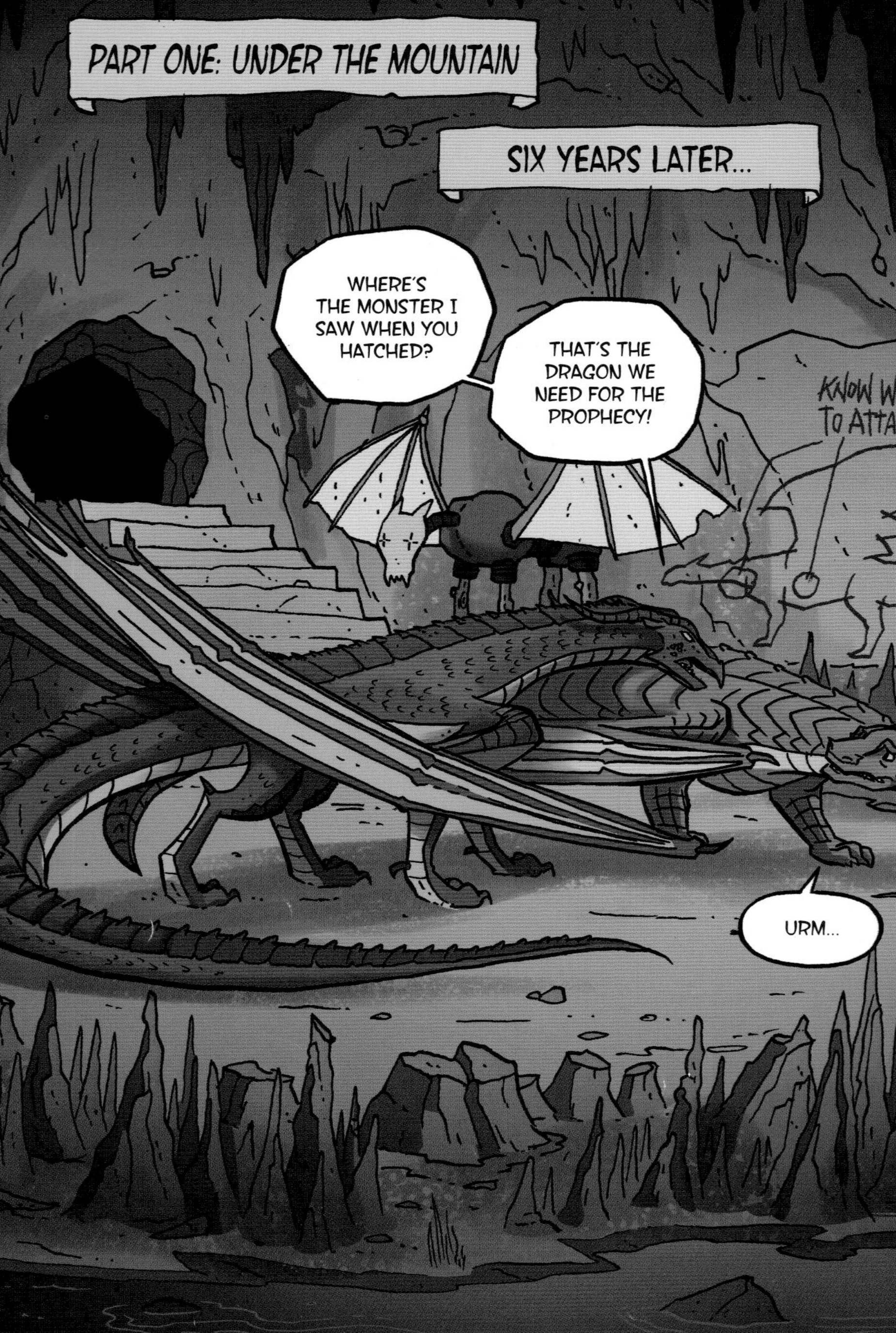
PART ONE: UNDER THE MOUNTAIN
SIX YEARS LATER...
WHERE'S THE MONSTER I SAW WHEN YOU HATCHED?
THAT'S THE DRAGON WE NEED FOR THE PROPHECY!
URM...

FIGHT!
I'M TRYING! MAYBE IF WE COULD STOP AND TALK—
OW! YOU SAID STOMPING TAILS WAS CHEATING!
I'M YOUR TEACHER. NOTHING I DO IS CHEATING.
ROLL RIGHT! USE YOUR FIRE!
FIGHT!
MAYBE WE COULD TRY FIGHTING WITHOUT ALL THE SHOUTING AND SEE—
UGH!

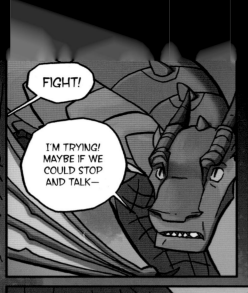

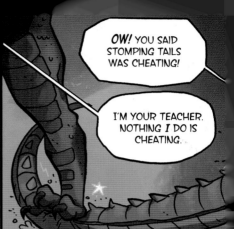

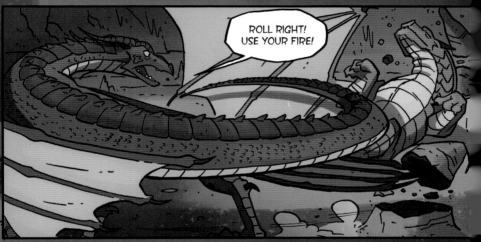

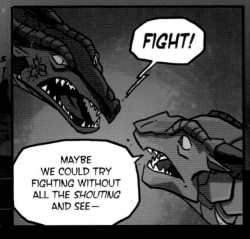

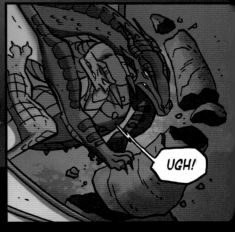

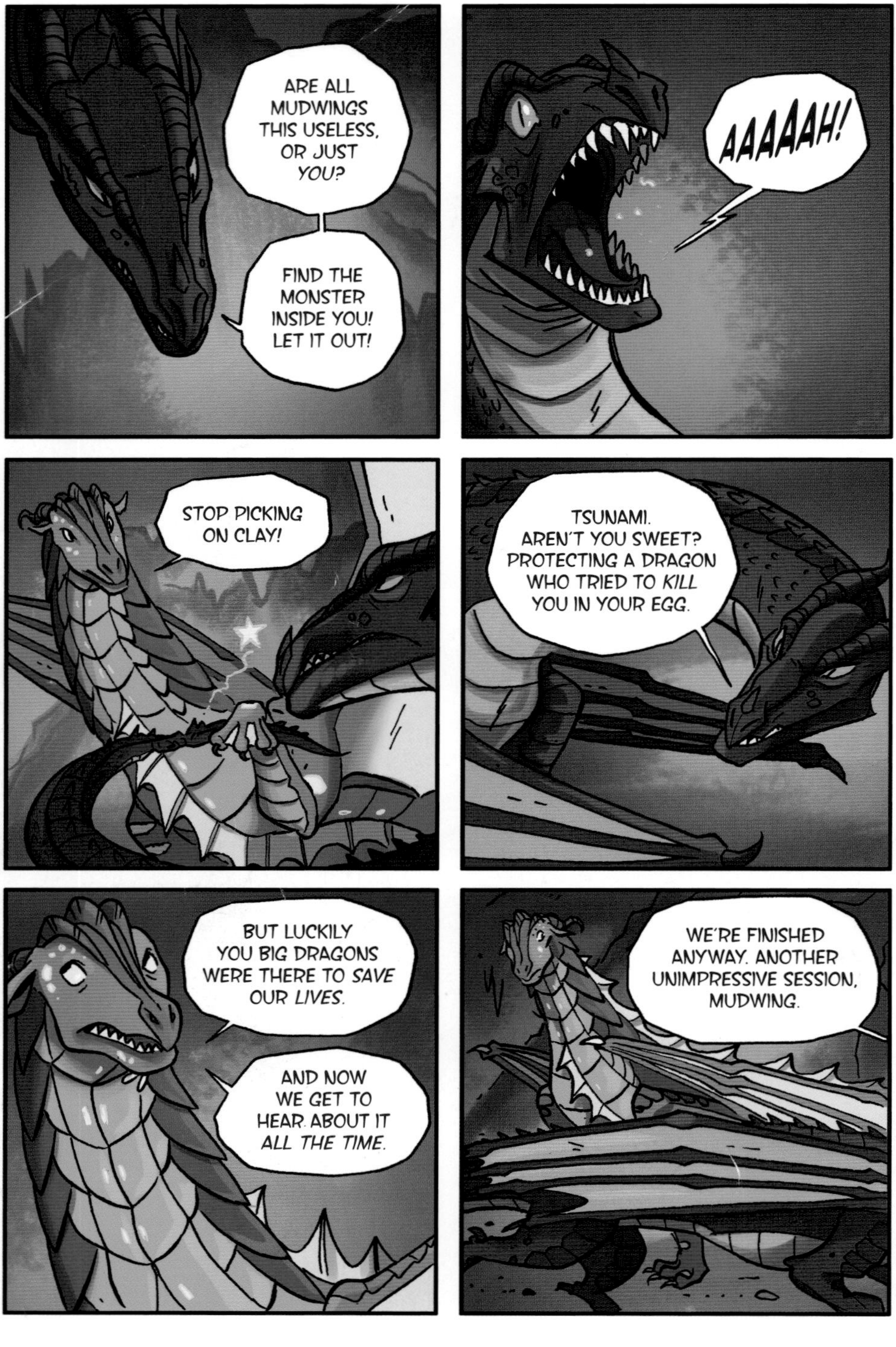
ARE ALL MUDWINGS THIS USELESS, OR JUST *YOU?*
FIND THE MONSTER INSIDE YOU! LET IT OUT!
AAAAAH!
STOP PICKING ON CLAY!
TSUNAMI. AREN'T YOU SWEET? PROTECTING A DRAGON WHO TRIED TO *KILL* YOU IN YOUR EGG.
BUT LUCKILY YOU BIG DRAGONS WERE THERE TO *SAVE* OUR *LIVES*.
AND NOW WE GET TO HEAR ABOUT IT *ALL THE TIME*.
WE'RE FINISHED ANYWAY. ANOTHER UNIMPRESSIVE SESSION, MUDWING.

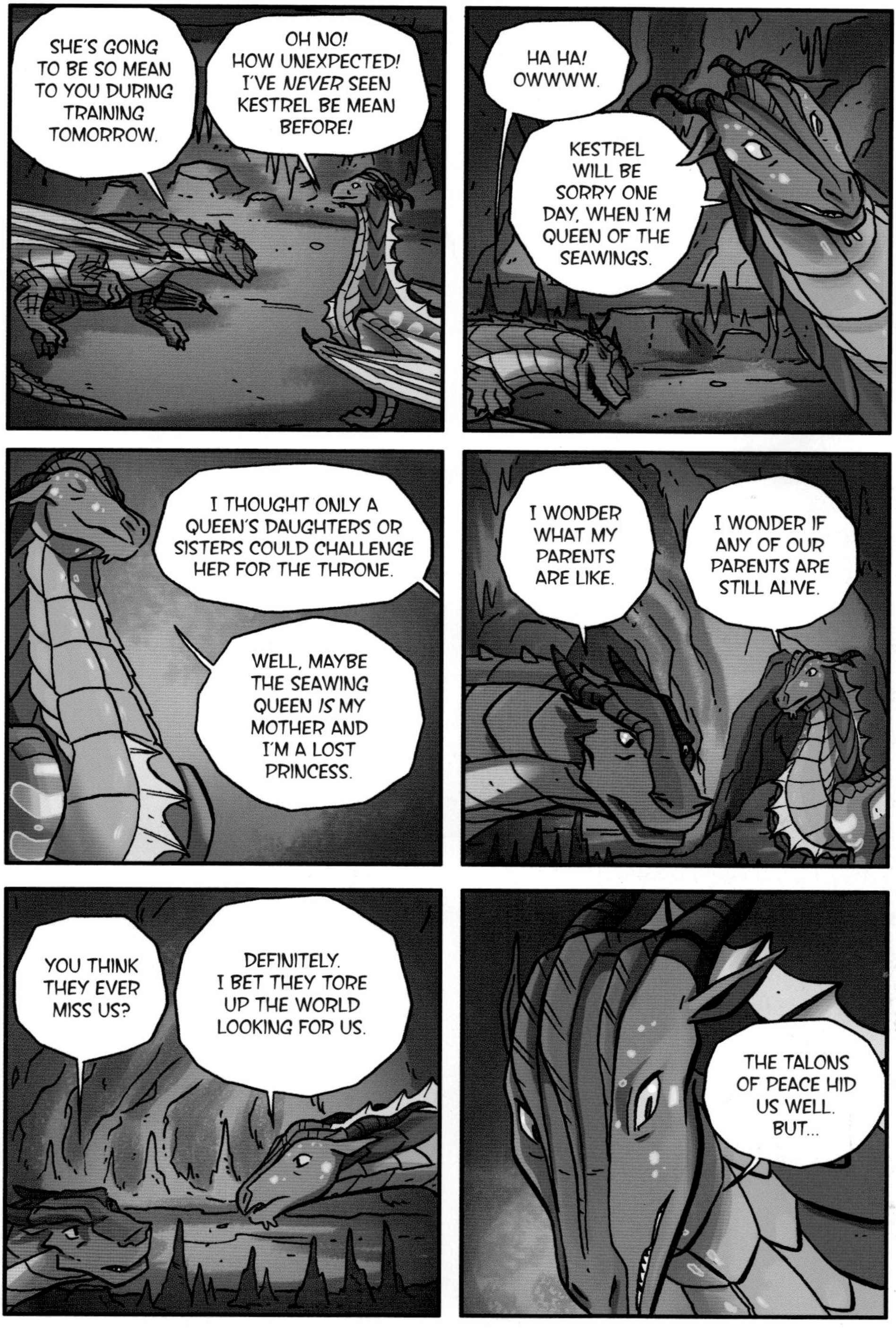
SHE'S GOING TO BE SO MEAN TO YOU DURING TRAINING TOMORROW.
OH NO! HOW UNEXPECTED! I'VE *NEVER* SEEN KESTREL BE MEAN BEFORE!
HA HA! OWWWW.
KESTREL WILL BE SORRY ONE DAY, WHEN I'M QUEEN OF THE SEAWINGS.
I THOUGHT ONLY A QUEEN'S DAUGHTERS OR SISTERS COULD CHALLENGE HER FOR THE THRONE.
WELL, MAYBE THE SEAWING QUEEN *IS* MY MOTHER AND I'M A LOST PRINCESS.
I WONDER WHAT MY PARENTS ARE LIKE.
I WONDER IF ANY OF OUR PARENTS ARE STILL ALIVE.
YOU THINK THEY EVER MISS US?
DEFINITELY. I BET THEY TORE UP THE WORLD LOOKING FOR US.
THE TALONS OF PEACE HID US WELL. BUT...

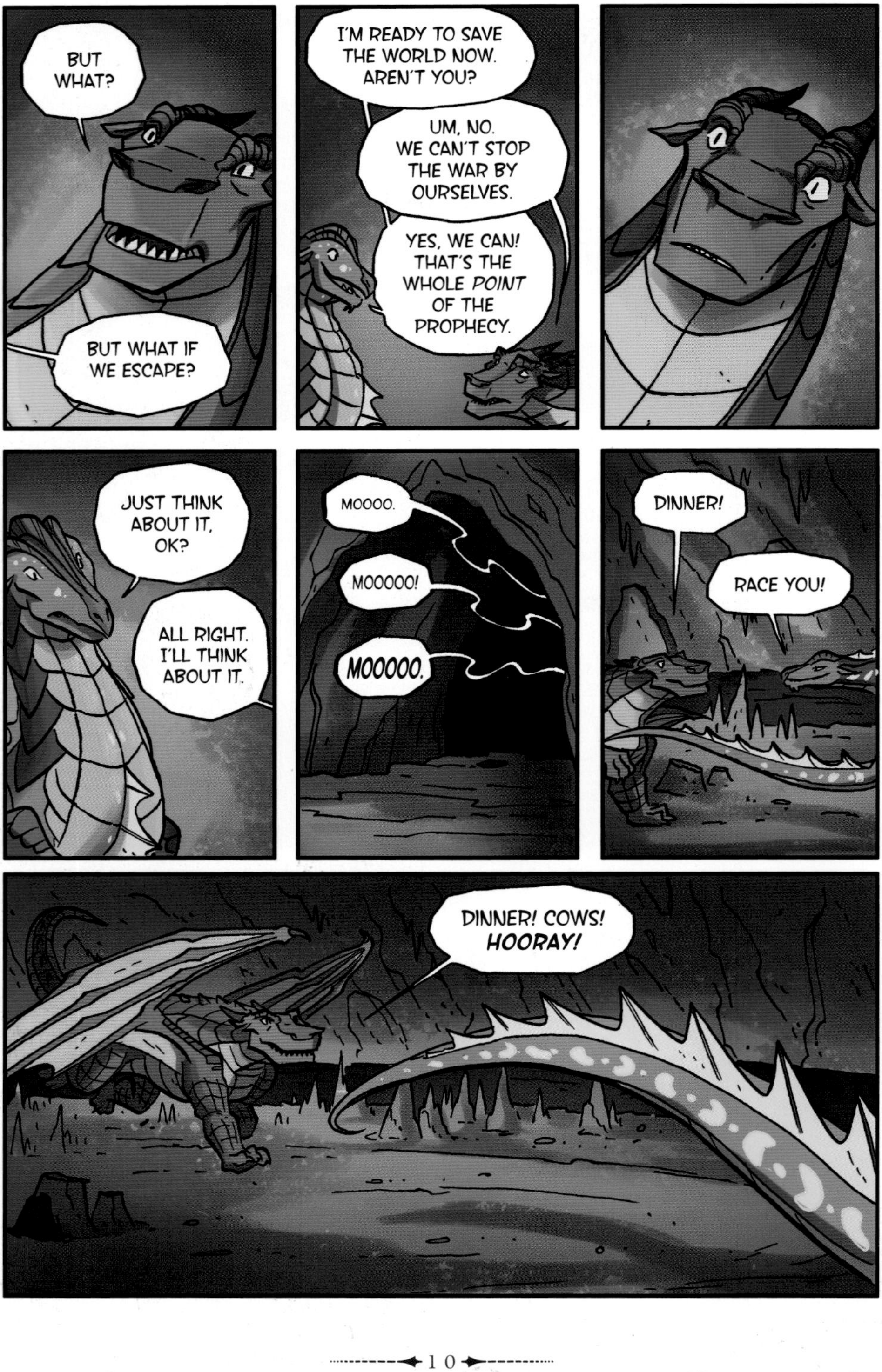
BUT WHAT?
BUT WHAT IF WE ESCAPE?
I'M READY TO SAVE THE WORLD NOW. AREN'T YOU?
UM, NO. WE CAN'T STOP THE WAR BY OURSELVES.
YES, WE CAN! THAT'S THE WHOLE *POINT* OF THE PROPHECY.
JUST THINK ABOUT IT, OK?
ALL RIGHT. I'LL THINK ABOUT IT.
MOOOO.
MOOOOO!
MOOOOO.
DINNER!
RACE YOU!
DINNER! COWS! ***HOORAY!***

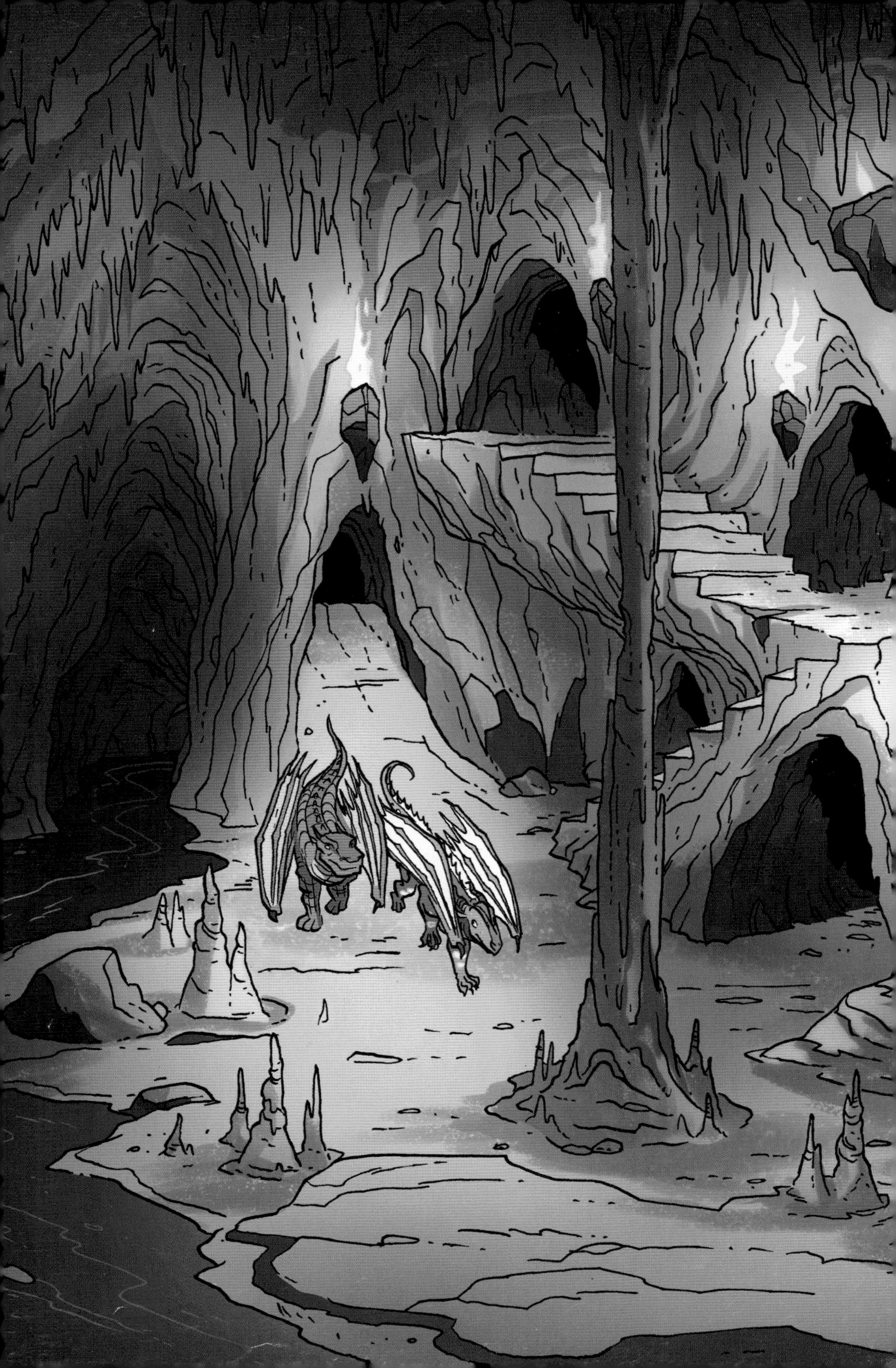

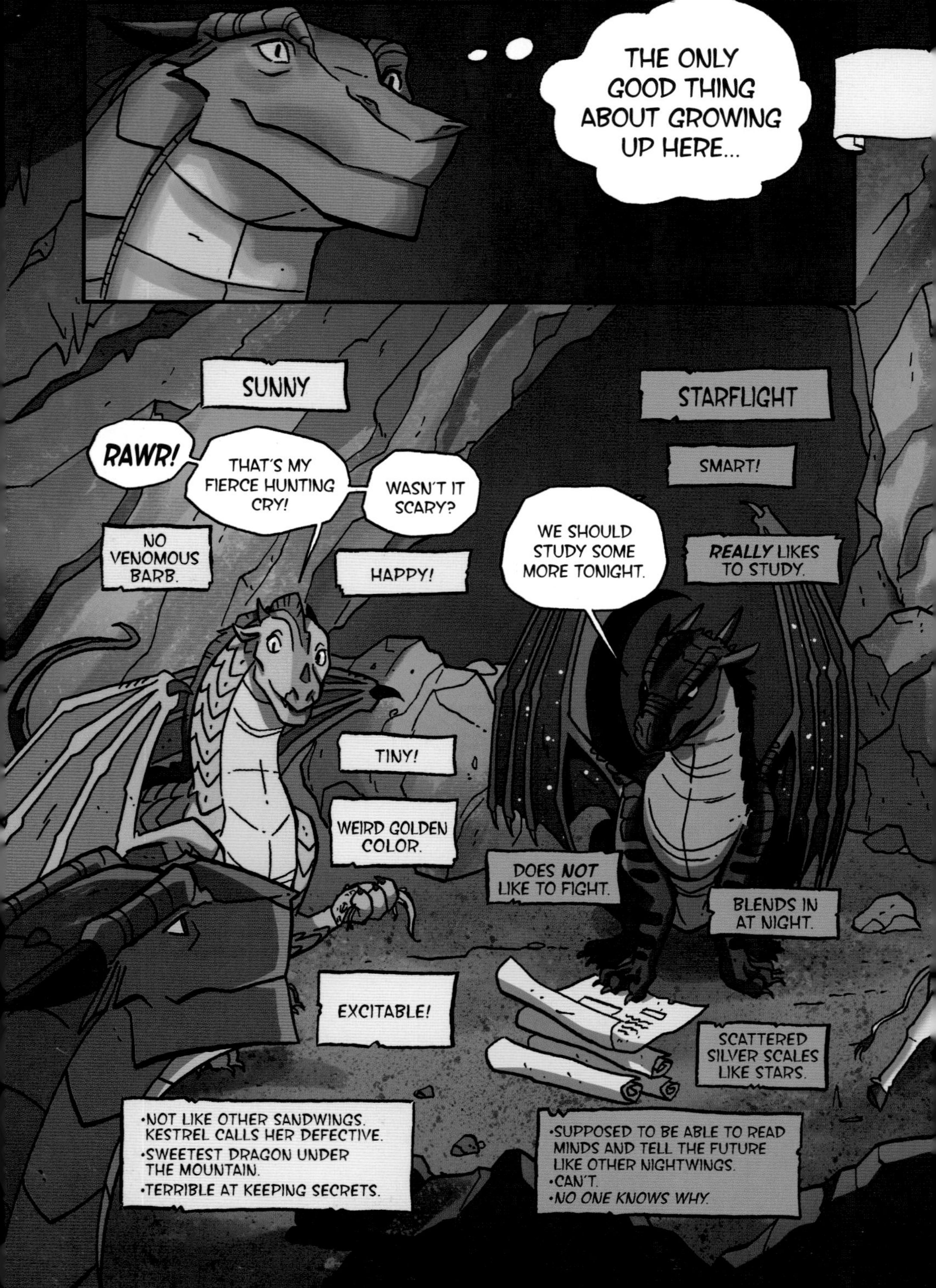
THE ONLY GOOD THING ABOUT GROWING UP HERE...
SUNNY
RAWR!
THAT'S MY FIERCE HUNTING CRY!
WASN'T IT SCARY?
NO VENOMOUS BARB.
HAPPY!
TINY!
WEIRD GOLDEN COLOR.
EXCITABLE!
STARFLIGHT
SMART!
WE SHOULD STUDY SOME MORE TONIGHT.
REALLY LIKES TO STUDY.
DOES NOT LIKE TO FIGHT.
BLENDS IN AT NIGHT.
SCATTERED SILVER SCALES LIKE STARS.
•NOT LIKE OTHER SANDWINGS. KESTREL CALLS HER DEFECTIVE.
•SWEETEST DRAGON UNDER THE MOUNTAIN.
•TERRIBLE AT KEEPING SECRETS.
•SUPPOSED TO BE ABLE TO READ MINDS AND TELL THE FUTURE LIKE OTHER NIGHTWINGS.
•CAN'T.
•NO ONE KNOWS WHY.

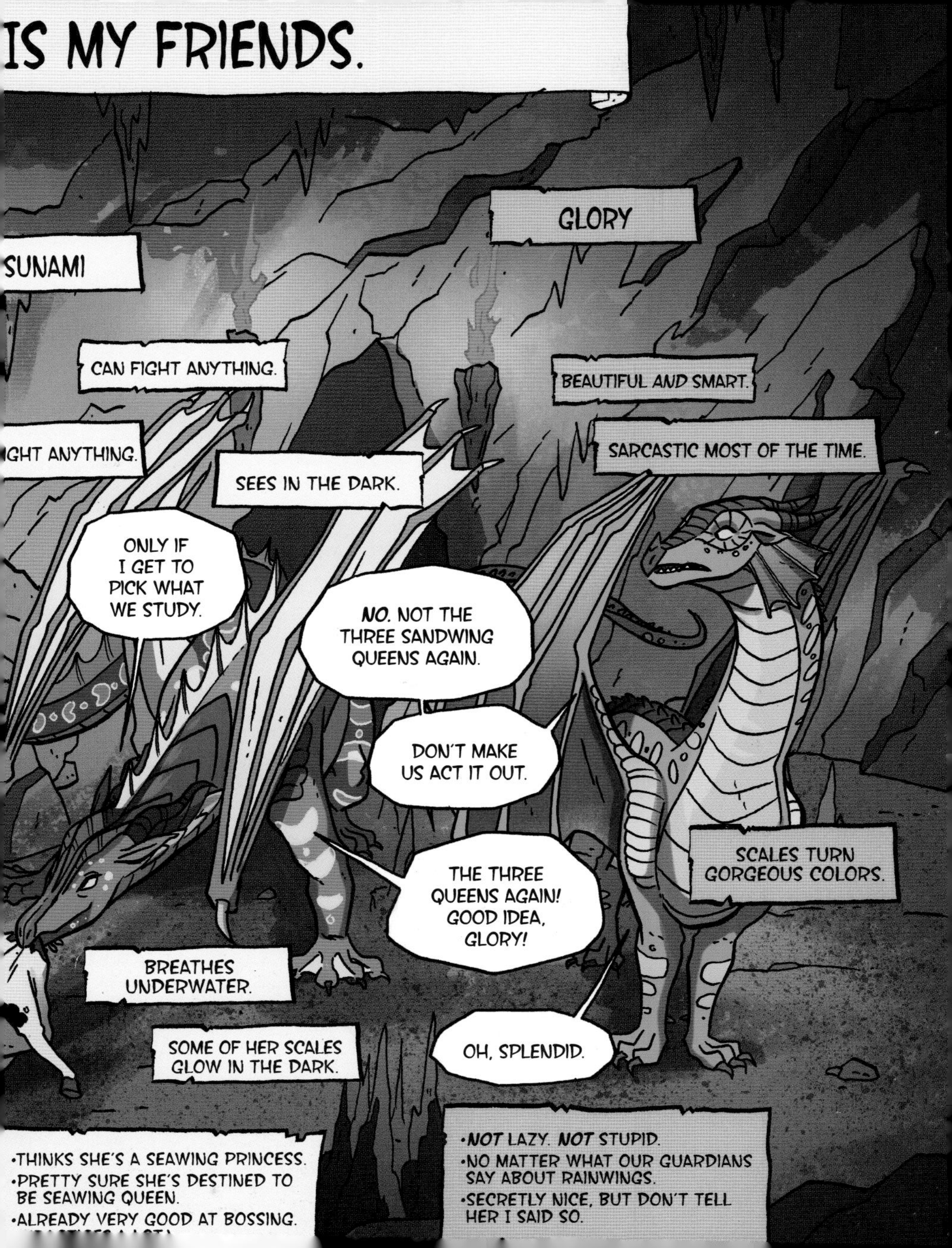
IS MY FRIENDS.
SUNAMI
CAN FIGHT ANYTHING.
GHT ANYTHING.
SEES IN THE DARK.
GLORY
BEAUTIFUL AND SMART.
SARCASTIC MOST OF THE TIME.
ONLY IF I GET TO PICK WHAT WE STUDY.
NO. NOT THE THREE SANDWING QUEENS AGAIN.
DON'T MAKE US ACT IT OUT.
THE THREE QUEENS AGAIN! GOOD IDEA, GLORY!
SCALES TURN GORGEOUS COLORS.
BREATHES UNDERWATER.
SOME OF HER SCALES GLOW IN THE DARK.
OH, SPLENDID.
•THINKS SHE'S A SEAWING PRINCESS.
•PRETTY SURE SHE'S DESTINED TO BE SEAWING QUEEN.
•ALREADY VERY GOOD AT BOSSING.
•NOT LAZY. NOT STUPID.
•NO MATTER WHAT OUR GUARDIANS SAY ABOUT RAINWINGS.
•SECRETLY NICE, BUT DON'T TELL HER I SAID SO.

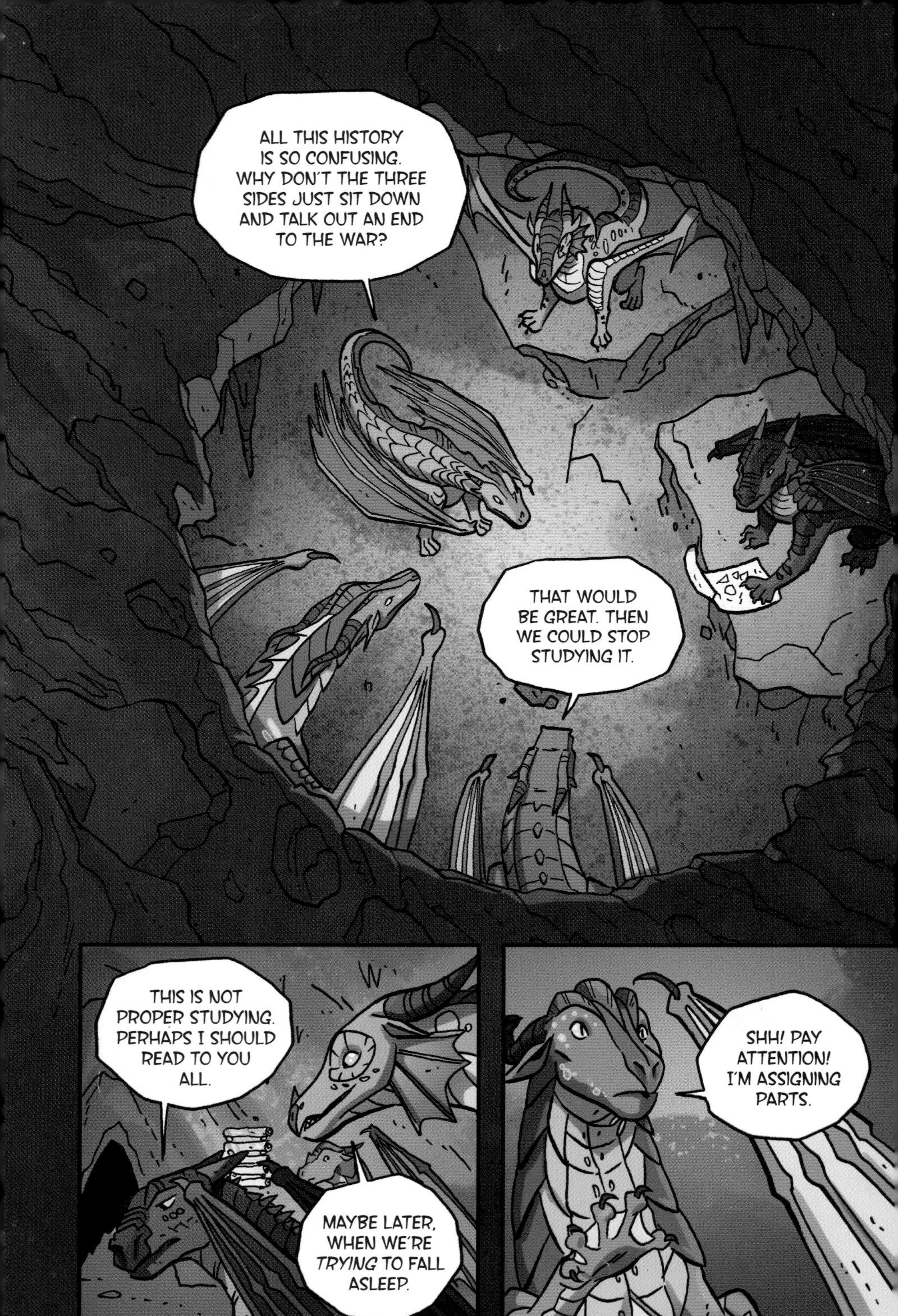
ALL THIS HISTORY IS SO CONFUSING. WHY DON'T THE THREE SIDES JUST SIT DOWN AND TALK OUT AN END TO THE WAR?
THAT WOULD BE GREAT. THEN WE COULD STOP STUDYING IT.
THIS IS NOT PROPER STUDYING. PERHAPS I SHOULD READ TO YOU ALL.
MAYBE LATER, WHEN WE'RE *TRYING* TO FALL ASLEEP.
SHH! PAY ATTENTION! I'M ASSIGNING PARTS.

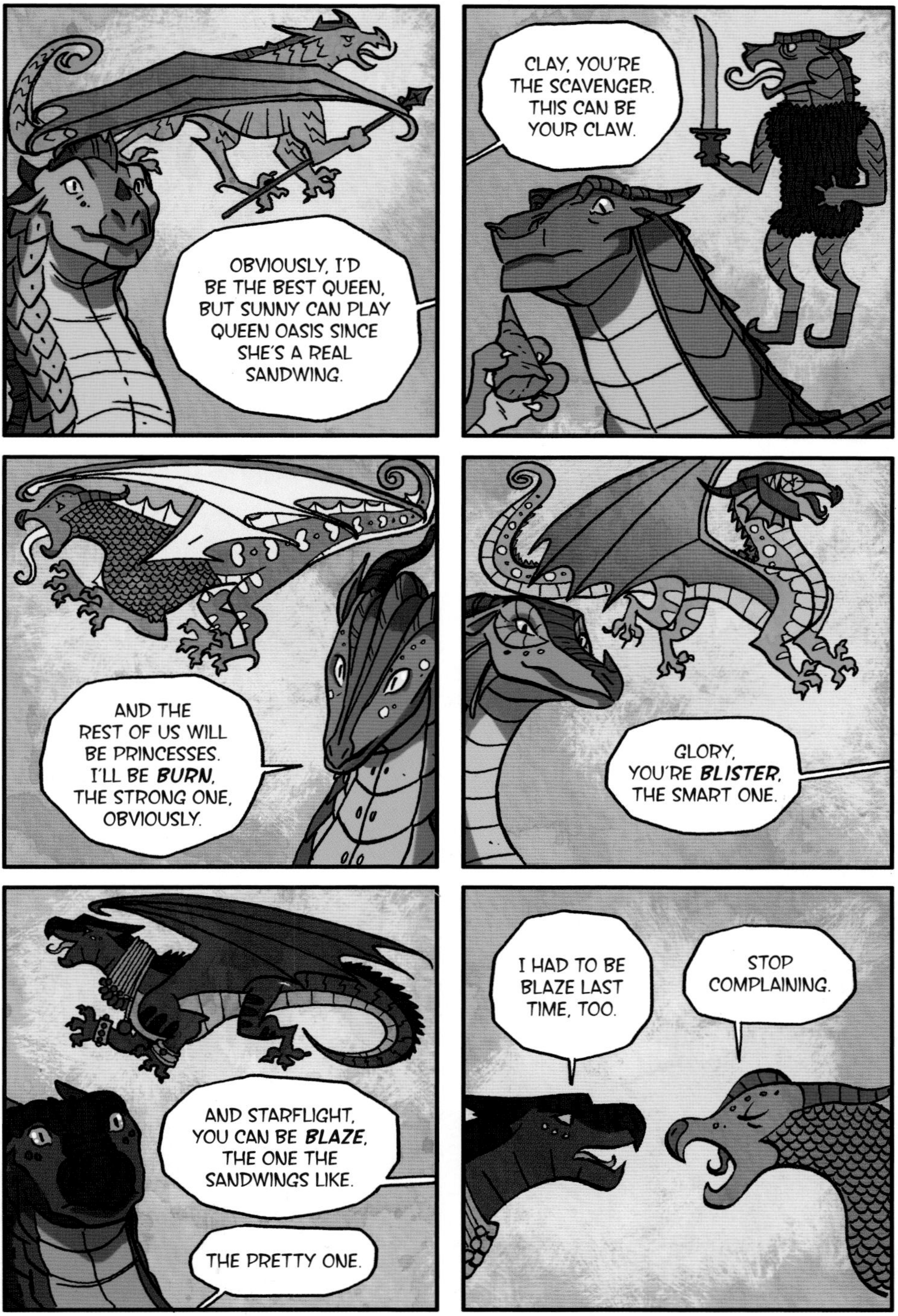
OBVIOUSLY, I'D BE THE BEST QUEEN, BUT SUNNY CAN PLAY QUEEN OASIS SINCE SHE'S A REAL SANDWING.
CLAY, YOU'RE THE SCAVENGER. THIS CAN BE YOUR CLAW.
AND THE REST OF US WILL BE PRINCESSES. I'LL BE **BURN**, THE STRONG ONE, OBVIOUSLY.
GLORY, YOU'RE **BLISTER**, THE SMART ONE.
AND STARFLIGHT, YOU CAN BE **BLAZE**, THE ONE THE SANDWINGS LIKE.
THE PRETTY ONE.
I HAD TO BE BLAZE LAST TIME, TOO.
STOP COMPLAINING.

HOW THE GREAT WAR BEGAN

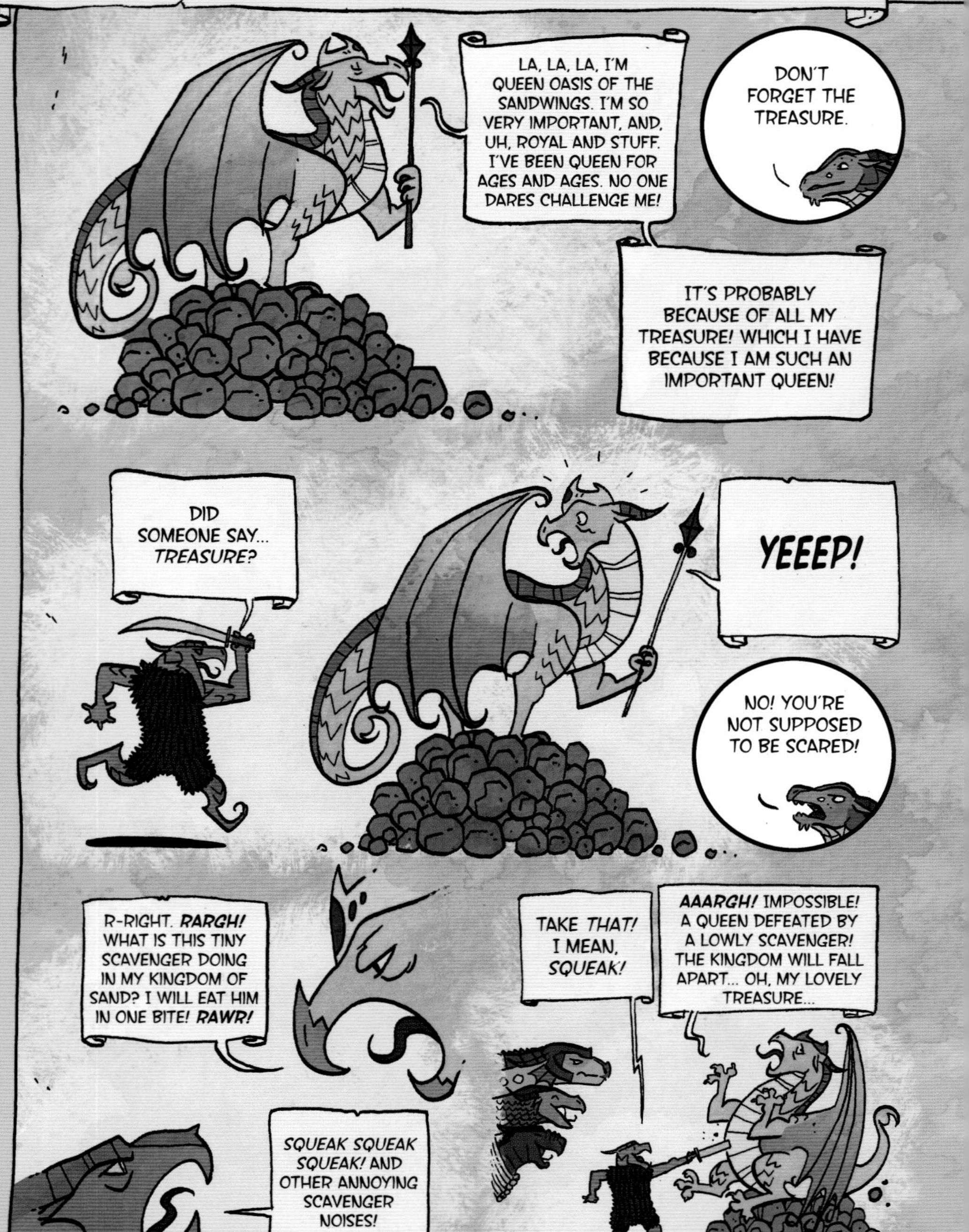

LA, LA, LA, I'M QUEEN OASIS OF THE SANDWINGS. I'M SO VERY IMPORTANT, AND, UH, ROYAL AND STUFF. I'VE BEEN QUEEN FOR AGES AND AGES. NO ONE DARES CHALLENGE ME!
DON'T FORGET THE TREASURE.
IT'S PROBABLY BECAUSE OF ALL MY TREASURE! WHICH I HAVE BECAUSE I AM SUCH AN IMPORTANT QUEEN!
DID SOMEONE SAY... *TREASURE?*
YEEEP!
NO! YOU'RE NOT SUPPOSED TO BE SCARED!
R-RIGHT. ***RARGH!*** WHAT IS THIS TINY SCAVENGER DOING IN MY KINGDOM OF SAND? I WILL EAT HIM IN ONE BITE! ***RAWR!***
SQUEAK SQUEAK SQUEAK! AND OTHER ANNOYING SCAVENGER NOISES!
TAKE *THAT!* I MEAN, *SQUEAK!*
AAARGH! IMPOSSIBLE! A QUEEN DEFEATED BY A LOWLY SCAVENGER! THE KINGDOM WILL FALL APART... OH, MY LOVELY TREASURE...

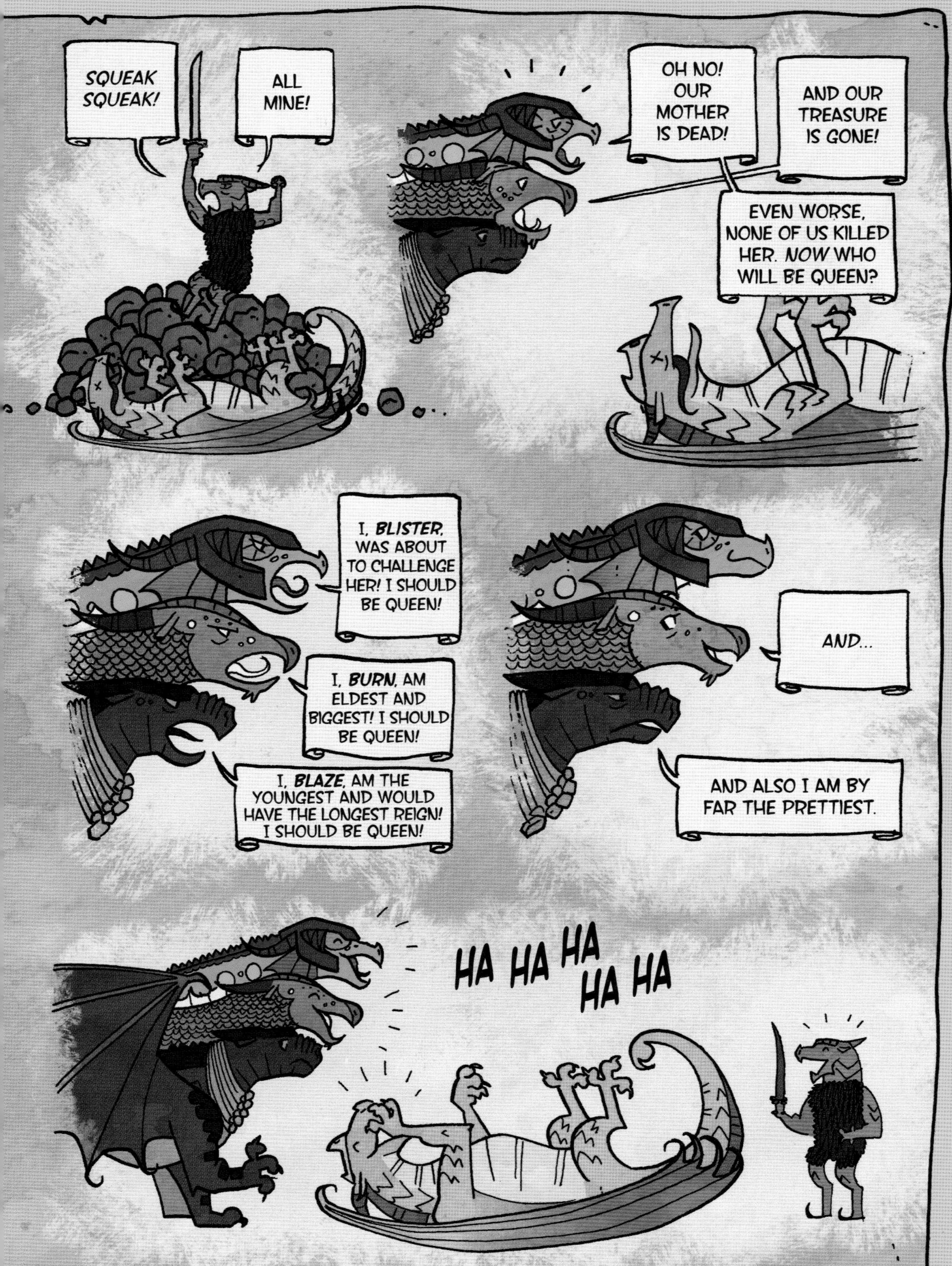

SQUEAK SQUEAK!
ALL MINE!
OH NO! OUR MOTHER IS DEAD!
AND OUR TREASURE IS GONE!
EVEN WORSE, NONE OF US KILLED HER. *NOW* WHO WILL BE QUEEN?
I, ***BLISTER***, WAS ABOUT TO CHALLENGE HER! I SHOULD BE QUEEN!
I, ***BURN***, AM ELDEST AND BIGGEST! I SHOULD BE QUEEN!
I, ***BLAZE***, AM THE YOUNGEST AND WOULD HAVE THE LONGEST REIGN! I SHOULD BE QUEEN!
AND...
AND ALSO I AM BY FAR THE PRETTIEST.
HA HA HA HA HA

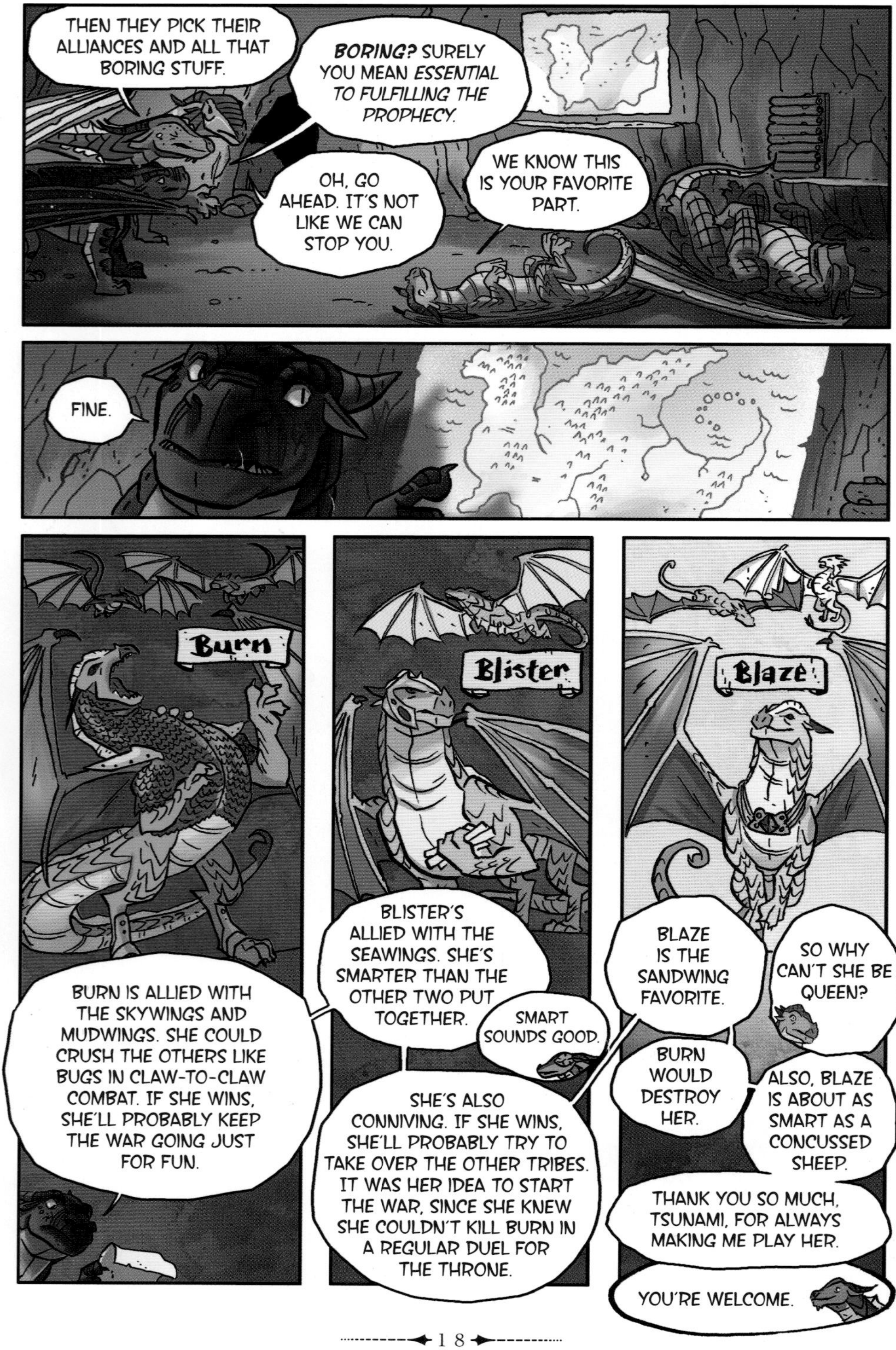
THEN THEY PICK THEIR ALLIANCES AND ALL THAT BORING STUFF.
BORING? SURELY YOU MEAN *ESSENTIAL TO FULFILLING THE PROPHECY.*
OH, GO AHEAD. IT'S NOT LIKE WE CAN STOP YOU.
WE KNOW THIS IS YOUR FAVORITE PART.
FINE.
Burn
Blister
Blaze
BURN IS ALLIED WITH THE SKYWINGS AND MUDWINGS. SHE COULD CRUSH THE OTHERS LIKE BUGS IN CLAW-TO-CLAW COMBAT. IF SHE WINS, SHE'LL PROBABLY KEEP THE WAR GOING JUST FOR FUN.
BLISTER'S ALLIED WITH THE SEAWINGS. SHE'S SMARTER THAN THE OTHER TWO PUT TOGETHER.
SMART SOUNDS GOOD.
SHE'S ALSO CONNIVING. IF SHE WINS, SHE'LL PROBABLY TRY TO TAKE OVER THE OTHER TRIBES. IT WAS HER IDEA TO START THE WAR, SINCE SHE KNEW SHE COULDN'T KILL BURN IN A REGULAR DUEL FOR THE THRONE.
BLAZE IS THE SANDWING FAVORITE.
SO WHY CAN'T SHE BE QUEEN?
BURN WOULD DESTROY HER.
ALSO, BLAZE IS ABOUT AS SMART AS A CONCUSSED SHEEP.
THANK YOU SO MUCH, TSUNAMI, FOR ALWAYS MAKING ME PLAY HER.
YOU'RE WELCOME.

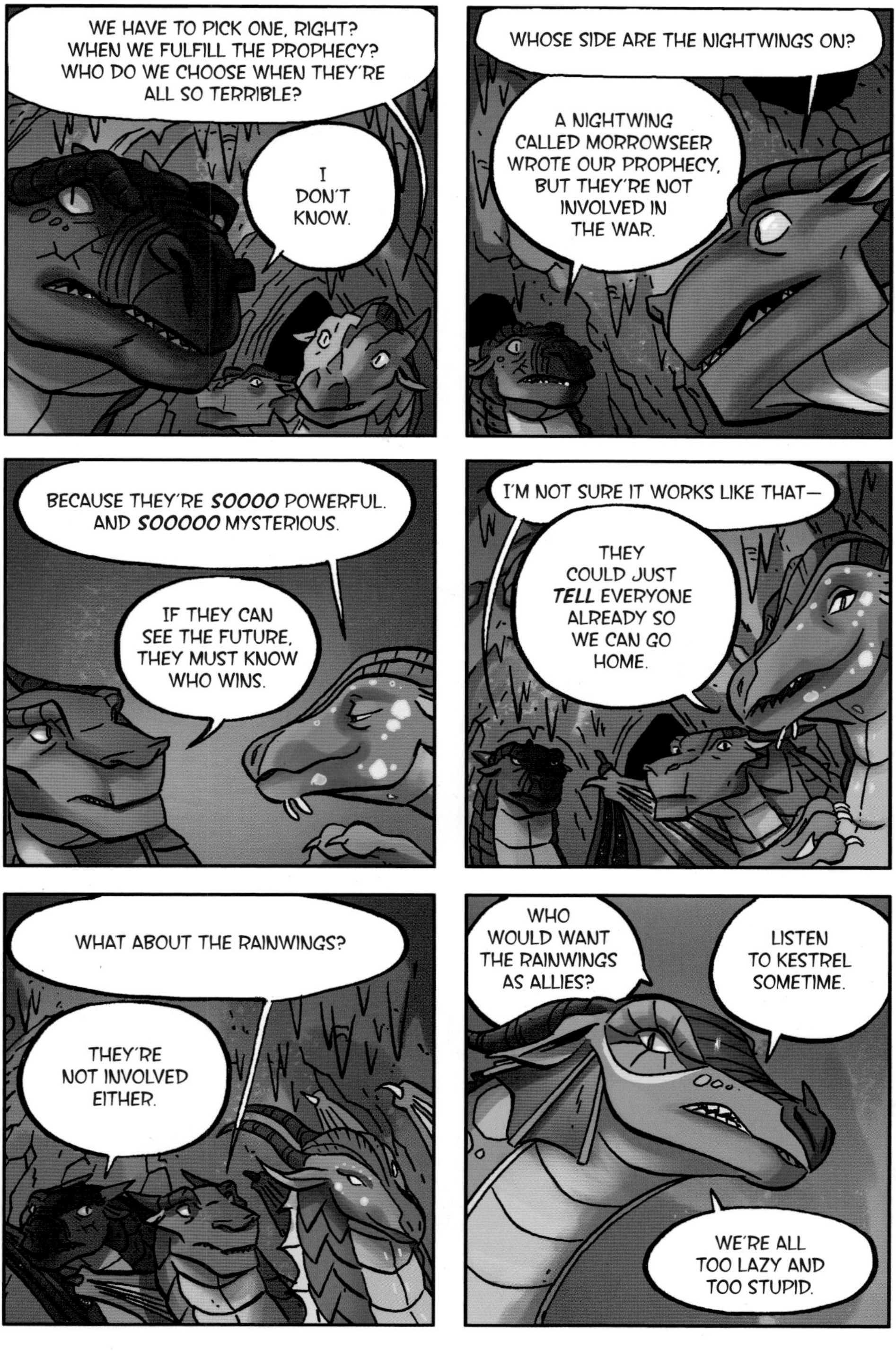
WE HAVE TO PICK ONE, RIGHT? WHEN WE FULFILL THE PROPHECY? WHO DO WE CHOOSE WHEN THEY'RE ALL SO TERRIBLE?
I DON'T KNOW.
WHOSE SIDE ARE THE NIGHTWINGS ON?
A NIGHTWING CALLED MORROWSEER WROTE OUR PROPHECY, BUT THEY'RE NOT INVOLVED IN THE WAR.
BECAUSE THEY'RE *SOOOO* POWERFUL. AND *SOOOOO* MYSTERIOUS.
IF THEY CAN SEE THE FUTURE, THEY MUST KNOW WHO WINS.
I'M NOT SURE IT WORKS LIKE THAT—
THEY COULD JUST *TELL* EVERYONE ALREADY SO WE CAN GO HOME.
WHAT ABOUT THE RAINWINGS?
THEY'RE NOT INVOLVED EITHER.
WHO WOULD WANT THE RAINWINGS AS ALLIES?
LISTEN TO KESTREL SOMETIME.
WE'RE ALL TOO LAZY AND TOO STUPID.

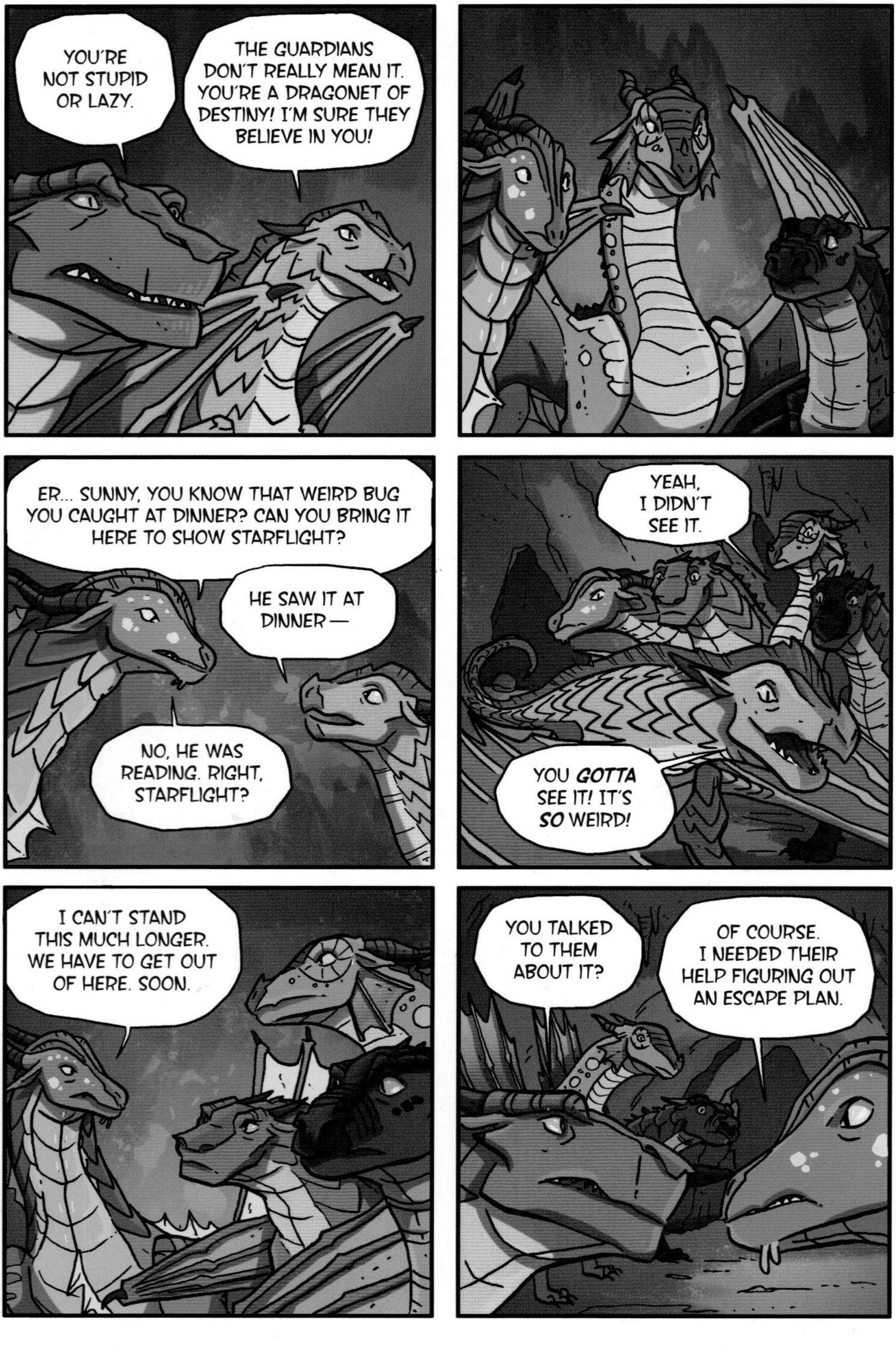
YOU'RE NOT STUPID OR LAZY.
THE GUARDIANS DON'T REALLY MEAN IT. YOU'RE A DRAGONET OF DESTINY! I'M SURE THEY BELIEVE IN YOU!
ER... SUNNY, YOU KNOW THAT WEIRD BUG YOU CAUGHT AT DINNER? CAN YOU BRING IT HERE TO SHOW STARFLIGHT?
HE SAW IT AT DINNER—
NO, HE WAS READING. RIGHT, STARFLIGHT?
YEAH, I DIDN'T SEE IT.
YOU **GOTTA** SEE IT! IT'S ***SO*** WEIRD!
I CAN'T STAND THIS MUCH LONGER. WE HAVE TO GET OUT OF HERE. SOON.
YOU TALKED TO THEM ABOUT IT?
OF COURSE. I NEEDED THEIR HELP FIGURING OUT AN ESCAPE PLAN.

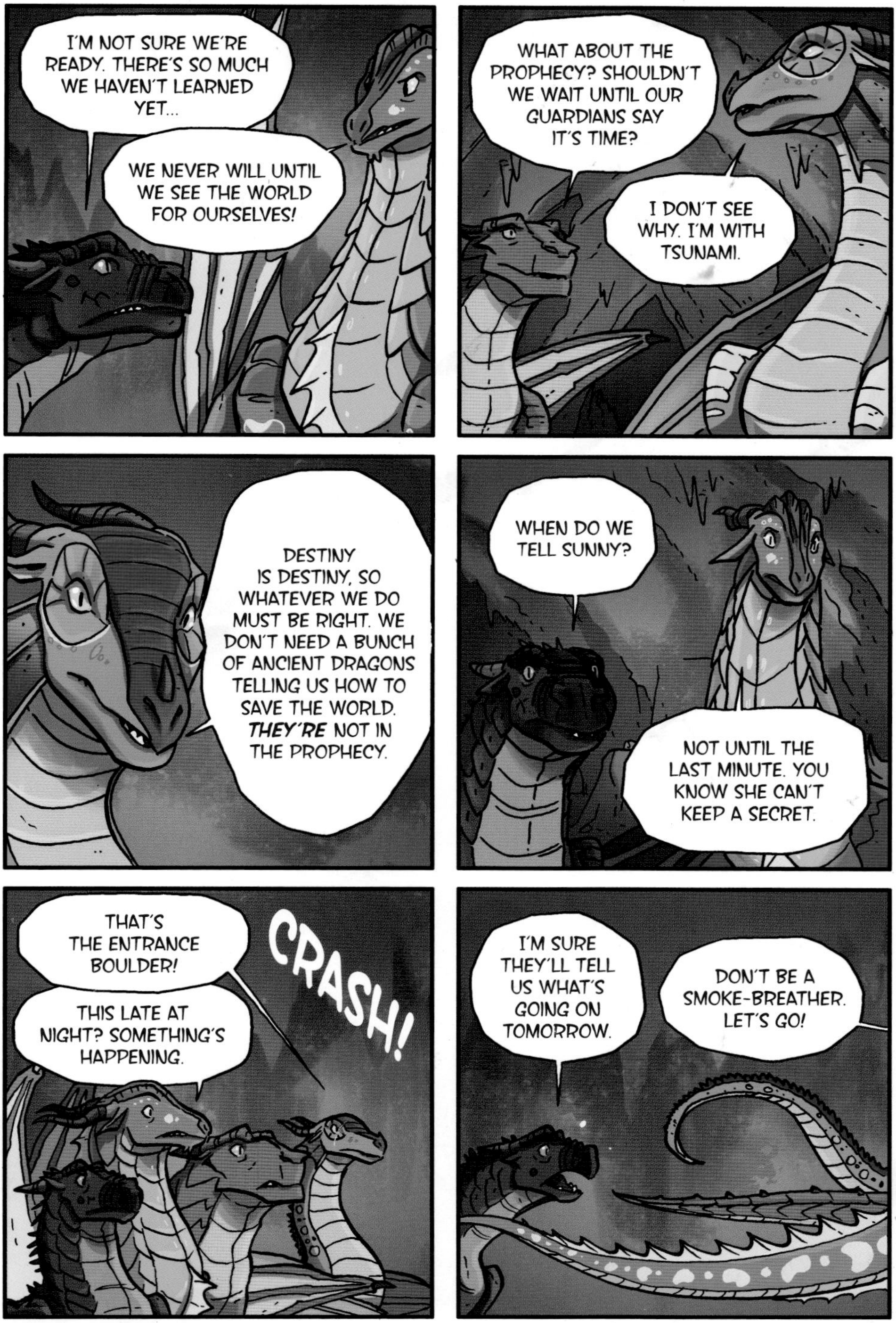
I'M NOT SURE WE'RE READY. THERE'S SO MUCH WE HAVEN'T LEARNED YET...
WE NEVER WILL UNTIL WE SEE THE WORLD FOR OURSELVES!
WHAT ABOUT THE PROPHECY? SHOULDN'T WE WAIT UNTIL OUR GUARDIANS SAY IT'S TIME?
I DON'T SEE WHY. I'M WITH TSUNAMI.
DESTINY IS DESTINY, SO WHATEVER WE DO MUST BE RIGHT. WE DON'T NEED A BUNCH OF ANCIENT DRAGONS TELLING US HOW TO SAVE THE WORLD. *THEY'RE* NOT IN THE PROPHECY.
WHEN DO WE TELL SUNNY?
NOT UNTIL THE LAST MINUTE. YOU KNOW SHE CAN'T KEEP A SECRET.
CRASH!
THAT'S THE ENTRANCE BOULDER!
THIS LATE AT NIGHT? SOMETHING'S HAPPENING.
I'M SURE THEY'LL TELL US WHAT'S GOING ON TOMORROW.
DON'T BE A SMOKE-BREATHER. LET'S GO!

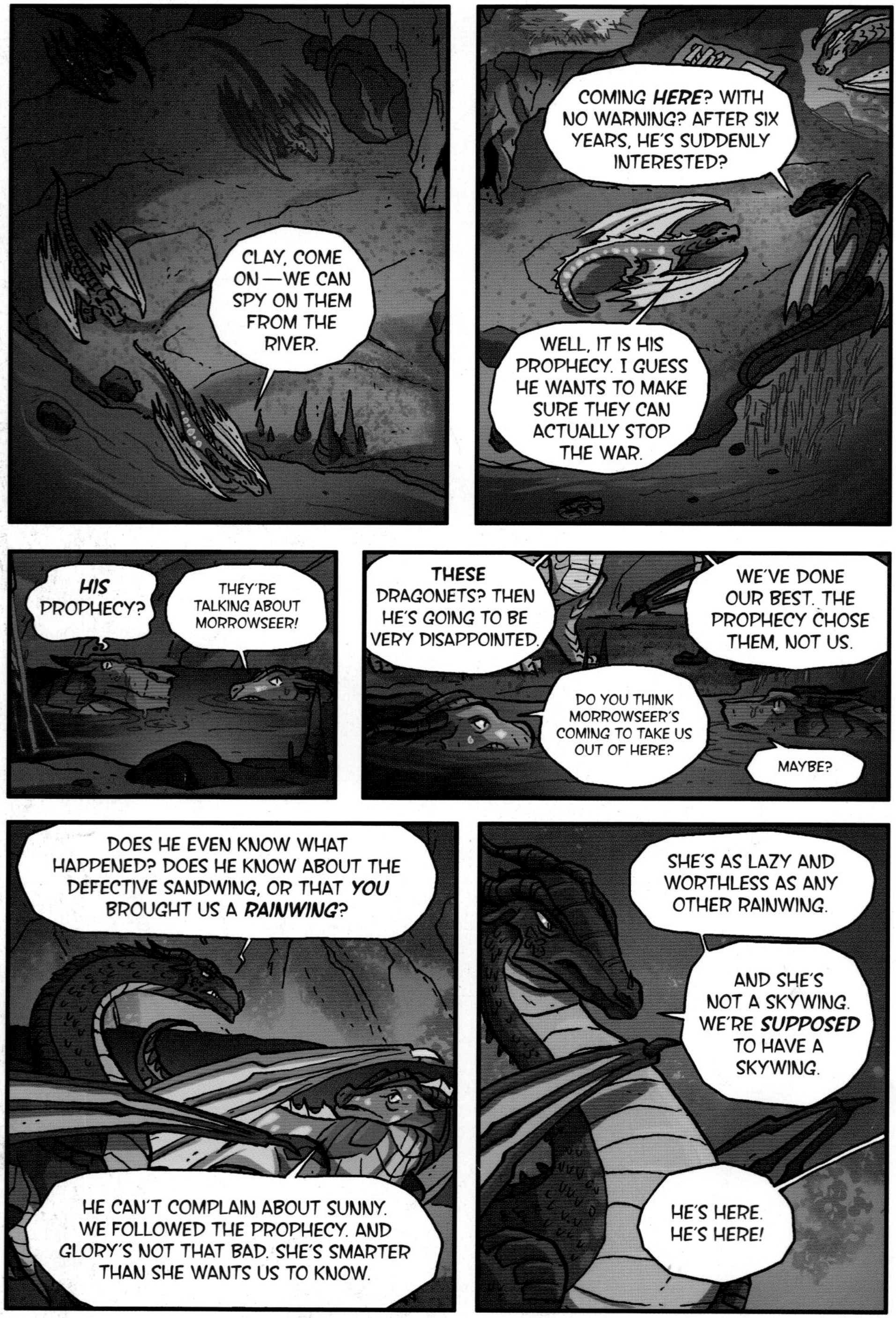
CLAY, COME ON—WE CAN SPY ON THEM FROM THE RIVER.
COMING HERE? WITH NO WARNING? AFTER SIX YEARS, HE'S SUDDENLY INTERESTED?
WELL, IT IS HIS PROPHECY. I GUESS HE WANTS TO MAKE SURE THEY CAN ACTUALLY STOP THE WAR.
HIS PROPHECY?
THEY'RE TALKING ABOUT MORROWSEER!
THESE DRAGONETS? THEN HE'S GOING TO BE VERY DISAPPOINTED.
WE'VE DONE OUR BEST. THE PROPHECY CHOSE THEM, NOT US.
DO YOU THINK MORROWSEER'S COMING TO TAKE US OUT OF HERE?
MAYBE?
DOES HE EVEN KNOW WHAT HAPPENED? DOES HE KNOW ABOUT THE DEFECTIVE SANDWING, OR THAT YOU BROUGHT US A RAINWING?
HE CAN'T COMPLAIN ABOUT SUNNY. WE FOLLOWED THE PROPHECY. AND GLORY'S NOT THAT BAD. SHE'S SMARTER THAN SHE WANTS US TO KNOW.
SHE'S AS LAZY AND WORTHLESS AS ANY OTHER RAINWING.
AND SHE'S NOT A SKYWING. WE'RE SUPPOSED TO HAVE A SKYWING.
HE'S HERE. HE'S HERE!

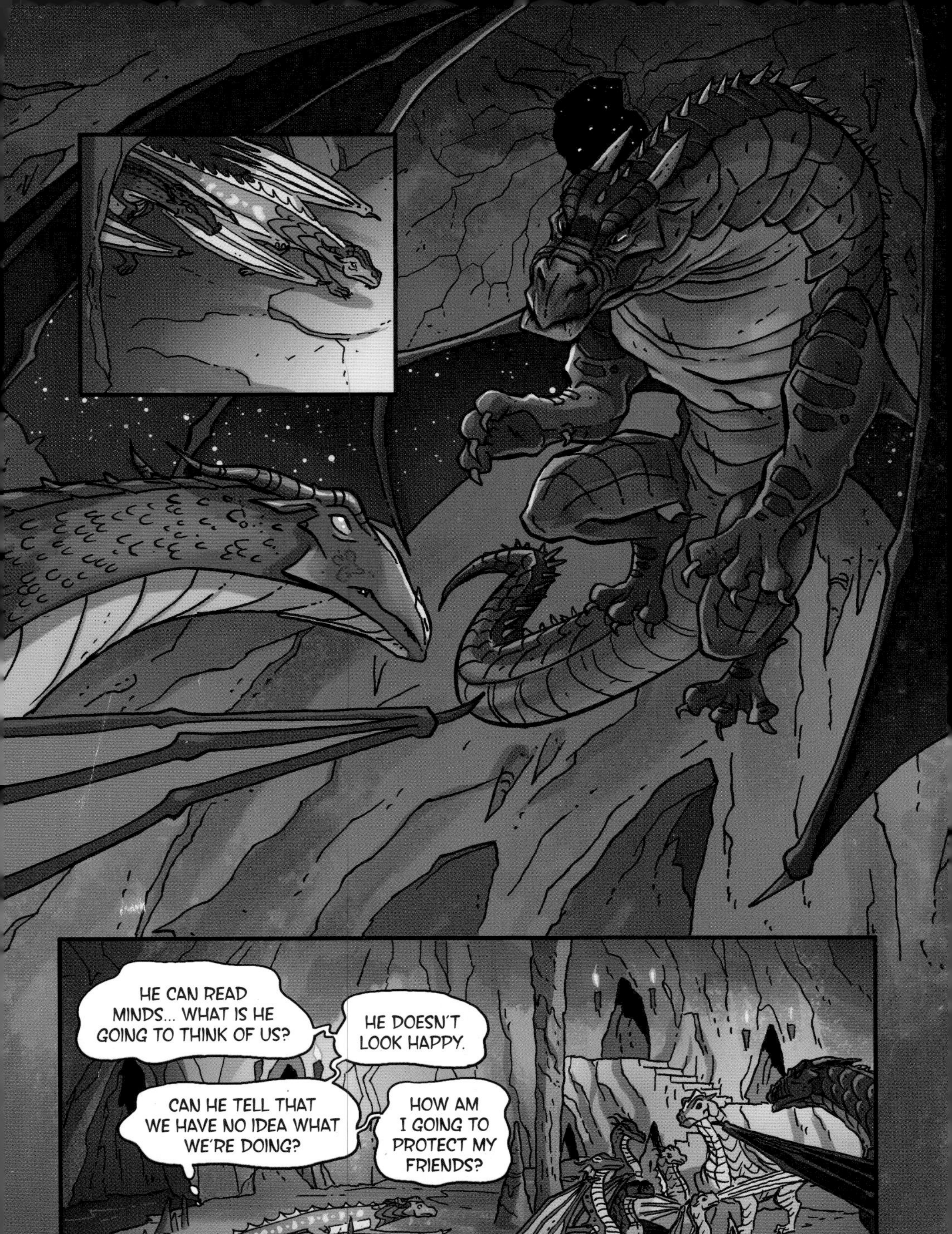

HE CAN READ MINDS... WHAT IS HE GOING TO THINK OF US?
HE DOESN'T LOOK HAPPY.
CAN HE TELL THAT WE HAVE NO IDEA WHAT WE'RE DOING?
HOW AM I GOING TO PROTECT MY FRIENDS?

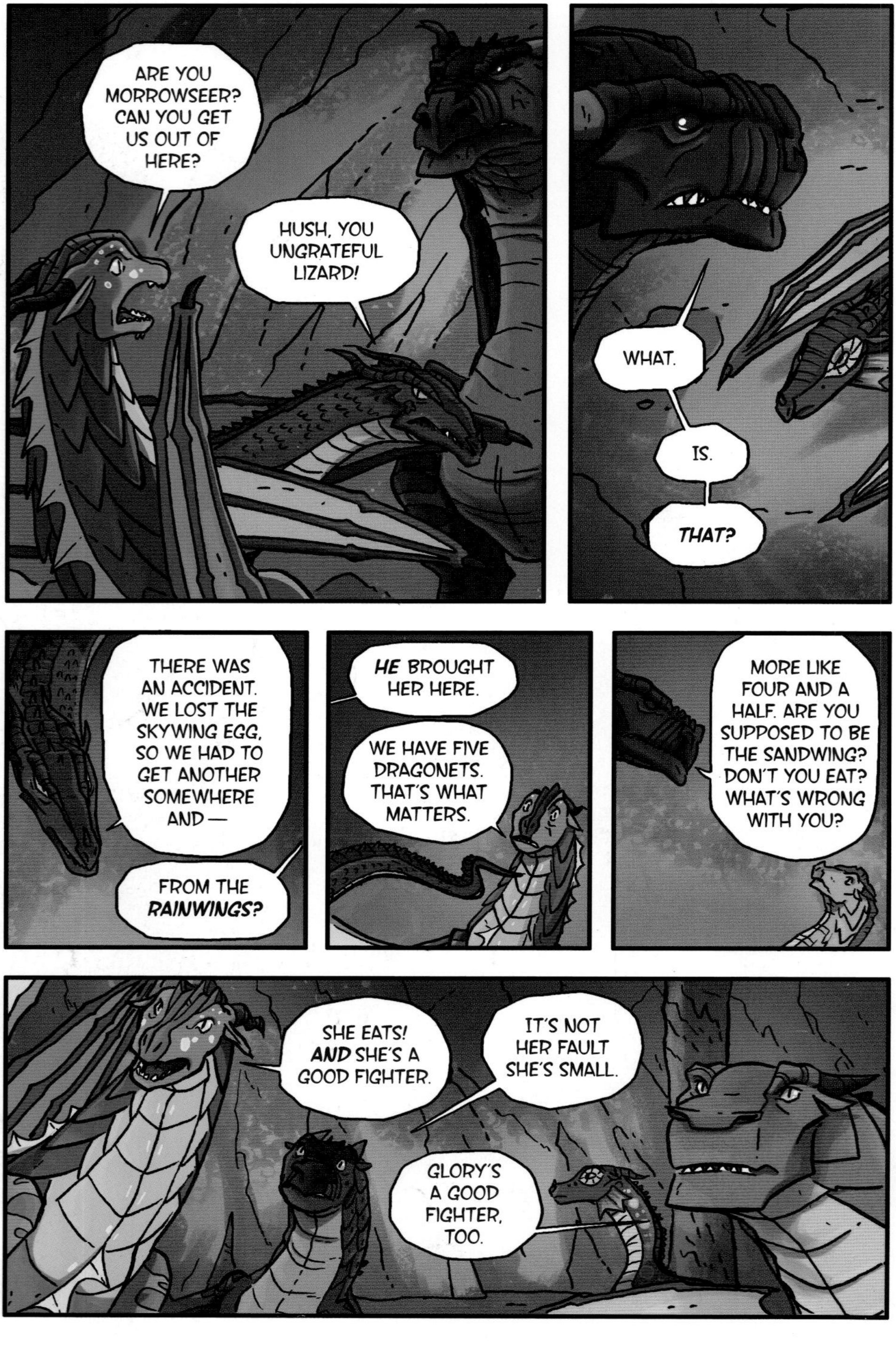
ARE YOU MORROWSEER? CAN YOU GET US OUT OF HERE?
HUSH, YOU UNGRATEFUL LIZARD!
WHAT.
IS.
THAT?
THERE WAS AN ACCIDENT. WE LOST THE SKYWING EGG, SO WE HAD TO GET ANOTHER SOMEWHERE AND—
FROM THE *RAINWINGS?*
HE BROUGHT HER HERE.
WE HAVE FIVE DRAGONETS. THAT'S WHAT MATTERS.
MORE LIKE FOUR AND A HALF. ARE YOU SUPPOSED TO BE THE SANDWING? DON'T YOU EAT? WHAT'S WRONG WITH YOU?
SHE EATS! *AND* SHE'S A GOOD FIGHTER.
IT'S NOT HER FAULT SHE'S SMALL.
GLORY'S A GOOD FIGHTER, TOO.

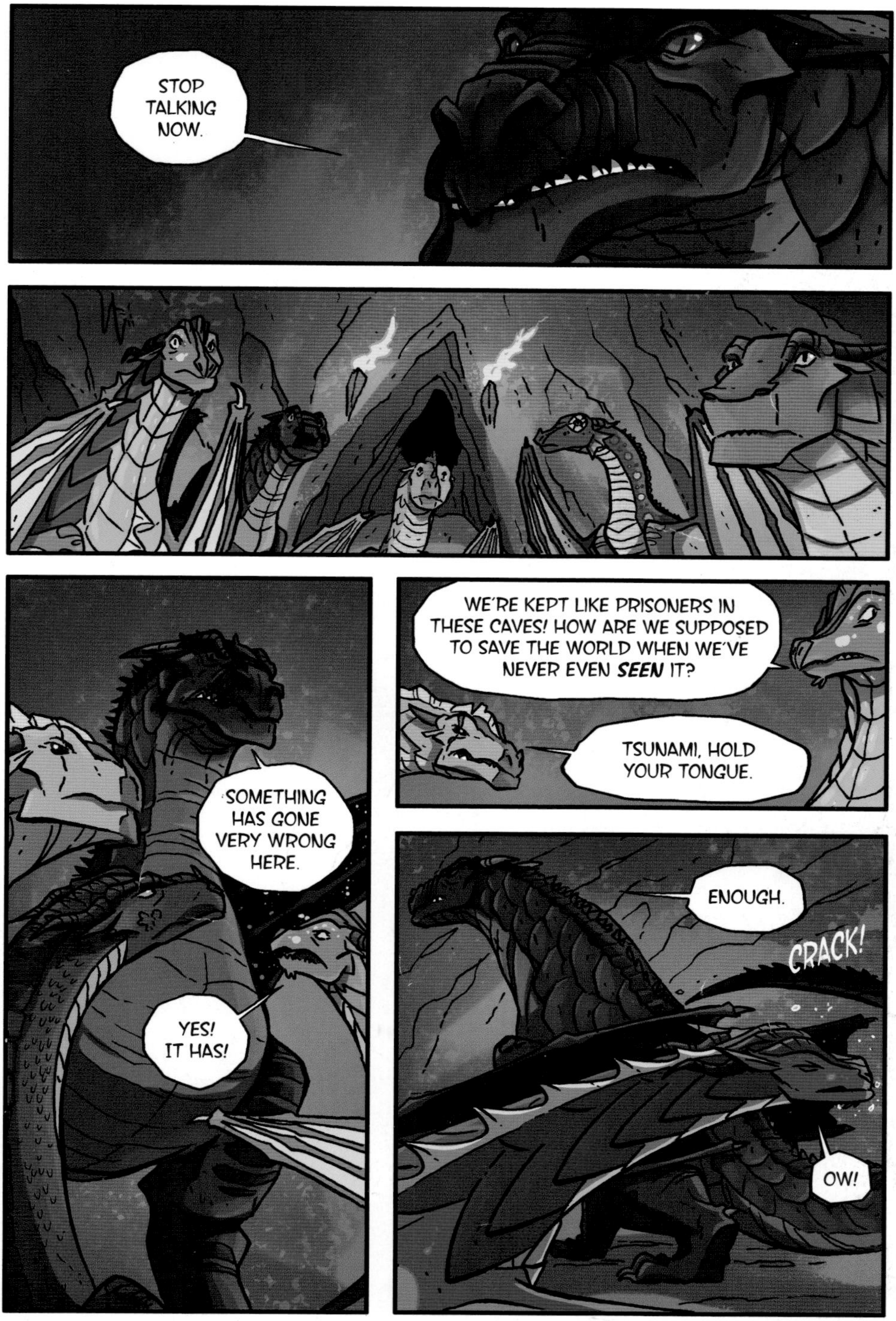
STOP TALKING NOW.
WE'RE KEPT LIKE PRISONERS IN THESE CAVES! HOW ARE WE SUPPOSED TO SAVE THE WORLD WHEN WE'VE NEVER EVEN **SEEN** IT?
TSUNAMI, HOLD YOUR TONGUE.
SOMETHING HAS GONE VERY WRONG HERE.
YES! IT HAS!
ENOUGH.
CRACK!
OW!

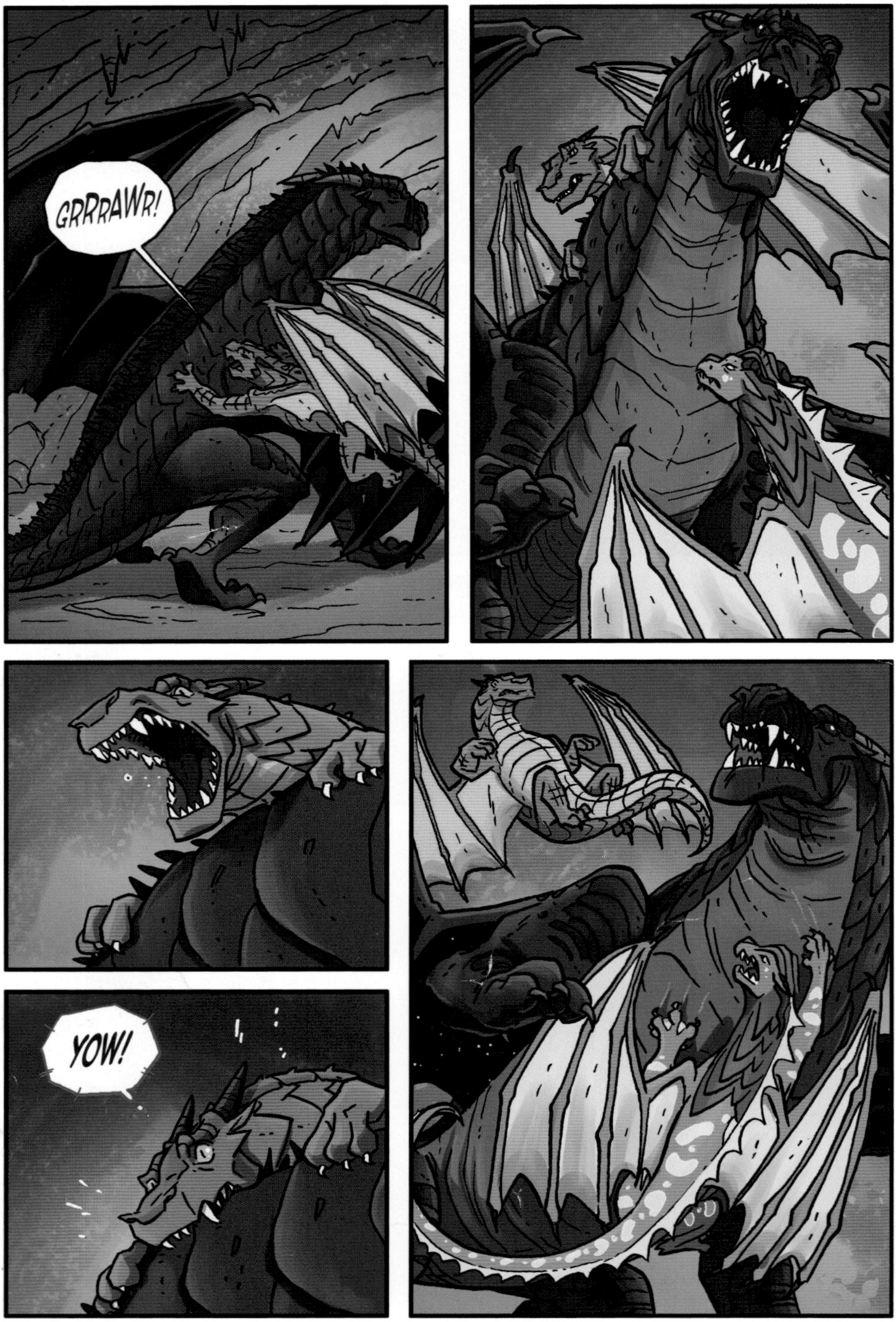
GRRRAWR!
YOW!

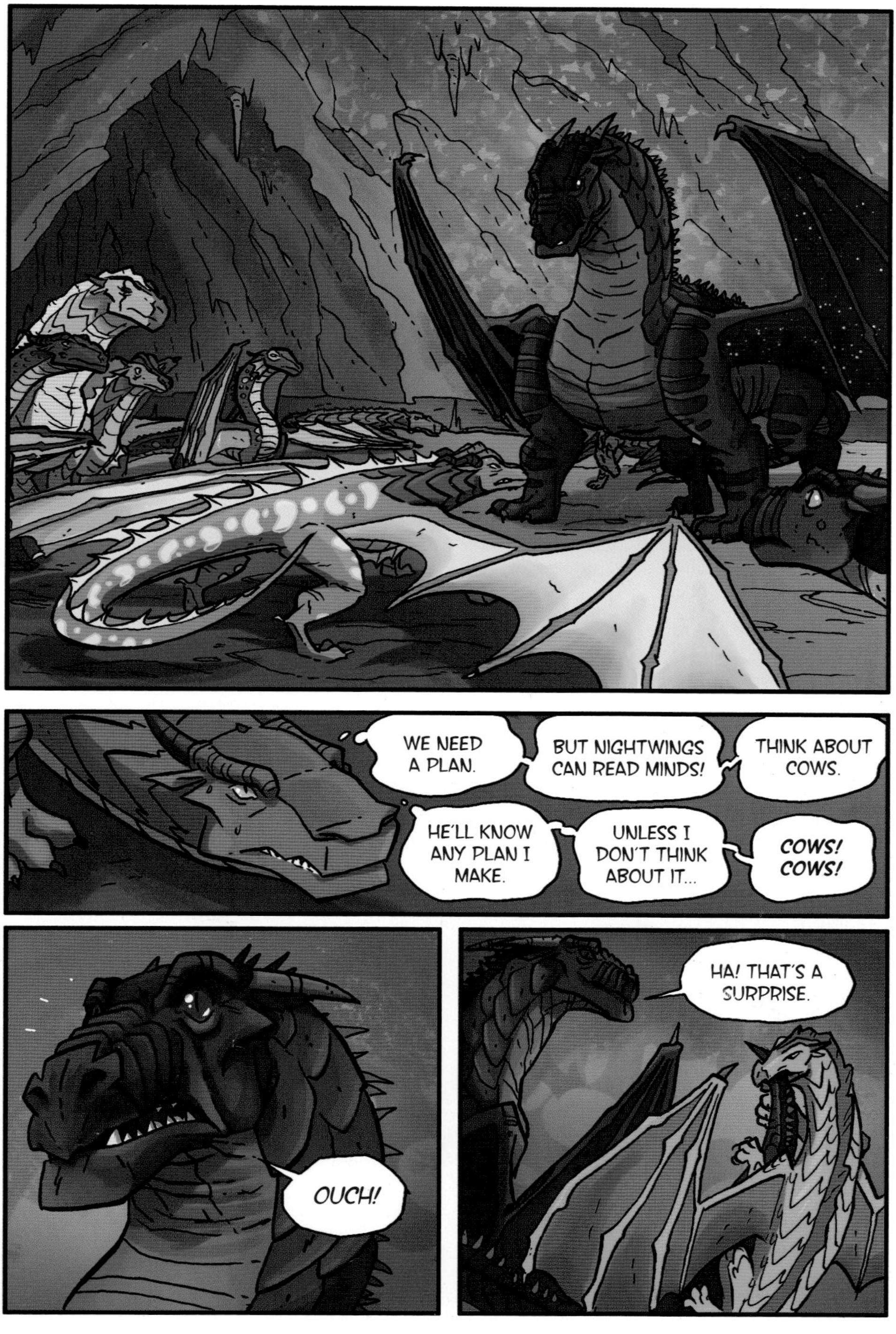
WE NEED A PLAN.
BUT NIGHTWINGS CAN READ MINDS!
THINK ABOUT COWS.
HE'LL KNOW ANY PLAN I MAKE.
UNLESS I DON'T THINK ABOUT IT...
COWS! COWS!
OUCH!
HA! THAT'S A SURPRISE.

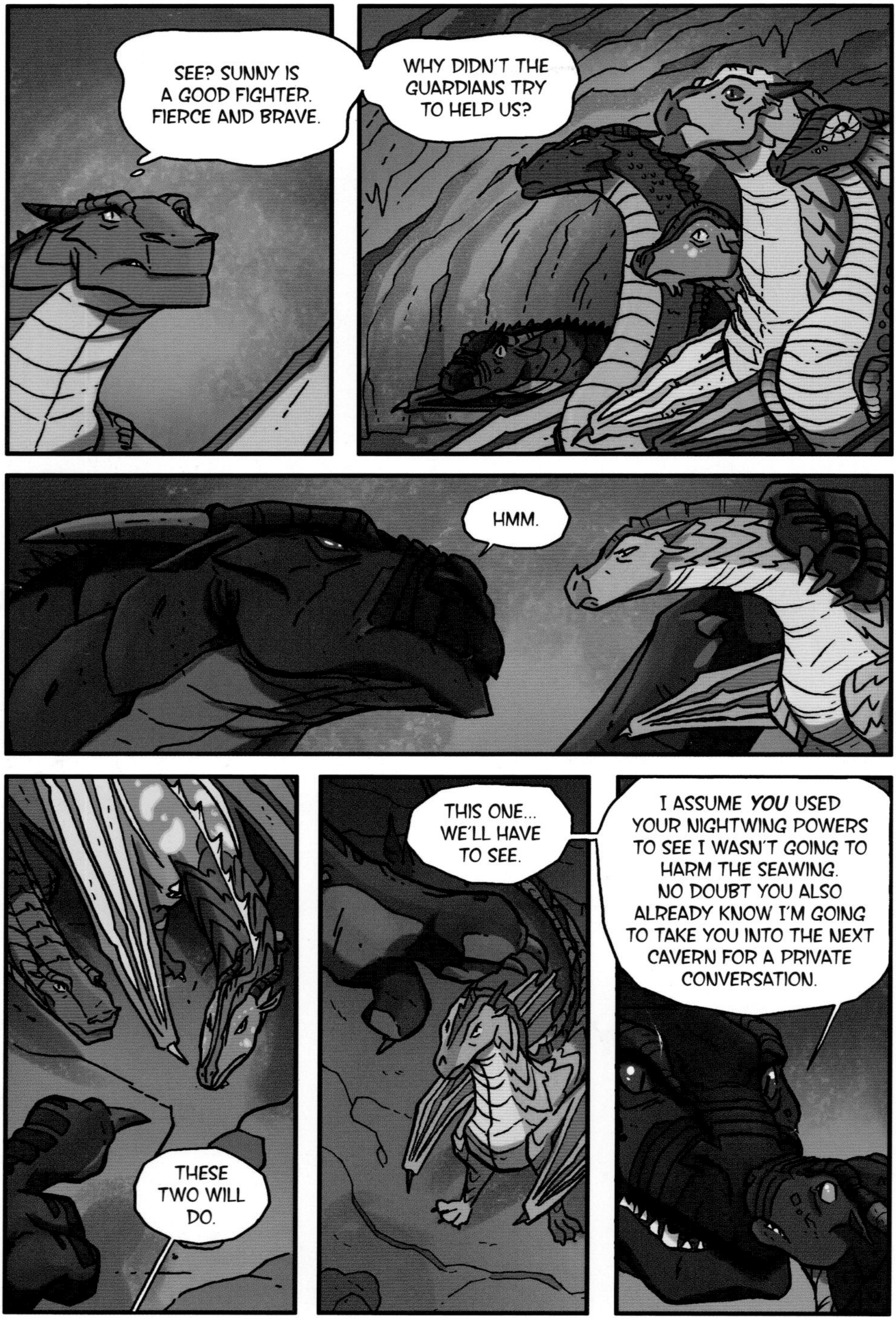
SEE? SUNNY IS A GOOD FIGHTER. FIERCE AND BRAVE.
WHY DIDN'T THE GUARDIANS TRY TO HELP US?
HMM.
THESE TWO WILL DO.
THIS ONE... WE'LL HAVE TO SEE.
I ASSUME *YOU* USED YOUR NIGHTWING POWERS TO SEE I WASN'T GOING TO HARM THE SEAWING. NO DOUBT YOU ALSO ALREADY KNOW I'M GOING TO TAKE YOU INTO THE NEXT CAVERN FOR A PRIVATE CONVERSATION.

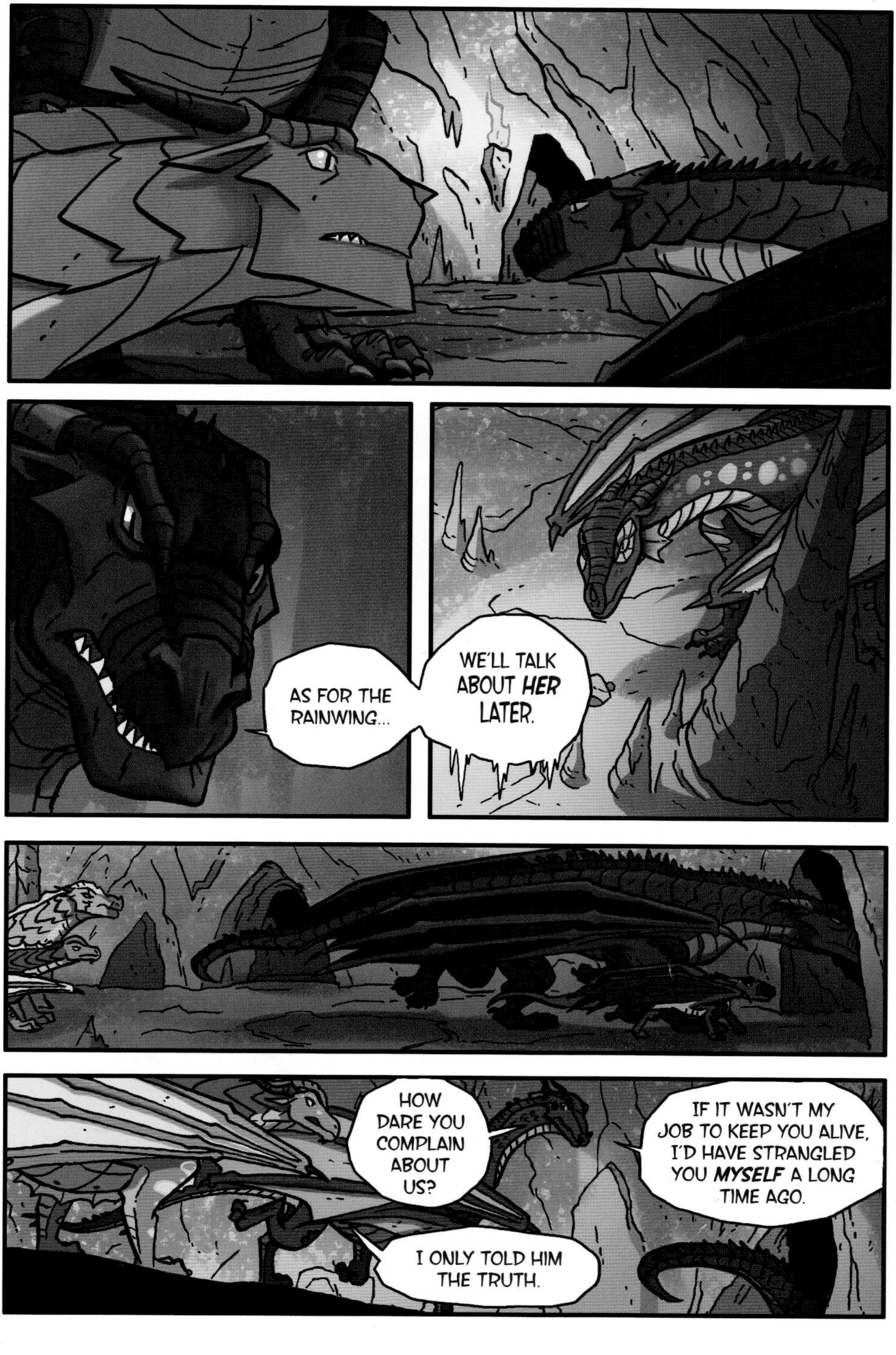
AS FOR THE RAINWING...
WE'LL TALK ABOUT *HER* LATER.
HOW DARE YOU COMPLAIN ABOUT US?
I ONLY TOLD HIM THE TRUTH.
IF IT WASN'T MY JOB TO KEEP YOU ALIVE, I'D HAVE STRANGLED YOU *MYSELF* A LONG TIME AGO.

WELL, *HE* WAS A *GREAT* HELP.

ARE YOU ALL RIGHT?

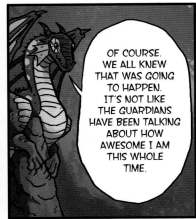

OF COURSE. WE ALL KNEW THAT WAS GOING TO HAPPEN. IT'S NOT LIKE THE GUARDIANS HAVE BEEN TALKING ABOUT HOW AWESOME I AM THIS WHOLE TIME.

WHY DIDN'T YOU FIGHT MORROWSEER? THEN THEY'D KNOW HOW BRAVE AND FIERCE YOU ARE.

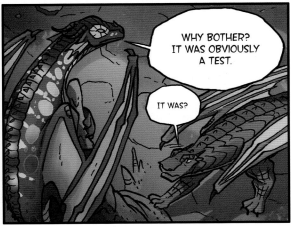

WHY BOTHER? IT WAS OBVIOUSLY A TEST.

IT WAS?

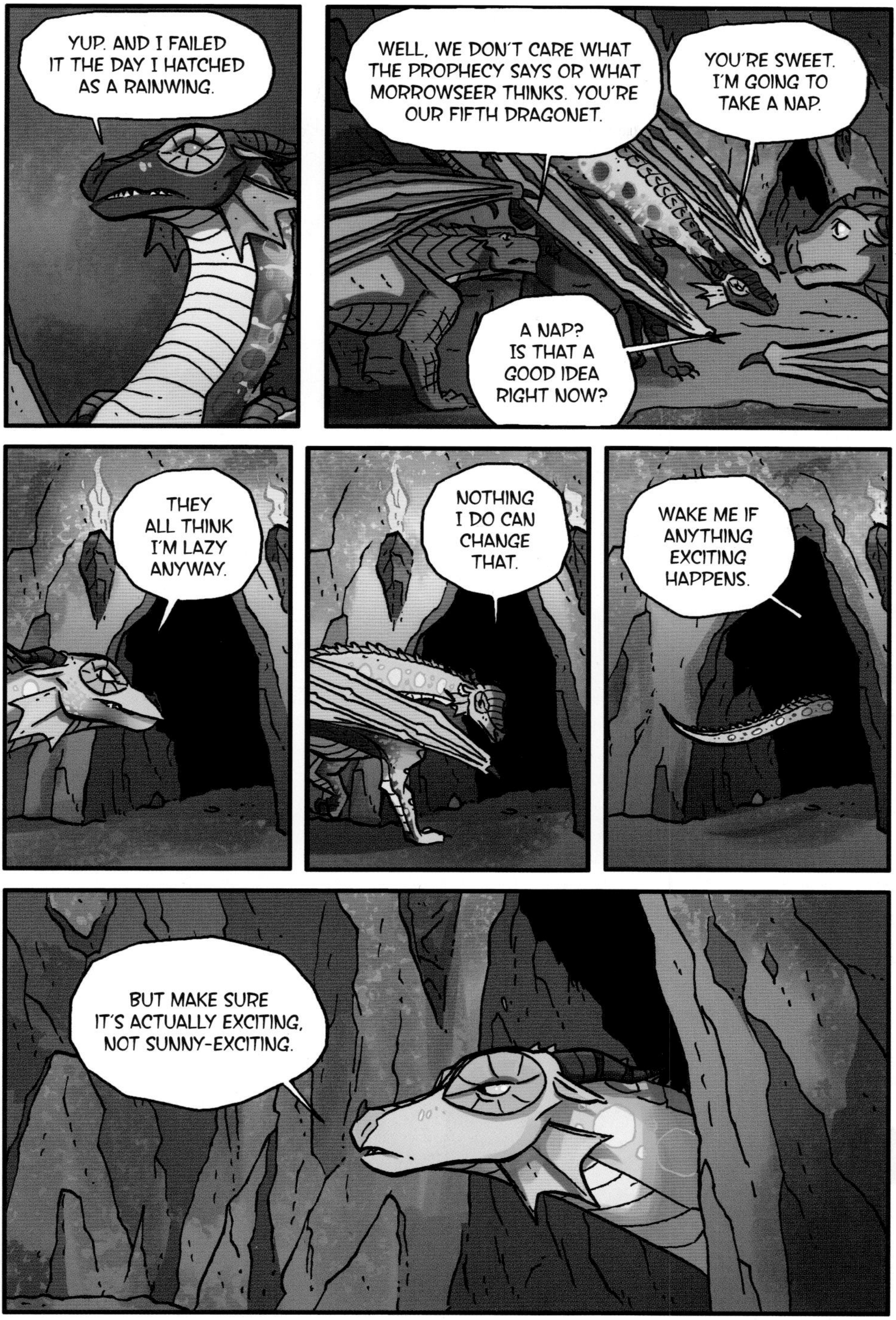
YUP. AND I FAILED IT THE DAY I HATCHED AS A RAINWING.
WELL, WE DON'T CARE WHAT THE PROPHECY SAYS OR WHAT MORROWSEER THINKS. YOU'RE OUR FIFTH DRAGONET.
YOU'RE SWEET. I'M GOING TO TAKE A NAP.
A NAP? IS THAT A GOOD IDEA RIGHT NOW?
THEY ALL THINK I'M LAZY ANYWAY.
NOTHING I DO CAN CHANGE THAT.
WAKE ME IF ANYTHING EXCITING HAPPENS.
BUT MAKE SURE IT'S ACTUALLY EXCITING, NOT SUNNY-EXCITING.

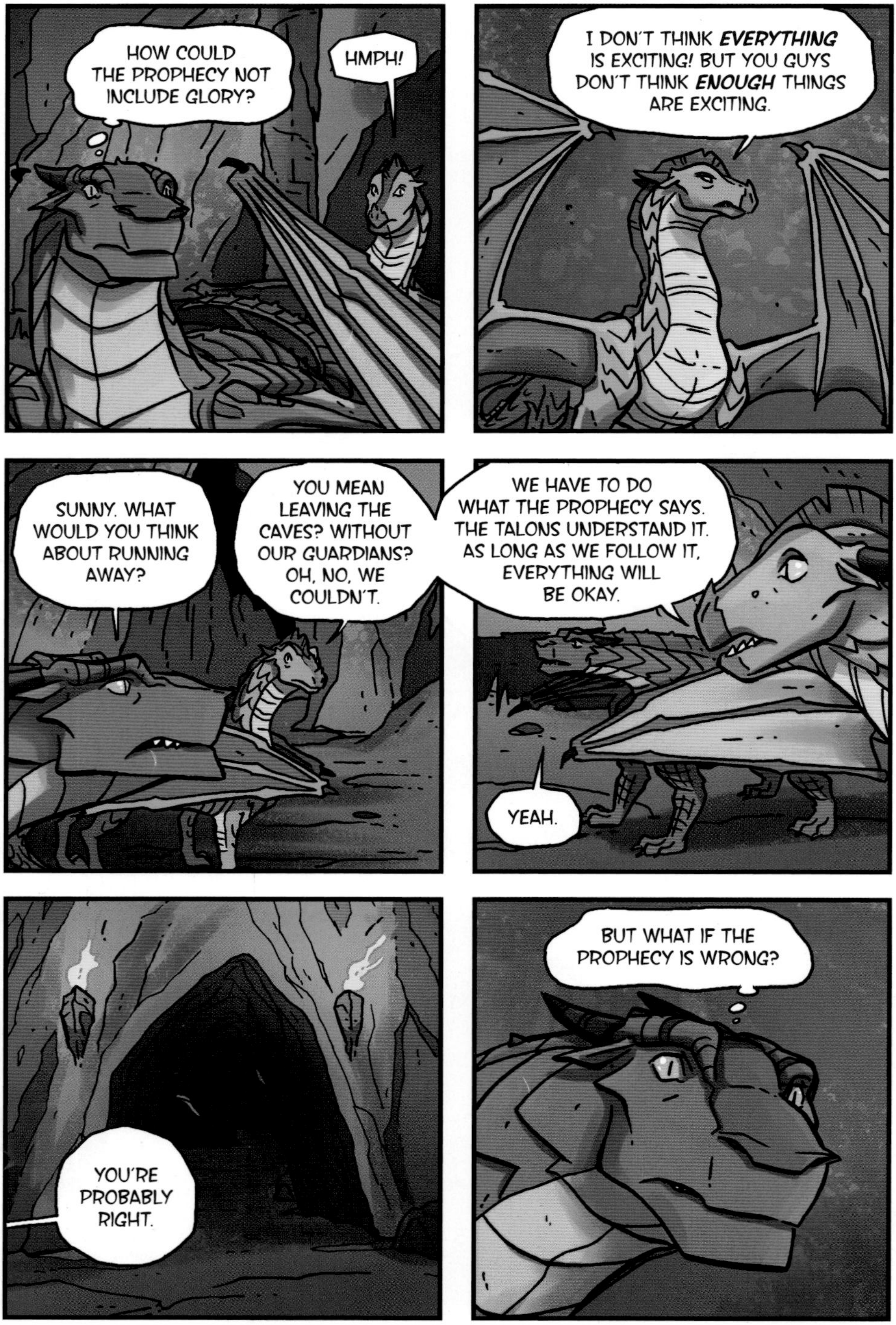
HOW COULD THE PROPHECY NOT INCLUDE GLORY?
HMPH!
I DON'T THINK EVERYTHING IS EXCITING! BUT YOU GUYS DON'T THINK ENOUGH THINGS ARE EXCITING.
SUNNY. WHAT WOULD YOU THINK ABOUT RUNNING AWAY?
YOU MEAN LEAVING THE CAVES? WITHOUT OUR GUARDIANS? OH, NO, WE COULDN'T.
WE HAVE TO DO WHAT THE PROPHECY SAYS. THE TALONS UNDERSTAND IT. AS LONG AS WE FOLLOW IT, EVERYTHING WILL BE OKAY.
YEAH.
YOU'RE PROBABLY RIGHT.
BUT WHAT IF THE PROPHECY IS WRONG?

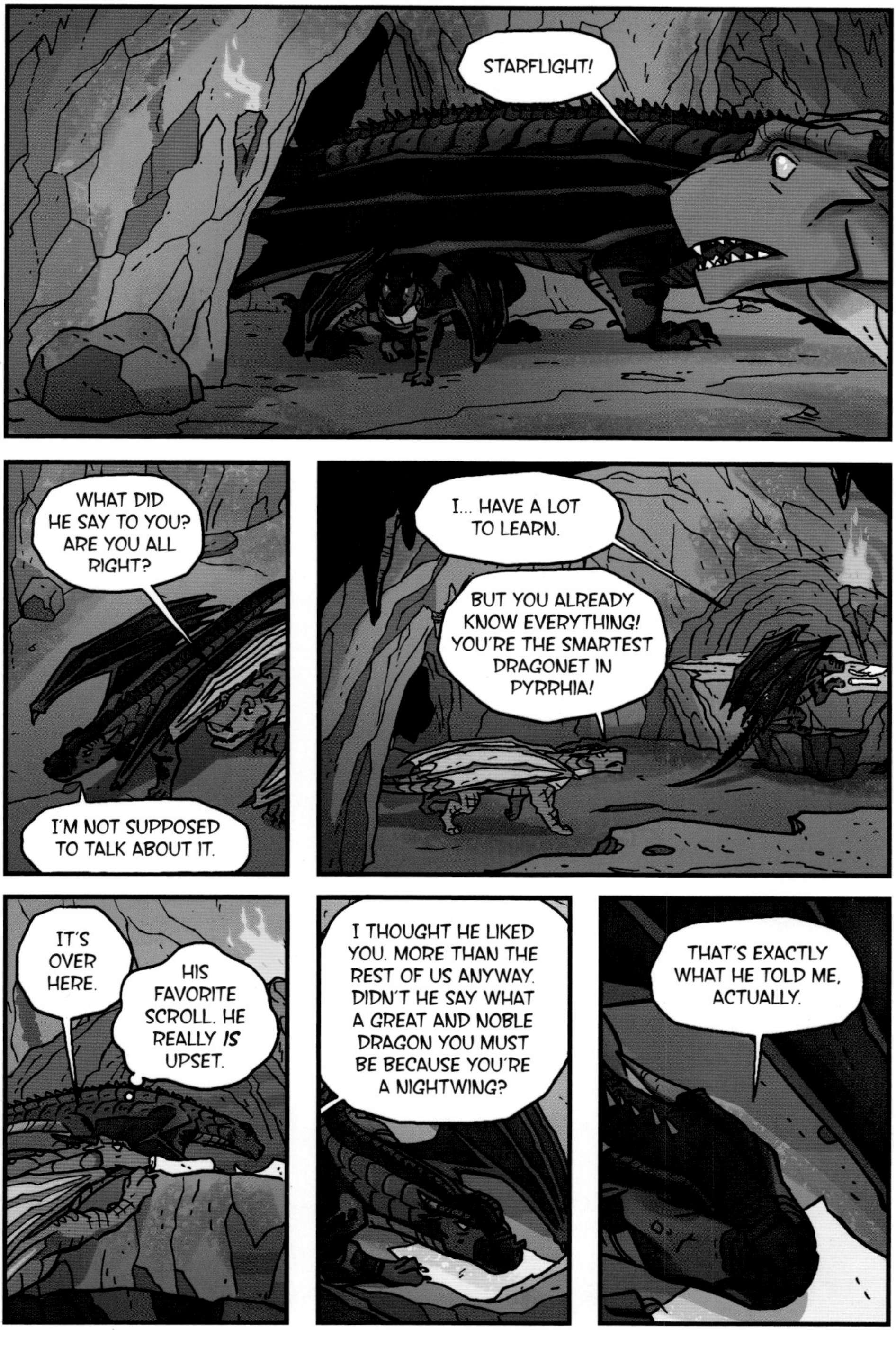
STARFLIGHT!
WHAT DID HE SAY TO YOU? ARE YOU ALL RIGHT?
I'M NOT SUPPOSED TO TALK ABOUT IT.
I... HAVE A LOT TO LEARN.
BUT YOU ALREADY KNOW EVERYTHING! YOU'RE THE SMARTEST DRAGONET IN PYRRHIA!
IT'S OVER HERE.
HIS FAVORITE SCROLL. HE REALLY *IS* UPSET.
I THOUGHT HE LIKED YOU. MORE THAN THE REST OF US ANYWAY. DIDN'T HE SAY WHAT A GREAT AND NOBLE DRAGON YOU MUST BE BECAUSE YOU'RE A NIGHTWING?
THAT'S EXACTLY WHAT HE TOLD ME, ACTUALLY.

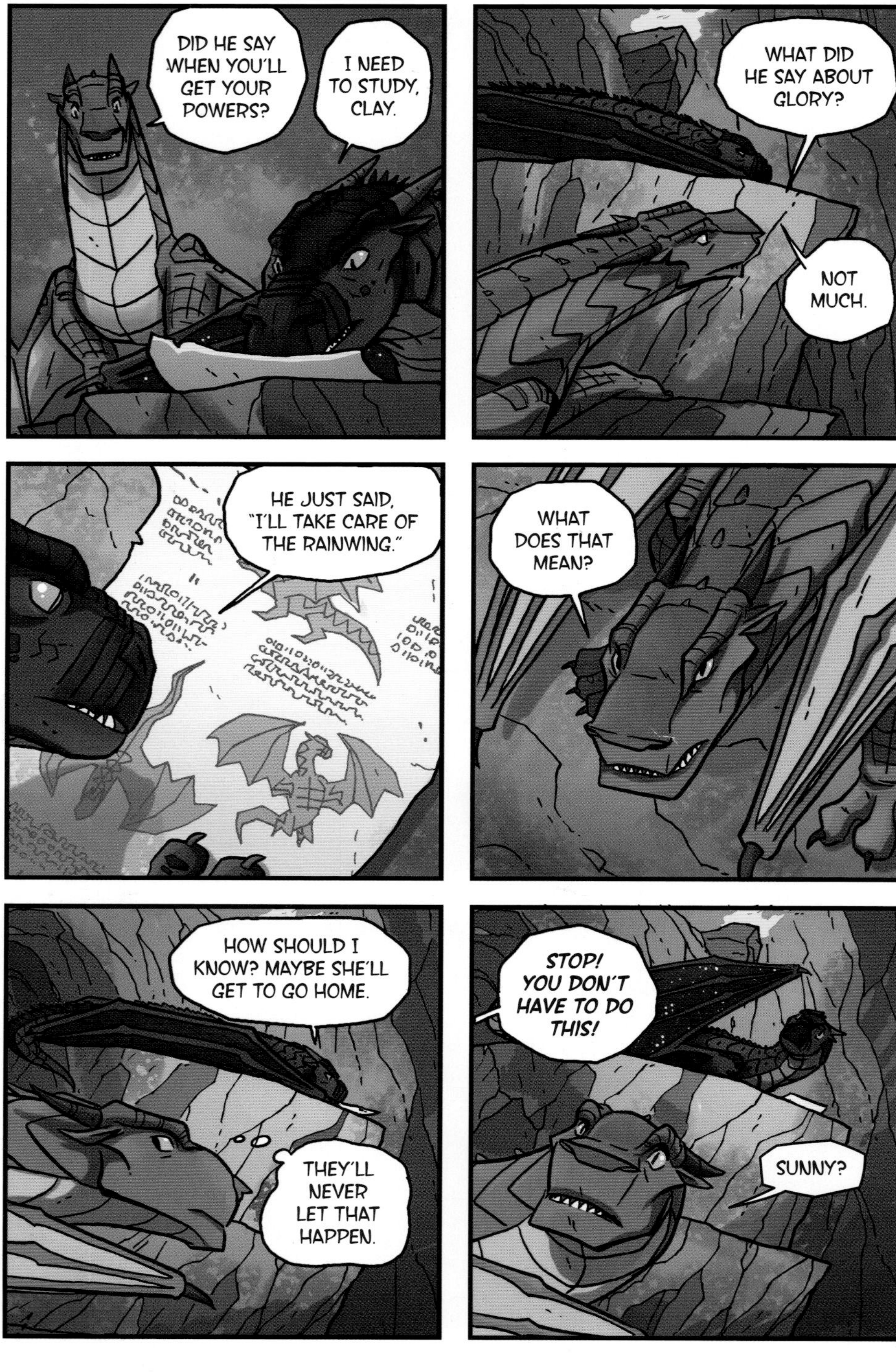
DID HE SAY WHEN YOU'LL GET YOUR POWERS?
I NEED TO STUDY, CLAY.
WHAT DID HE SAY ABOUT GLORY?
NOT MUCH.
HE JUST SAID, "I'LL TAKE CARE OF THE RAINWING."
WHAT DOES THAT MEAN?
HOW SHOULD I KNOW? MAYBE SHE'LL GET TO GO HOME.
THEY'LL NEVER LET THAT HAPPEN.
STOP! YOU DON'T HAVE TO DO THIS!
SUNNY?

WHAT ARE YOU DOING? LET HER GO!

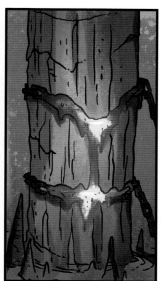

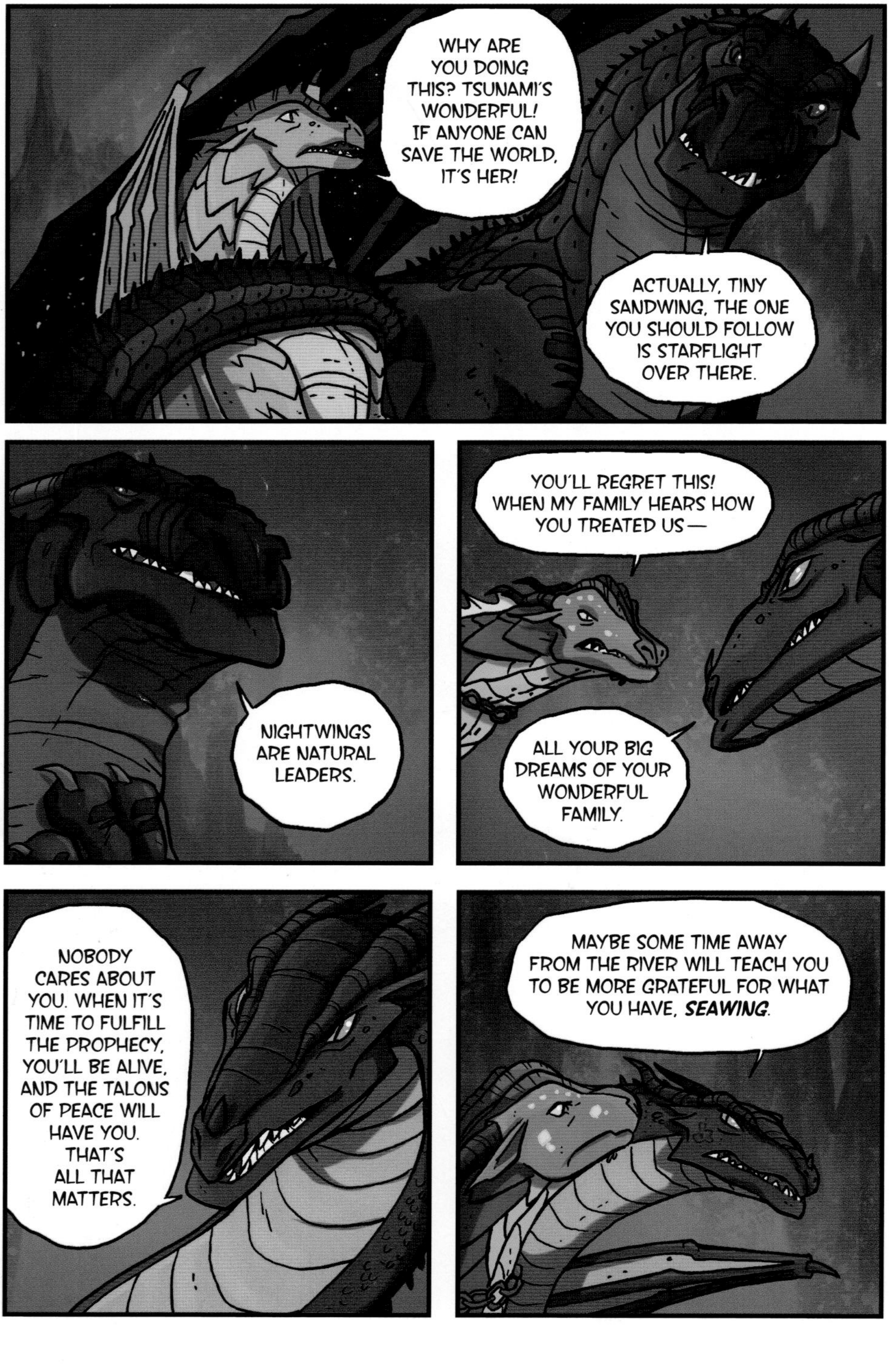
WHY ARE YOU DOING THIS? TSUNAMI'S WONDERFUL! IF ANYONE CAN SAVE THE WORLD, IT'S HER!
ACTUALLY, TINY SANDWING, THE ONE YOU SHOULD FOLLOW IS STARFLIGHT OVER THERE.
NIGHTWINGS ARE NATURAL LEADERS.
YOU'LL REGRET THIS! WHEN MY FAMILY HEARS HOW YOU TREATED US—
ALL YOUR BIG DREAMS OF YOUR WONDERFUL FAMILY.
NOBODY CARES ABOUT YOU. WHEN IT'S TIME TO FULFILL THE PROPHECY, YOU'LL BE ALIVE, AND THE TALONS OF PEACE WILL HAVE YOU. THAT'S ALL THAT MATTERS.
MAYBE SOME TIME AWAY FROM THE RIVER WILL TEACH YOU TO BE MORE GRATEFUL FOR WHAT YOU HAVE, ***SEAWING***.

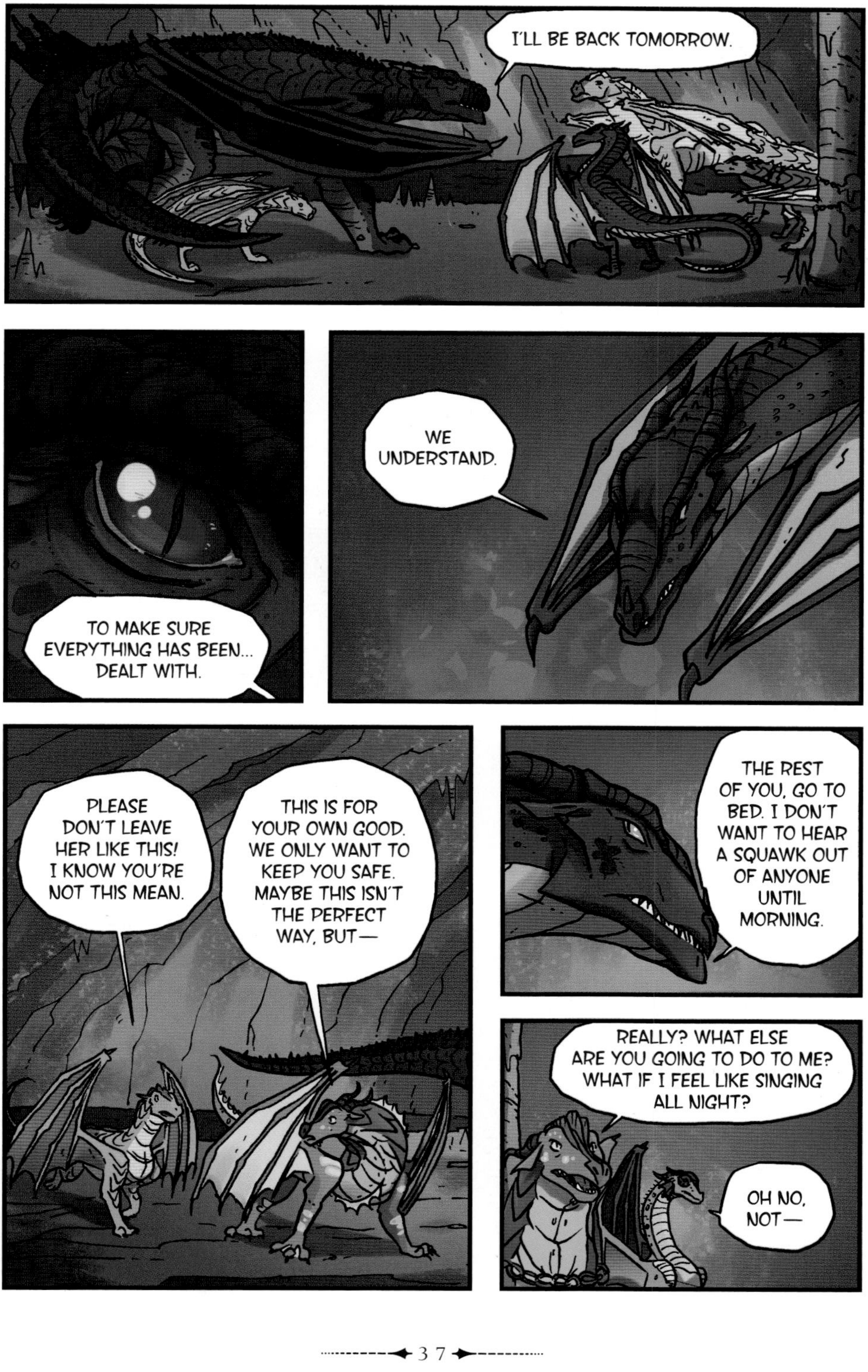
I'LL BE BACK TOMORROW.
TO MAKE SURE EVERYTHING HAS BEEN... DEALT WITH.
WE UNDERSTAND.
PLEASE DON'T LEAVE HER LIKE THIS! I KNOW YOU'RE NOT THIS MEAN.
THIS IS FOR YOUR OWN GOOD. WE ONLY WANT TO KEEP YOU SAFE. MAYBE THIS ISN'T THE PERFECT WAY, BUT—
THE REST OF YOU, GO TO BED. I DON'T WANT TO HEAR A SQUAWK OUT OF ANYONE UNTIL MORNING.
REALLY? WHAT ELSE ARE YOU GOING TO DO TO ME? WHAT IF I FEEL LIKE SINGING ALL NIGHT?
OH NO, NOT—

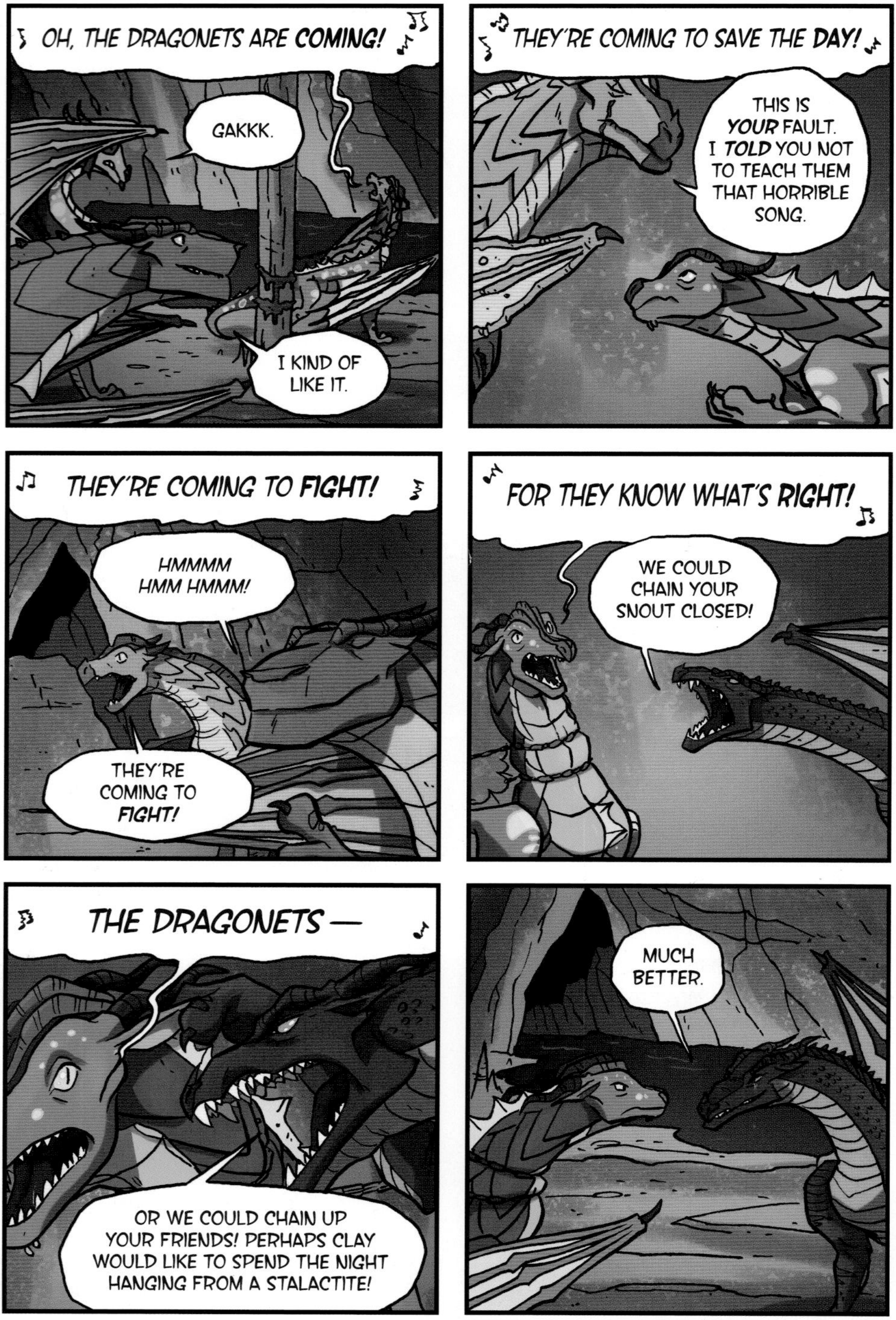
OH, THE DRAGONETS ARE COMING!
GAKKK.
I KIND OF LIKE IT.
THEY'RE COMING TO SAVE THE DAY!
THIS IS YOUR FAULT. I TOLD YOU NOT TO TEACH THEM THAT HORRIBLE SONG.
THEY'RE COMING TO FIGHT!
HMMMM HMM HMMM!
THEY'RE COMING TO FIGHT!
FOR THEY KNOW WHAT'S RIGHT!
WE COULD CHAIN YOUR SNOUT CLOSED!
THE DRAGONETS —
OR WE COULD CHAIN UP YOUR FRIENDS! PERHAPS CLAY WOULD LIKE TO SPEND THE NIGHT HANGING FROM A STALACTITE!
MUCH BETTER.

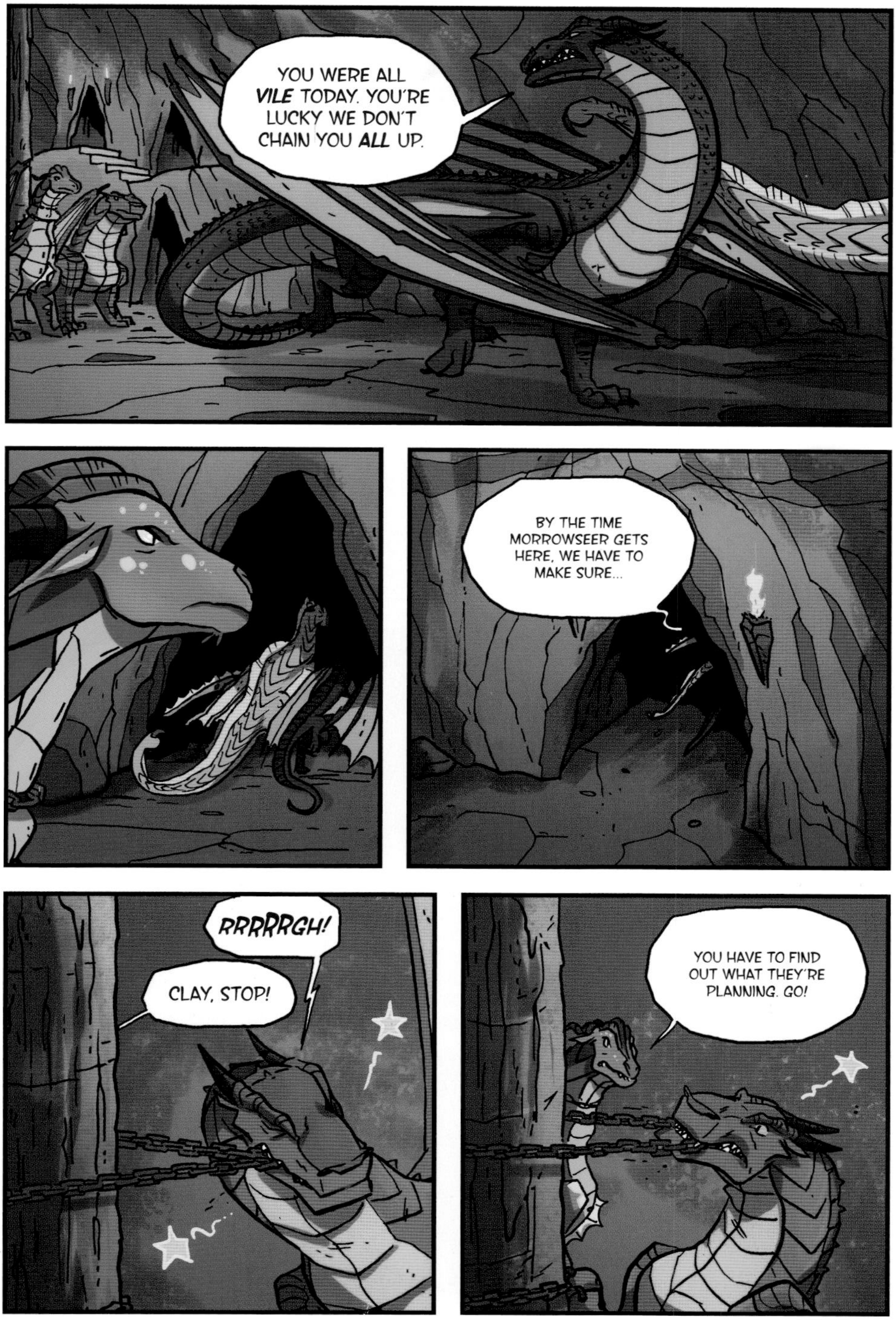
YOU WERE ALL VILE TODAY. YOU'RE LUCKY WE DON'T CHAIN YOU ALL UP.
BY THE TIME MORROWSEER GETS HERE, WE HAVE TO MAKE SURE...
RRRRRGH!
CLAY, STOP!
YOU HAVE TO FIND OUT WHAT THEY'RE PLANNING. GO!

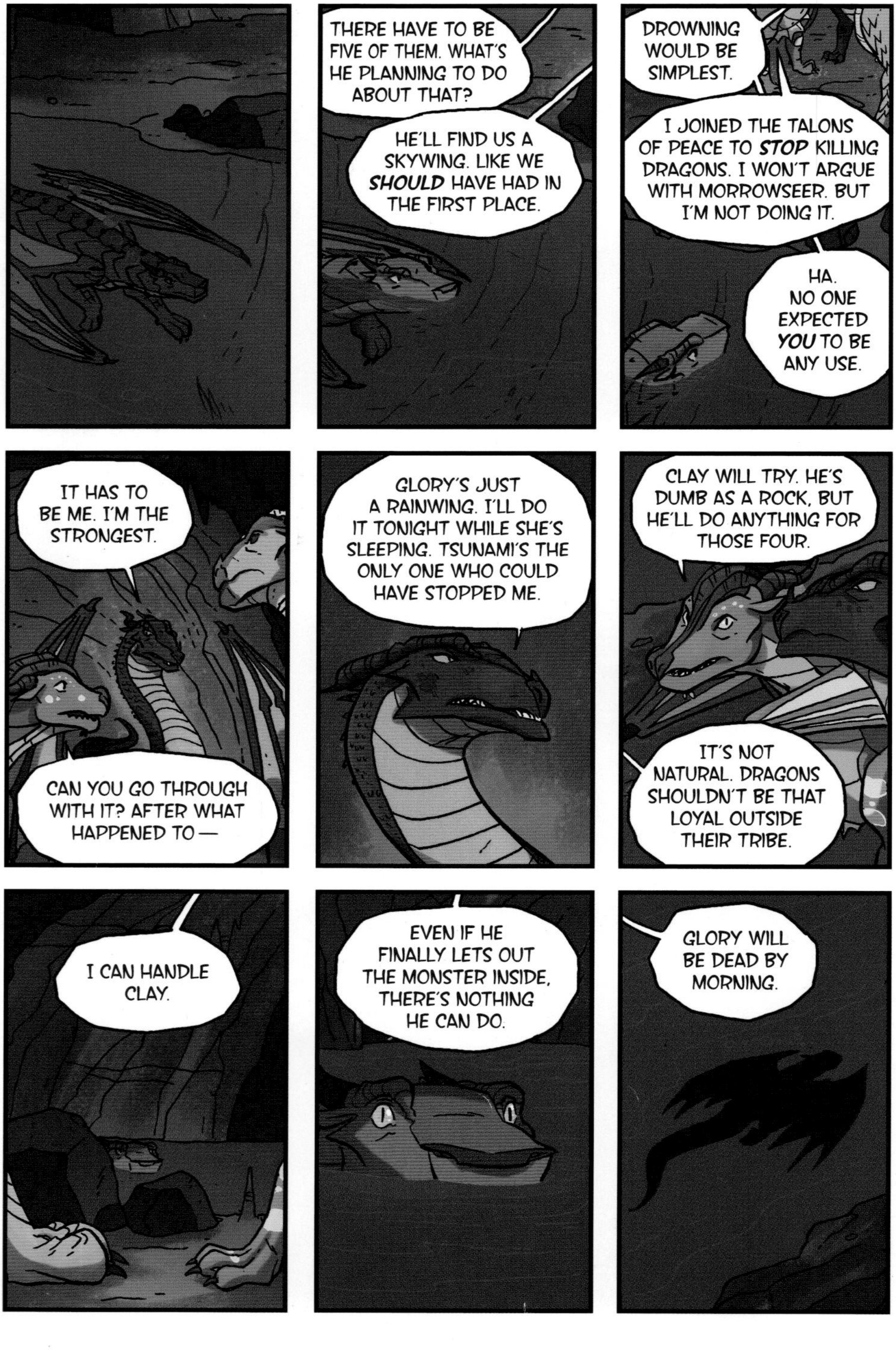
THERE HAVE TO BE FIVE OF THEM. WHAT'S HE PLANNING TO DO ABOUT THAT?
HE'LL FIND US A SKYWING. LIKE WE SHOULD HAVE HAD IN THE FIRST PLACE.
DROWNING WOULD BE SIMPLEST.
I JOINED THE TALONS OF PEACE TO STOP KILLING DRAGONS. I WON'T ARGUE WITH MORROWSEER. BUT I'M NOT DOING IT.
HA. NO ONE EXPECTED YOU TO BE ANY USE.
IT HAS TO BE ME. I'M THE STRONGEST.
CAN YOU GO THROUGH WITH IT? AFTER WHAT HAPPENED TO—
GLORY'S JUST A RAINWING. I'LL DO IT TONIGHT WHILE SHE'S SLEEPING. TSUNAMI'S THE ONLY ONE WHO COULD HAVE STOPPED ME.
CLAY WILL TRY. HE'S DUMB AS A ROCK, BUT HE'LL DO ANYTHING FOR THOSE FOUR.
IT'S NOT NATURAL. DRAGONS SHOULDN'T BE THAT LOYAL OUTSIDE THEIR TRIBE.
I CAN HANDLE CLAY.
EVEN IF HE FINALLY LETS OUT THE MONSTER INSIDE, THERE'S NOTHING HE CAN DO.
GLORY WILL BE DEAD BY MORNING.

THEY WOULDN'T!

THEY DEFINITELY WOULD. THEY'LL DO ANYTHING FOR THE PROPHECY.

BUT WE WON'T LET THEM.

YOU DON'T HAVE TO GET INVOLVED. IT'S MY PROBLEM, NOT YOURS.

ALL OF YOU TOGETHER ARE NO MATCH FOR KESTREL. AND I CAN'T DO ANYTHING!

SO WE ESCAPE.

ESCAPE?

WE HAVE TO GET OUT. TONIGHT. RIGHT NOW.

IF ESCAPE WERE THAT EASY, WE'D ALREADY BE GONE.

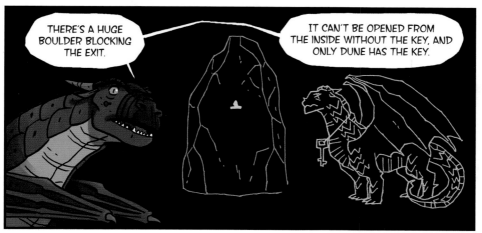

THERE'S A HUGE BOULDER BLOCKING THE EXIT.

IT CAN'T BE OPENED FROM THE INSIDE WITHOUT THE KEY, AND ONLY DUNE HAS THE KEY.

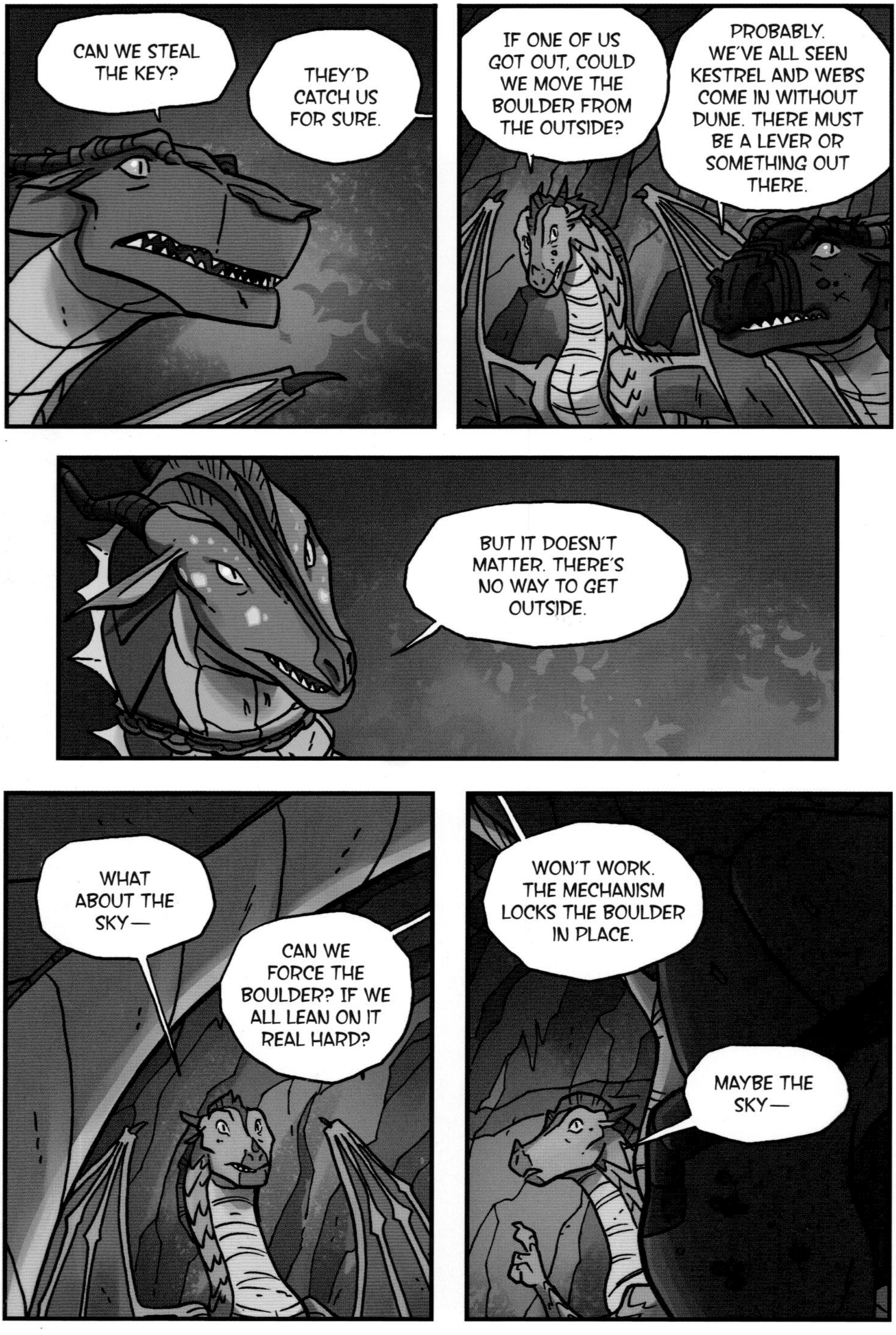
CAN WE STEAL THE KEY?
THEY'D CATCH US FOR SURE.
IF ONE OF US GOT OUT, COULD WE MOVE THE BOULDER FROM THE OUTSIDE?
PROBABLY. WE'VE ALL SEEN KESTREL AND WEBS COME IN WITHOUT DUNE. THERE MUST BE A LEVER OR SOMETHING OUT THERE.
BUT IT DOESN'T MATTER. THERE'S NO WAY TO GET OUTSIDE.
WHAT ABOUT THE SKY—
CAN WE FORCE THE BOULDER? IF WE ALL LEAN ON IT REAL HARD?
WON'T WORK. THE MECHANISM LOCKS THE BOULDER IN PLACE.
MAYBE THE SKY—

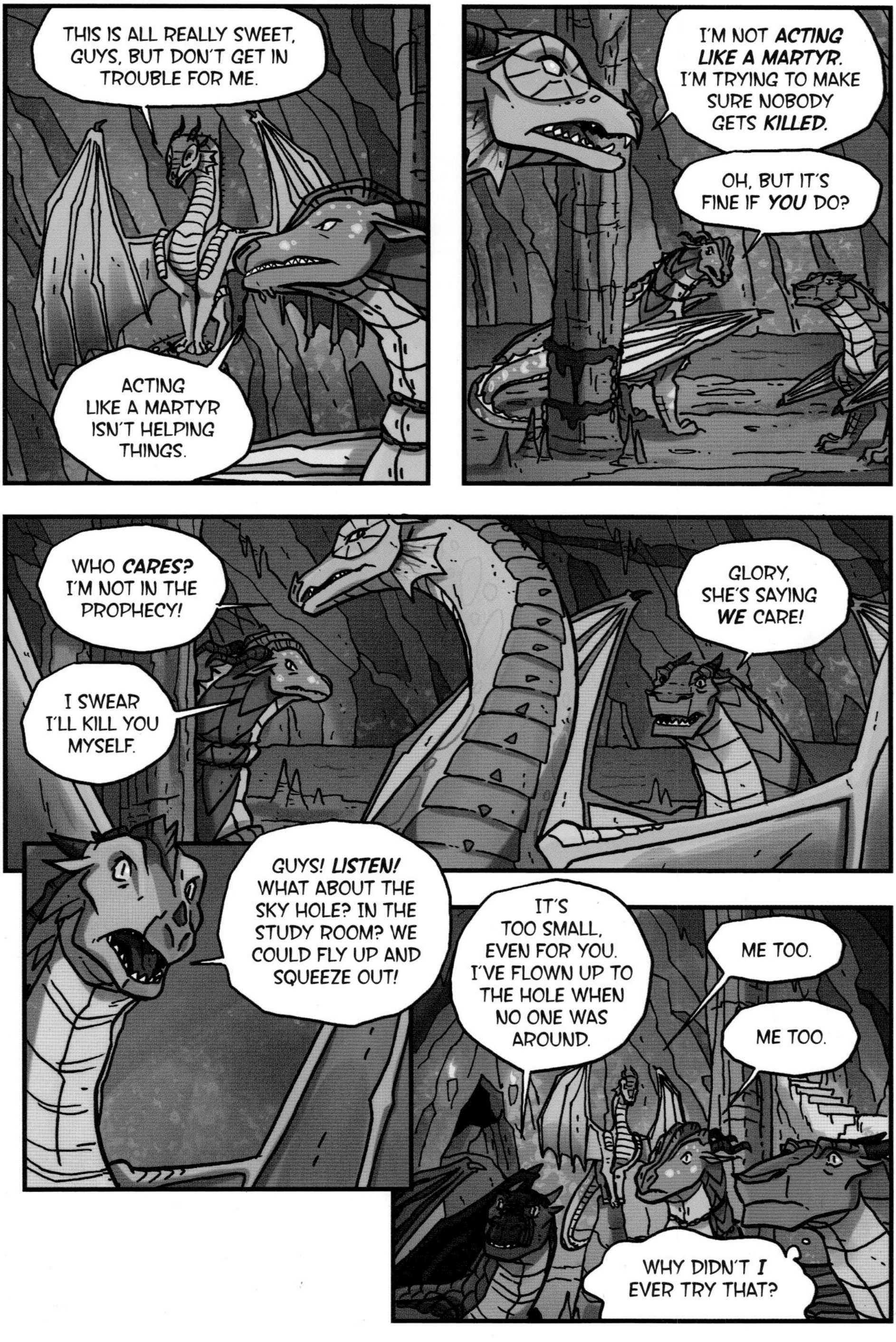
THIS IS ALL REALLY SWEET, GUYS, BUT DON'T GET IN TROUBLE FOR ME.
ACTING LIKE A MARTYR ISN'T HELPING THINGS.
I'M NOT ACTING LIKE A MARTYR. I'M TRYING TO MAKE SURE NOBODY GETS KILLED.
OH, BUT IT'S FINE IF YOU DO?
WHO CARES? I'M NOT IN THE PROPHECY!
I SWEAR I'LL KILL YOU MYSELF.
GLORY, SHE'S SAYING WE CARE!
GUYS! LISTEN! WHAT ABOUT THE SKY HOLE? IN THE STUDY ROOM? WE COULD FLY UP AND SQUEEZE OUT!
IT'S TOO SMALL, EVEN FOR YOU. I'VE FLOWN UP TO THE HOLE WHEN NO ONE WAS AROUND.
ME TOO.
ME TOO.
WHY DIDN'T I EVER TRY THAT?

YOU HAVE AN IDEA. I CAN TELL. YOU'VE BEEN WORKING ON AN ESCAPE PLAN FOREVER.

FOREVER? WHY DIDN'T ANYONE TELL ME?

IT'S TOO DANGEROUS. IT WAS SUPPOSED TO BE ME.

THE RIVER?

DO YOU KNOW WHERE IT GOES?

I FOUND A GAP UNDER THE WALL IN THE TRAINING CAVE. IT'S VERY TIGHT. I'VE NEVER GONE THROUGH IN CASE I COULDN'T GET BACK.

I'LL GO. WITH YOU TIED UP, I'M THE BEST SWIMMER.

CLAY, YOU CAN'T!

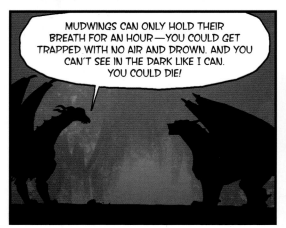

MUDWINGS CAN ONLY HOLD THEIR BREATH FOR AN HOUR—YOU COULD GET TRAPPED WITH NO AIR AND DROWN. AND YOU CAN'T SEE IN THE DARK LIKE I CAN. YOU COULD DIE!

GLORY *WILL* DIE IF I DON'T. RIGHT? THERE'S NO OTHER WAY.

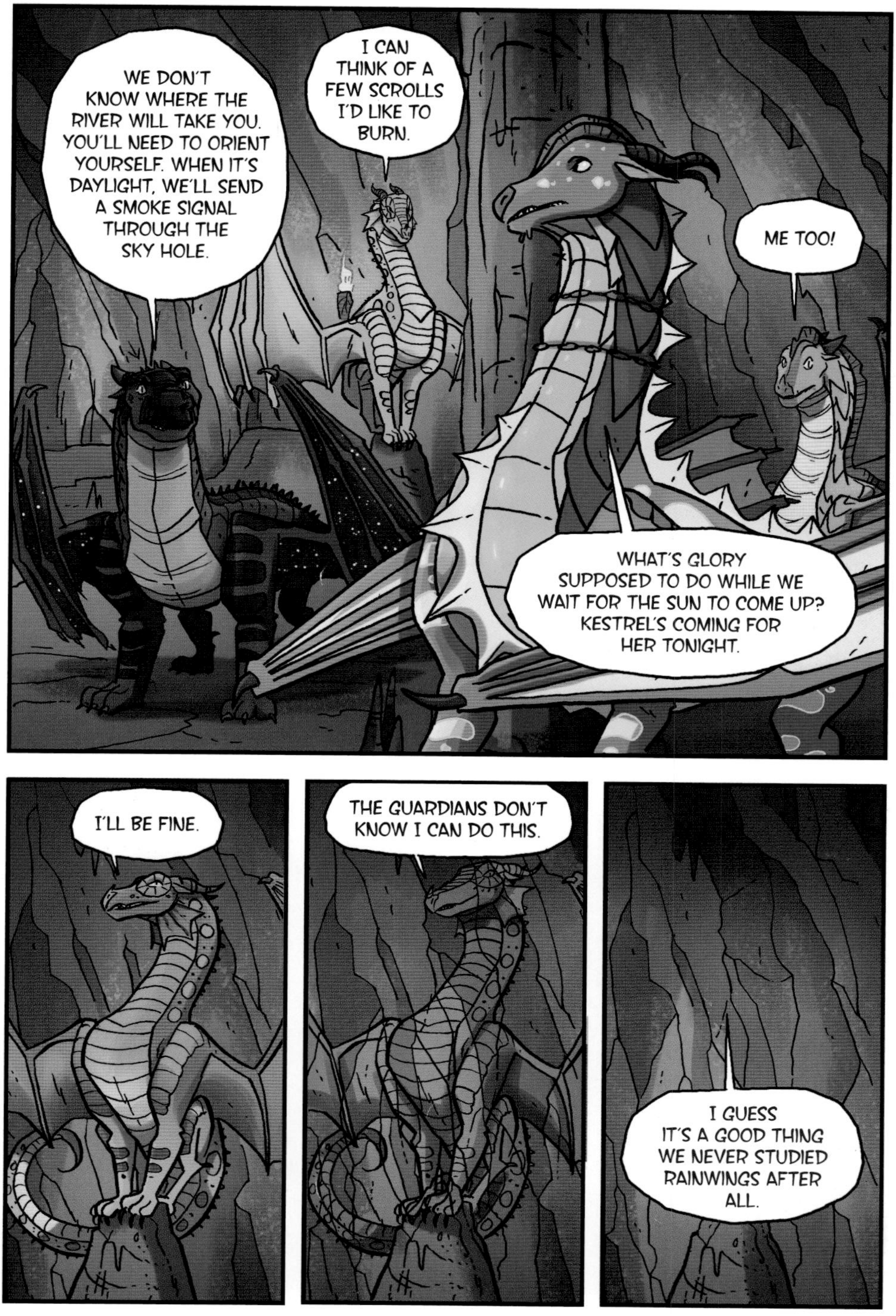
WE DON'T KNOW WHERE THE RIVER WILL TAKE YOU. YOU'LL NEED TO ORIENT YOURSELF. WHEN IT'S DAYLIGHT, WE'LL SEND A SMOKE SIGNAL THROUGH THE SKY HOLE.
I CAN THINK OF A FEW SCROLLS I'D LIKE TO BURN.
ME TOO!
WHAT'S GLORY SUPPOSED TO DO WHILE WE WAIT FOR THE SUN TO COME UP? KESTREL'S COMING FOR HER TONIGHT.
I'LL BE FINE.
THE GUARDIANS DON'T KNOW I CAN DO THIS.
I GUESS IT'S A GOOD THING WE NEVER STUDIED RAINWINGS AFTER ALL.

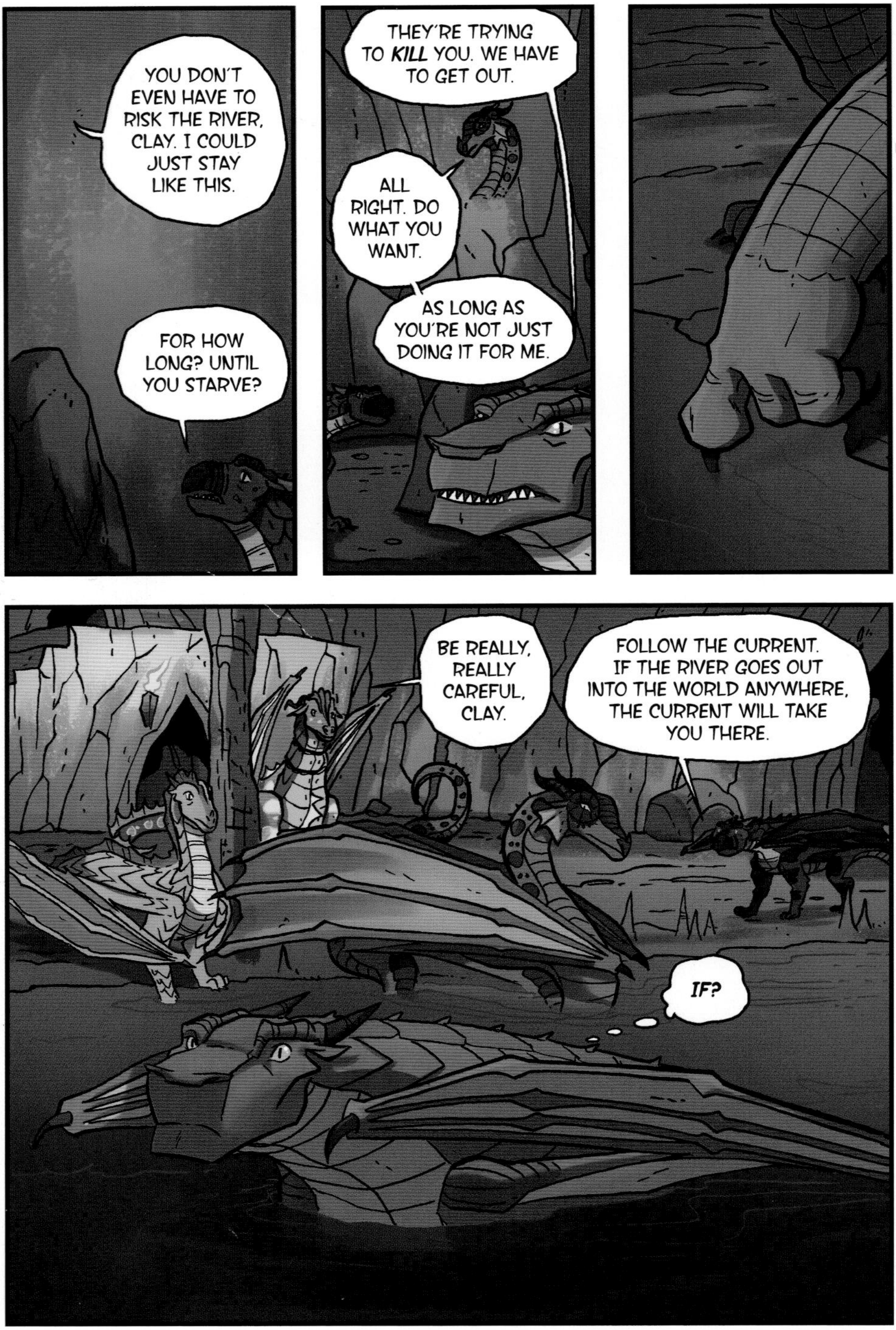
YOU DON'T EVEN HAVE TO RISK THE RIVER, CLAY. I COULD JUST STAY LIKE THIS.
FOR HOW LONG? UNTIL YOU STARVE?
THEY'RE TRYING TO KILL YOU. WE HAVE TO GET OUT.
ALL RIGHT. DO WHAT YOU WANT.
AS LONG AS YOU'RE NOT JUST DOING IT FOR ME.
BE REALLY, REALLY CAREFUL, CLAY.
FOLLOW THE CURRENT. IF THE RIVER GOES OUT INTO THE WORLD ANYWHERE, THE CURRENT WILL TAKE YOU THERE.
IF?

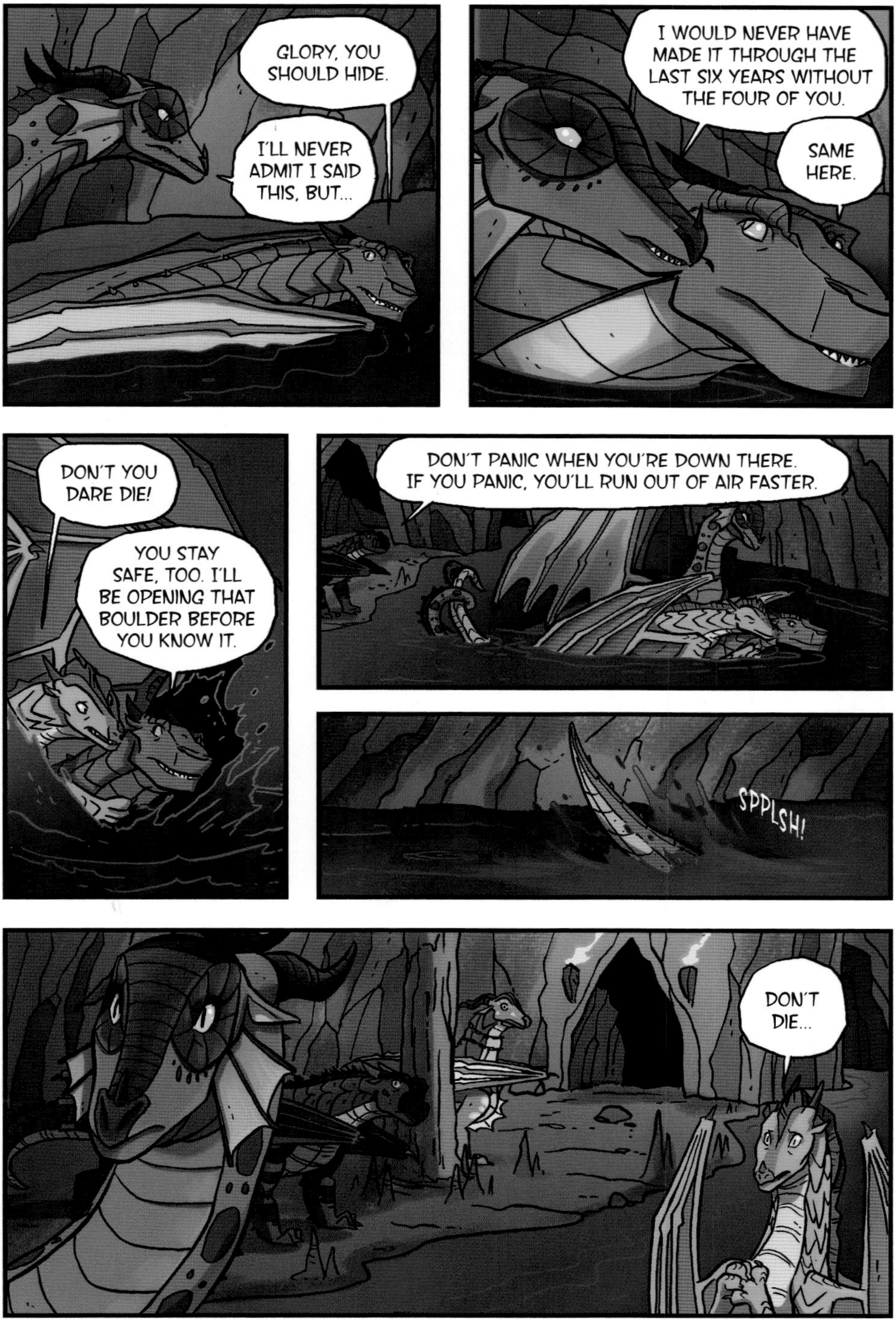
GLORY, YOU SHOULD HIDE.
I'LL NEVER ADMIT I SAID THIS, BUT...
I WOULD NEVER HAVE MADE IT THROUGH THE LAST SIX YEARS WITHOUT THE FOUR OF YOU.
SAME HERE.
DON'T YOU DARE DIE!
YOU STAY SAFE, TOO. I'LL BE OPENING THAT BOULDER BEFORE YOU KNOW IT.
DON'T PANIC WHEN YOU'RE DOWN THERE. IF YOU PANIC, YOU'LL RUN OUT OF AIR FASTER.
SPPLSH!
DON'T DIE...

THERE, THAT DARK PATCH. THAT'S THE WAY OUT.

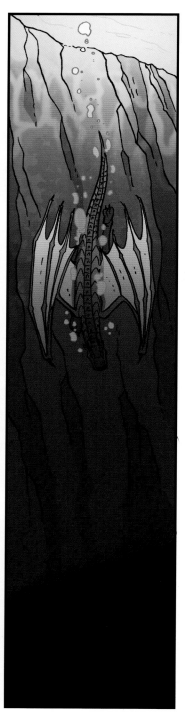

IT'S SO SMALL!

INHALE!

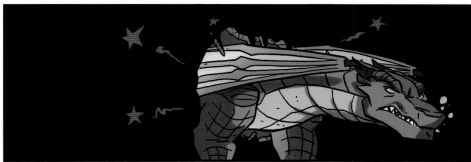

DON'T PANIC.
DON'T PANIC.
DON'T—

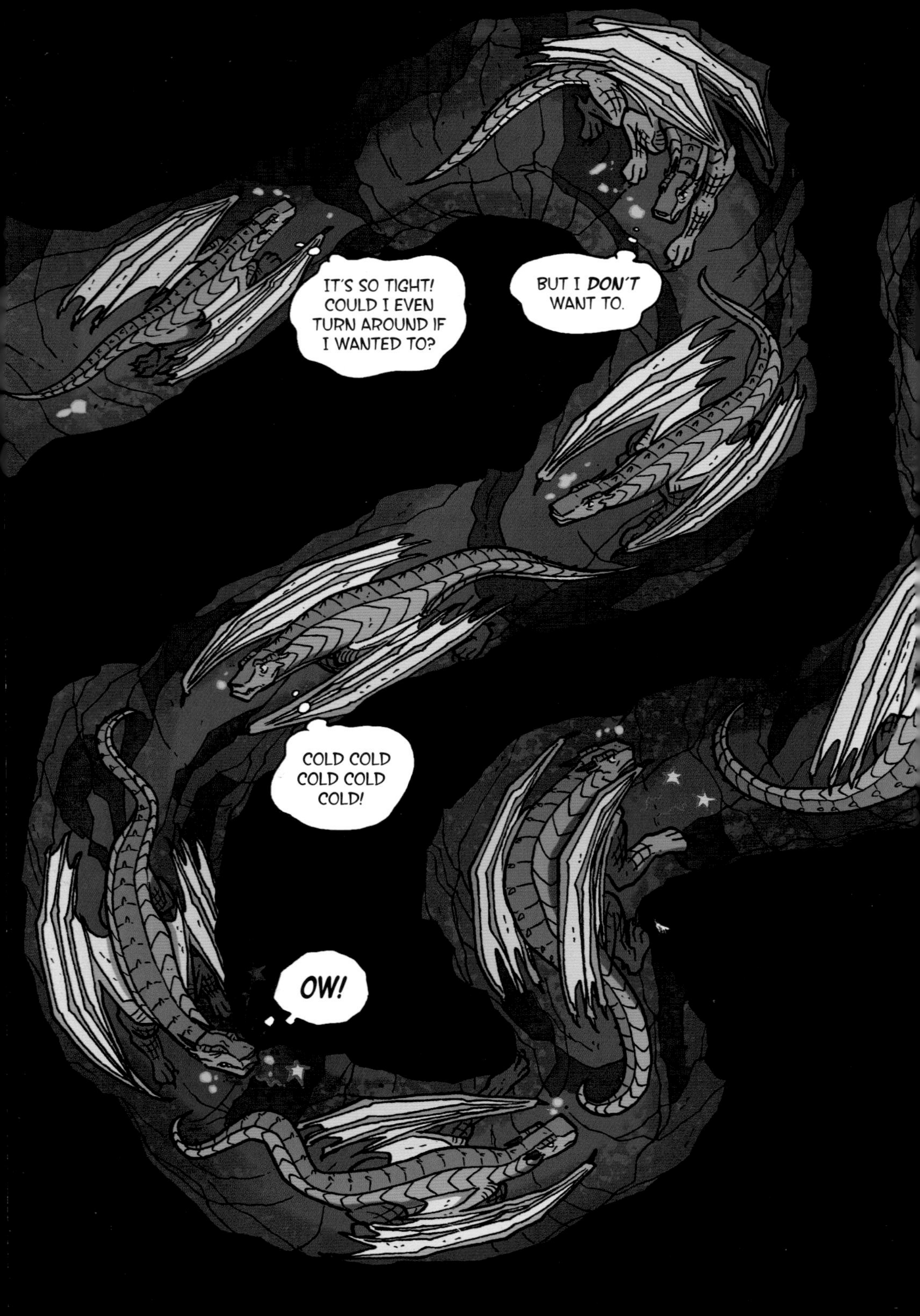
IT'S SO TIGHT! COULD I EVEN TURN AROUND IF I WANTED TO?
BUT I *DON'T* WANT TO.
COLD COLD COLD COLD COLD!
OW!

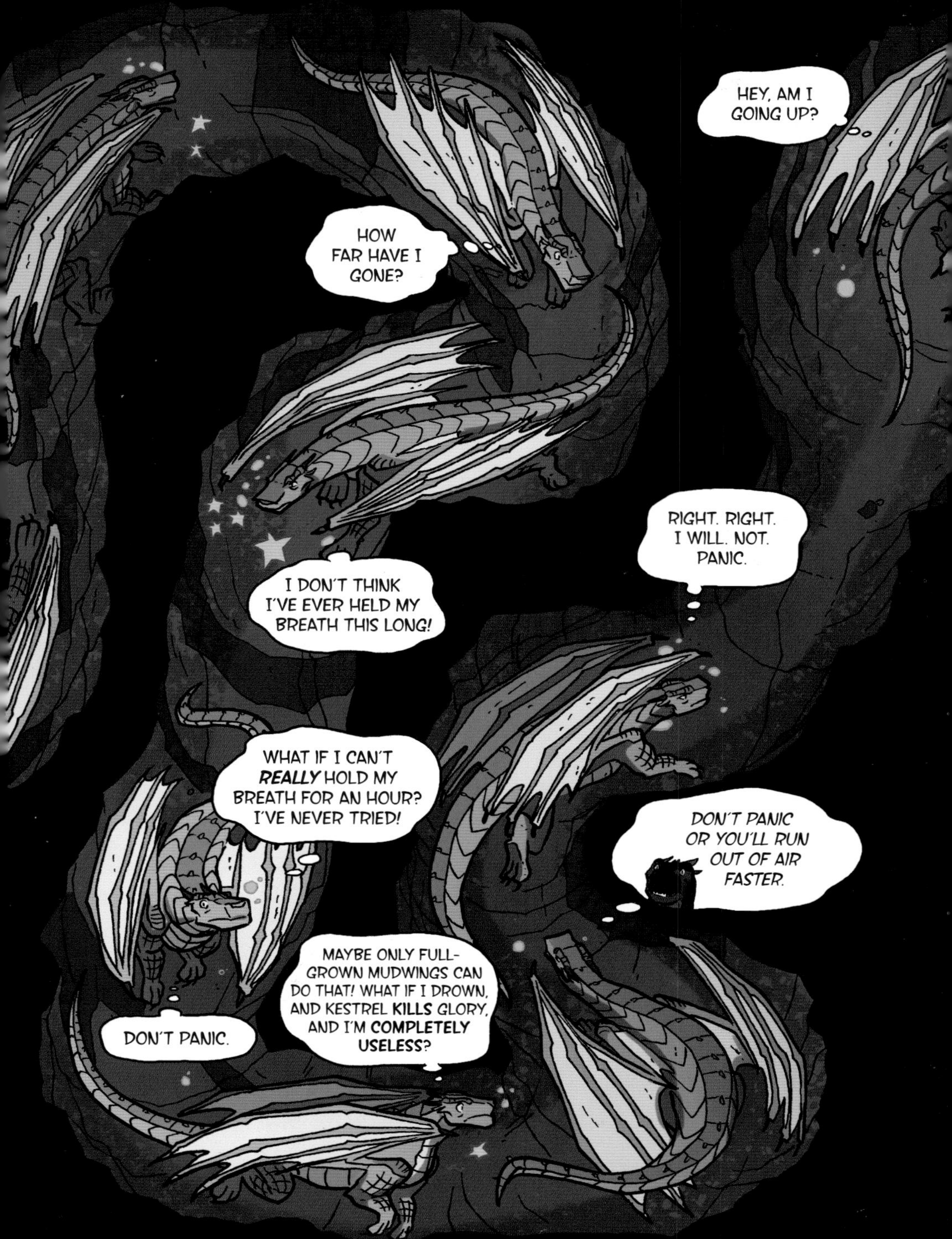
HOW FAR HAVE I GONE?
I DON'T THINK I'VE EVER HELD MY BREATH THIS LONG!
WHAT IF I CAN'T *REALLY* HOLD MY BREATH FOR AN HOUR? I'VE NEVER TRIED!
MAYBE ONLY FULL-GROWN MUDWINGS CAN DO THAT! WHAT IF I DROWN, AND KESTREL **KILLS** GLORY, AND I'M **COMPLETELY USELESS**?
DON'T PANIC.
DON'T PANIC OR YOU'LL RUN OUT OF AIR FASTER.
RIGHT. RIGHT. I WILL. NOT. PANIC.
HEY, AM I GOING UP?

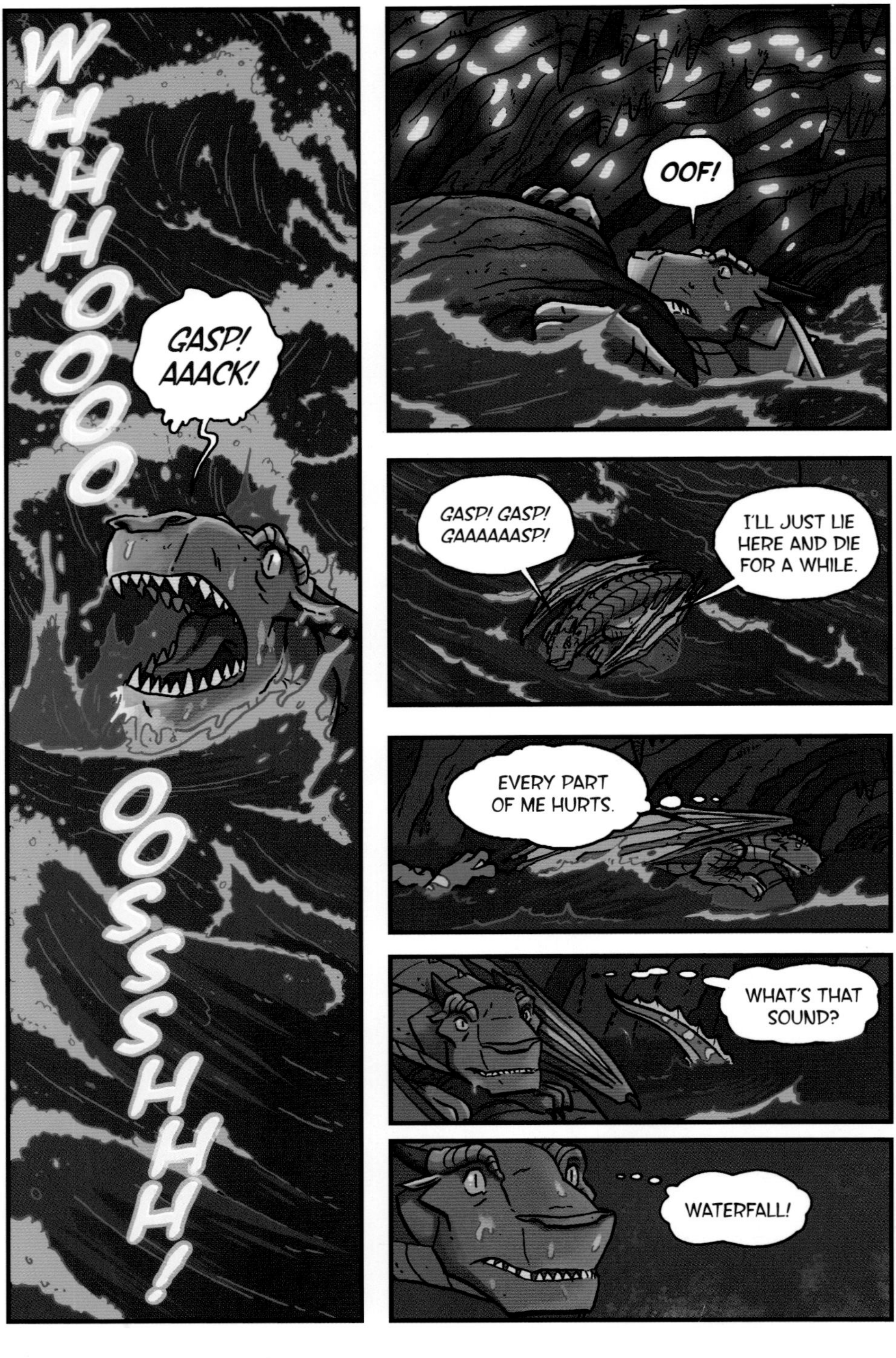
WHHOOOOO
GASP! AAACK!
OOSSSHHH!
OOF!
GASP! GASP! GAAAAAASP!
I'LL JUST LIE HERE AND DIE FOR A WHILE.
EVERY PART OF ME HURTS.
WHAT'S THAT SOUND?
WATERFALL!

I'LL HAVE TO APPROACH THE WATERFALL SLOWLY AND CARE —

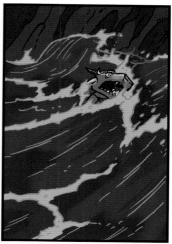

AAAAAAAH!

DON'T PANIC DON'T PANIC DON'T—

WATCH OUT, CLAY! IT'S REALLY DANGEROUS! YOU MIGHT STUB A CLAW!

WHATEVER YOU DO, DON'T LET GO!

HA. HA.

C'MON. THE EXIT'S THIS WAY.

HOW DID YOU GET HERE?

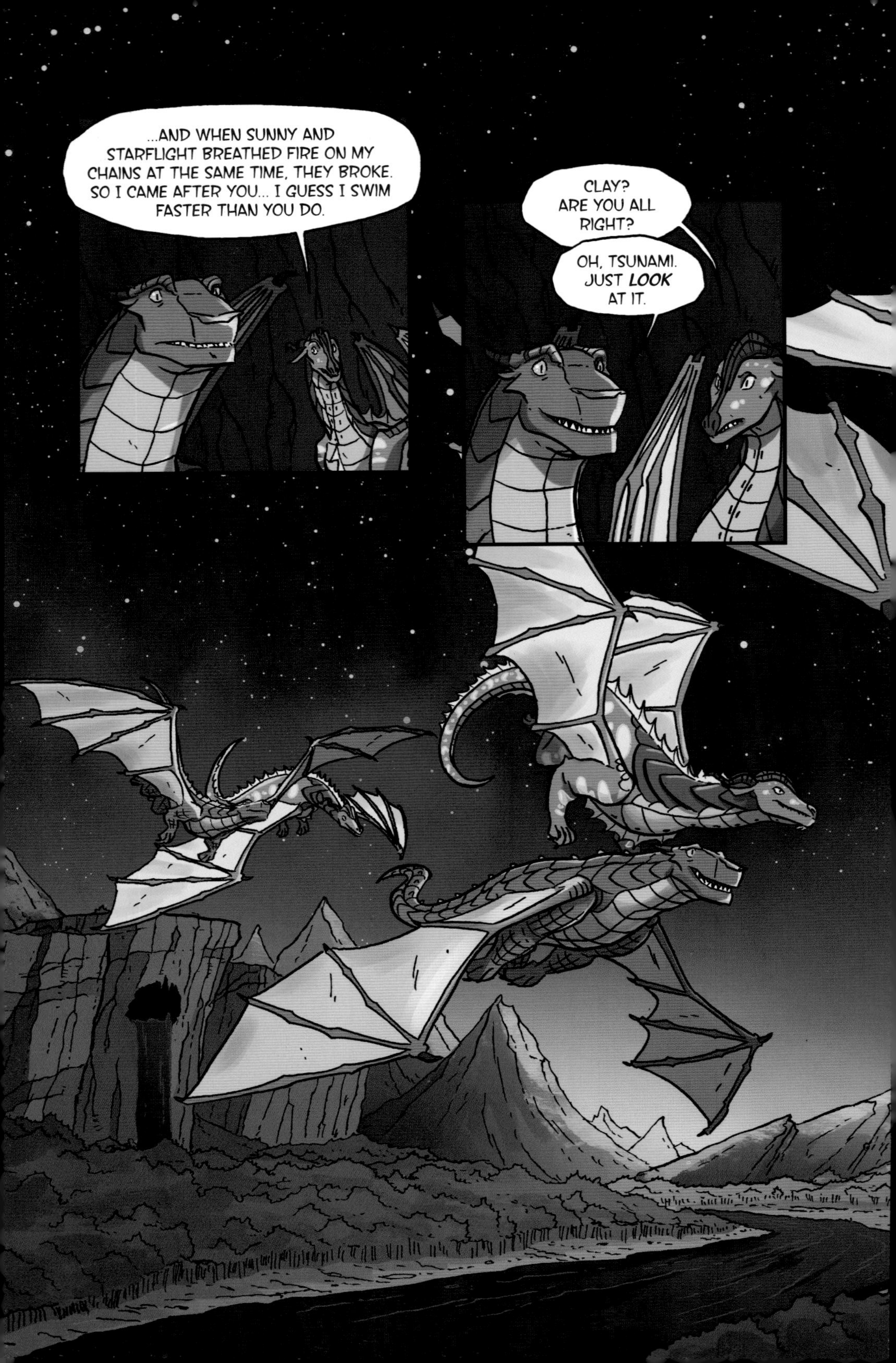
...AND WHEN SUNNY AND STARFLIGHT BREATHED FIRE ON MY CHAINS AT THE SAME TIME, THEY BROKE. SO I CAME AFTER YOU... I GUESS I SWIM FASTER THAN YOU DO.
CLAY? ARE YOU ALL RIGHT?
OH, TSUNAMI. JUST **LOOK** AT IT.

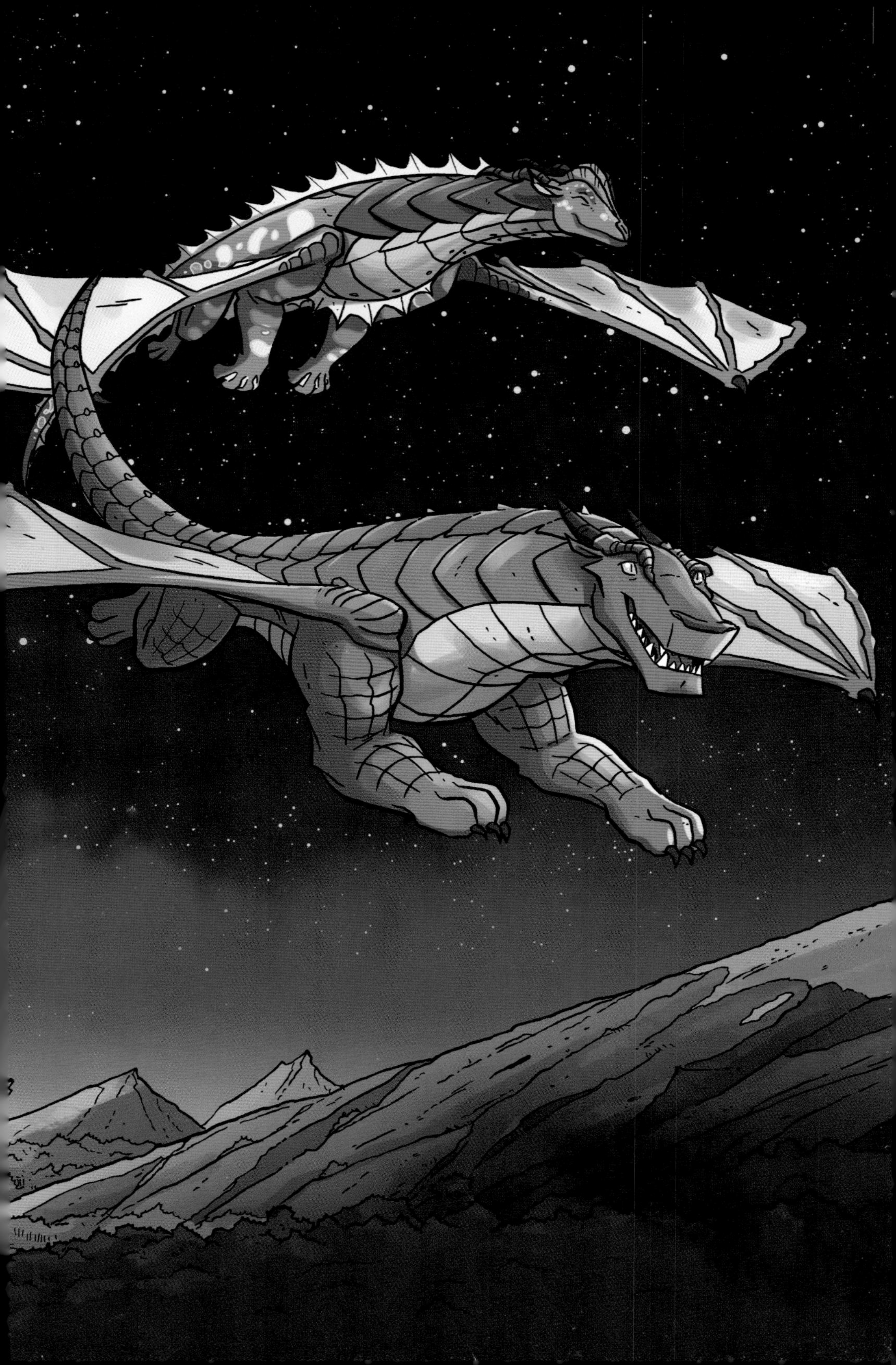

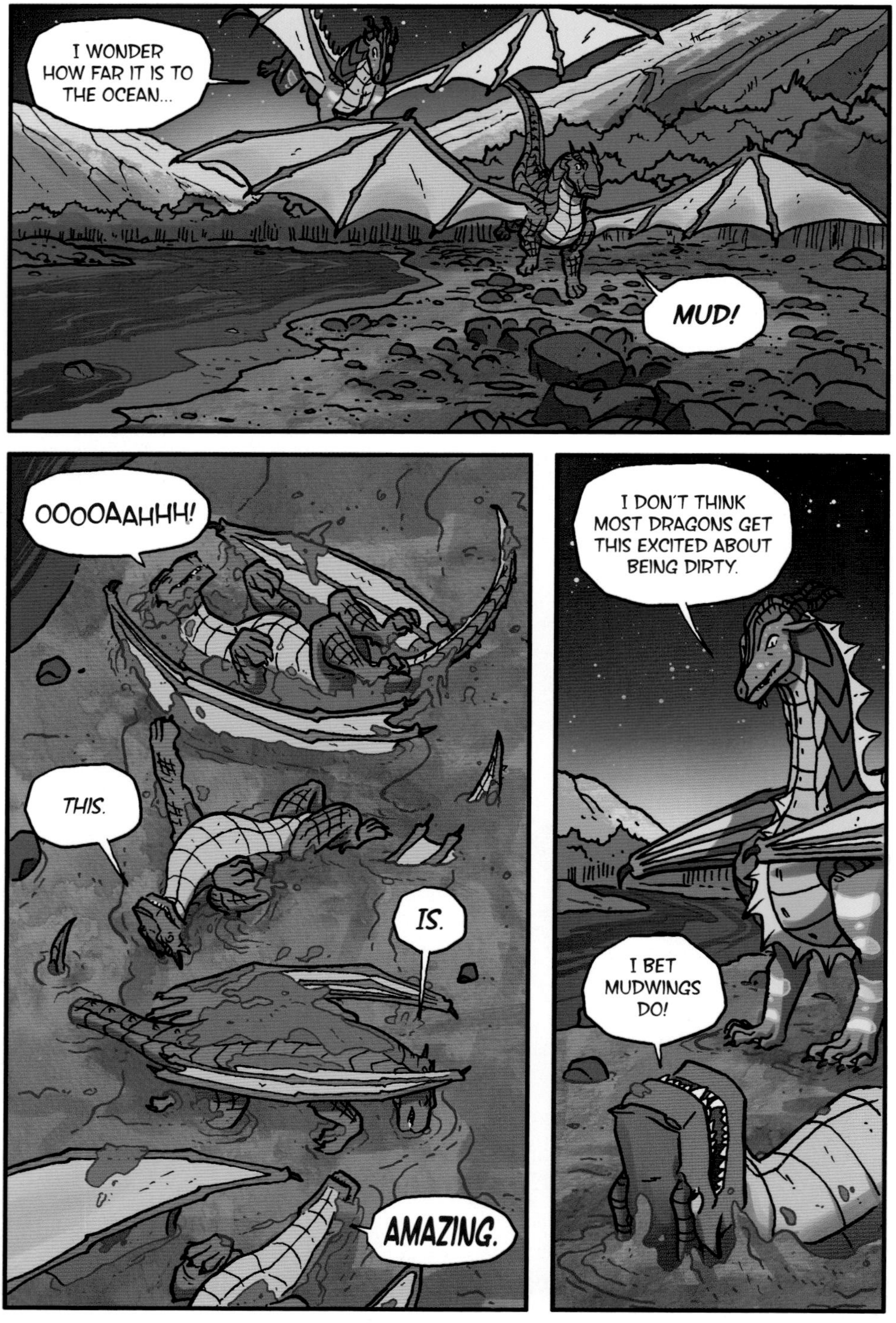
I WONDER HOW FAR IT IS TO THE OCEAN...
MUD!
OOOOAAHHH!
THIS.
IS.
AMAZING.
I DON'T THINK MOST DRAGONS GET THIS EXCITED ABOUT BEING DIRTY.
I BET MUDWINGS DO!

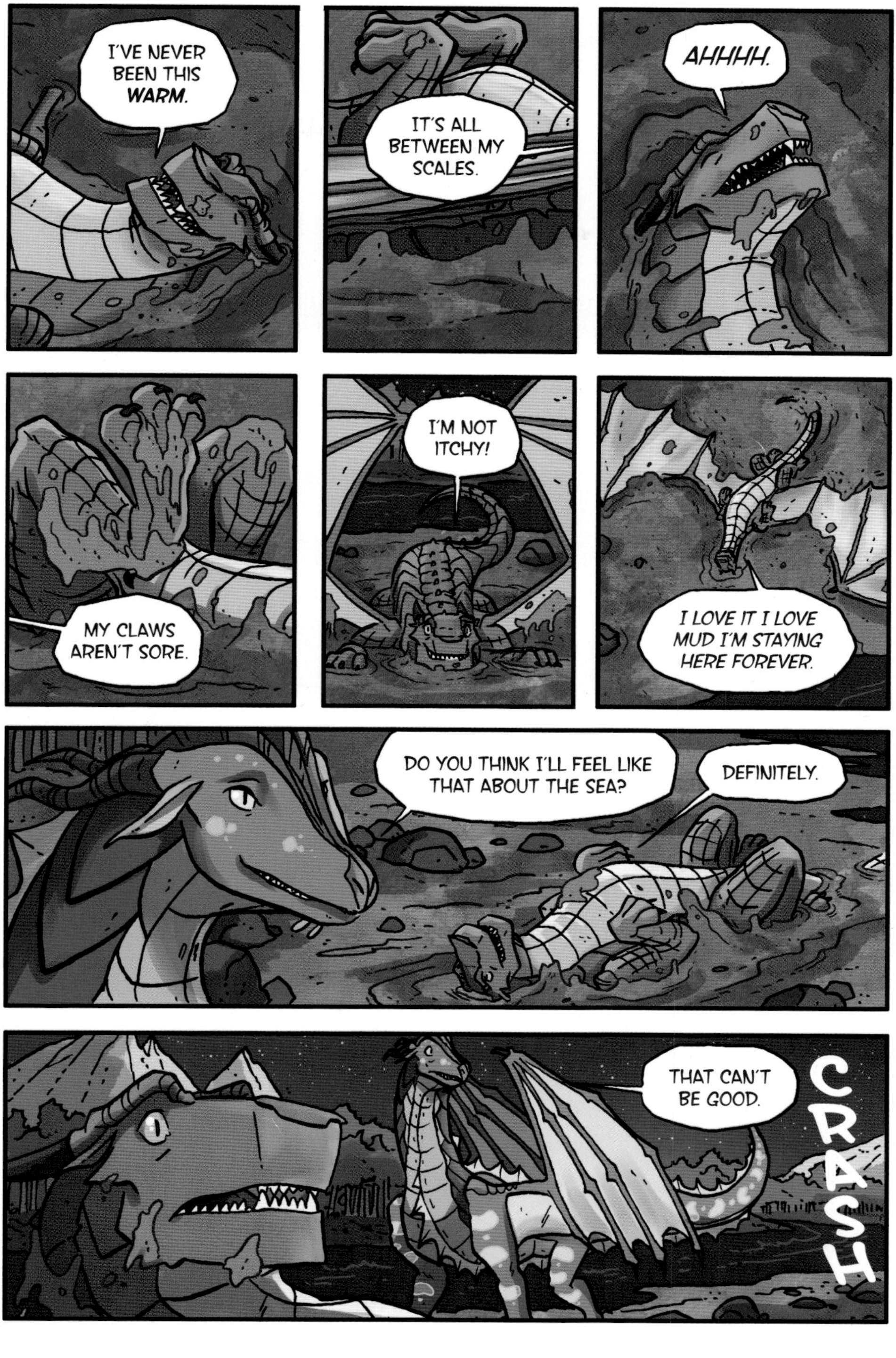
I'VE NEVER BEEN THIS WARM.
IT'S ALL BETWEEN MY SCALES.
AHHHH.
MY CLAWS AREN'T SORE.
I'M NOT ITCHY!
I LOVE IT I LOVE MUD I'M STAYING HERE FOREVER.
DO YOU THINK I'LL FEEL LIKE THAT ABOUT THE SEA?
DEFINITELY.
THAT CAN'T BE GOOD.
CRASH

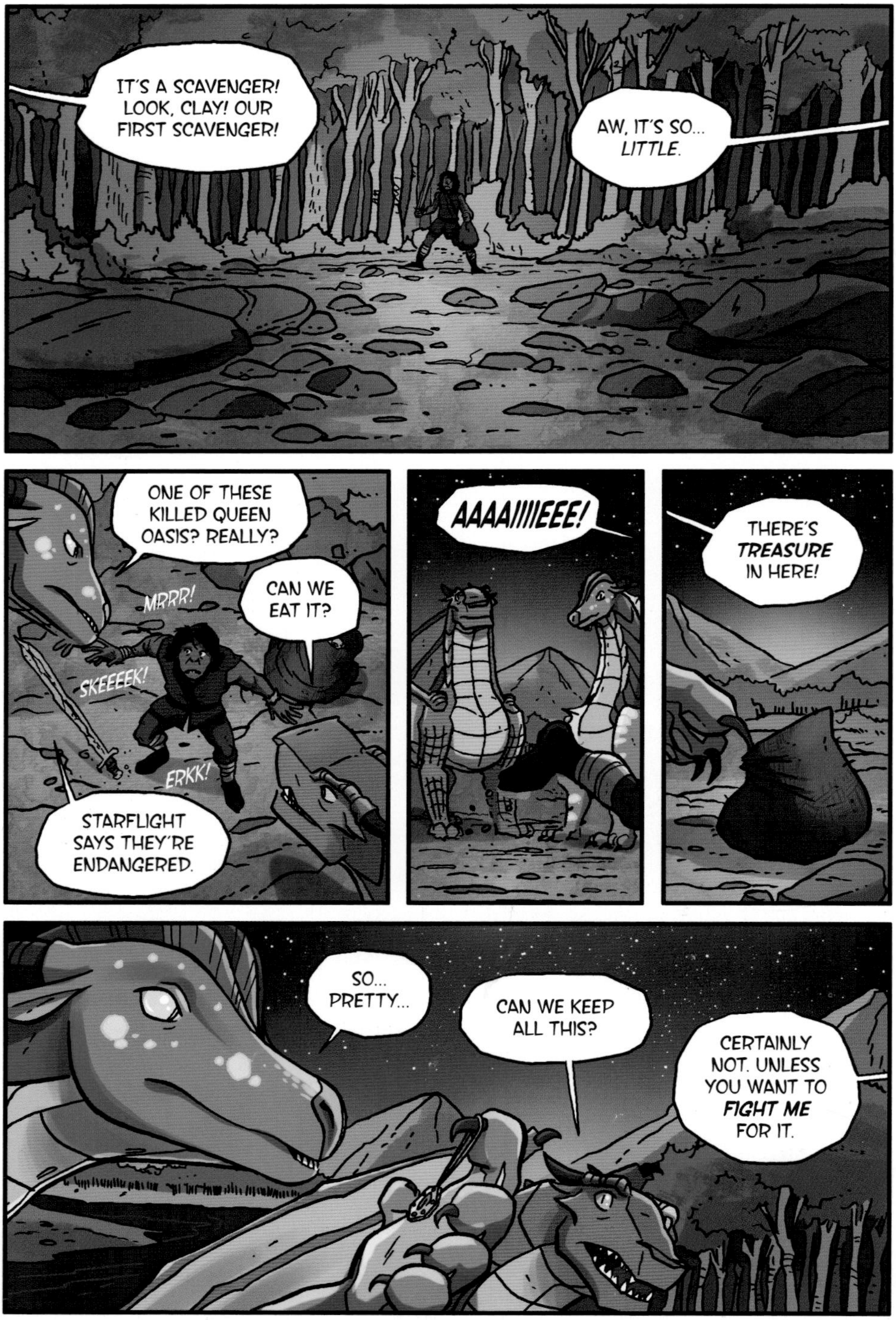
IT'S A SCAVENGER! LOOK, CLAY! OUR FIRST SCAVENGER!
AW, IT'S SO... *LITTLE*.
ONE OF THESE KILLED QUEEN OASIS? REALLY?
MRRR!
CAN WE EAT IT?
SKEEEEK!
ERKK!
STARFLIGHT SAYS THEY'RE ENDANGERED.
AAAAIIIIIEEE!
THERE'S **TREASURE** IN HERE!
SO... PRETTY...
CAN WE KEEP ALL THIS?
CERTAINLY NOT. UNLESS YOU WANT TO ***FIGHT ME*** FOR IT.

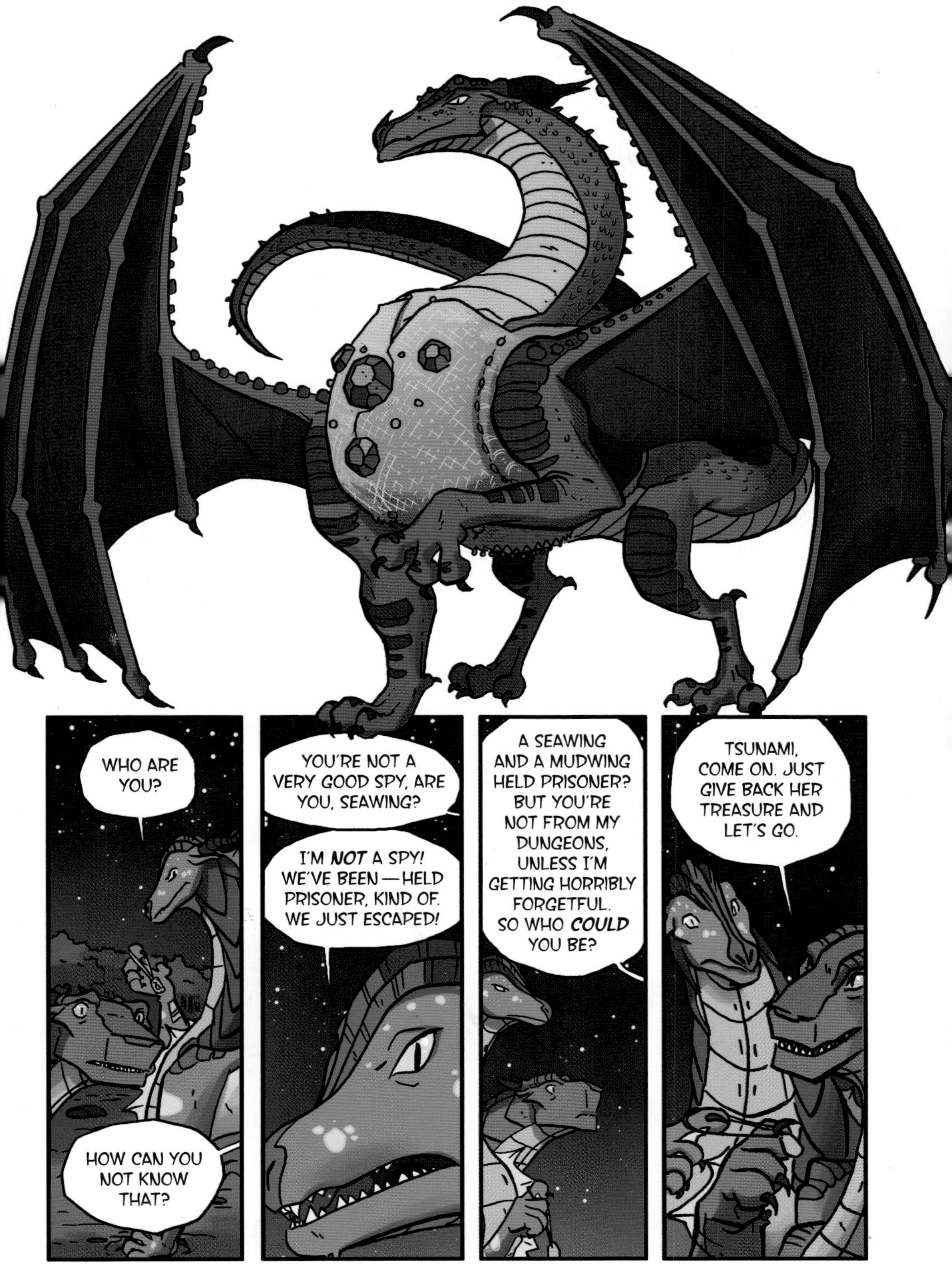
WHO ARE YOU?
HOW CAN YOU NOT KNOW THAT?
YOU'RE NOT A VERY GOOD SPY, ARE YOU, SEAWING?
I'M **NOT** A SPY! WE'VE BEEN — HELD PRISONER, KIND OF. WE JUST ESCAPED!
A SEAWING AND A MUDWING HELD PRISONER? BUT YOU'RE NOT FROM MY DUNGEONS, UNLESS I'M GETTING HORRIBLY FORGETFUL. SO WHO **COULD** YOU BE?
TSUNAMI, COME ON. JUST GIVE BACK HER TREASURE AND LET'S GO.

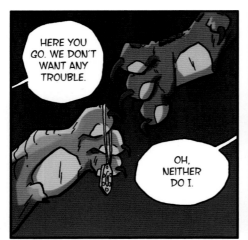

HERE YOU GO. WE DON'T WANT ANY TROUBLE.

OH, NEITHER DO I.

THAT'S WHY IT MAKES ME *SO SAD* WHEN TROUBLE KEEPS COMING TO ME.

NOBODY TOUCHES MY TREASURE!

WE DIDN'T KNOW! WE DON'T EVEN KNOW WHO YOU ARE!

OH, DIDN'T I SAY? MY NAME IS SCARLET.

BUT YOU MAY CALL ME *YOUR MAJESTY* IF YOU WANT TO LIVE.

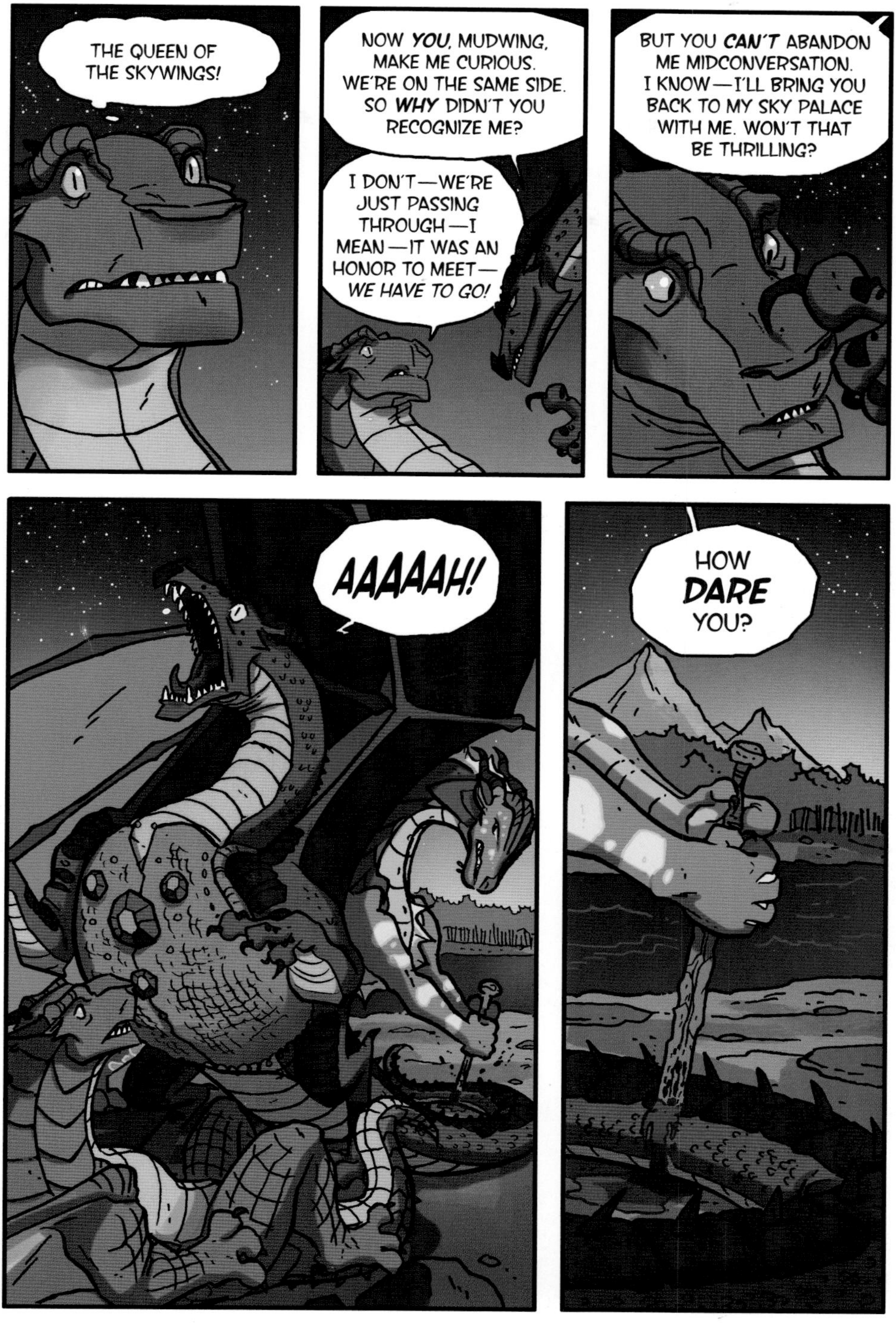
THE QUEEN OF THE SKYWINGS!
NOW *YOU*, MUDWING, MAKE ME CURIOUS. WE'RE ON THE SAME SIDE. SO *WHY* DIDN'T YOU RECOGNIZE ME?
I DON'T—WE'RE JUST PASSING THROUGH—I MEAN—IT WAS AN HONOR TO MEET— *WE HAVE TO GO!*
BUT YOU *CAN'T* ABANDON ME MIDCONVERSATION. I KNOW—I'LL BRING YOU BACK TO MY SKY PALACE WITH ME. WON'T THAT BE THRILLING?
AAAAAH!
HOW **DARE** YOU?

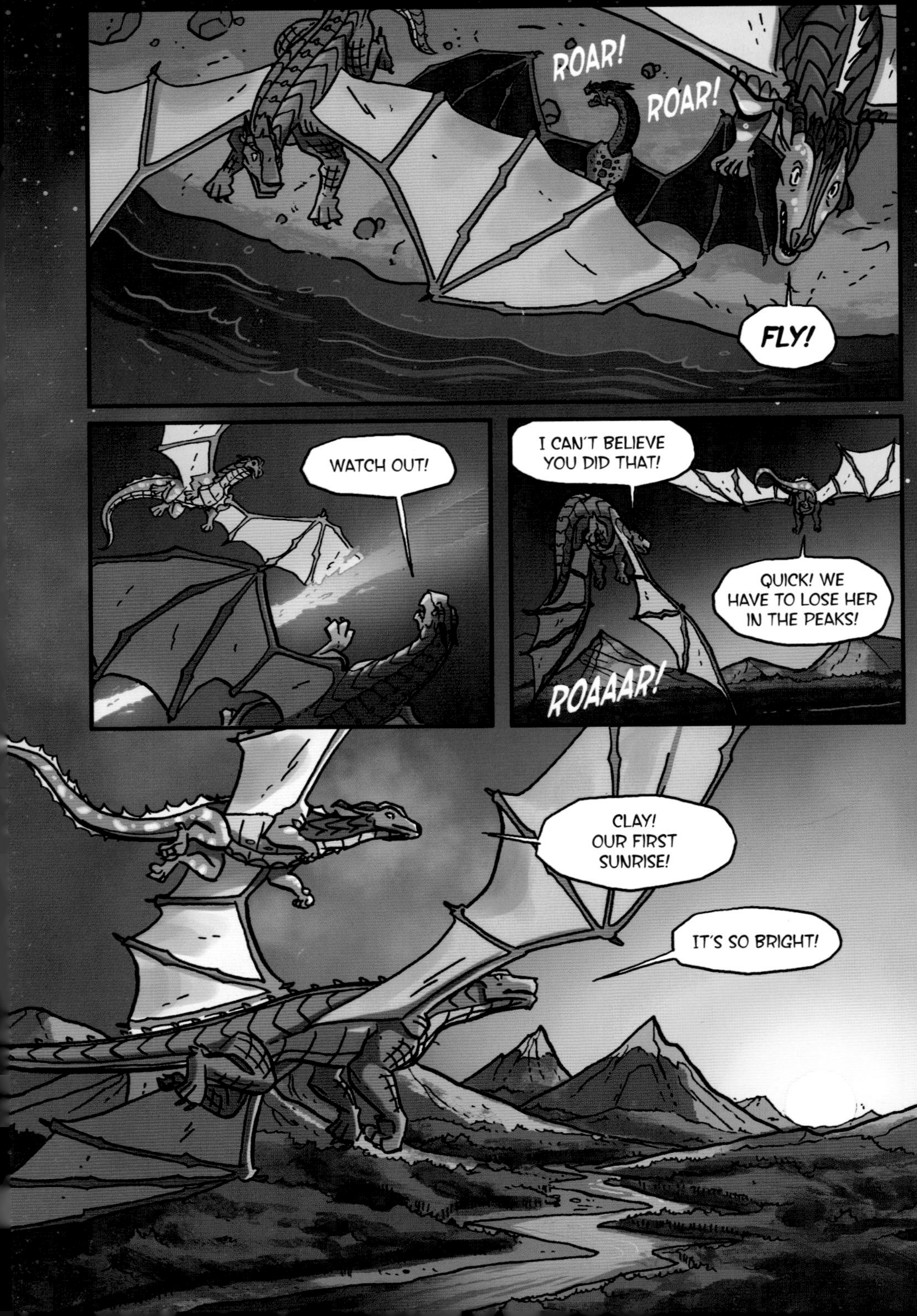
ROAR!
ROAR!
FLY!
WATCH OUT!
I CAN'T BELIEVE YOU DID THAT!
QUICK! WE HAVE TO LOSE HER IN THE PEAKS!
ROAAAR!
CLAY! OUR FIRST SUNRISE!
IT'S SO BRIGHT!

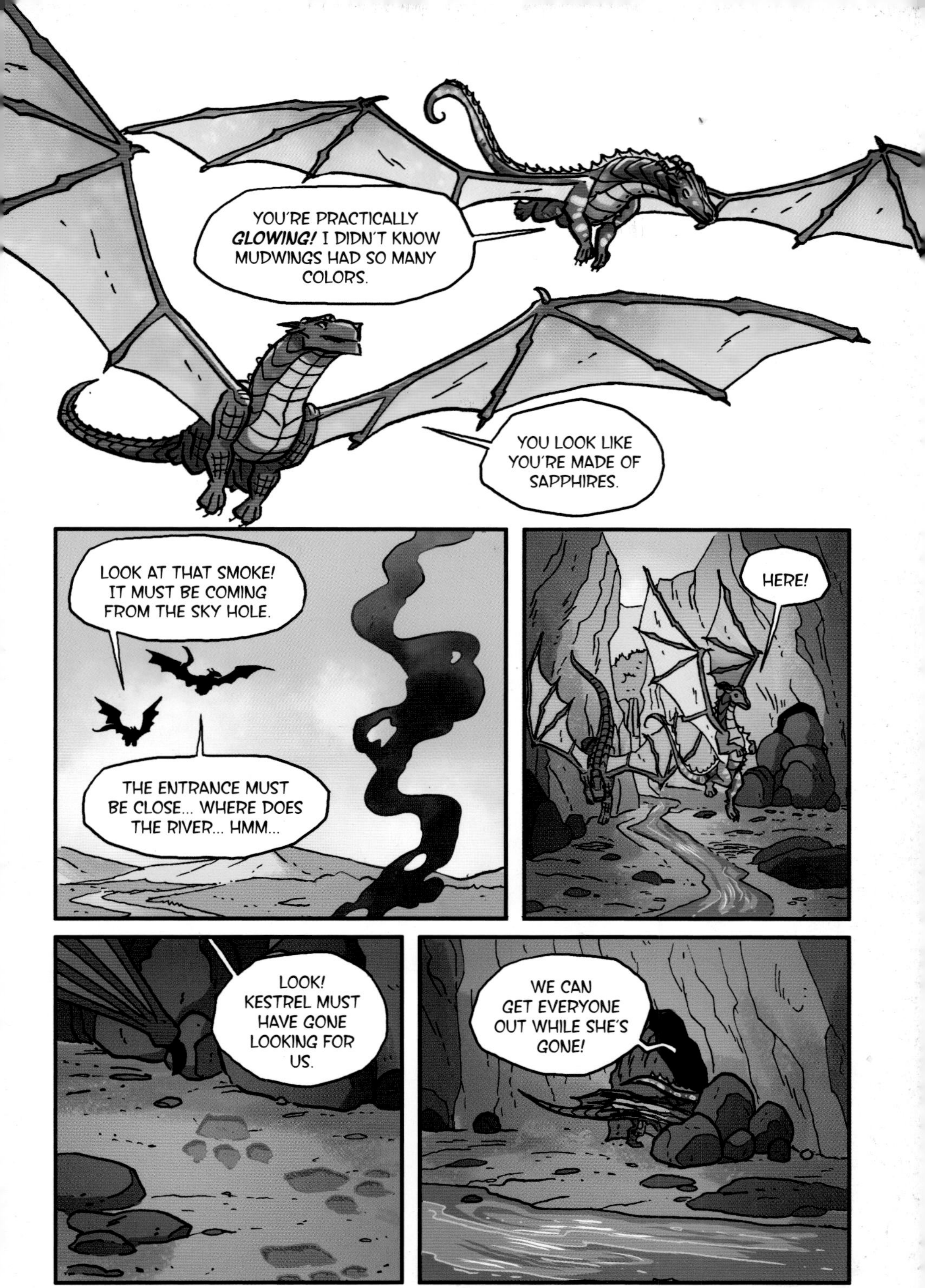
YOU'RE PRACTICALLY **GLOWING!** I DIDN'T KNOW MUDWINGS HAD SO MANY COLORS.
YOU LOOK LIKE YOU'RE MADE OF SAPPHIRES.
LOOK AT THAT SMOKE! IT MUST BE COMING FROM THE SKY HOLE.
THE ENTRANCE MUST BE CLOSE... WHERE DOES THE RIVER... HMM...
HERE!
LOOK! KESTREL MUST HAVE GONE LOOKING FOR US.
WE CAN GET EVERYONE OUT WHILE SHE'S GONE!

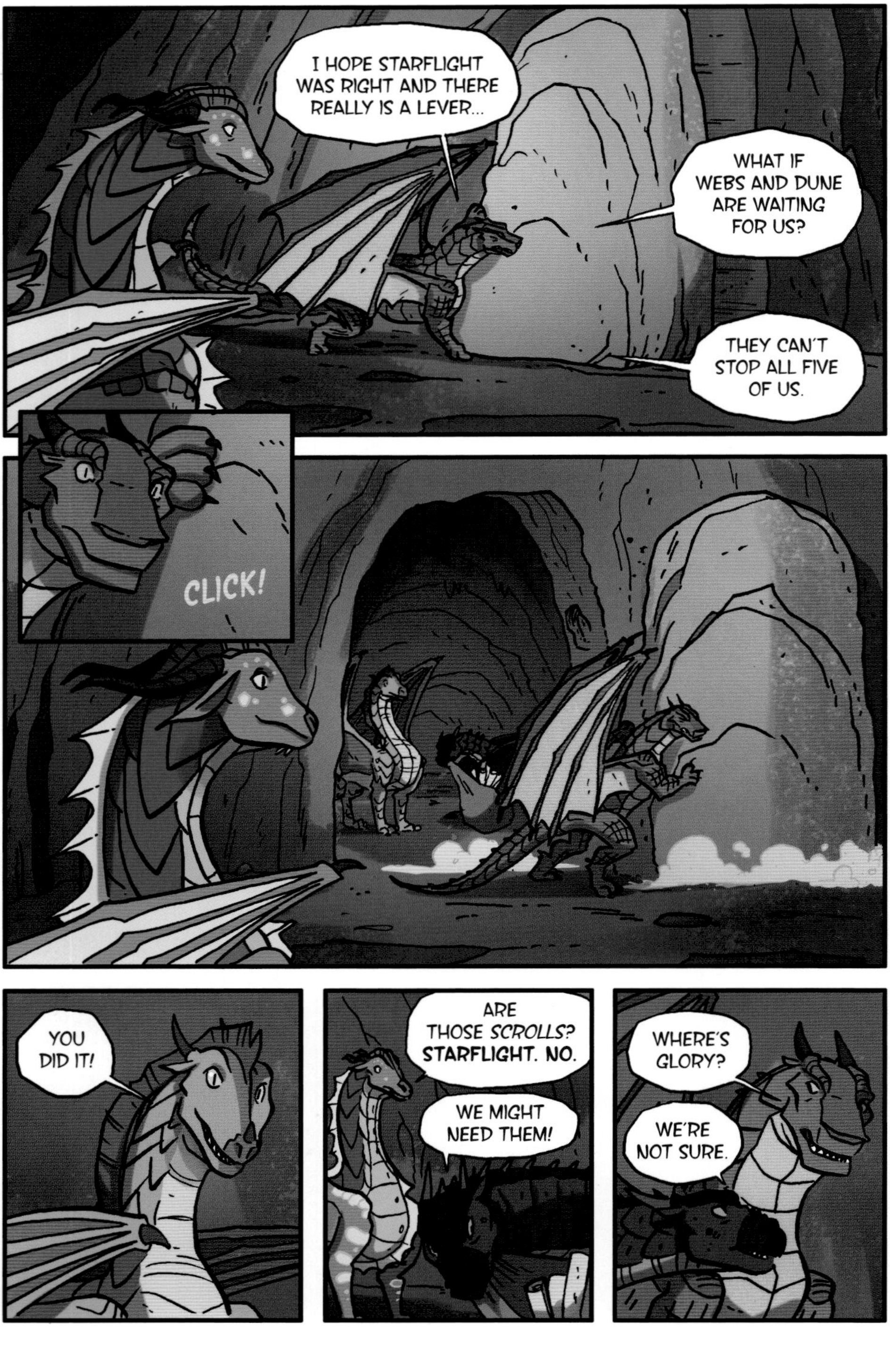
I HOPE STARFLIGHT WAS RIGHT AND THERE REALLY IS A LEVER...
WHAT IF WEBS AND DUNE ARE WAITING FOR US?
THEY CAN'T STOP ALL FIVE OF US.
CLICK!
YOU DID IT!
ARE THOSE *SCROLLS*? **STARFLIGHT. NO.**
WE MIGHT NEED THEM!
WHERE'S GLORY?
WE'RE NOT SURE.

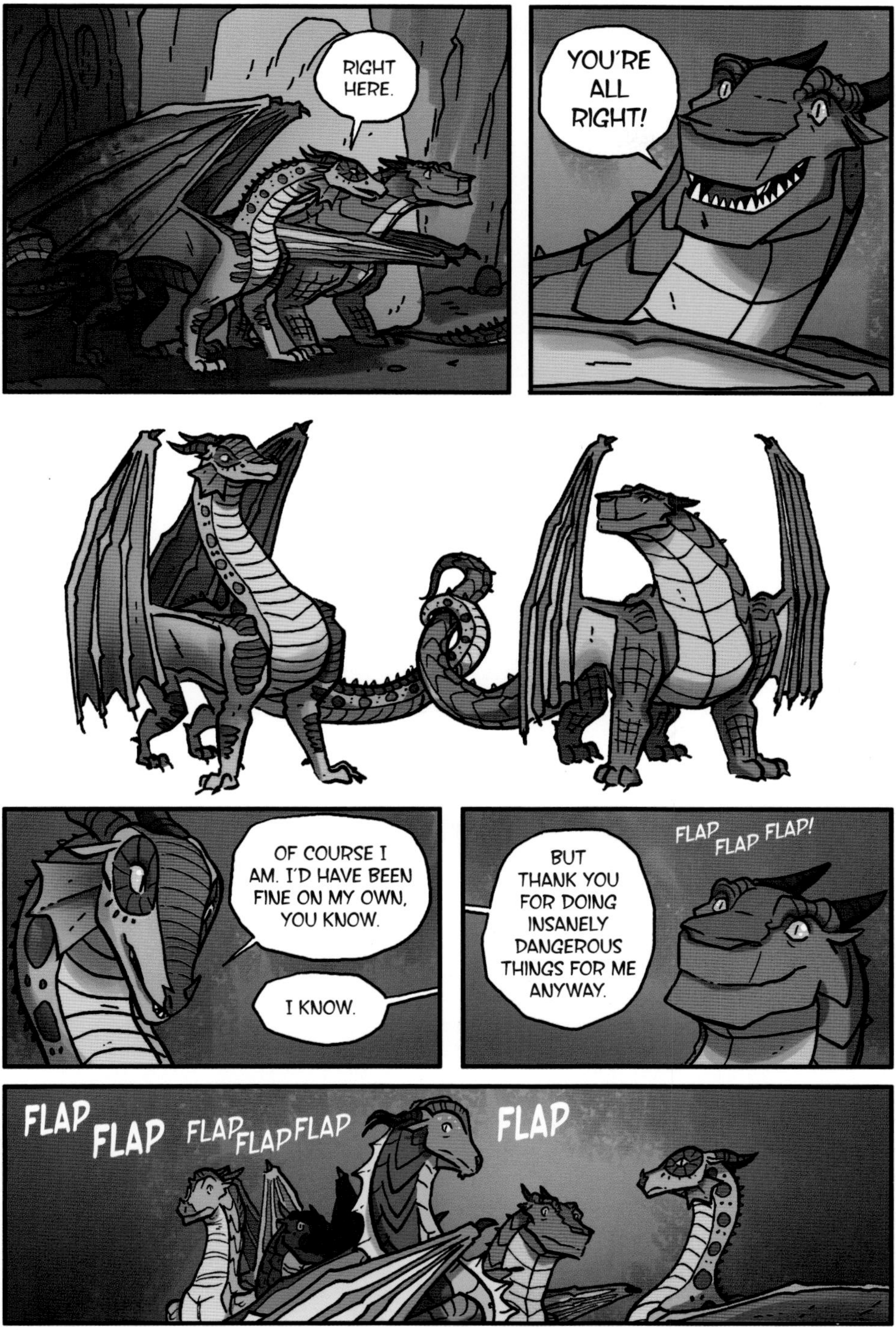

RIGHT HERE.
YOU'RE ALL RIGHT!
OF COURSE I AM. I'D HAVE BEEN FINE ON MY OWN, YOU KNOW.
I KNOW.
BUT THANK YOU FOR DOING INSANELY DANGEROUS THINGS FOR ME ANYWAY.
FLAP FLAP FLAP!
FLAP FLAP FLAP FLAP FLAP
FLAP

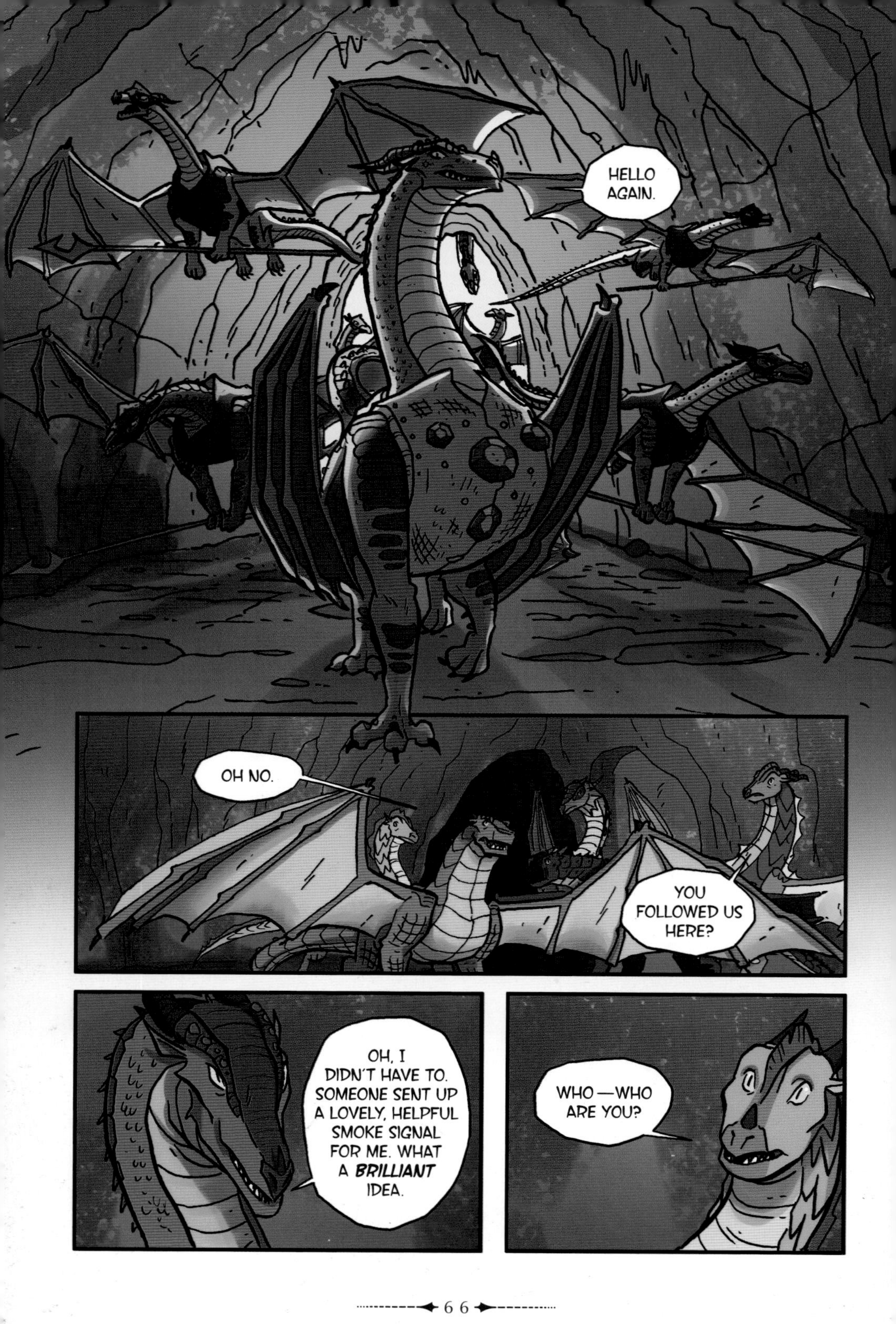
HELLO AGAIN.
OH NO.
YOU FOLLOWED US HERE?
OH, I DIDN'T HAVE TO. SOMEONE SENT UP A LOVELY, HELPFUL SMOKE SIGNAL FOR ME. WHAT A **BRILLIANT** IDEA.
WHO—WHO ARE YOU?

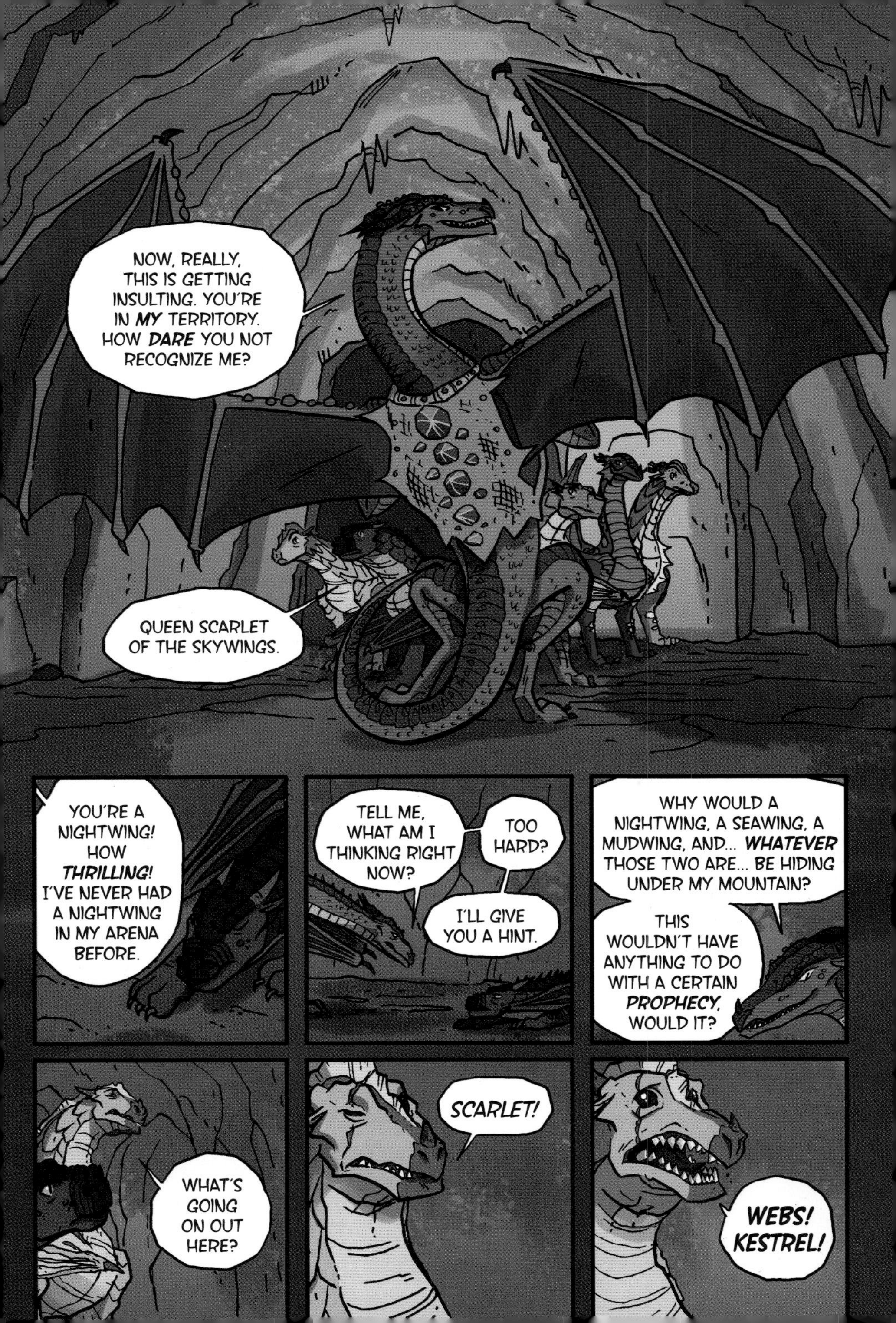
NOW, REALLY, THIS IS GETTING INSULTING. YOU'RE IN MY TERRITORY. HOW DARE YOU NOT RECOGNIZE ME?
QUEEN SCARLET OF THE SKYWINGS.
YOU'RE A NIGHTWING! HOW THRILLING! I'VE NEVER HAD A NIGHTWING IN MY ARENA BEFORE.
TELL ME, WHAT AM I THINKING RIGHT NOW?
TOO HARD?
I'LL GIVE YOU A HINT.
WHY WOULD A NIGHTWING, A SEAWING, A MUDWING, AND... WHATEVER THOSE TWO ARE... BE HIDING UNDER MY MOUNTAIN?
THIS WOULDN'T HAVE ANYTHING TO DO WITH A CERTAIN PROPHECY, WOULD IT?
WHAT'S GOING ON OUT HERE?
SCARLET!
WEBS! KESTREL!

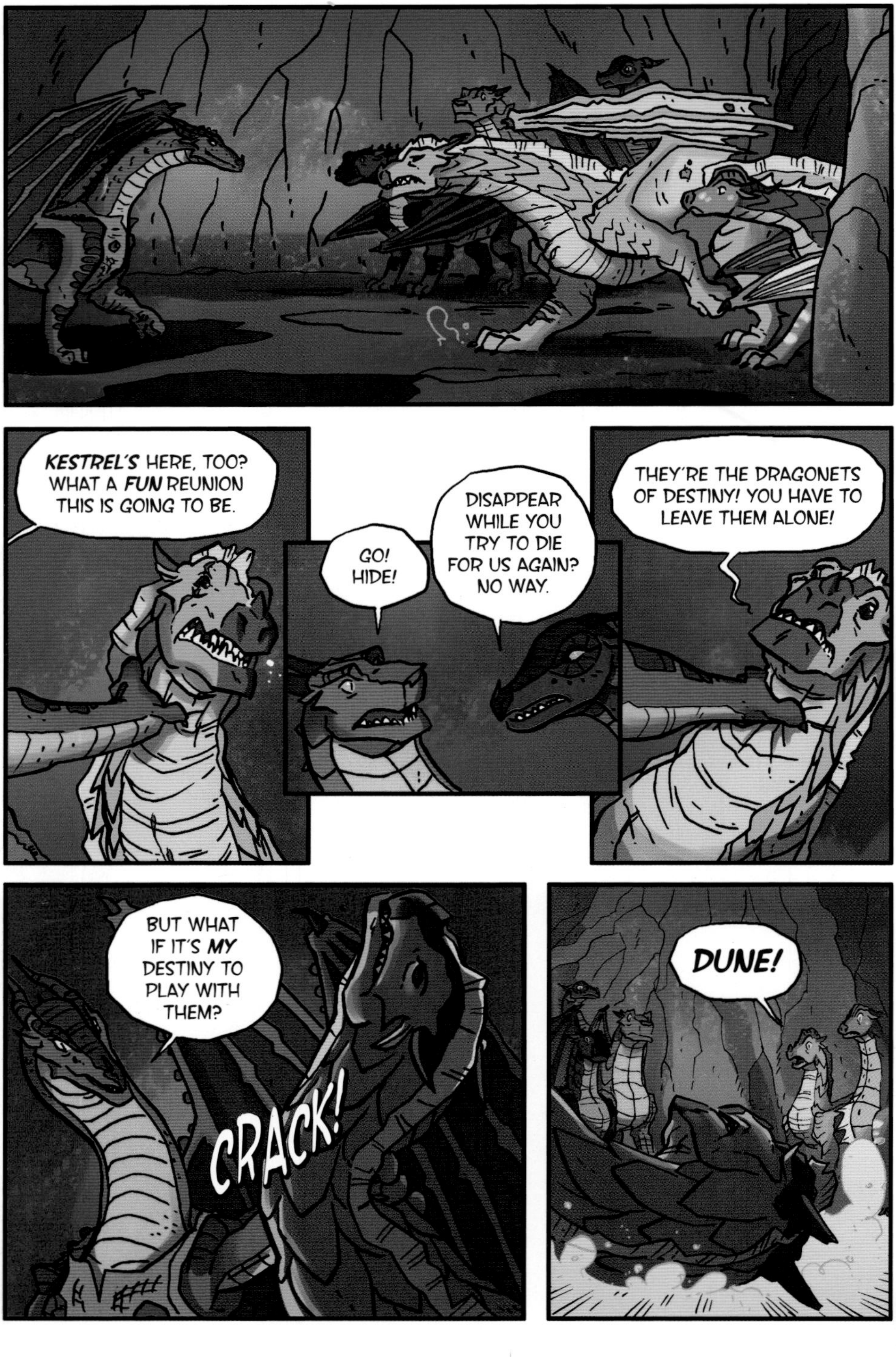
KESTREL'S HERE, TOO? WHAT A FUN REUNION THIS IS GOING TO BE.
GO! HIDE!
DISAPPEAR WHILE YOU TRY TO DIE FOR US AGAIN? NO WAY.
THEY'RE THE DRAGONETS OF DESTINY! YOU HAVE TO LEAVE THEM ALONE!
BUT WHAT IF IT'S MY DESTINY TO PLAY WITH THEM?
CRACK!
DUNE!

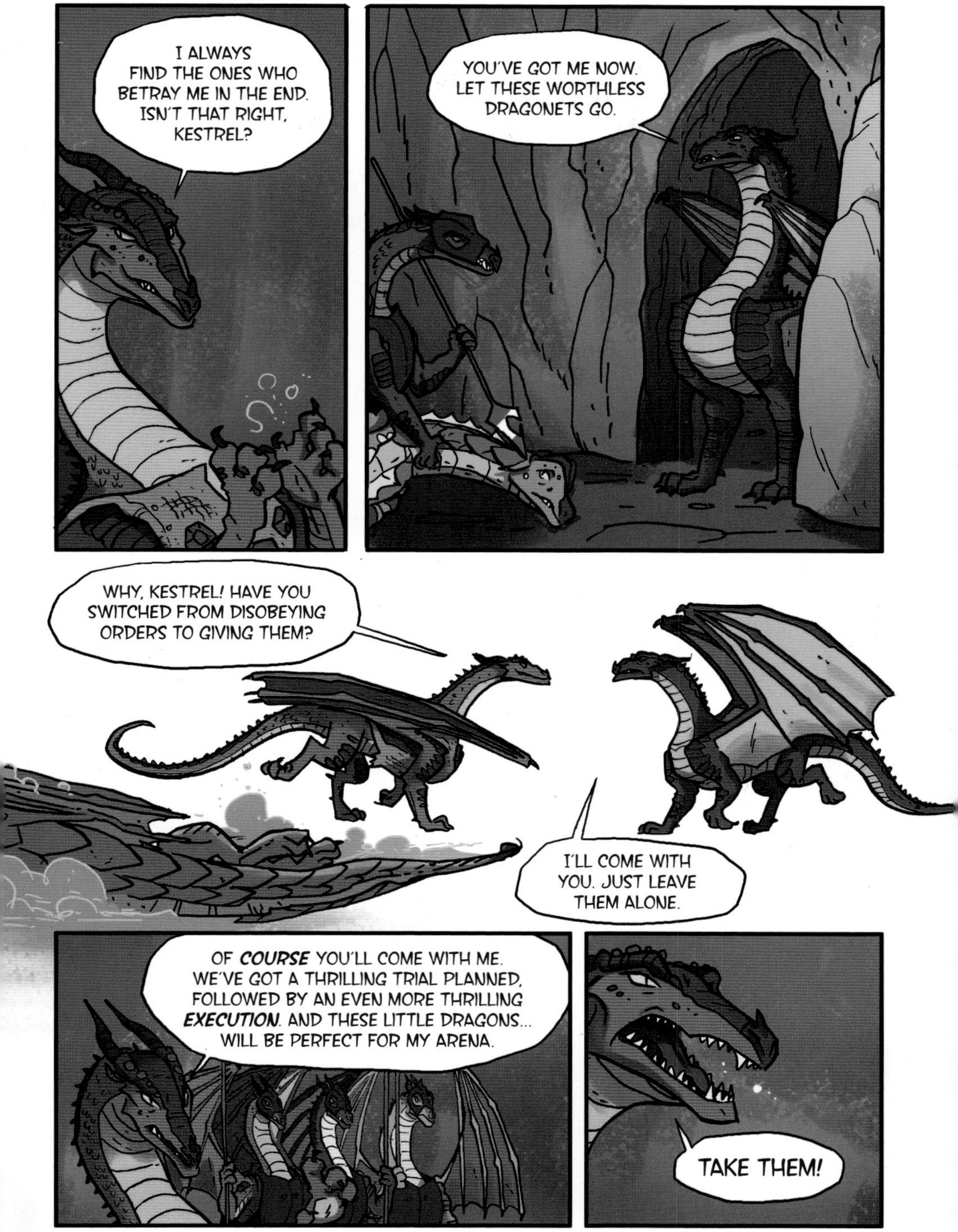
I ALWAYS FIND THE ONES WHO BETRAY ME IN THE END. ISN'T THAT RIGHT, KESTREL?
YOU'VE GOT ME NOW. LET THESE WORTHLESS DRAGONETS GO.
WHY, KESTREL! HAVE YOU SWITCHED FROM DISOBEYING ORDERS TO GIVING THEM?
I'LL COME WITH YOU. JUST LEAVE THEM ALONE.
OF ***COURSE*** YOU'LL COME WITH ME. WE'VE GOT A THRILLING TRIAL PLANNED, FOLLOWED BY AN EVEN MORE THRILLING ***EXECUTION***. AND THESE LITTLE DRAGONS... WILL BE PERFECT FOR MY ARENA.
TAKE THEM!

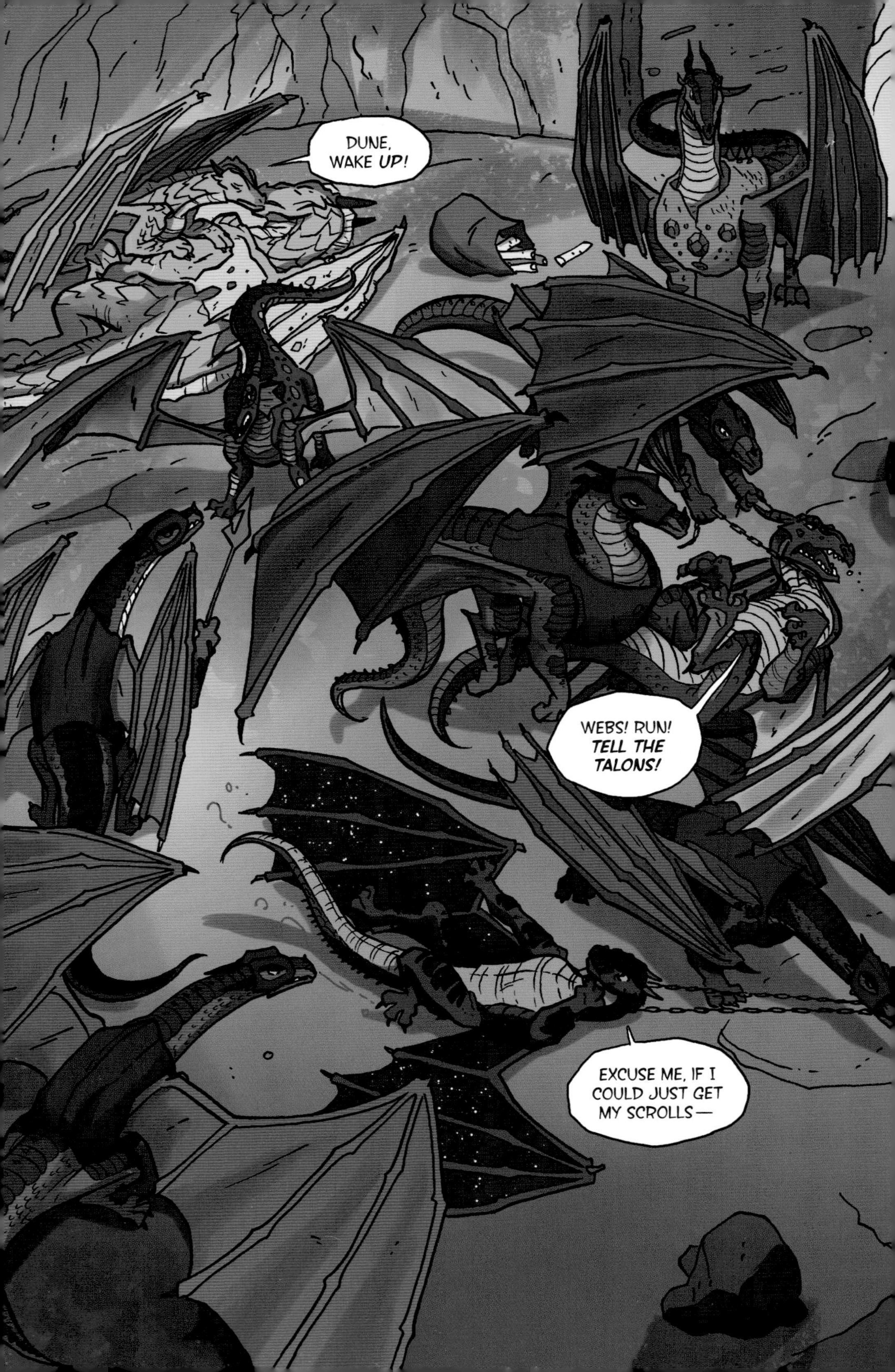
DUNE, WAKE *UP*!
WEBS! RUN! ***TELL THE TALONS!***
EXCUSE ME, IF I COULD JUST GET MY SCROLLS—

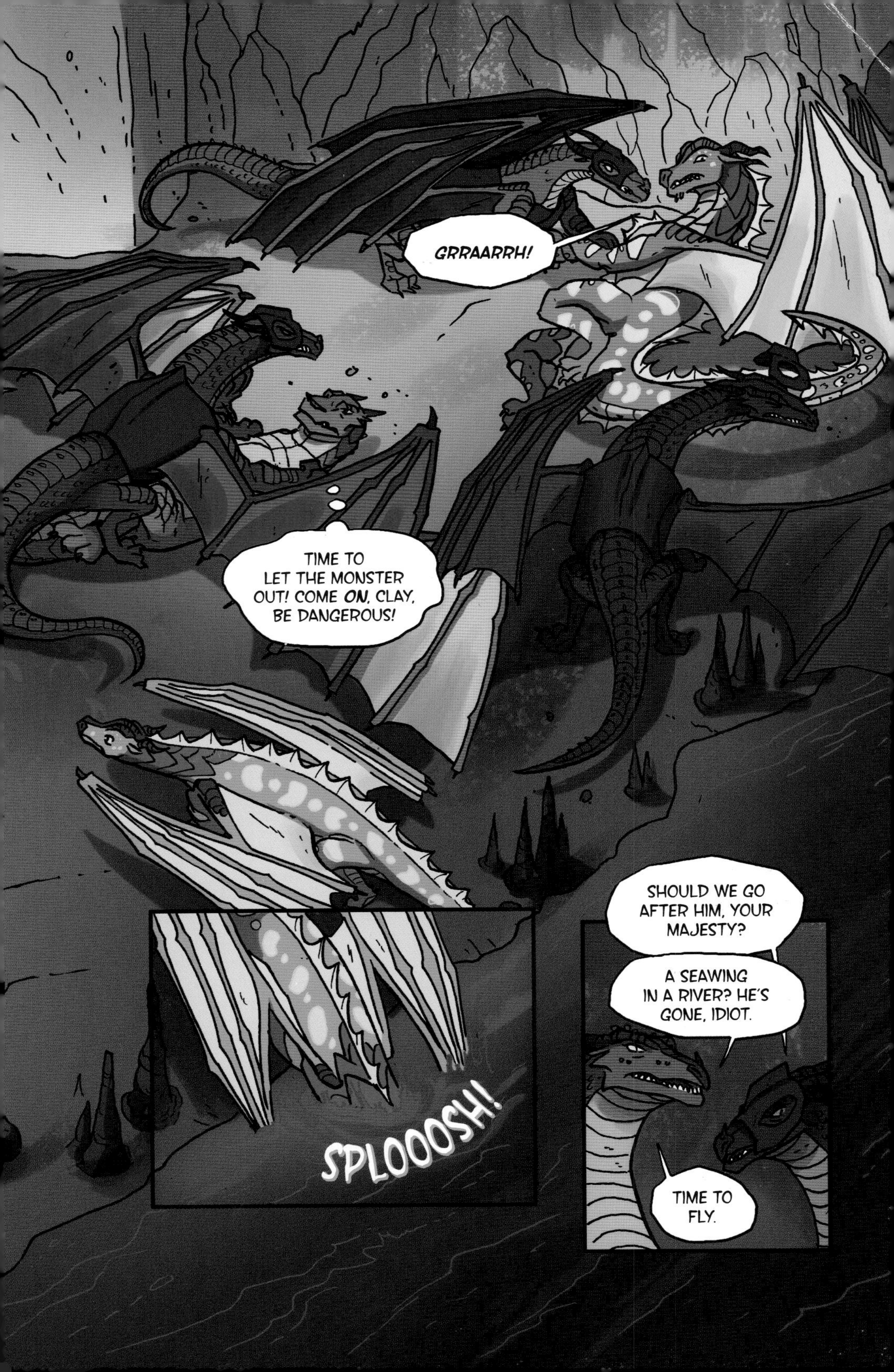
GRRAARRH!
TIME TO LET THE MONSTER OUT! COME *ON*, CLAY, BE DANGEROUS!
SPLOOOSH!
SHOULD WE GO AFTER HIM, YOUR MAJESTY?
A SEAWING IN A RIVER? HE'S GONE, IDIOT.
TIME TO FLY.

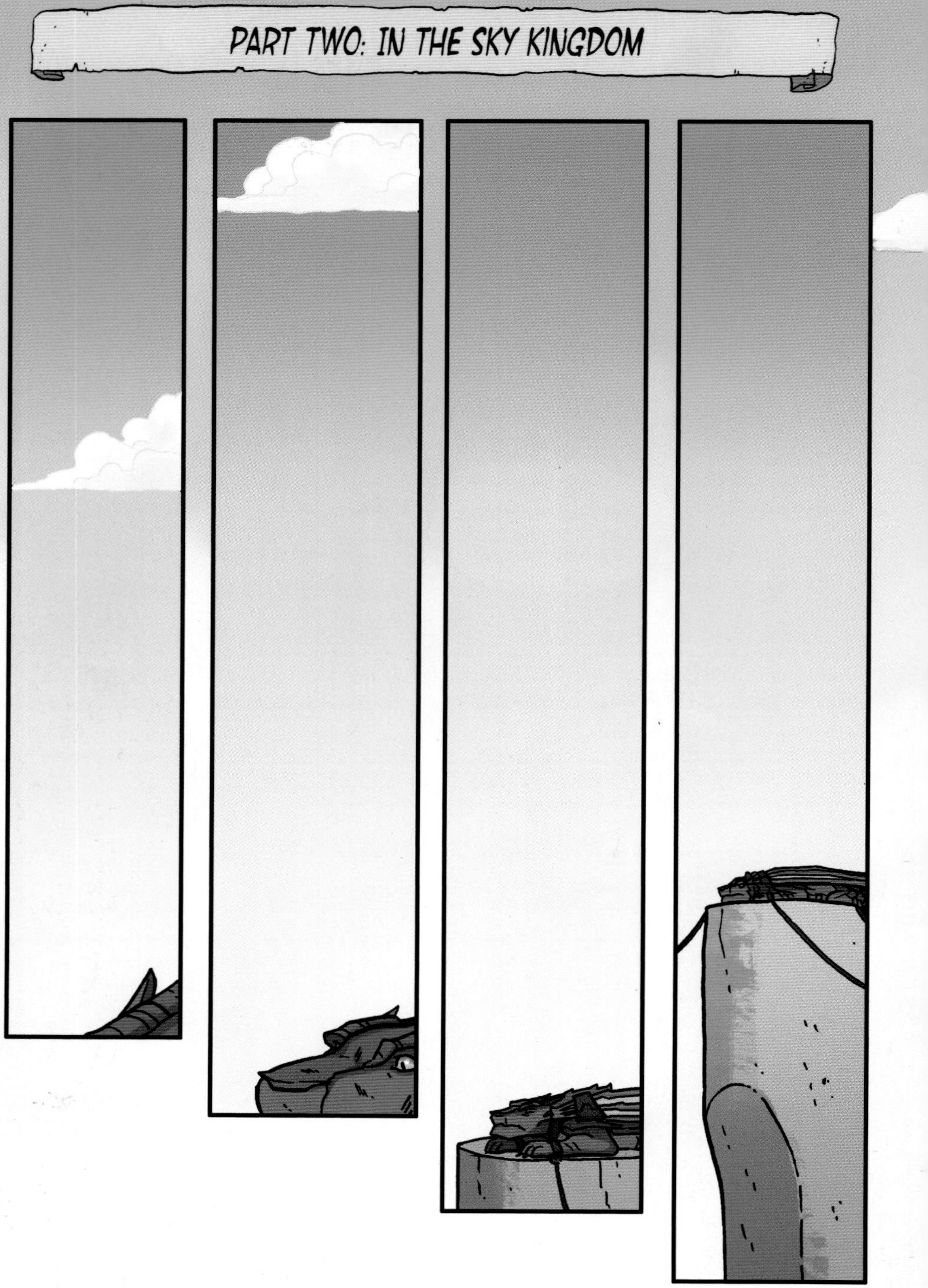
PART TWO: IN THE SKY KINGDOM

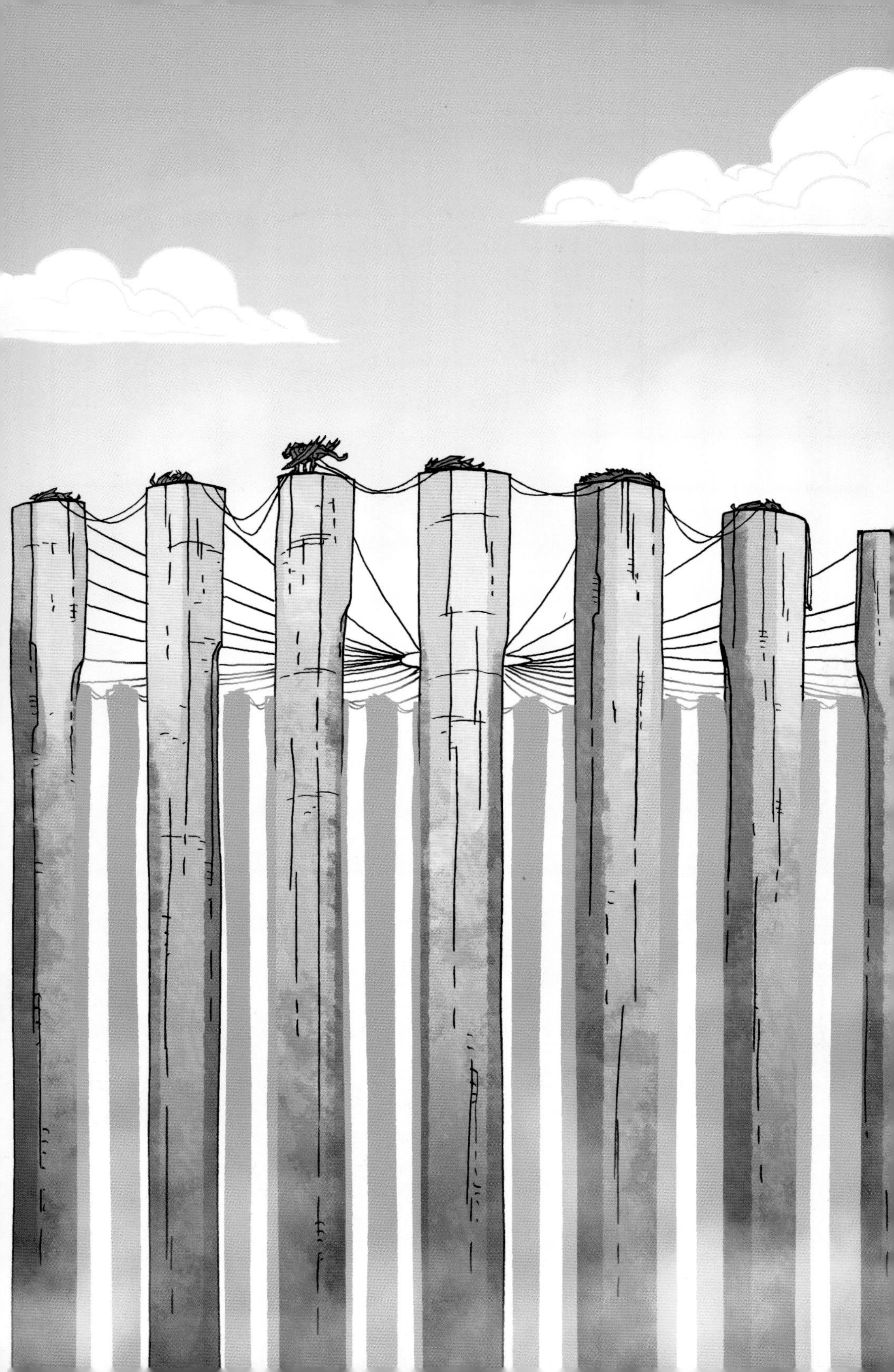

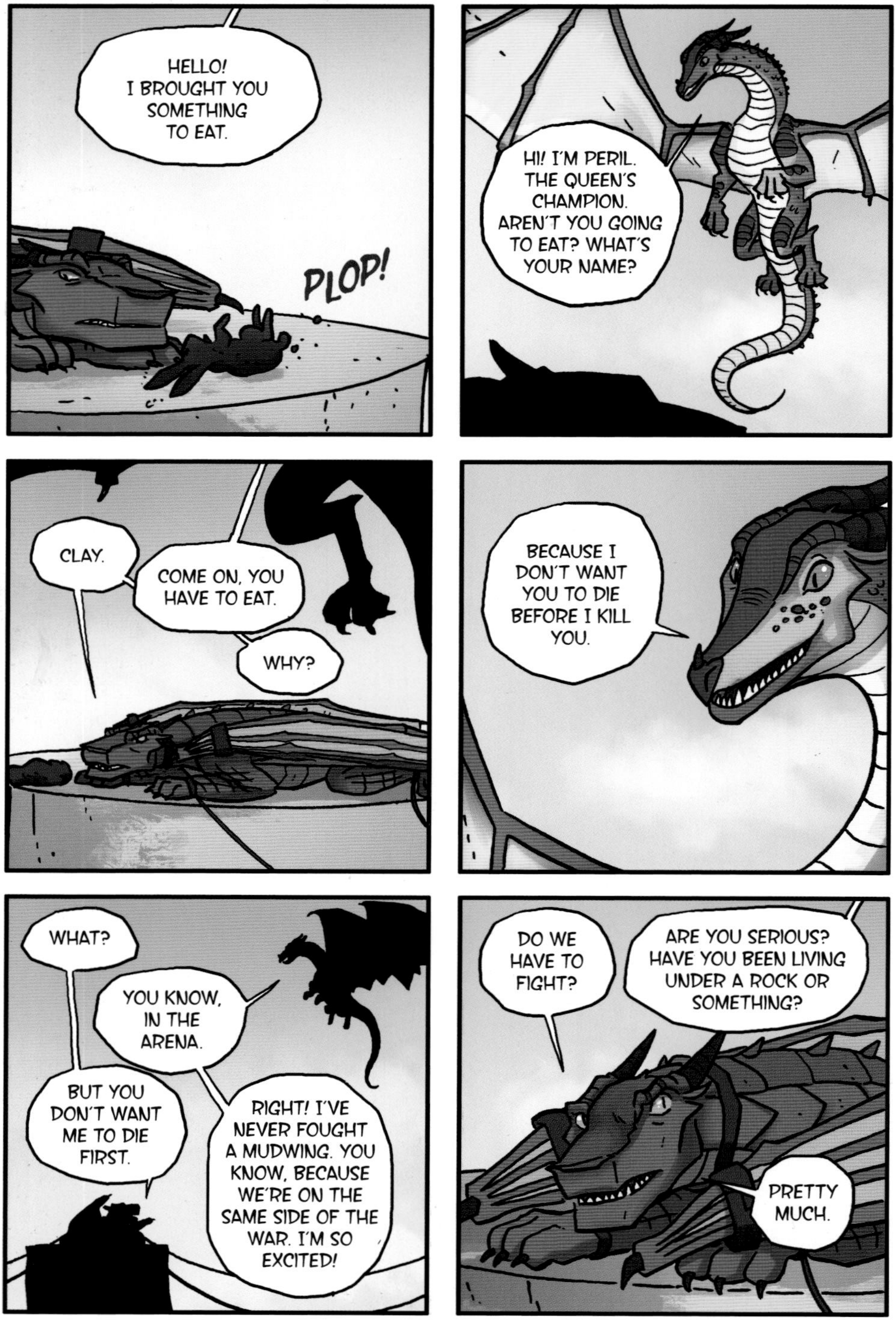
HELLO! I BROUGHT YOU SOMETHING TO EAT.
PLOP!
HI! I'M PERIL. THE QUEEN'S CHAMPION. AREN'T YOU GOING TO EAT? WHAT'S YOUR NAME?
CLAY.
COME ON, YOU HAVE TO EAT.
WHY?
BECAUSE I DON'T WANT YOU TO DIE BEFORE I KILL YOU.
WHAT?
YOU KNOW, IN THE ARENA.
BUT YOU DON'T WANT ME TO DIE FIRST.
RIGHT! I'VE NEVER FOUGHT A MUDWING. YOU KNOW, BECAUSE WE'RE ON THE SAME SIDE OF THE WAR. I'M SO EXCITED!
DO WE HAVE TO FIGHT?
ARE YOU SERIOUS? HAVE YOU BEEN LIVING UNDER A ROCK OR SOMETHING?
PRETTY MUCH.

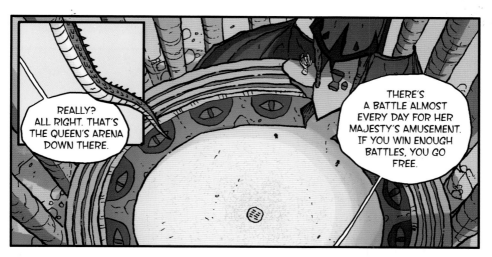

REALLY? ALL RIGHT. THAT'S THE QUEEN'S ARENA DOWN THERE.

THERE'S A BATTLE ALMOST EVERY DAY FOR HER MAJESTY'S AMUSEMENT. IF YOU WIN ENOUGH BATTLES, YOU GO FREE.

HOW MANY IS THAT?

I DON'T KNOW. NO ONE'S EVER DONE IT. AFTER A DRAGON HAS A FEW WINS, HER MAJESTY SENDS ME IN. I ALWAYS KILL THEM. I'M REALLY DANGEROUS.

I CAN'T WAIT TO FIGHT THE NIGHTWING! NOBODY KNOWS WHAT THAT WILL BE LIKE. WHAT IF HE CAN READ MY MIND AND KNOWS WHAT I'M GOING TO DO BEFORE I DO IT?

STARFLIGHT! WHERE IS HE?

SOMEWHERE OVER THERE.

WHAT ABOUT TSUNAMI?

THE SEAWING? BORING. I'VE FOUGHT PLENTY OF SEAWINGS.

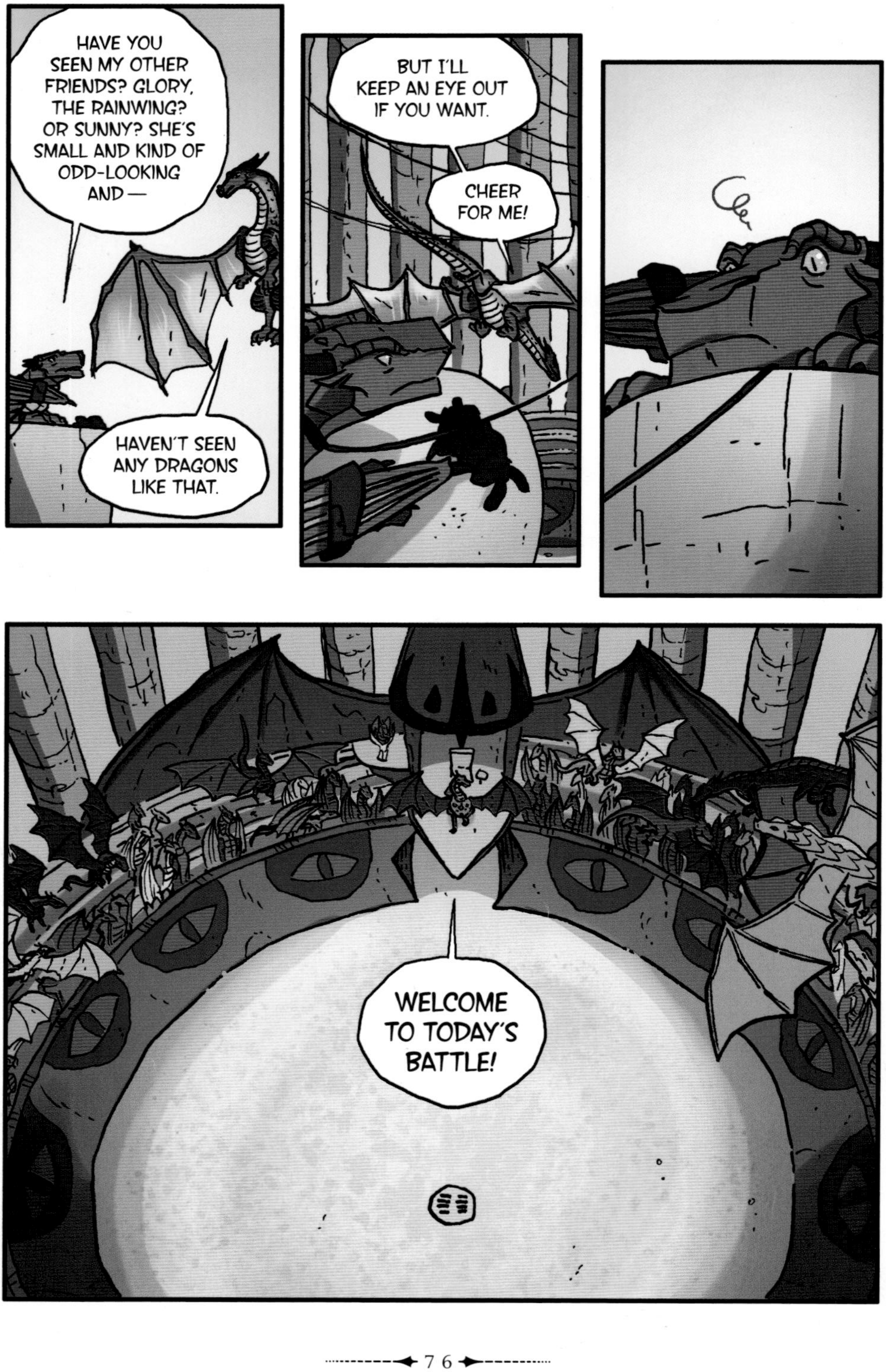

HAVE YOU SEEN MY OTHER FRIENDS? GLORY, THE RAINWING? OR SUNNY? SHE'S SMALL AND KIND OF ODD-LOOKING AND—
HAVEN'T SEEN ANY DRAGONS LIKE THAT.
BUT I'LL KEEP AN EYE OUT IF YOU WANT.
CHEER FOR ME!
WELCOME TO TODAY'S BATTLE!

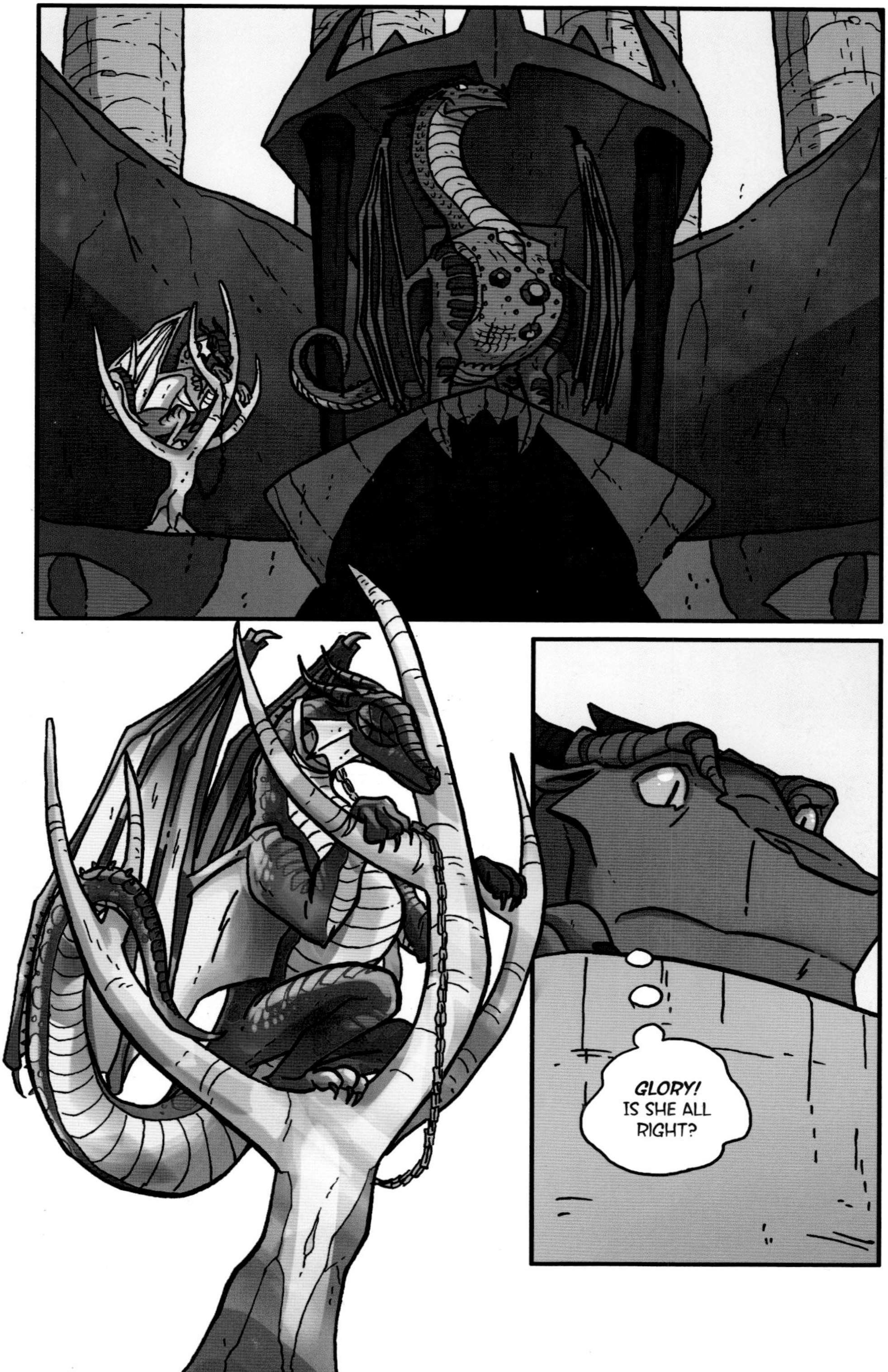
GLORY!
IS SHE ALL
RIGHT?

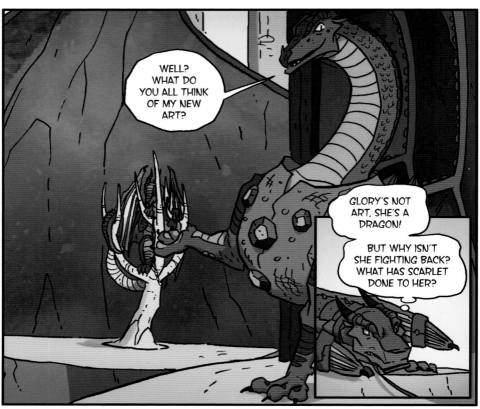

WELL? WHAT DO YOU ALL THINK OF MY NEW ART?

GLORY'S NOT ART, SHE'S A DRAGON!

BUT WHY ISN'T SHE FIGHTING BACK? WHAT HAS SCARLET DONE TO HER?

BRING IN THE COMBATANTS!

YAY!

HUZZAH!

FIGHT!

FIGHT!

FIGHT!

GET *OFF* ME!

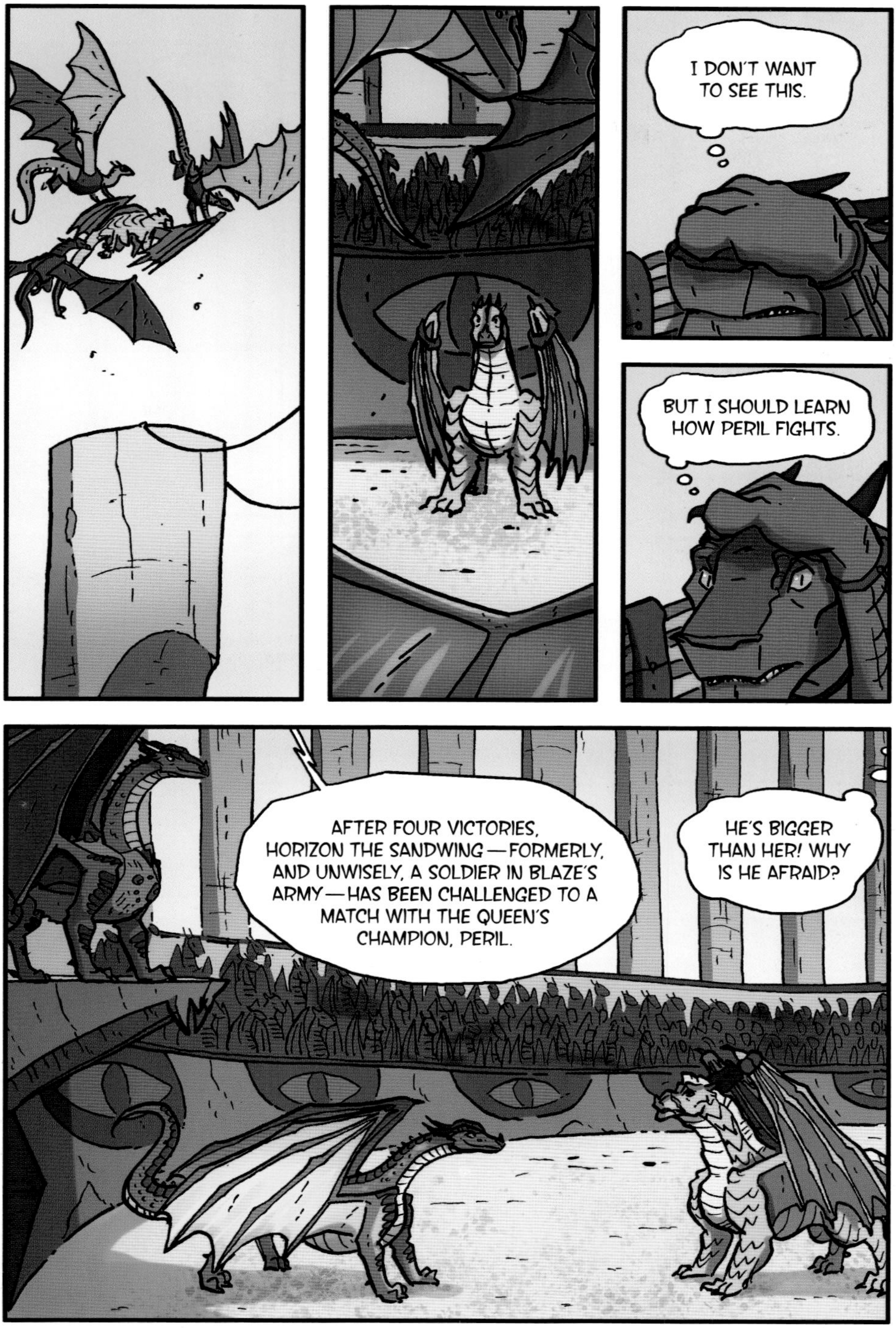

I DON'T WANT TO SEE THIS.
BUT I SHOULD LEARN HOW PERIL FIGHTS.
AFTER FOUR VICTORIES, HORIZON THE SANDWING—FORMERLY, AND UNWISELY, A SOLDIER IN BLAZE'S ARMY—HAS BEEN CHALLENGED TO A MATCH WITH THE QUEEN'S CHAMPION, PERIL.
HE'S BIGGER THAN HER! WHY IS HE AFRAID?

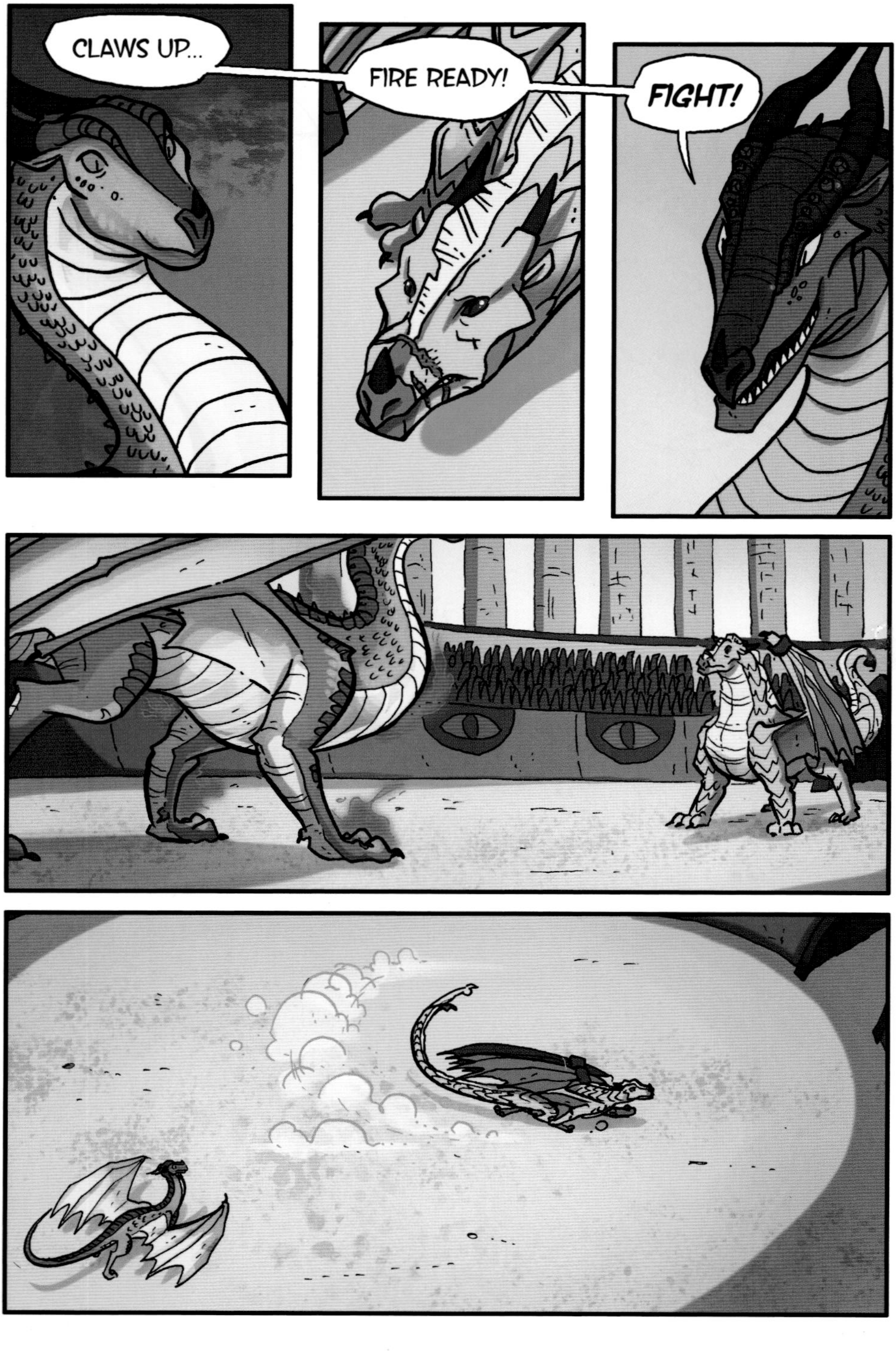
CLAWS UP...
FIRE READY!
FIGHT!

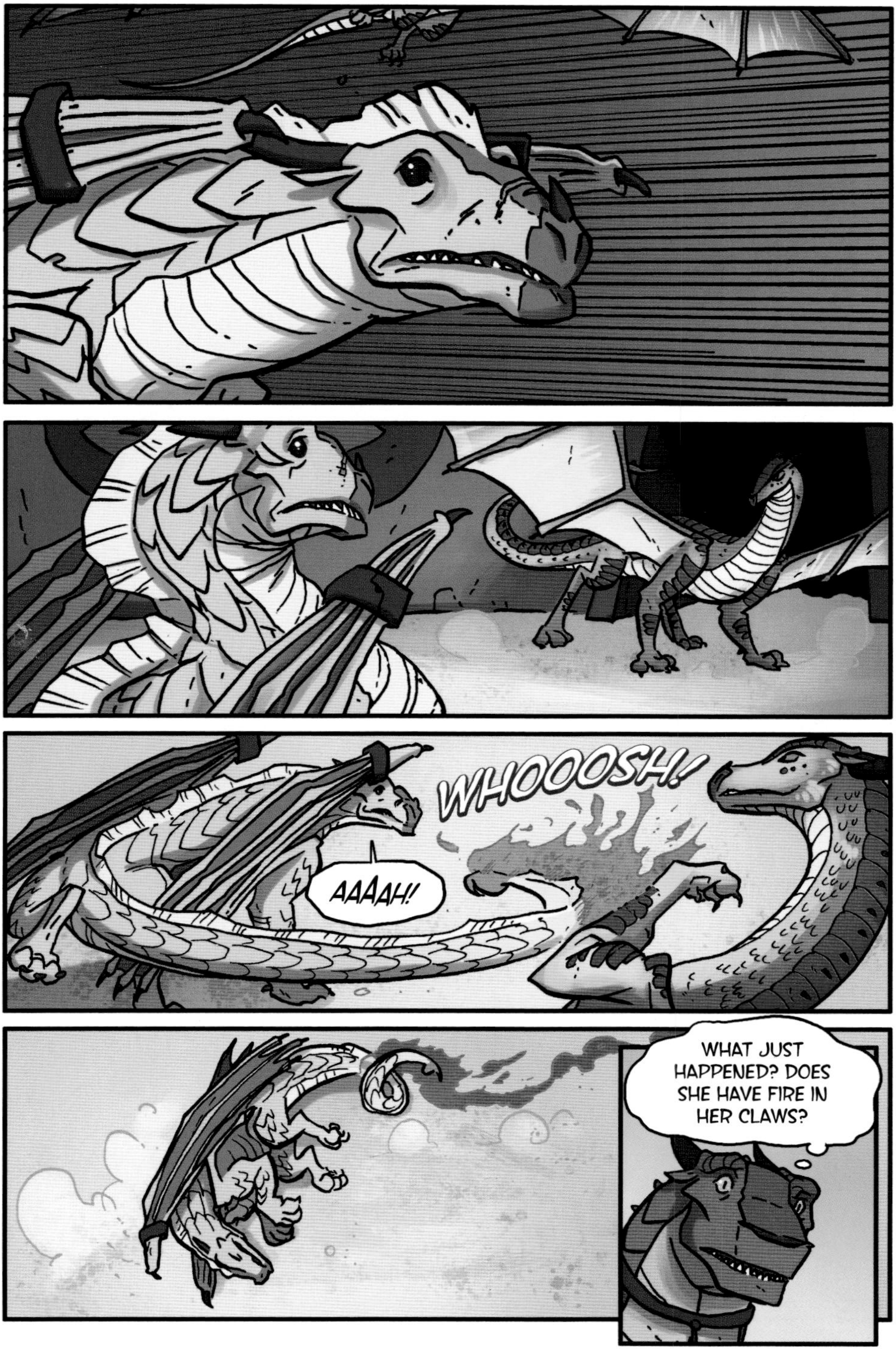
WHOOOOSH!
AAAAH!
WHAT JUST HAPPENED? DOES SHE HAVE FIRE IN HER CLAWS?

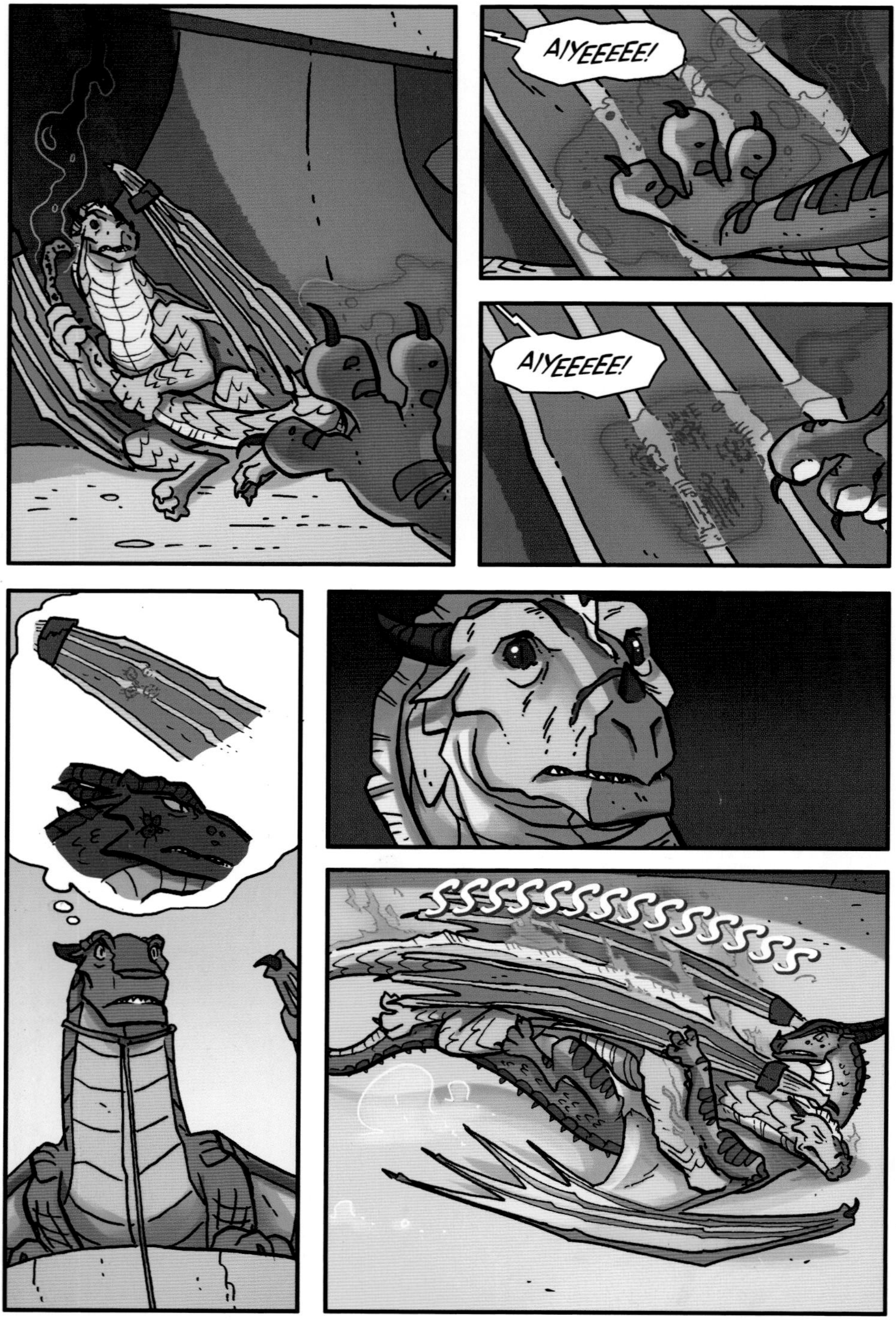
AIYEEEEE!
AIYEEEEE!
SSSSSSSSSSSSSSSS

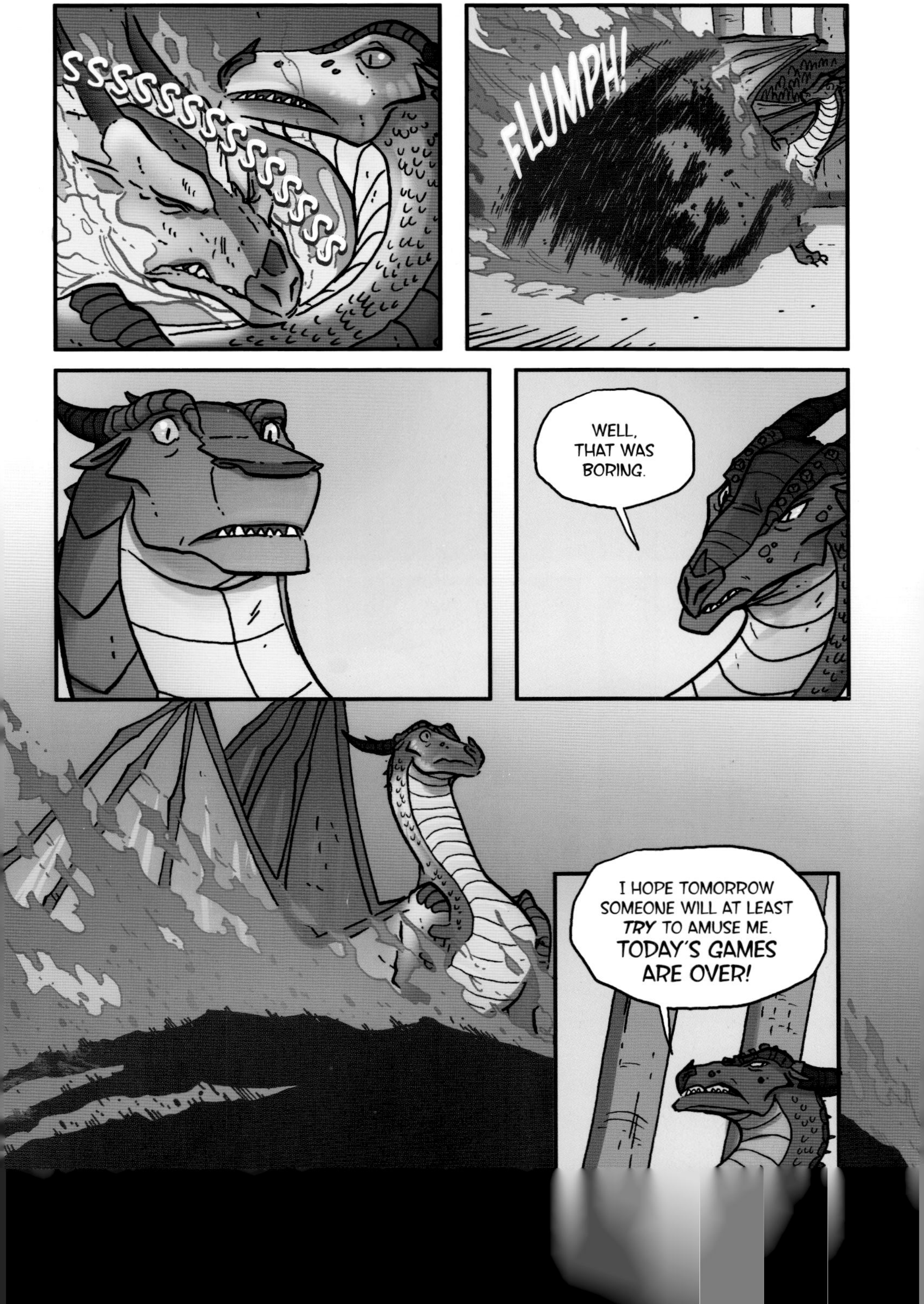
SSSSSSSSSSSSSSSSSS
FLUMPH!
WELL, THAT WAS BORING.
I HOPE TOMORROW SOMEONE WILL AT LEAST *TRY* TO AMUSE ME.
TODAY'S GAMES ARE OVER!

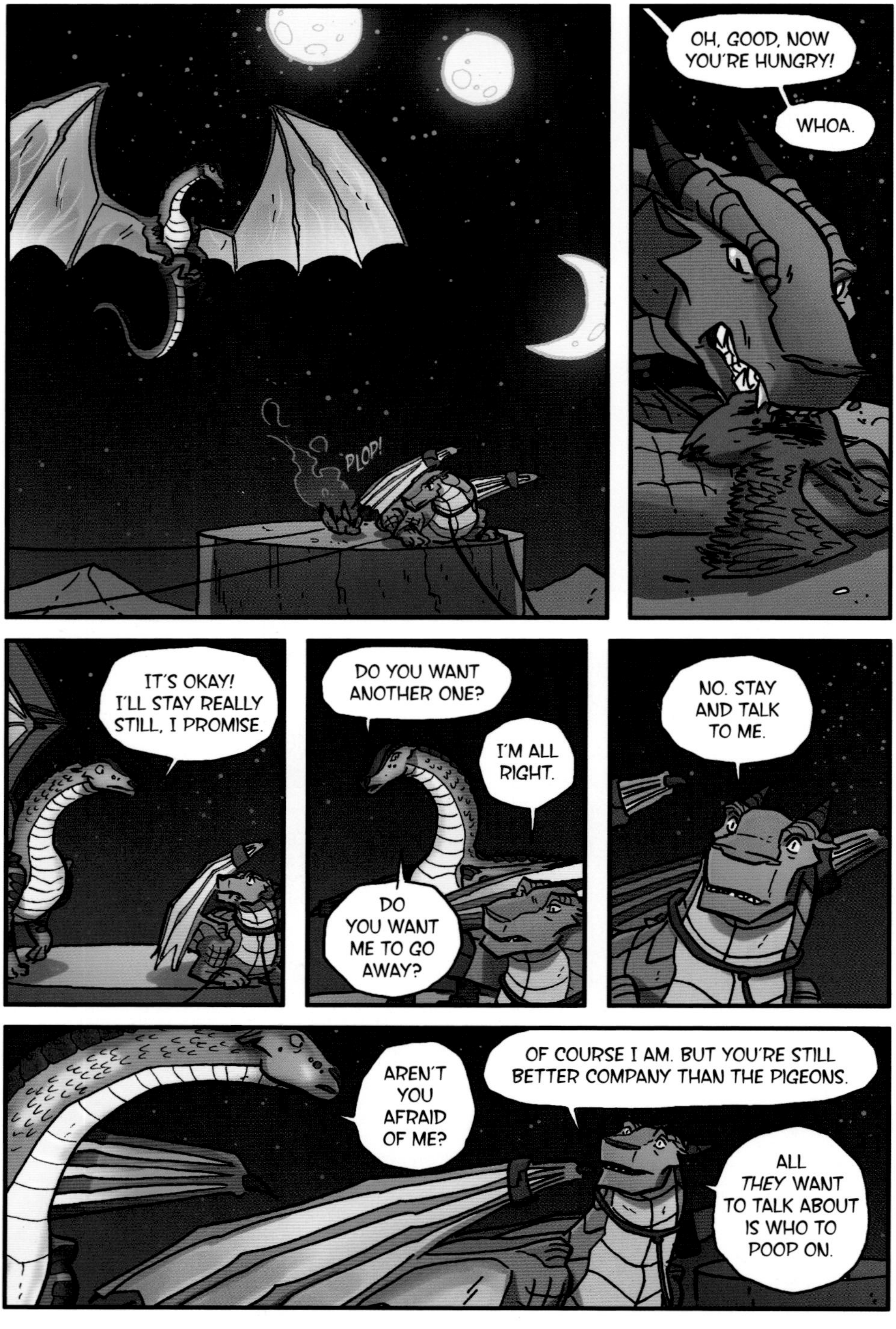
PLOP!
OH, GOOD, NOW YOU'RE HUNGRY!
WHOA.
IT'S OKAY! I'LL STAY REALLY STILL, I PROMISE.
DO YOU WANT ANOTHER ONE?
I'M ALL RIGHT.
DO YOU WANT ME TO GO AWAY?
NO. STAY AND TALK TO ME.
AREN'T YOU AFRAID OF ME?
OF COURSE I AM. BUT YOU'RE STILL BETTER COMPANY THAN THE PIGEONS.
ALL *THEY* WANT TO TALK ABOUT IS WHO TO POOP ON.

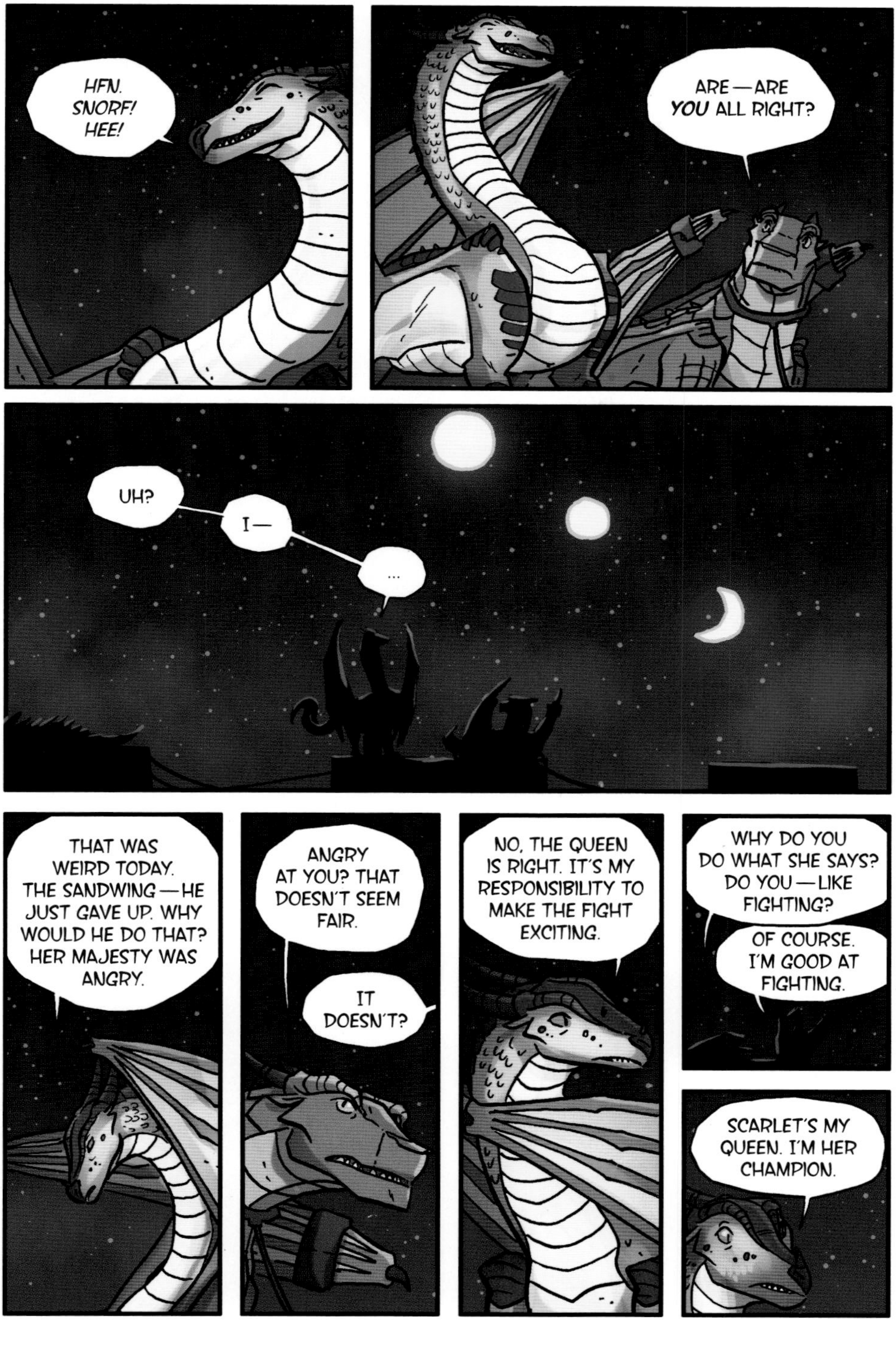
HFN. SNORF! HEE!
ARE—ARE *YOU* ALL RIGHT?
UH?
I—
...
THAT WAS WEIRD TODAY. THE SANDWING—HE JUST GAVE UP. WHY WOULD HE DO THAT? HER MAJESTY WAS ANGRY.
ANGRY AT YOU? THAT DOESN'T SEEM FAIR.
IT DOESN'T?
NO, THE QUEEN IS RIGHT. IT'S MY RESPONSIBILITY TO MAKE THE FIGHT EXCITING.
WHY DO YOU DO WHAT SHE SAYS? DO YOU—LIKE FIGHTING?
OF COURSE. I'M GOOD AT FIGHTING.
SCARLET'S MY QUEEN. I'M HER CHAMPION.

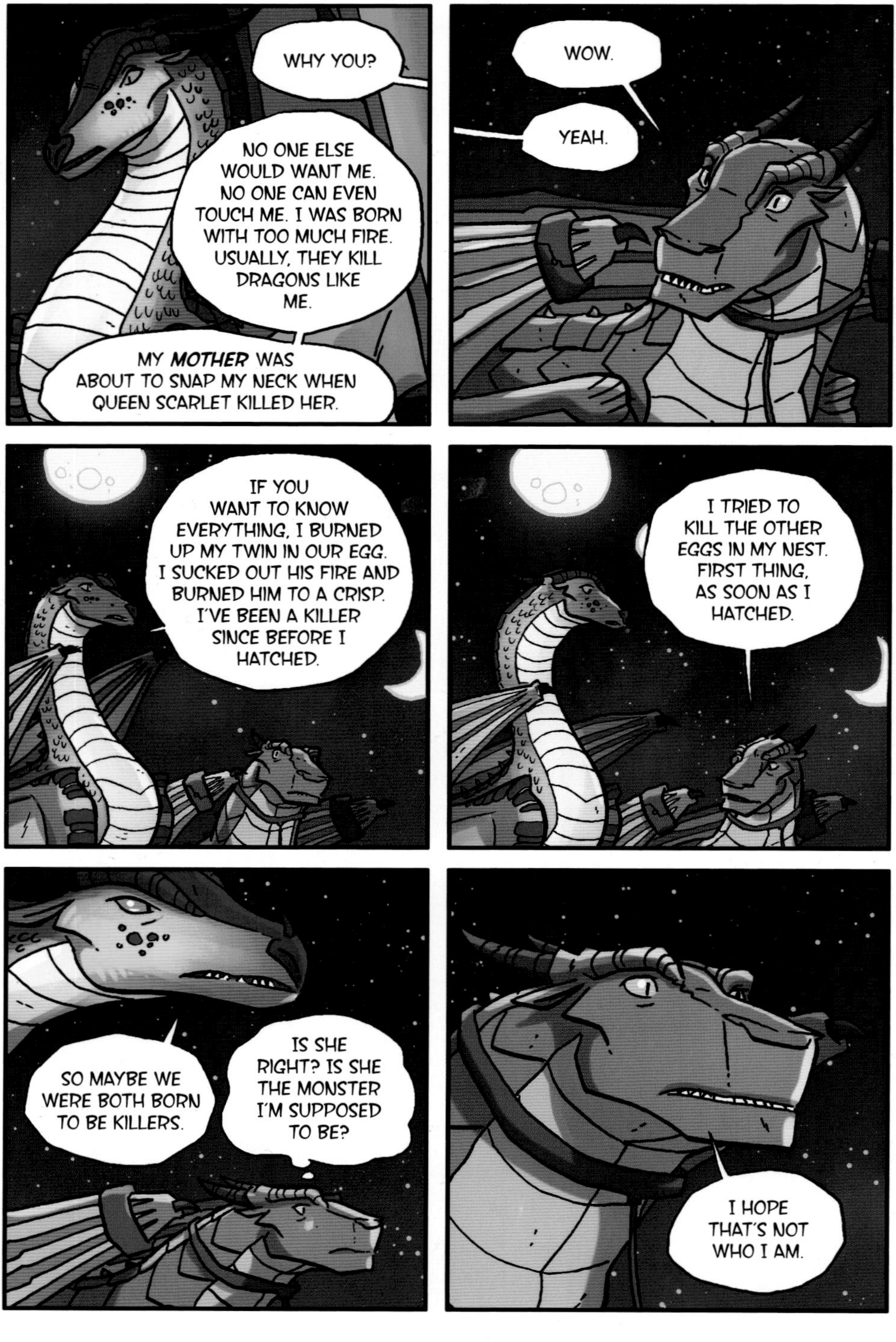
WHY YOU?
NO ONE ELSE WOULD WANT ME. NO ONE CAN EVEN TOUCH ME. I WAS BORN WITH TOO MUCH FIRE. USUALLY, THEY KILL DRAGONS LIKE ME.
MY *MOTHER* WAS ABOUT TO SNAP MY NECK WHEN QUEEN SCARLET KILLED HER.
WOW.
YEAH.
IF YOU WANT TO KNOW EVERYTHING, I BURNED UP MY TWIN IN OUR EGG. I SUCKED OUT HIS FIRE AND BURNED HIM TO A CRISP. I'VE BEEN A KILLER SINCE BEFORE I HATCHED.
I TRIED TO KILL THE OTHER EGGS IN MY NEST. FIRST THING, AS SOON AS I HATCHED.
SO MAYBE WE WERE BOTH BORN TO BE KILLERS.
IS SHE RIGHT? IS SHE THE MONSTER I'M SUPPOSED TO BE?
I HOPE THAT'S NOT WHO I AM.

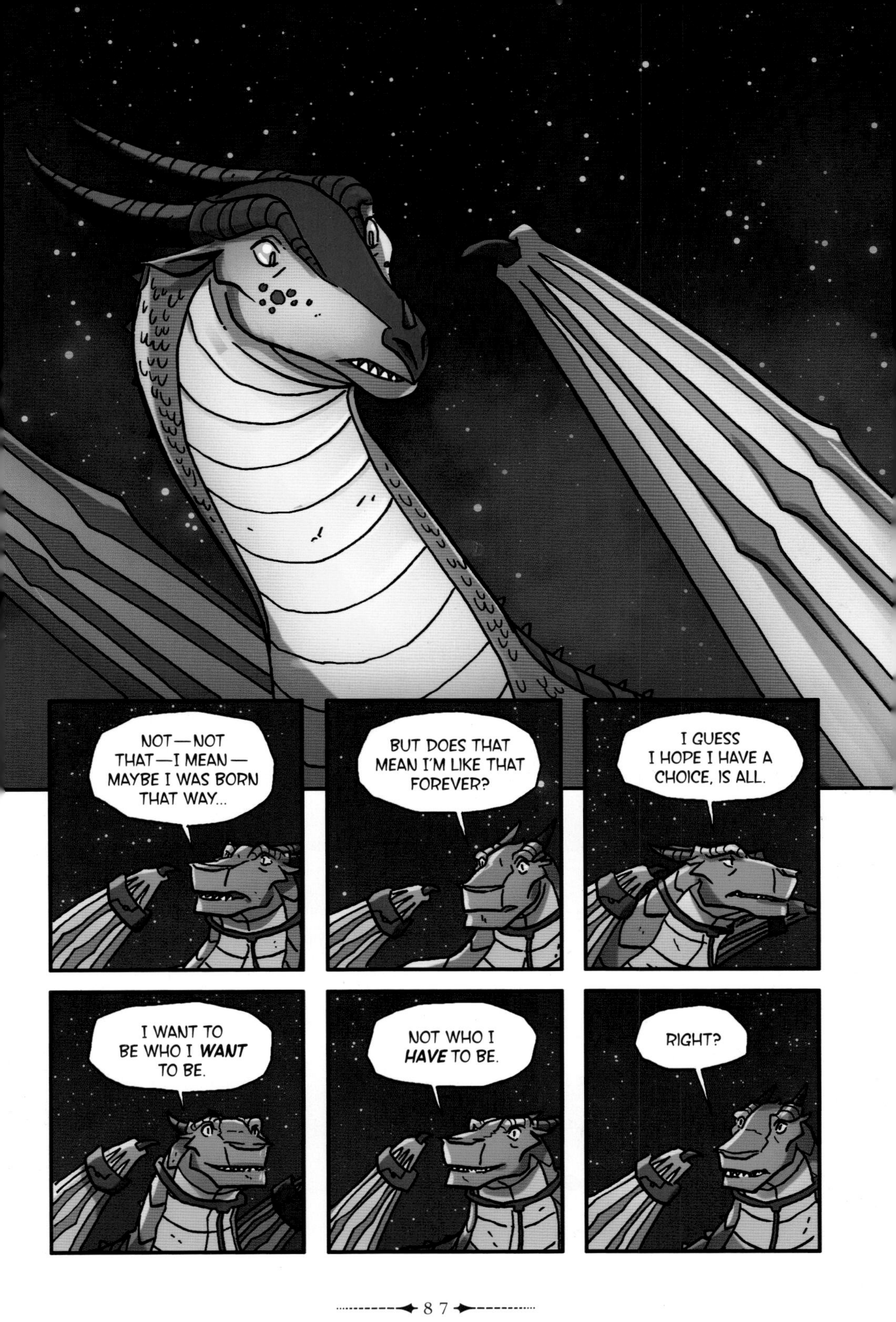
NOT—NOT THAT—I MEAN—MAYBE I WAS BORN THAT WAY...
BUT DOES THAT MEAN I'M LIKE THAT FOREVER?
I GUESS I HOPE I HAVE A CHOICE, IS ALL.
I WANT TO BE WHO I *WANT* TO BE.
NOT WHO I *HAVE* TO BE.
RIGHT?

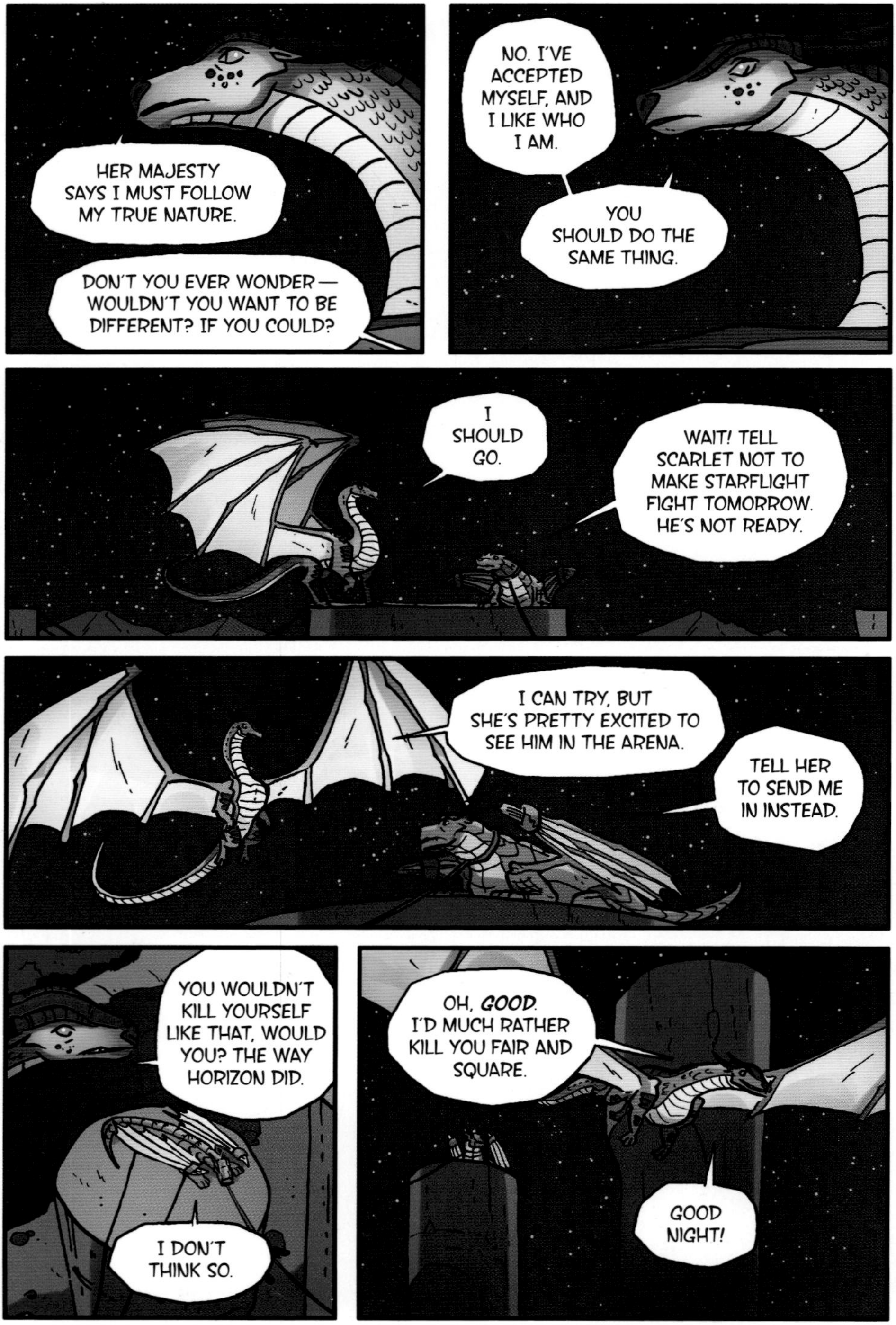
HER MAJESTY SAYS I MUST FOLLOW MY TRUE NATURE.
DON'T YOU EVER WONDER— WOULDN'T YOU WANT TO BE DIFFERENT? IF YOU COULD?
NO. I'VE ACCEPTED MYSELF, AND I LIKE WHO I AM.
YOU SHOULD DO THE SAME THING.
I SHOULD GO.
WAIT! TELL SCARLET NOT TO MAKE STARFLIGHT FIGHT TOMORROW. HE'S NOT READY.
I CAN TRY, BUT SHE'S PRETTY EXCITED TO SEE HIM IN THE ARENA.
TELL HER TO SEND ME IN INSTEAD.
YOU WOULDN'T KILL YOURSELF LIKE THAT, WOULD YOU? THE WAY HORIZON DID.
I DON'T THINK SO.
OH, ***GOOD***. I'D MUCH RATHER KILL YOU FAIR AND SQUARE.
GOOD NIGHT!

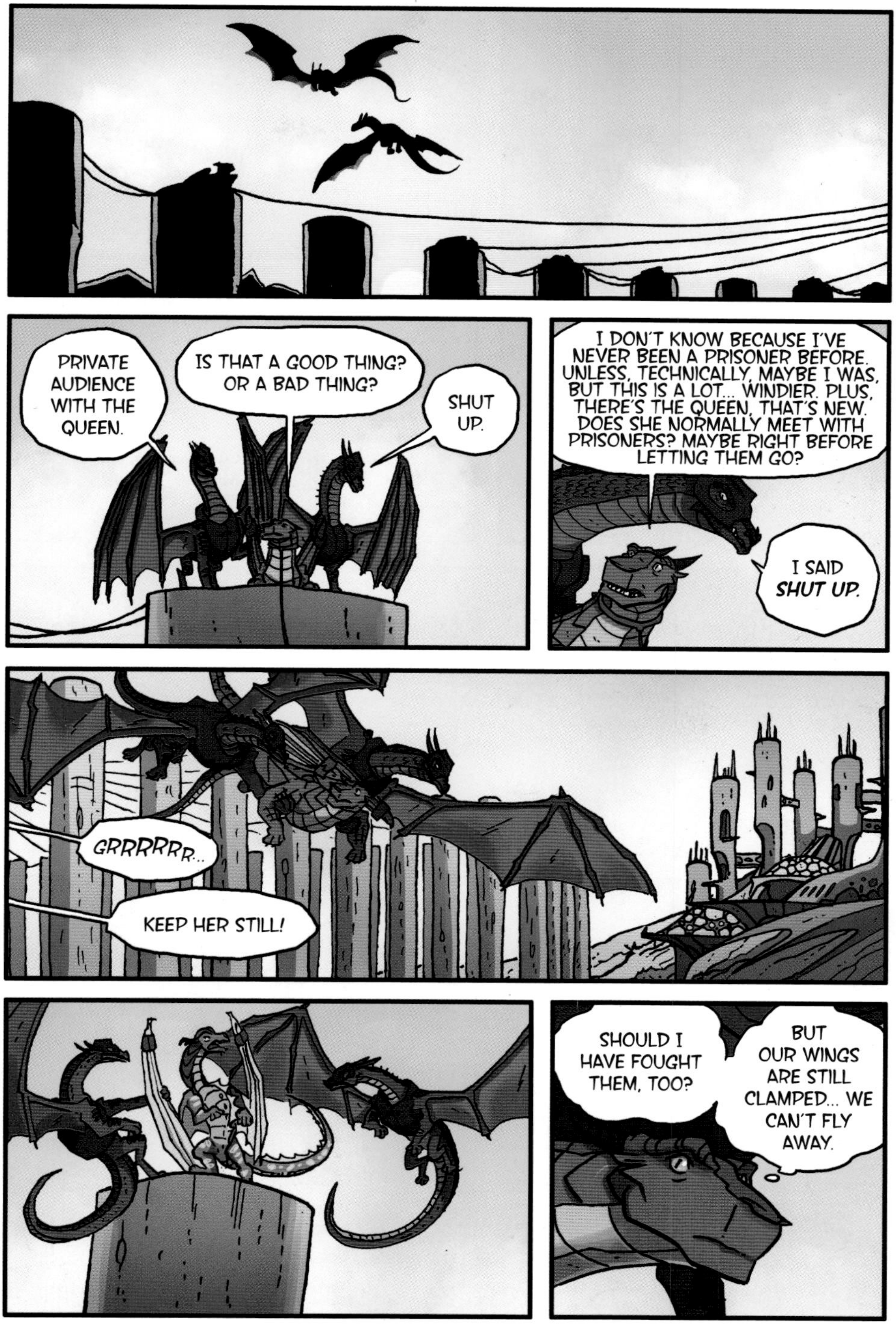
PRIVATE AUDIENCE WITH THE QUEEN.
IS THAT A GOOD THING? OR A BAD THING?
SHUT UP.
I DON'T KNOW BECAUSE I'VE NEVER BEEN A PRISONER BEFORE. UNLESS, TECHNICALLY, MAYBE I WAS, BUT THIS IS A LOT... WINDIER. PLUS, THERE'S THE QUEEN, THAT'S NEW. DOES SHE NORMALLY MEET WITH PRISONERS? MAYBE RIGHT BEFORE LETTING THEM GO?
I SAID *SHUT UP.*
GRRRRRR...
KEEP HER STILL!
SHOULD I HAVE FOUGHT THEM, TOO?
BUT OUR WINGS ARE STILL CLAMPED... WE CAN'T FLY AWAY.

KESTREL!

ANOTHER **WORD** AND THERE'S GOING TO BE AN **UNFORTUNATE ACCIDENT.**

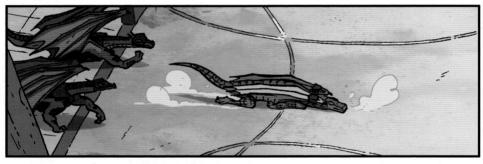

ARE YOU ALL RIGHT?

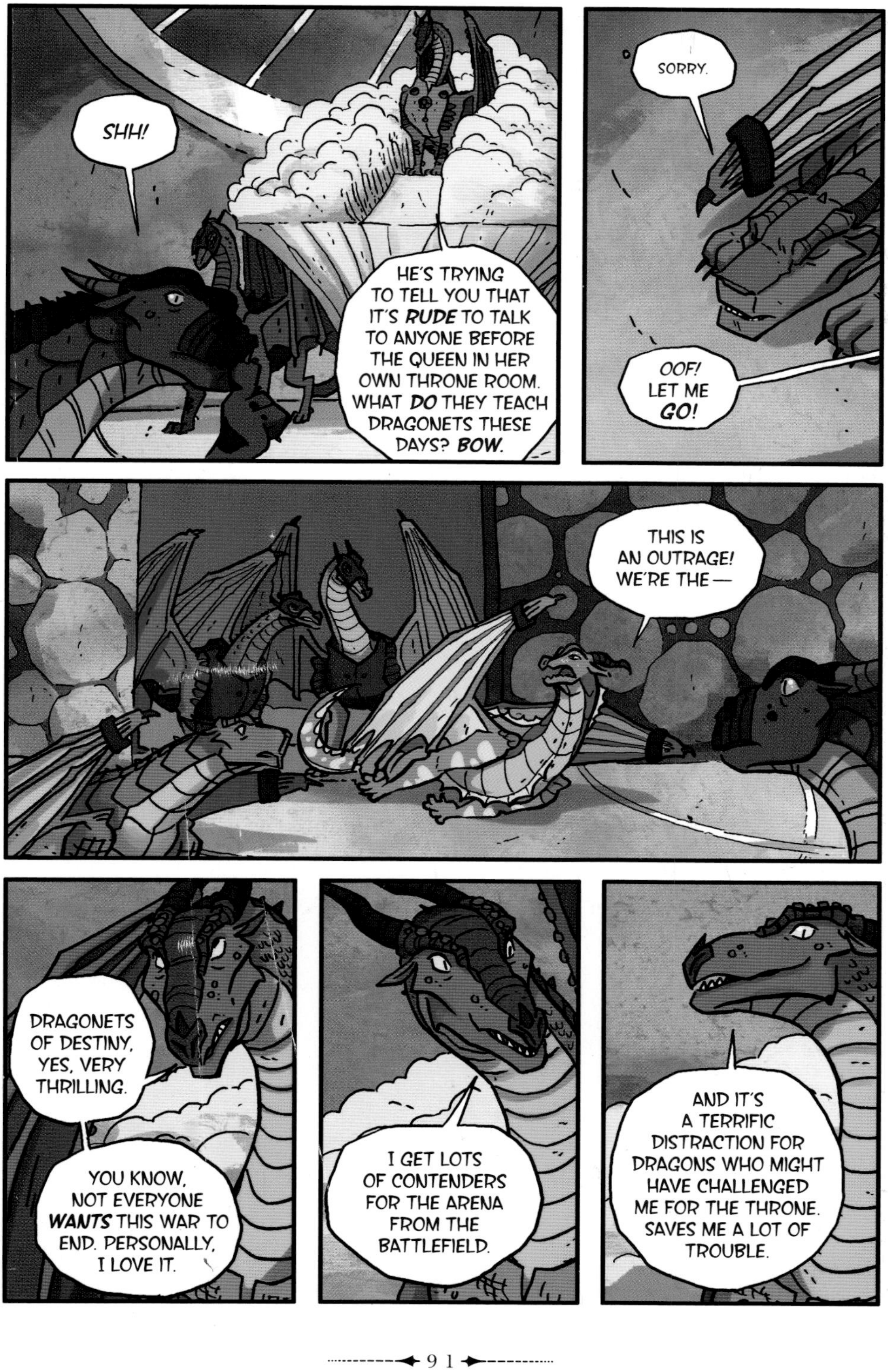
SHH!
HE'S TRYING TO TELL YOU THAT IT'S ***RUDE*** TO TALK TO ANYONE BEFORE THE QUEEN IN HER OWN THRONE ROOM. WHAT ***DO*** THEY TEACH DRAGONETS THESE DAYS? ***BOW.***
SORRY.
OOF! LET ME ***GO!***
THIS IS AN OUTRAGE! WE'RE THE —
DRAGONETS OF DESTINY, YES, VERY THRILLING.
YOU KNOW, NOT EVERYONE ***WANTS*** THIS WAR TO END. PERSONALLY, I LOVE IT.
I GET LOTS OF CONTENDERS FOR THE ARENA FROM THE BATTLEFIELD.
AND IT'S A TERRIFIC DISTRACTION FOR DRAGONS WHO MIGHT HAVE CHALLENGED ME FOR THE THRONE. SAVES ME A LOT OF TROUBLE.

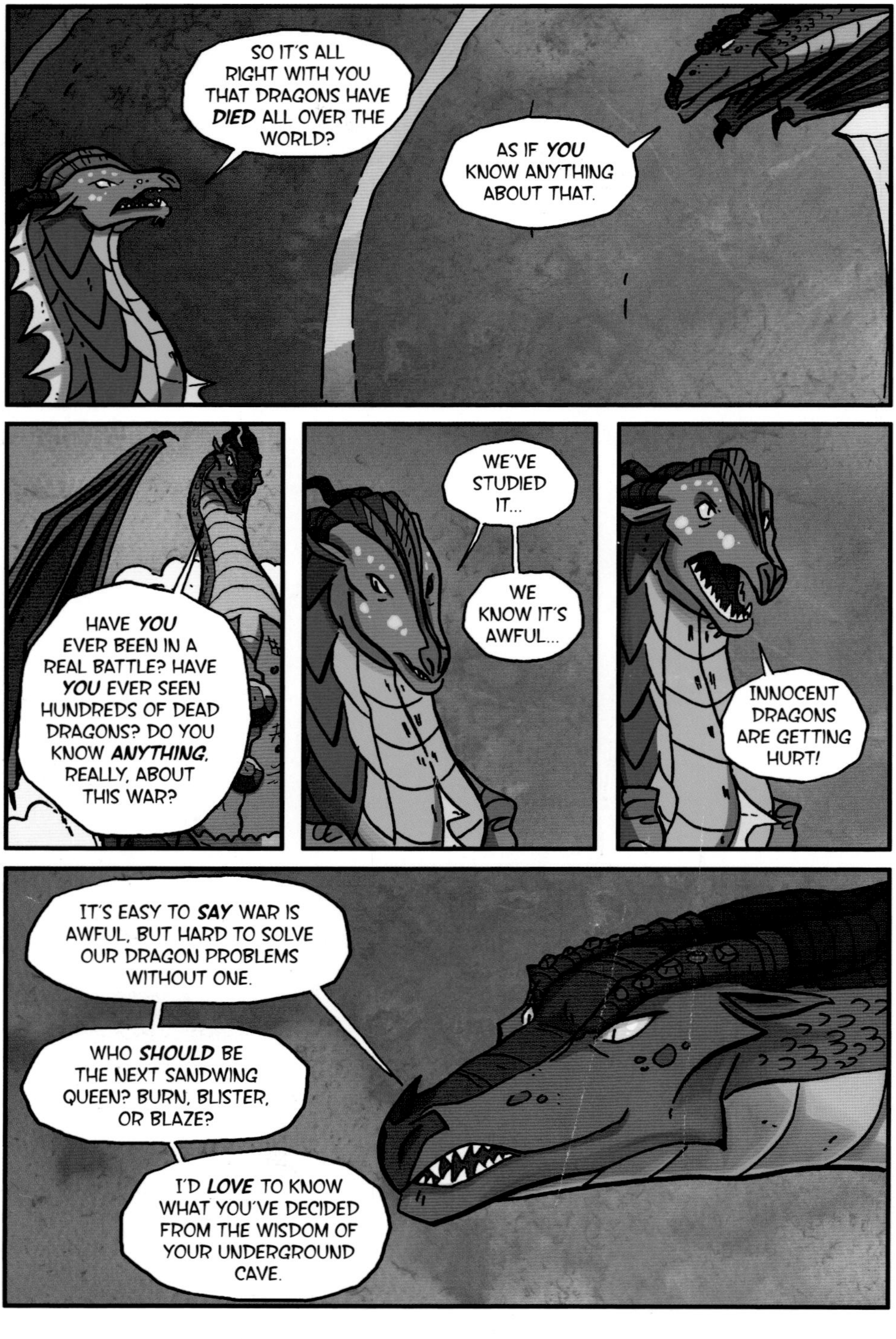
SO IT'S ALL RIGHT WITH YOU THAT DRAGONS HAVE ***DIED*** ALL OVER THE WORLD?
AS IF ***YOU*** KNOW ANYTHING ABOUT THAT.
HAVE ***YOU*** EVER BEEN IN A REAL BATTLE? HAVE ***YOU*** EVER SEEN HUNDREDS OF DEAD DRAGONS? DO YOU KNOW ***ANYTHING***, REALLY, ABOUT THIS WAR?
WE'VE STUDIED IT...
WE KNOW IT'S AWFUL...
INNOCENT DRAGONS ARE GETTING HURT!
IT'S EASY TO ***SAY*** WAR IS AWFUL, BUT HARD TO SOLVE OUR DRAGON PROBLEMS WITHOUT ONE.
WHO ***SHOULD*** BE THE NEXT SANDWING QUEEN? BURN, BLISTER, OR BLAZE?
I'D ***LOVE*** TO KNOW WHAT YOU'VE DECIDED FROM THE WISDOM OF YOUR UNDERGROUND CAVE.

THAT WASN'T OUR FAULT! WE *WANTED* TO BE OUT IN THE WORLD.

THAT'S WHAT YOU THINK. HILARIOUS. AS IF YOU'D HAVE SURVIVED THIS LONG OUT THERE.

YOUR GUARDIANS *DID* TELL YOU WHAT HAPPENED TO ALL THE SKYWING DRAGONETS BORN ON THE BRIGHTEST NIGHT, DIDN'T THEY?

I WON'T GO INTO DETAILS, BUT IT WAS VERY SAD.

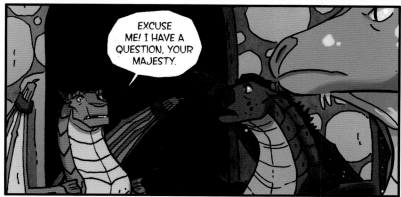

EXCUSE *ME!* I HAVE A QUESTION, YOUR MAJESTY.

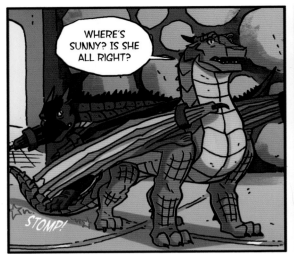

WHERE'S SUNNY? IS SHE ALL RIGHT?

STOMP!

OH, THE ODD-LOOKING SANDWING. I THINK BURN WILL LIKE HER VERY MUCH.

SHE COLLECTS CURIOSITIES. YOU SHOULD SEE HER PALACE. IT'S QUITE HORRIFYING.

FULL OF TWO-HEADED LIZARDS...

...AND SEVEN-TOED DRAGON TALONS...

...AND STUFFED SCAVENGERS WITH WEIRD PALE SKIN...

...YOUR LITTLE FRIEND WILL FIT RIGHT IN.

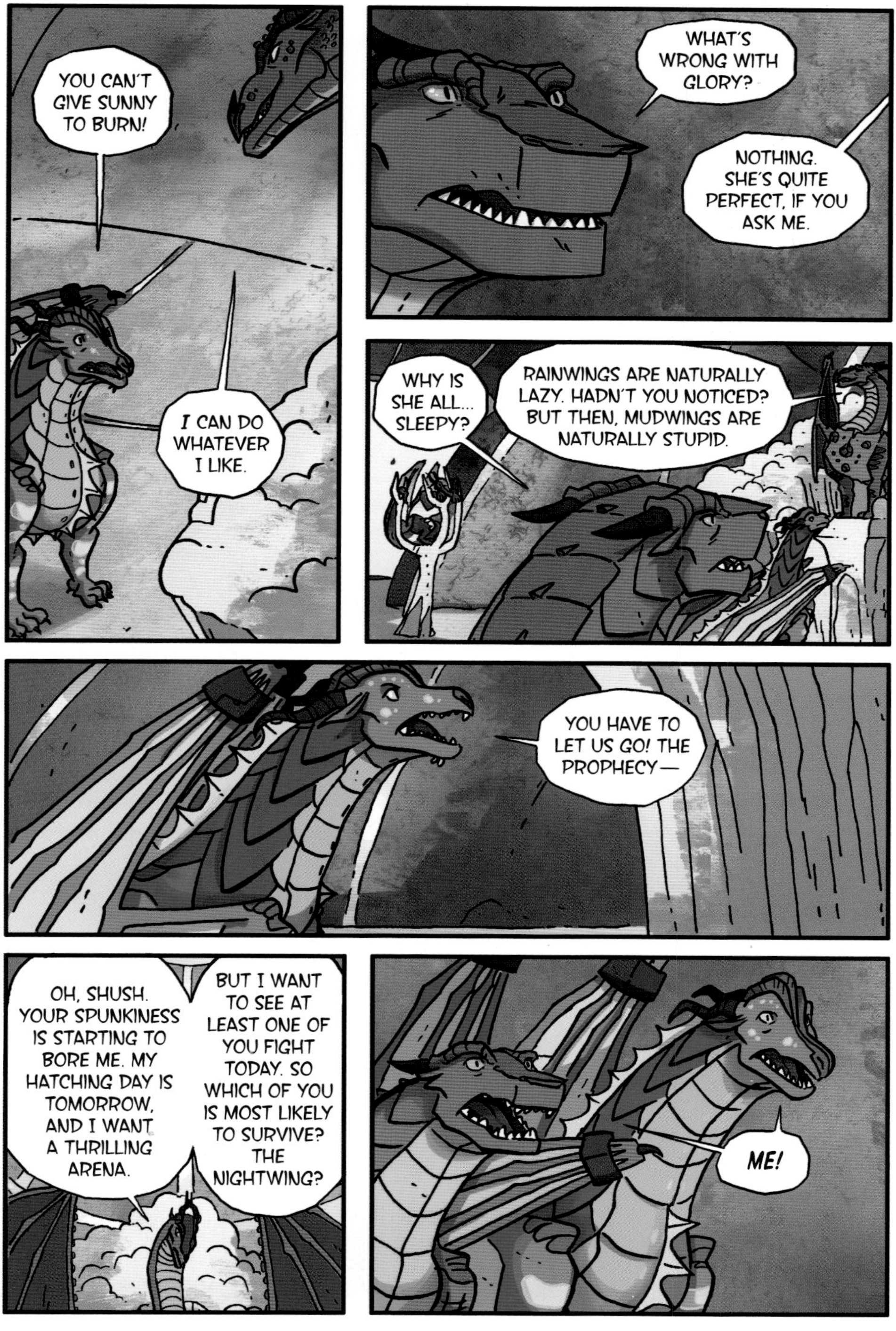

YOU CAN'T GIVE SUNNY TO BURN!
I CAN DO WHATEVER I LIKE.
WHAT'S WRONG WITH GLORY?
NOTHING. SHE'S QUITE PERFECT, IF YOU ASK ME.
WHY IS SHE ALL... SLEEPY?
RAINWINGS ARE NATURALLY LAZY. HADN'T YOU NOTICED? BUT THEN, MUDWINGS ARE NATURALLY STUPID.
YOU HAVE TO LET US GO! THE PROPHECY—
OH, SHUSH. YOUR SPUNKINESS IS STARTING TO BORE ME. MY HATCHING DAY IS TOMORROW, AND I WANT A THRILLING ARENA.
BUT I WANT TO SEE AT LEAST ONE OF YOU FIGHT TODAY. SO WHICH OF YOU IS MOST LIKELY TO SURVIVE? THE NIGHTWING?
ME!

ADORABLE. BUT SERIOUSLY.

YOU'RE DELUSIONAL. I BEAT YOU ALL THE TIME.

A MUDWING WOULD BE MORE EXCITING THAN JUST ANOTHER SEAWING, WOULDN'T IT?

I LOVE YOUR ENTHUSIASM, DRAGONETS!

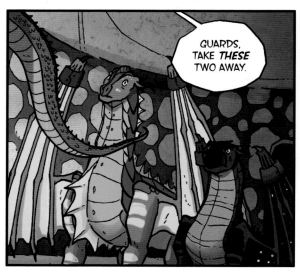

GUARDS, TAKE *THESE* TWO AWAY.

AS FOR THIS ONE... PREPARE HIM FOR THE ARENA.

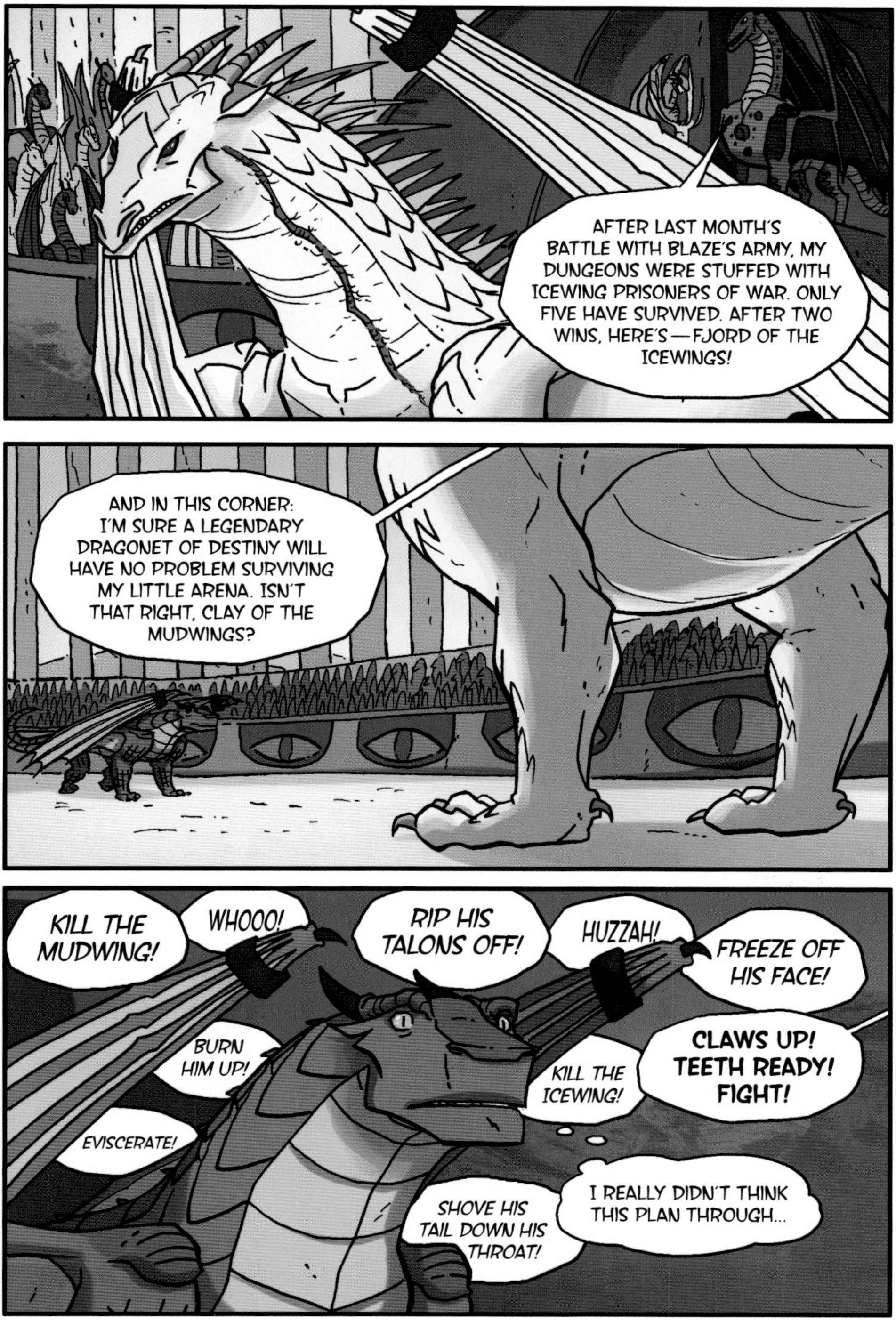
AFTER LAST MONTH'S BATTLE WITH BLAZE'S ARMY, MY DUNGEONS WERE STUFFED WITH ICEWING PRISONERS OF WAR. ONLY FIVE HAVE SURVIVED. AFTER TWO WINS, HERE'S—FJORD OF THE ICEWINGS!
AND IN THIS CORNER: I'M SURE A LEGENDARY DRAGONET OF DESTINY WILL HAVE NO PROBLEM SURVIVING MY LITTLE ARENA. ISN'T THAT RIGHT, CLAY OF THE MUDWINGS?
KILL THE MUDWING!
WHOOO!
RIP HIS TALONS OFF!
HUZZAH!
FREEZE OFF HIS FACE!
BURN HIM UP!
CLAWS UP! TEETH READY! FIGHT!
KILL THE ICEWING!
EVISCERATE!
SHOVE HIS TAIL DOWN HIS THROAT!
I REALLY DIDN'T THINK THIS PLAN THROUGH...

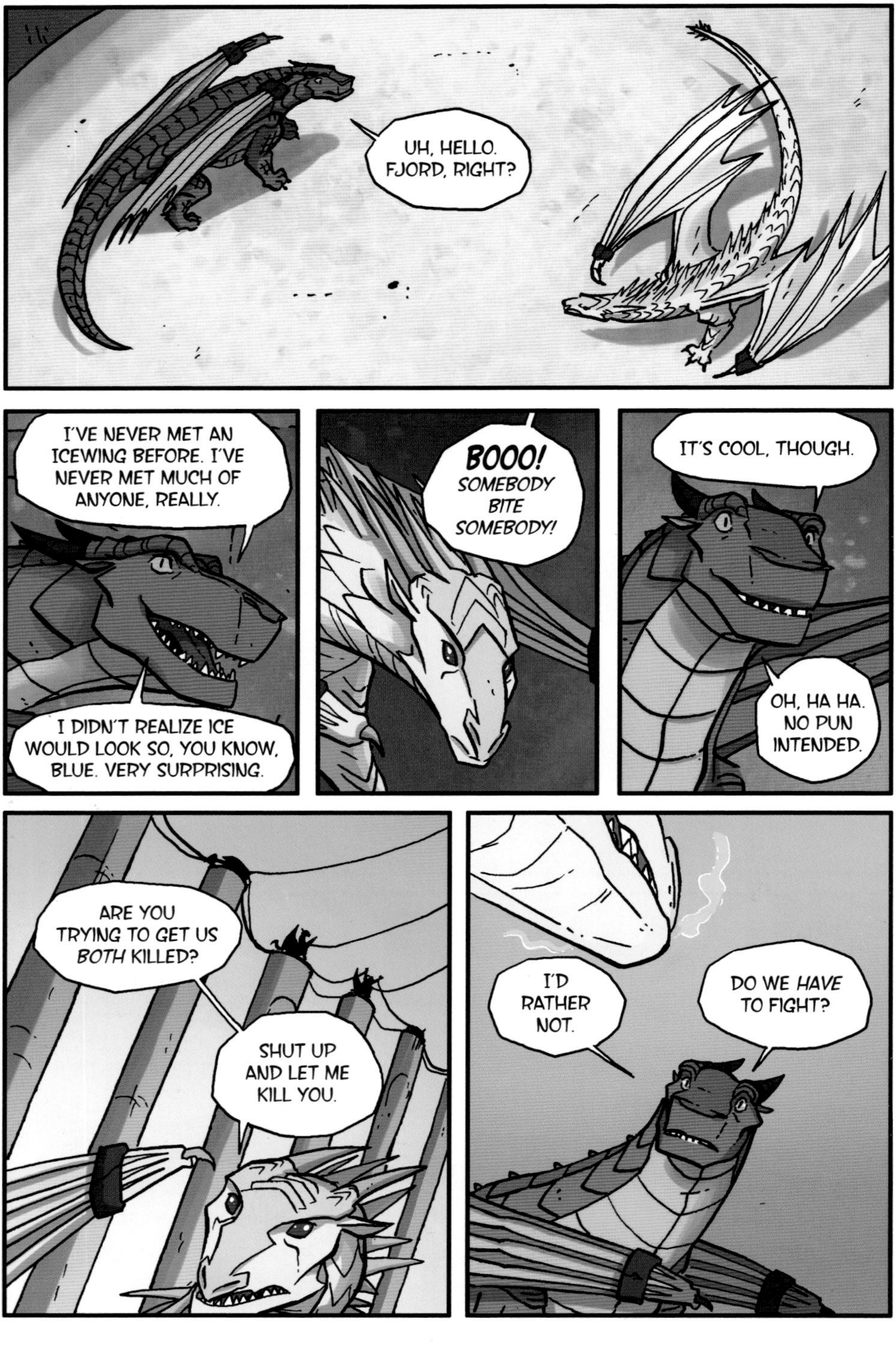
UH, HELLO. FJORD, RIGHT?
I'VE NEVER MET AN ICEWING BEFORE. I'VE NEVER MET MUCH OF ANYONE, REALLY.
I DIDN'T REALIZE ICE WOULD LOOK SO, YOU KNOW, BLUE. VERY SURPRISING.
BOOO! SOMEBODY BITE SOMEBODY!
IT'S COOL, THOUGH.
OH, HA HA. NO PUN INTENDED.
ARE YOU TRYING TO GET US BOTH KILLED?
SHUT UP AND LET ME KILL YOU.
I'D RATHER NOT.
DO WE HAVE TO FIGHT?

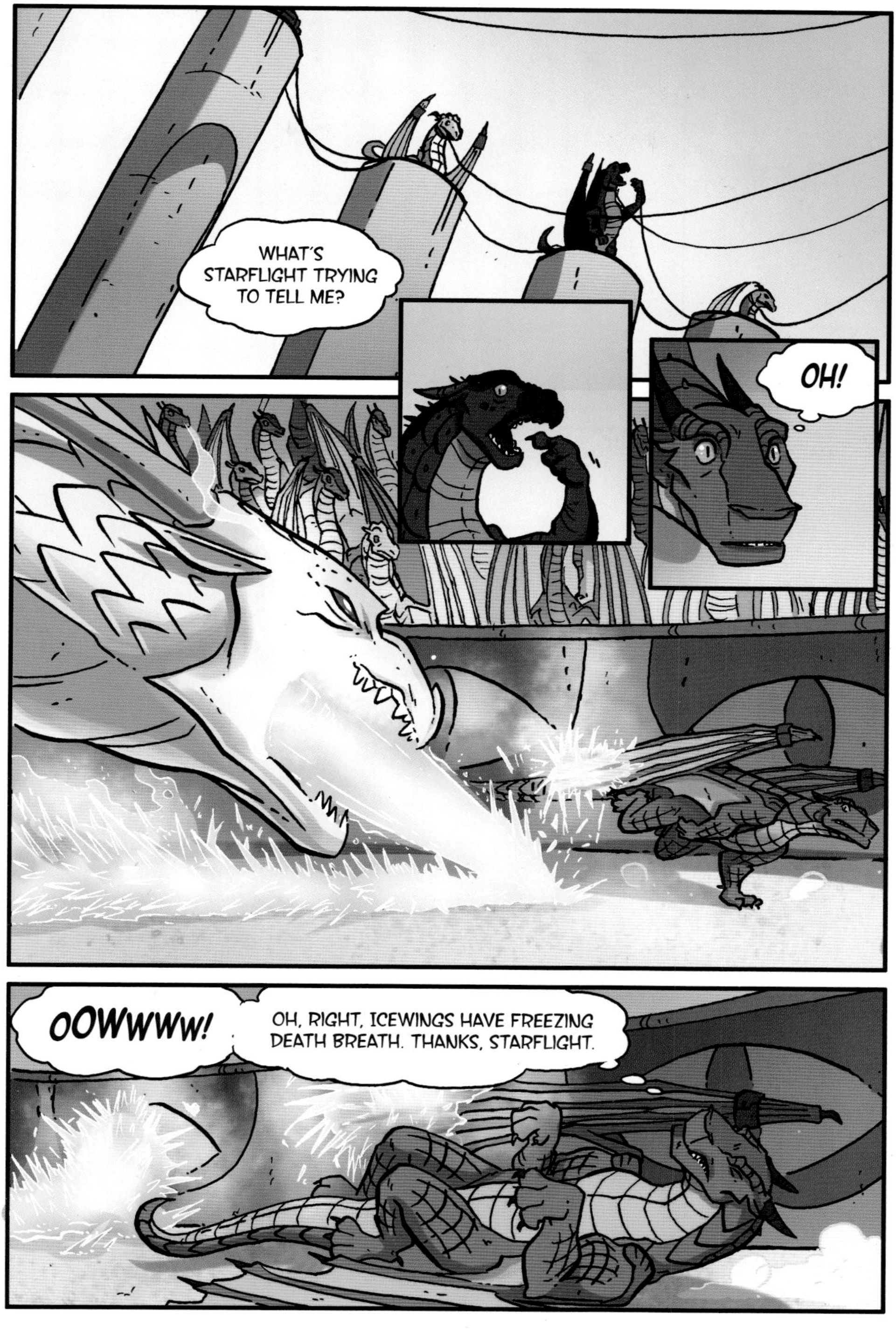
WHAT'S STARFLIGHT TRYING TO TELL ME?
OH!
OOWWWW!
OH, RIGHT, ICEWINGS HAVE FREEZING DEATH BREATH. THANKS, STARFLIGHT.

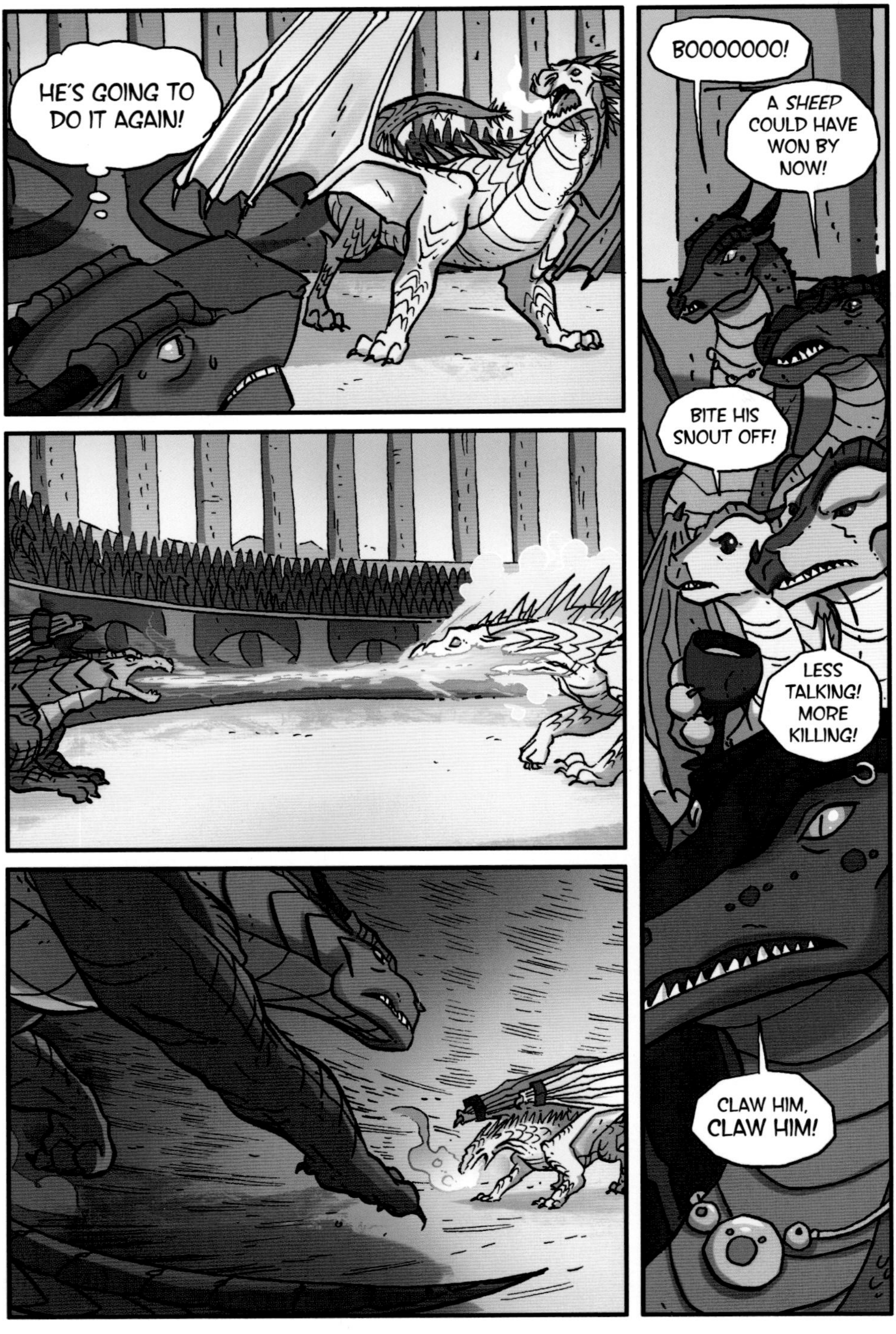
HE'S GOING TO DO IT AGAIN!
BOOOOOOO!
A *SHEEP* COULD HAVE WON BY NOW!
BITE HIS SNOUT OFF!
LESS TALKING! MORE KILLING!
CLAW HIM, CLAW HIM!

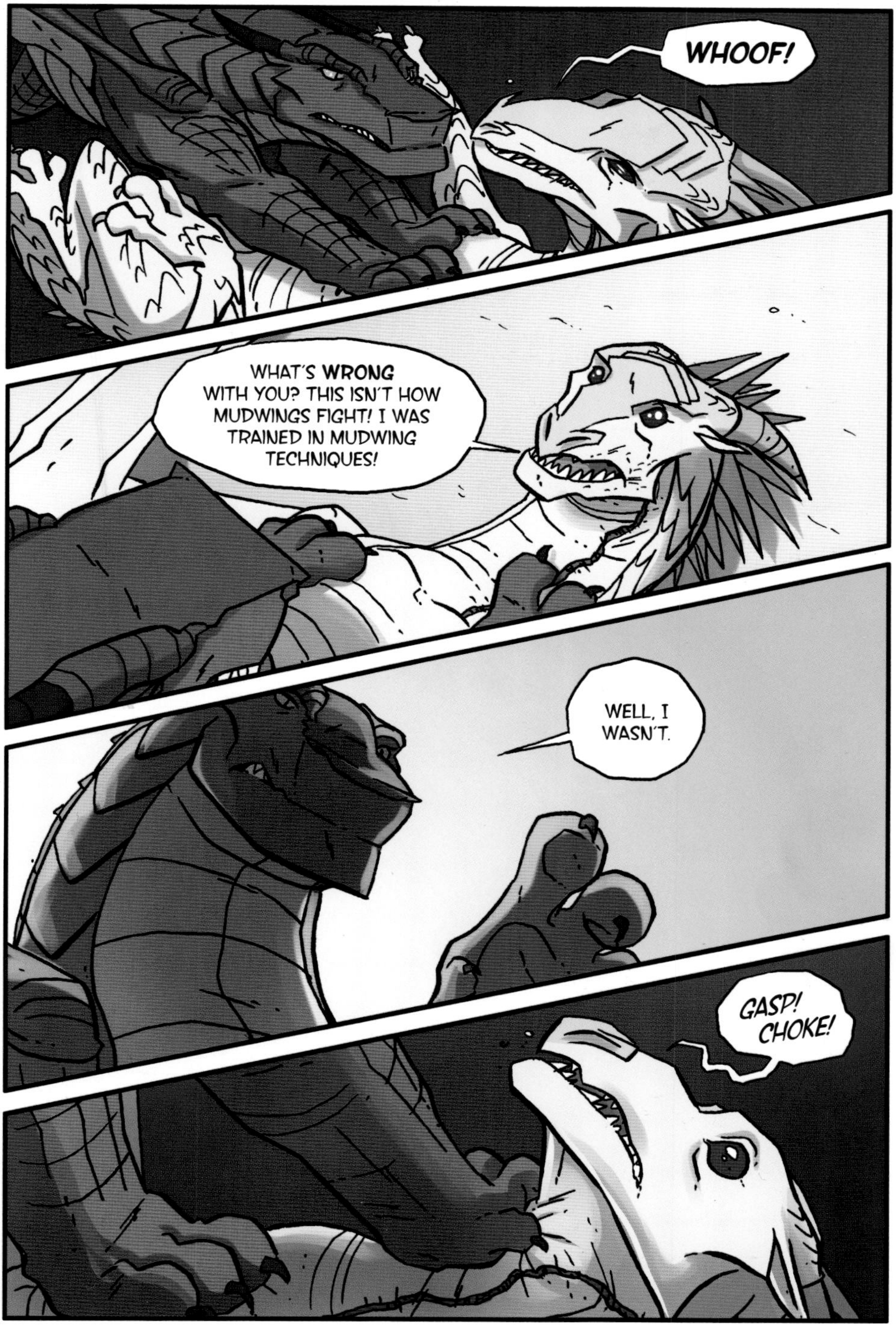
WHOOF!
WHAT'S **WRONG** WITH YOU? THIS ISN'T HOW MUDWINGS FIGHT! I WAS TRAINED IN MUDWING TECHNIQUES!
WELL, I WASN'T.
GASP! CHOKE!

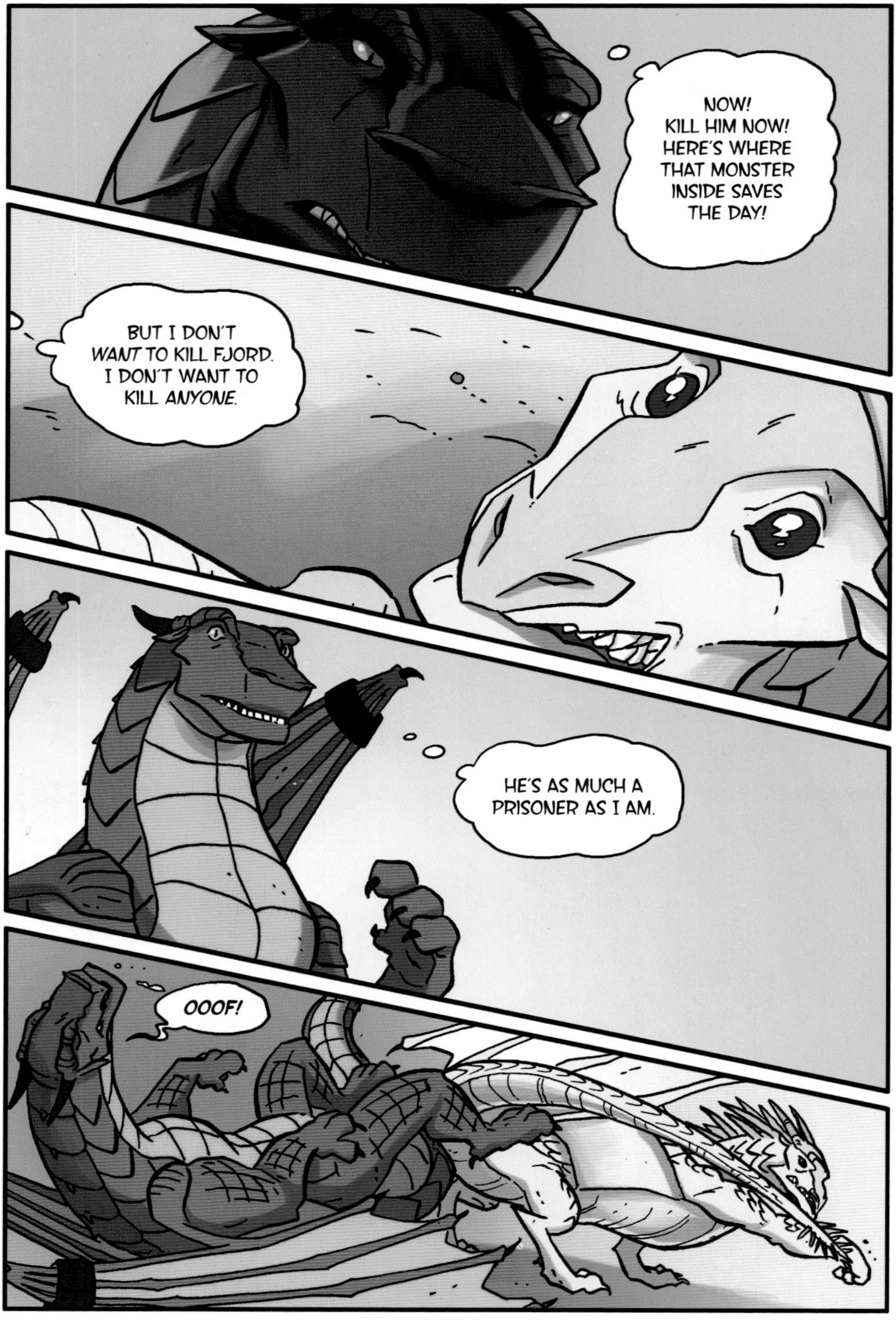
NOW!
KILL HIM NOW!
HERE'S WHERE
THAT MONSTER
INSIDE SAVES
THE DAY!
BUT I DON'T
WANT TO KILL FJORD.
I DON'T WANT TO
KILL *ANYONE*.
HE'S AS MUCH A
PRISONER AS I AM.
OOOF!

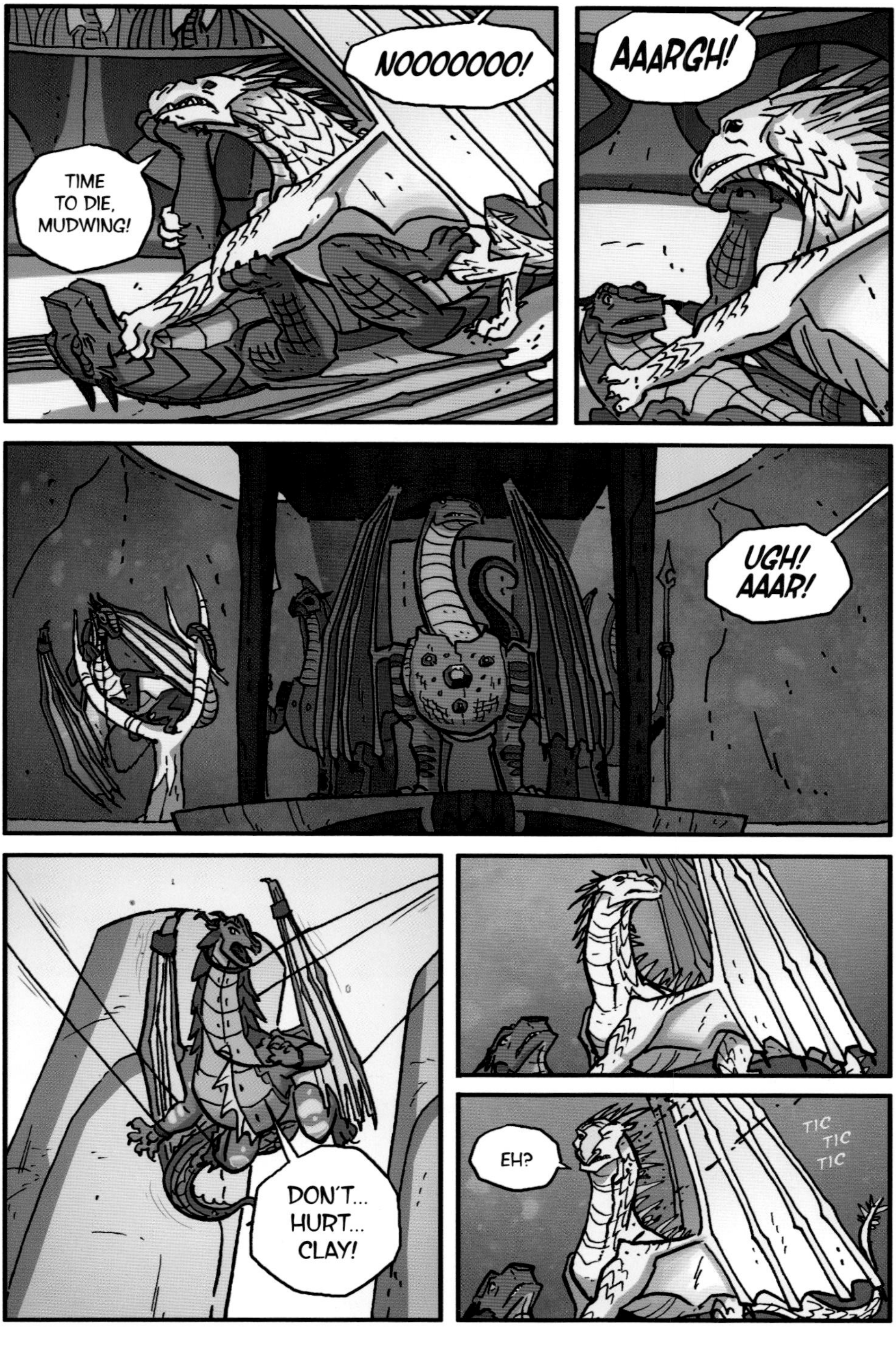
NOOOOOOO!
TIME TO DIE, MUDWING!
AAARGH!
UGH! AAAR!
DON'T... HURT... CLAY!
EH?
TIC TIC TIC

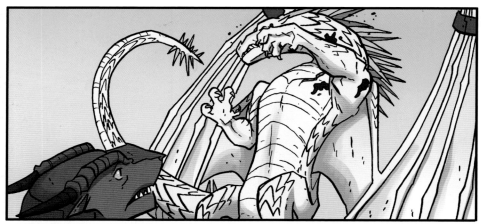

EEEYYYYdAAHHHH!!!

HSSSSSSSS

HELP ME! MAKE IT *STOPPPPP!*

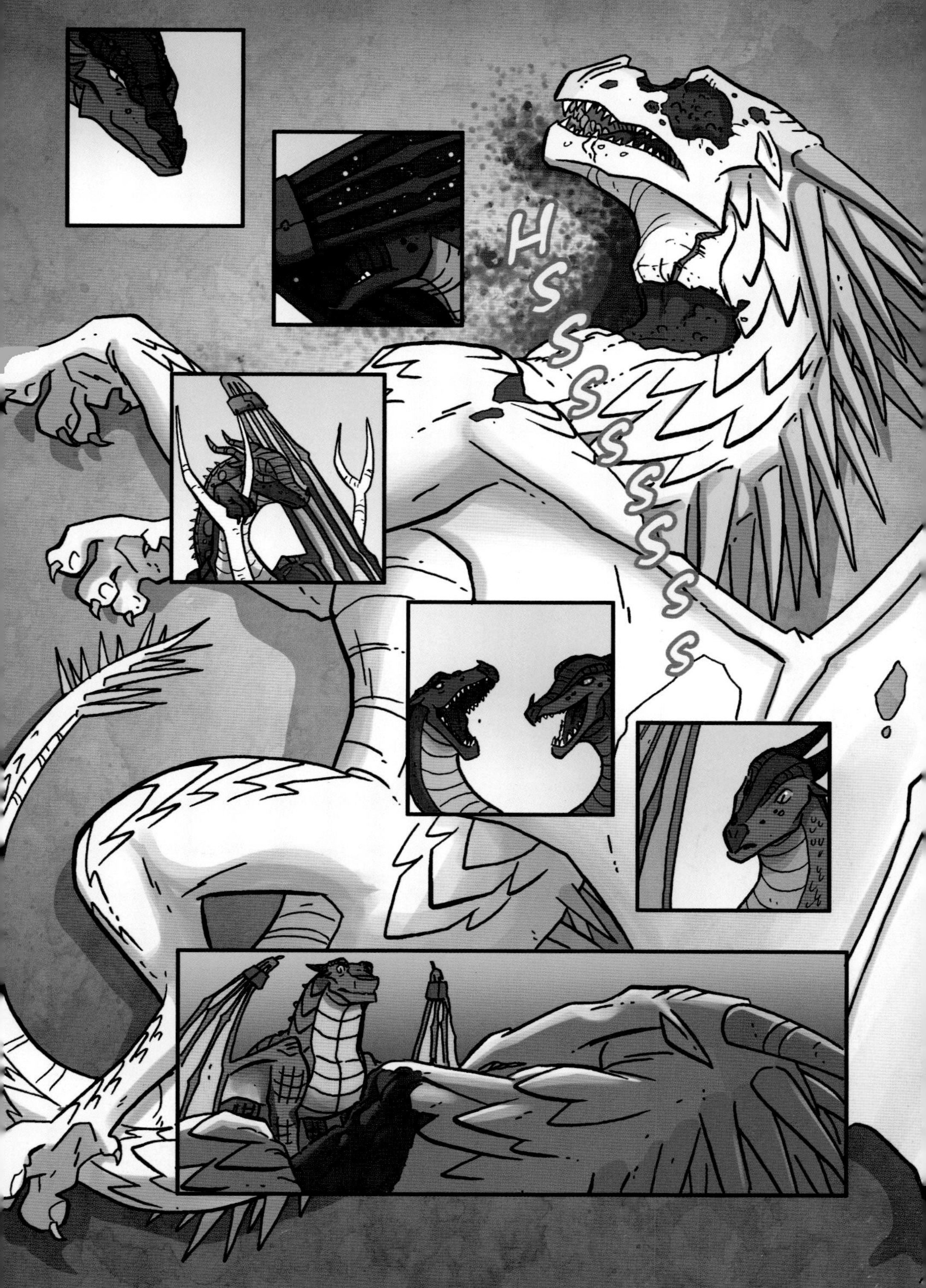
HSSSSSSSS

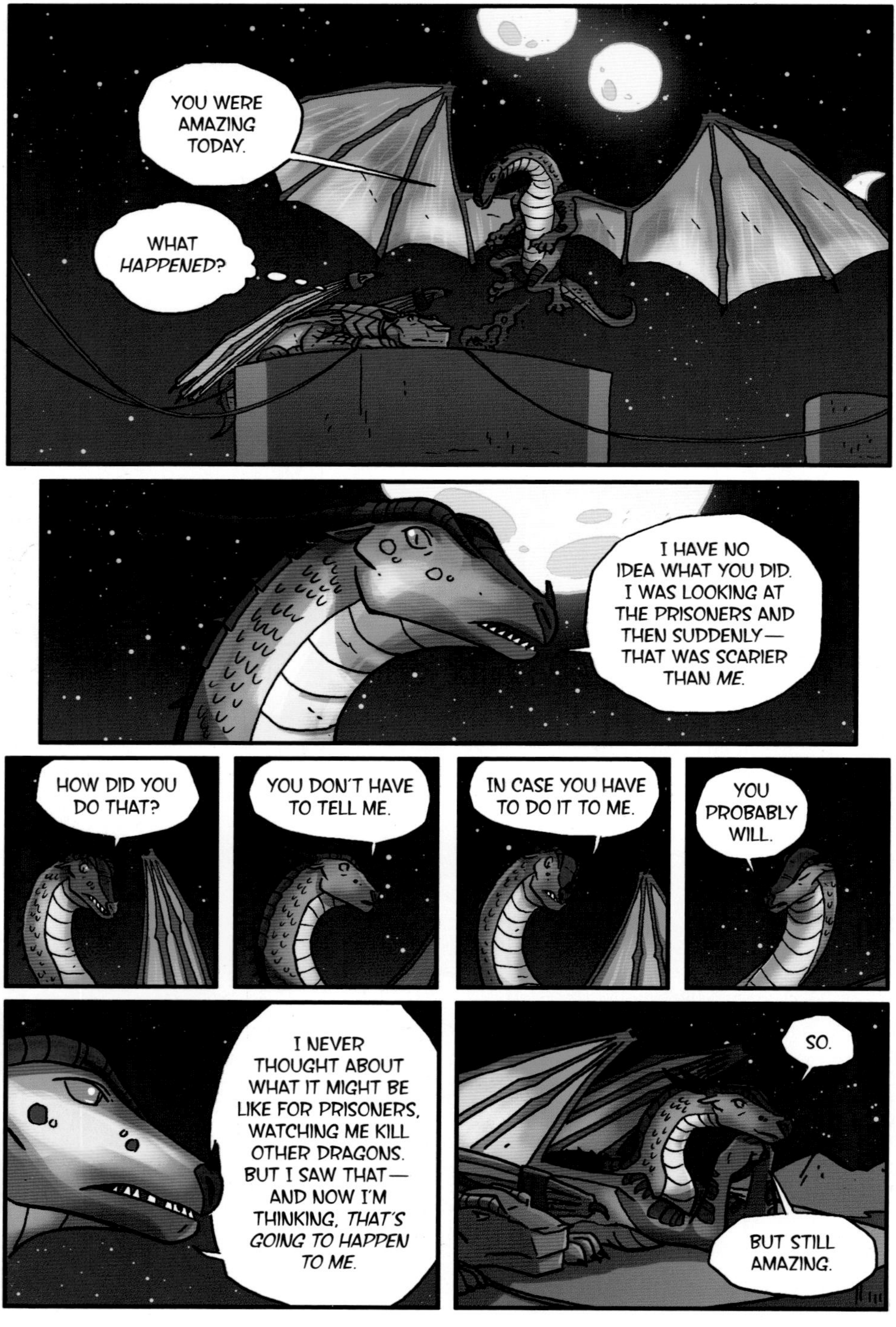
YOU WERE AMAZING TODAY.
WHAT *HAPPENED?*
I HAVE NO IDEA WHAT YOU DID. I WAS LOOKING AT THE PRISONERS AND THEN SUDDENLY— THAT WAS SCARIER THAN *ME.*
HOW DID YOU DO THAT?
YOU DON'T HAVE TO TELL ME.
IN CASE YOU HAVE TO DO IT TO ME.
YOU PROBABLY WILL.
I NEVER THOUGHT ABOUT WHAT IT MIGHT BE LIKE FOR PRISONERS, WATCHING ME KILL OTHER DRAGONS. BUT I SAW THAT— AND NOW I'M THINKING, *THAT'S GOING TO HAPPEN TO ME.*
SO.
BUT STILL AMAZING.

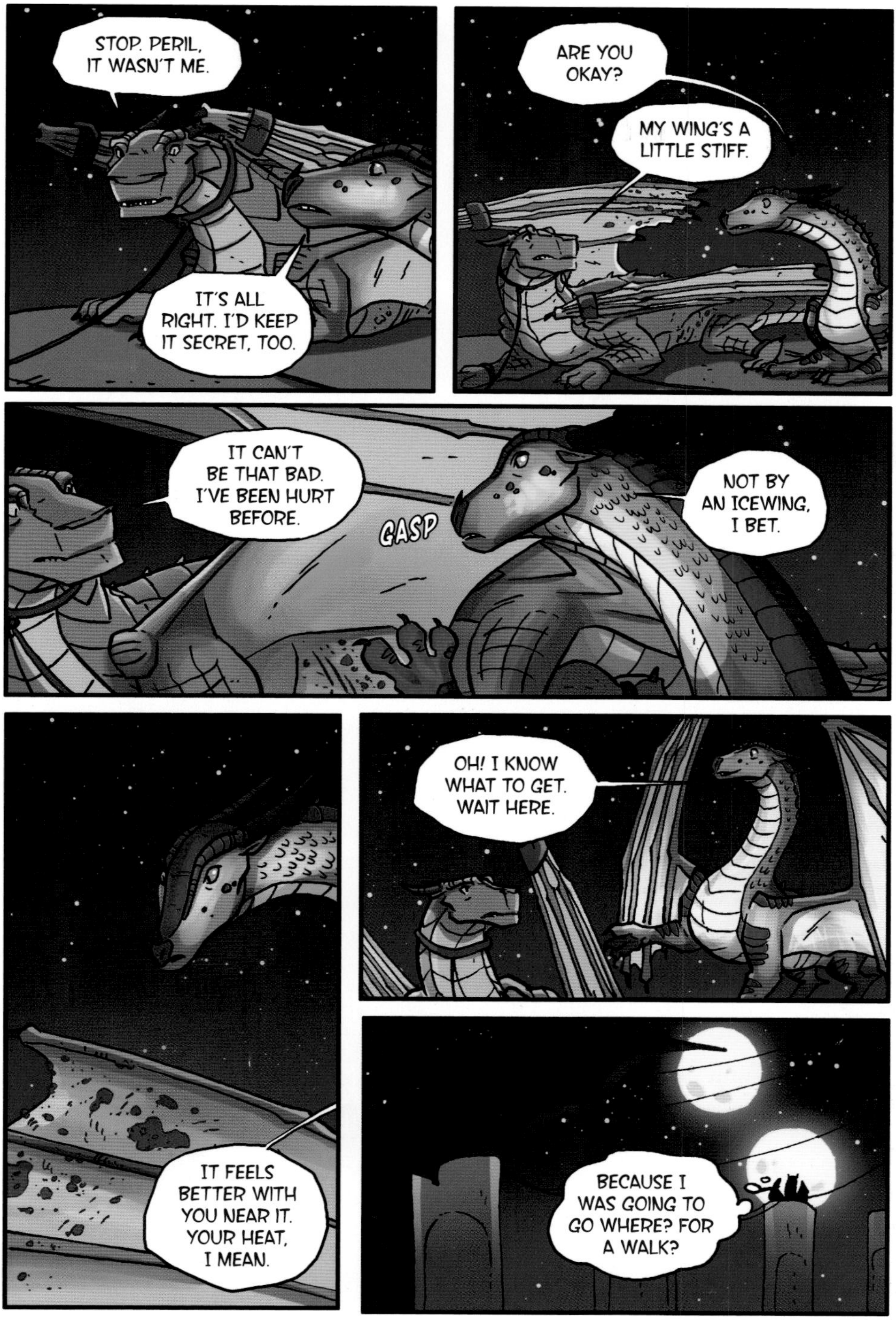
STOP. PERIL, IT WASN'T ME.
IT'S ALL RIGHT. I'D KEEP IT SECRET, TOO.
ARE YOU OKAY?
MY WING'S A LITTLE STIFF.
IT CAN'T BE THAT BAD. I'VE BEEN HURT BEFORE.
GASP
NOT BY AN ICEWING, I BET.
IT FEELS BETTER WITH YOU NEAR IT. YOUR HEAT, I MEAN.
OH! I KNOW WHAT TO GET. WAIT HERE.
BECAUSE I WAS GOING TO GO WHERE? FOR A WALK?

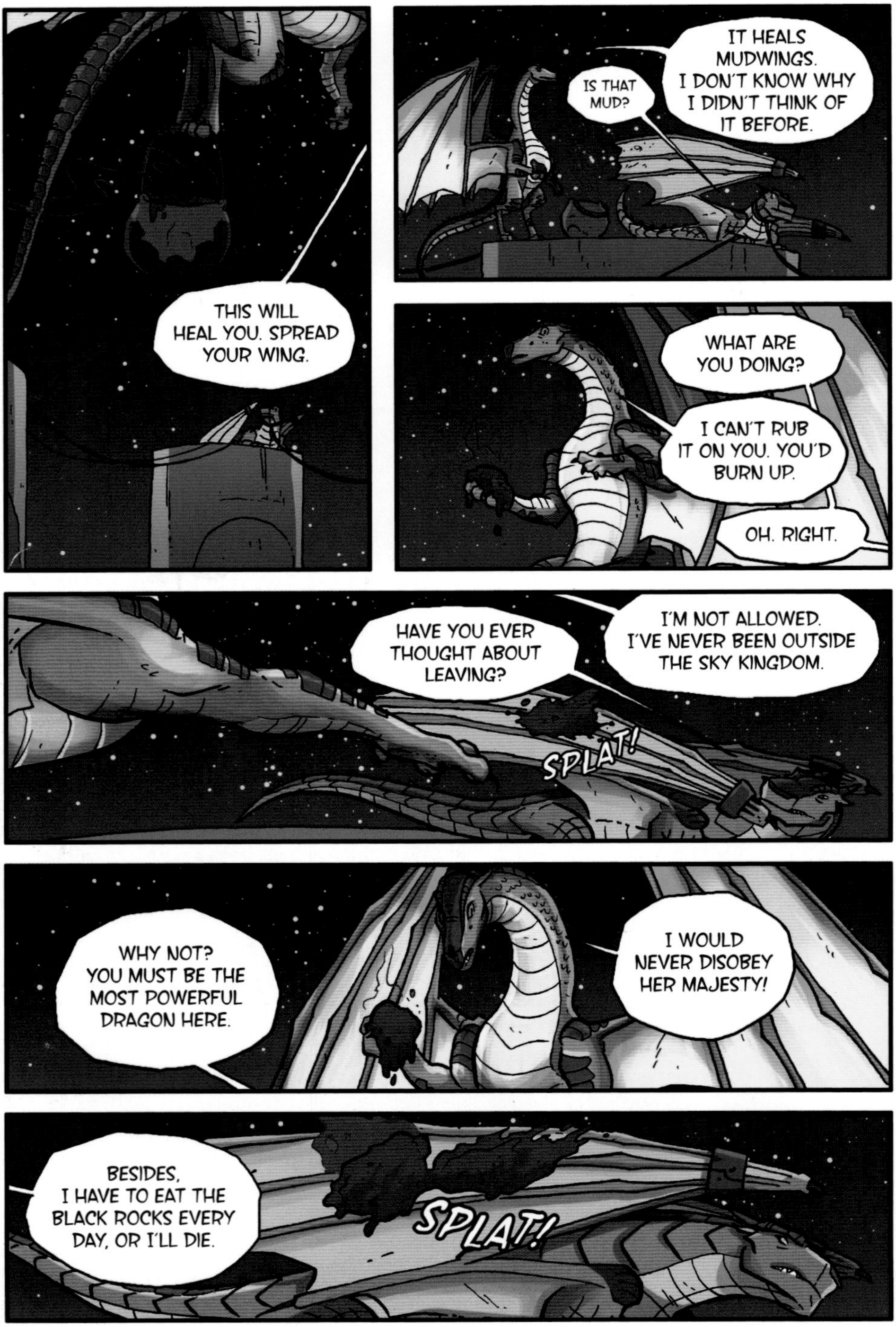
THIS WILL HEAL YOU. SPREAD YOUR WING.
IS THAT MUD?
IT HEALS MUDWINGS. I DON'T KNOW WHY I DIDN'T THINK OF IT BEFORE.
WHAT ARE YOU DOING?
I CAN'T RUB IT ON YOU. YOU'D BURN UP.
OH. RIGHT.
HAVE YOU EVER THOUGHT ABOUT LEAVING?
I'M NOT ALLOWED. I'VE NEVER BEEN OUTSIDE THE SKY KINGDOM.
SPLAT!
WHY NOT? YOU MUST BE THE MOST POWERFUL DRAGON HERE.
I WOULD NEVER DISOBEY HER MAJESTY!
BESIDES, I HAVE TO EAT THE BLACK ROCKS EVERY DAY, OR I'LL DIE.
SPLAT!

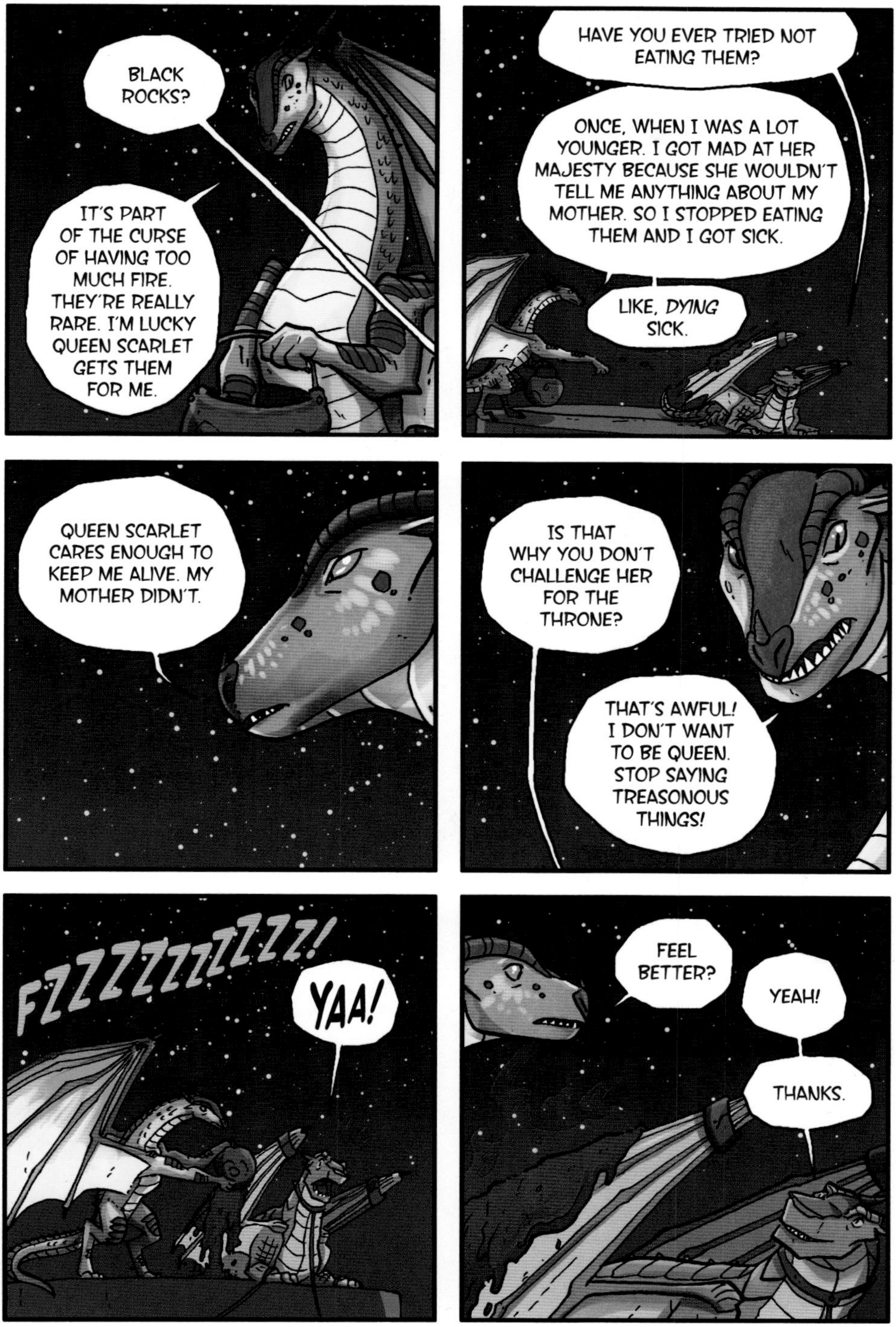
BLACK ROCKS?
IT'S PART OF THE CURSE OF HAVING TOO MUCH FIRE. THEY'RE REALLY RARE. I'M LUCKY QUEEN SCARLET GETS THEM FOR ME.
HAVE YOU EVER TRIED NOT EATING THEM?
ONCE, WHEN I WAS A LOT YOUNGER. I GOT MAD AT HER MAJESTY BECAUSE SHE WOULDN'T TELL ME ANYTHING ABOUT MY MOTHER. SO I STOPPED EATING THEM AND I GOT SICK.
LIKE, *DYING* SICK.
QUEEN SCARLET CARES ENOUGH TO KEEP ME ALIVE. MY MOTHER DIDN'T.
IS THAT WHY YOU DON'T CHALLENGE HER FOR THE THRONE?
THAT'S AWFUL! I DON'T WANT TO BE QUEEN. STOP SAYING TREASONOUS THINGS!
FZZZZZZZZZZZ!
YAA!
FEEL BETTER?
YEAH!
THANKS.

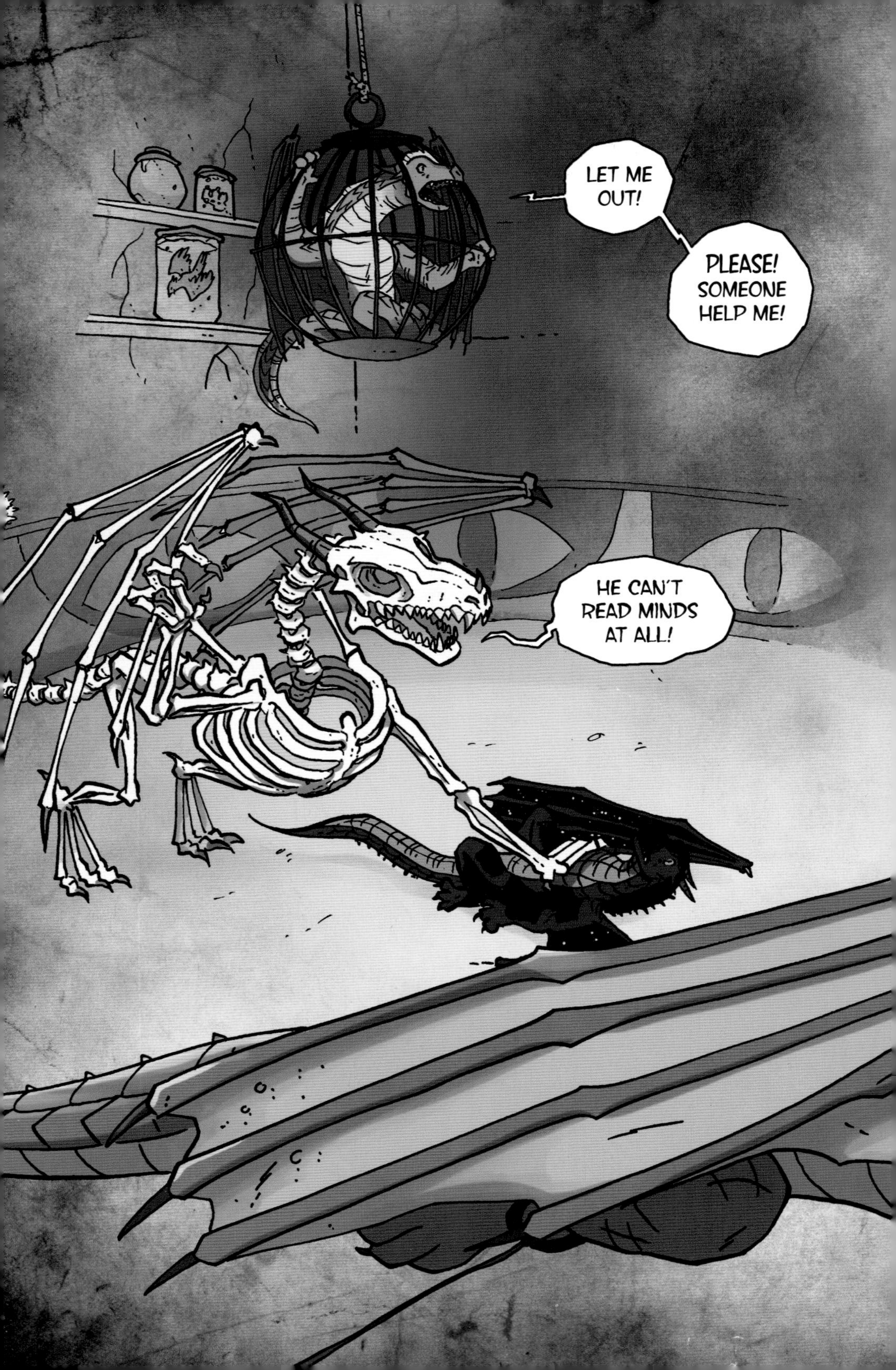
LET ME OUT!
PLEASE! SOMEONE HELP ME!
HE CAN'T READ MINDS AT ALL!

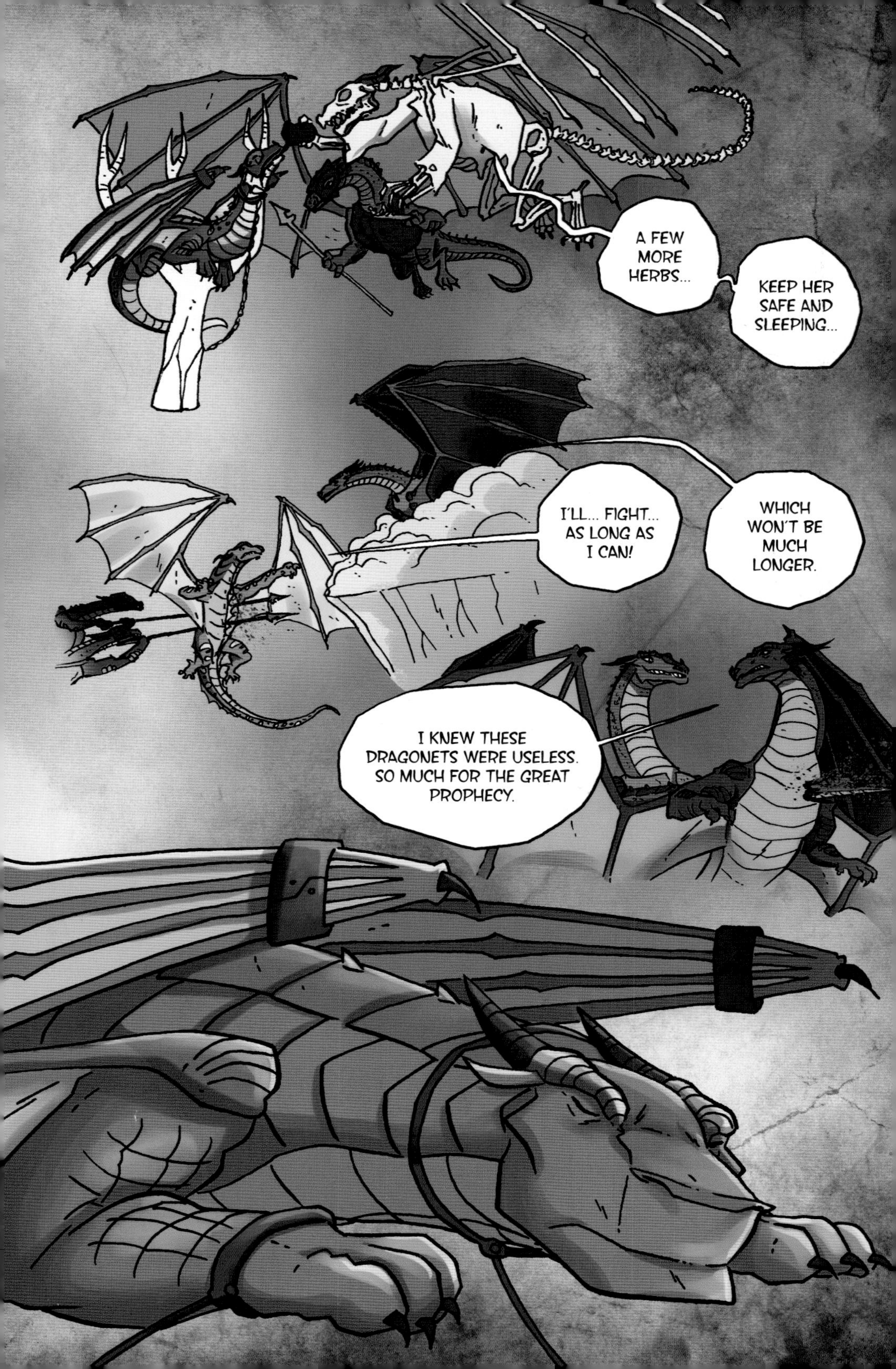
A FEW MORE HERBS...
KEEP HER SAFE AND SLEEPING...
I'LL... FIGHT... AS LONG AS I CAN!
WHICH WON'T BE MUCH LONGER.
I KNEW THESE DRAGONETS WERE USELESS. SO MUCH FOR THE GREAT PROPHECY.

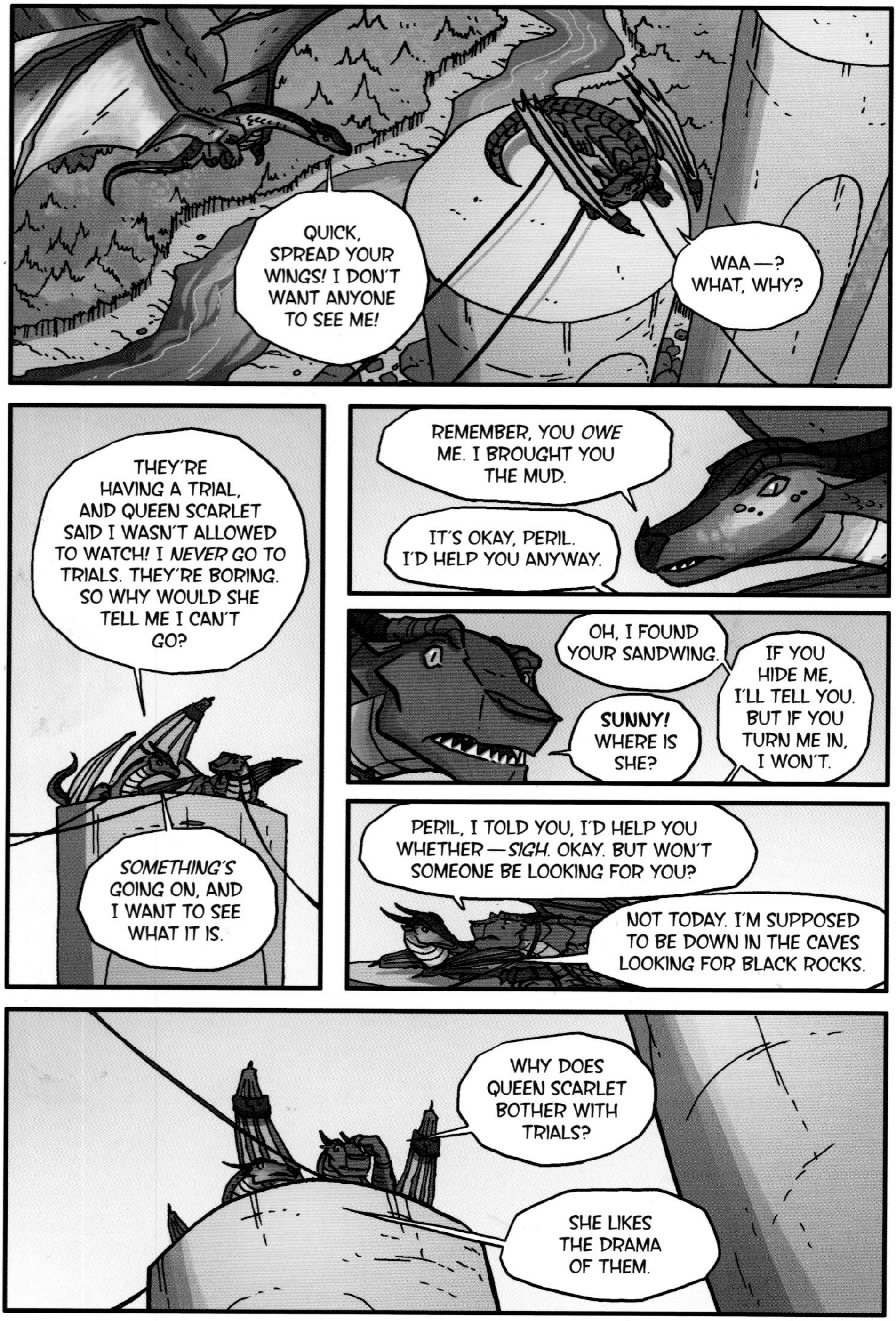
QUICK, SPREAD YOUR WINGS! I DON'T WANT ANYONE TO SEE ME!
WAA—? WHAT, WHY?
THEY'RE HAVING A TRIAL, AND QUEEN SCARLET SAID I WASN'T ALLOWED TO WATCH! I *NEVER* GO TO TRIALS. THEY'RE BORING. SO WHY WOULD SHE TELL ME I CAN'T GO?
SOMETHING'S GOING ON, AND I WANT TO SEE WHAT IT IS.
REMEMBER, YOU *OWE* ME. I BROUGHT YOU THE MUD.
IT'S OKAY, PERIL. I'D HELP YOU ANYWAY.
OH, I FOUND YOUR SANDWING.
SUNNY! WHERE IS SHE?
IF YOU HIDE ME, I'LL TELL YOU. BUT IF YOU TURN ME IN, I WON'T.
PERIL, I TOLD YOU, I'D HELP YOU WHETHER—*SIGH*. OKAY. BUT WON'T SOMEONE BE LOOKING FOR YOU?
NOT TODAY. I'M SUPPOSED TO BE DOWN IN THE CAVES LOOKING FOR BLACK ROCKS.
WHY DOES QUEEN SCARLET BOTHER WITH TRIALS?
SHE LIKES THE DRAMA OF THEM.

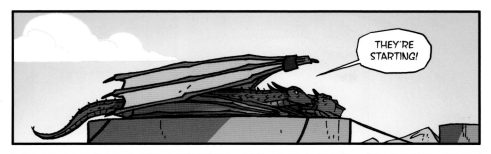

THEY'RE STARTING!

THAT'S VERMILION, QUEEN SCARLET'S OLDEST SON. HE ALWAYS ARGUES FOR THE PROSECUTION.

YOU LOOK PARTICULARLY DEADLY TODAY, YOUR MAJESTY.

YES, YES, I KNOW I DO.

WHERE'S OUR DEFENDANT? SOMEONE FETCH HER!

AND THE OLD ONE'S OSPREY. HE LOST HIS WINGS IN THE WAR. HE'S MY FRIEND, BUT HE TALKS LIKE A SCROLL.

SO DOES MY FRIEND STARFLIGHT.

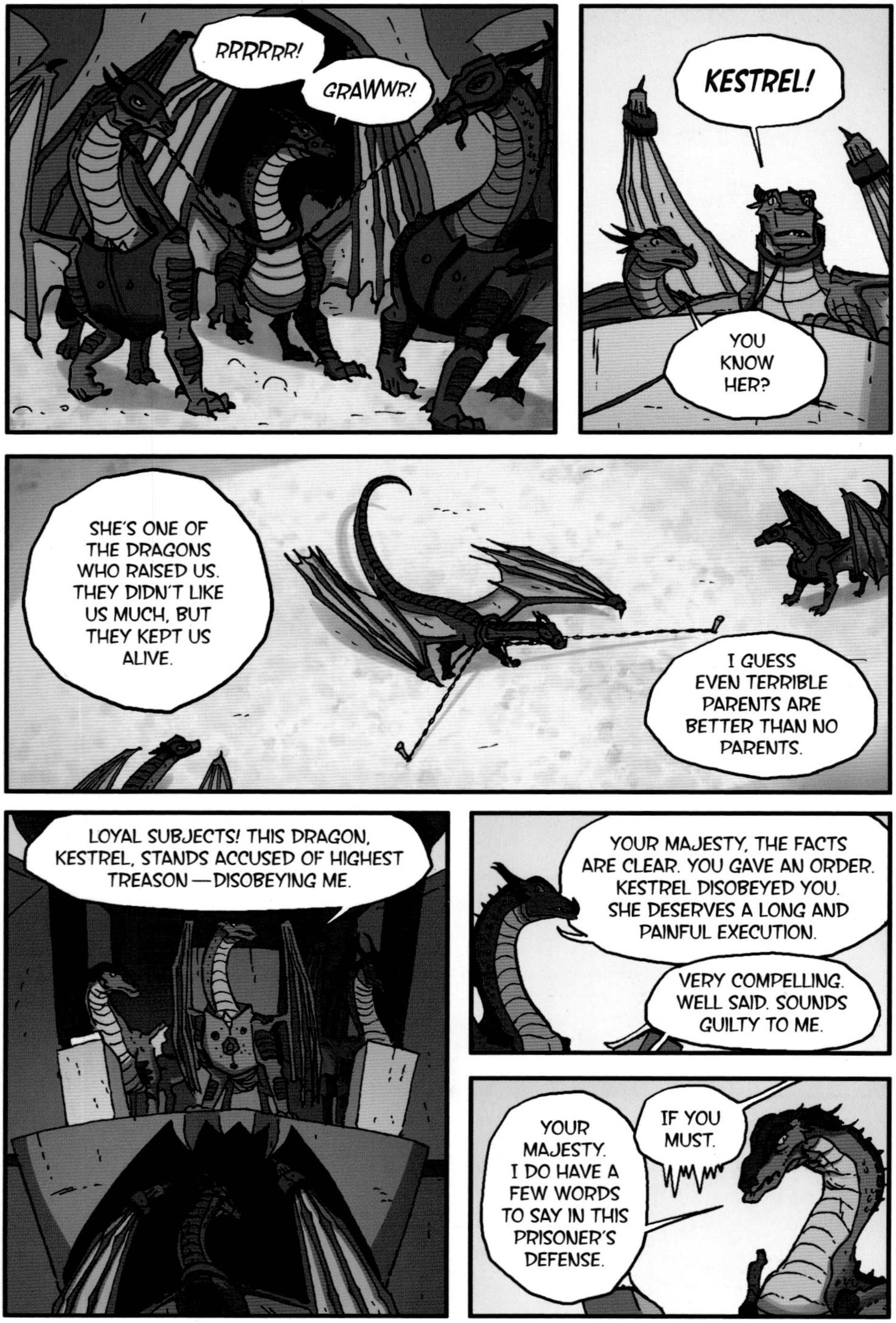
RRRRRR!
GRAWWR!
KESTREL!
YOU KNOW HER?
SHE'S ONE OF THE DRAGONS WHO RAISED US. THEY DIDN'T LIKE US MUCH, BUT THEY KEPT US ALIVE.
I GUESS EVEN TERRIBLE PARENTS ARE BETTER THAN NO PARENTS.
LOYAL SUBJECTS! THIS DRAGON, KESTREL, STANDS ACCUSED OF HIGHEST TREASON — DISOBEYING ME.
YOUR MAJESTY, THE FACTS ARE CLEAR. YOU GAVE AN ORDER. KESTREL DISOBEYED YOU. SHE DESERVES A LONG AND PAINFUL EXECUTION.
VERY COMPELLING. WELL SAID. SOUNDS GUILTY TO ME.
YOUR MAJESTY. I DO HAVE A FEW WORDS TO SAY IN THIS PRISONER'S DEFENSE.
IF YOU MUST.

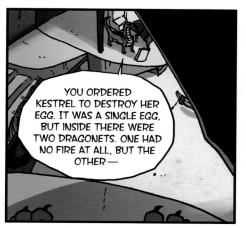

YOU ORDERED KESTREL TO DESTROY HER EGG. IT WAS A SINGLE EGG, BUT INSIDE THERE WERE TWO DRAGONETS. ONE HAD NO FIRE AT ALL, BUT THE OTHER—

HAD TOO MUCH.

TOO MUCH FIRE? LIKE YOU?

NO OTHER DRAGONETS LIKE ME HAVE HATCHED IN YEARS AND YEARS...

IS KESTREL... YOUR MOTHER?

MY MOTHER IS DEAD! QUEEN SCARLET KILLED HER TO SAVE ME!

MAYBE THAT WAS A LIE.

WE *KNOW* ALL THIS. SKIP TO THE PART WHERE WE EXECUTE HER.

YOU ORDERED HER TO DESTROY THE DEFECTIVE EGG. HOWEVER, SHE FLED WITH IT—

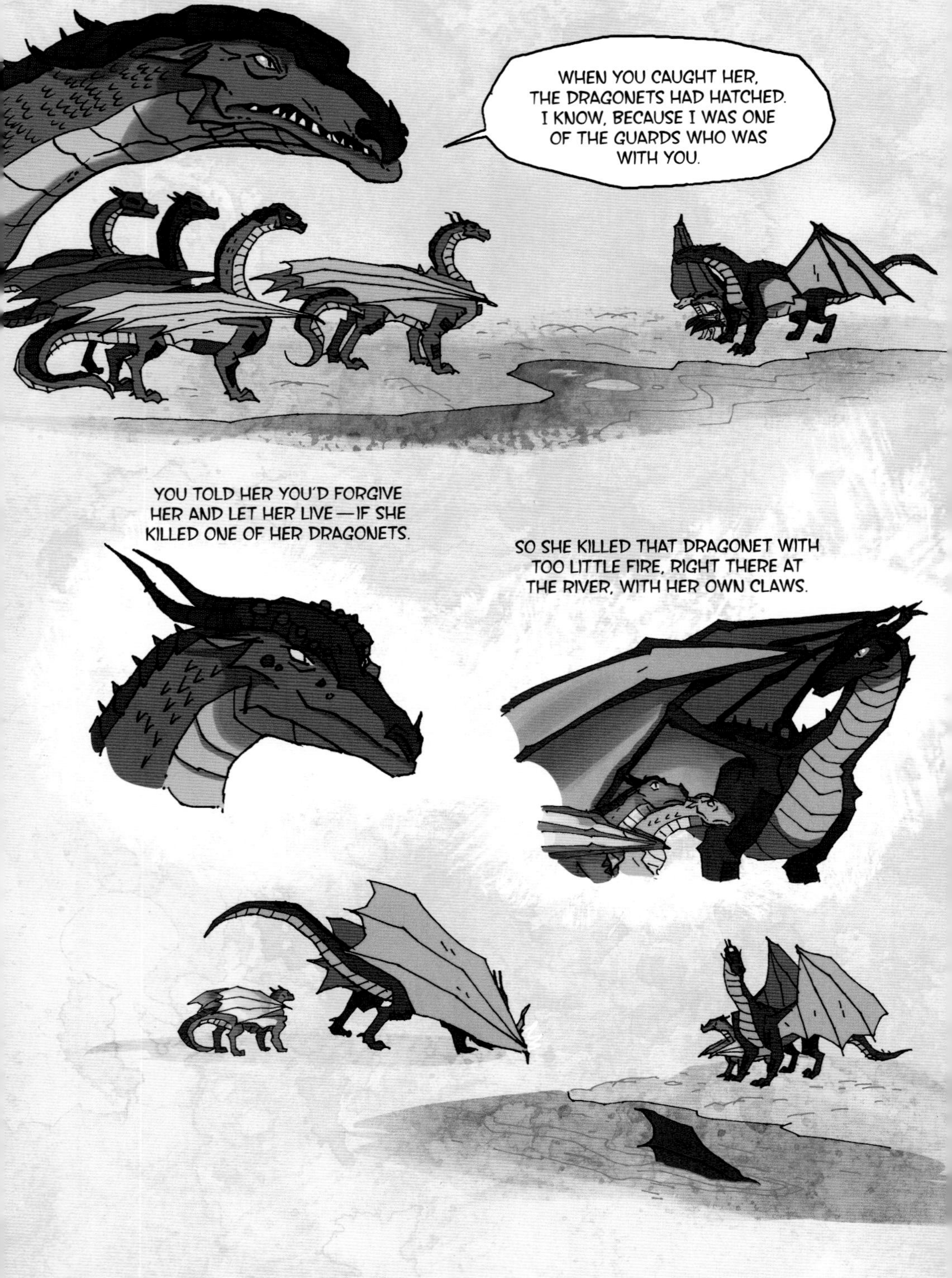
WHEN YOU CAUGHT HER, THE DRAGONETS HAD HATCHED. I KNOW, BECAUSE I WAS ONE OF THE GUARDS WHO WAS WITH YOU.
YOU TOLD HER YOU'D FORGIVE HER AND LET HER LIVE—IF SHE KILLED ONE OF HER DRAGONETS.
SO SHE KILLED THAT DRAGONET WITH TOO LITTLE FIRE, RIGHT THERE AT THE RIVER, WITH HER OWN CLAWS.

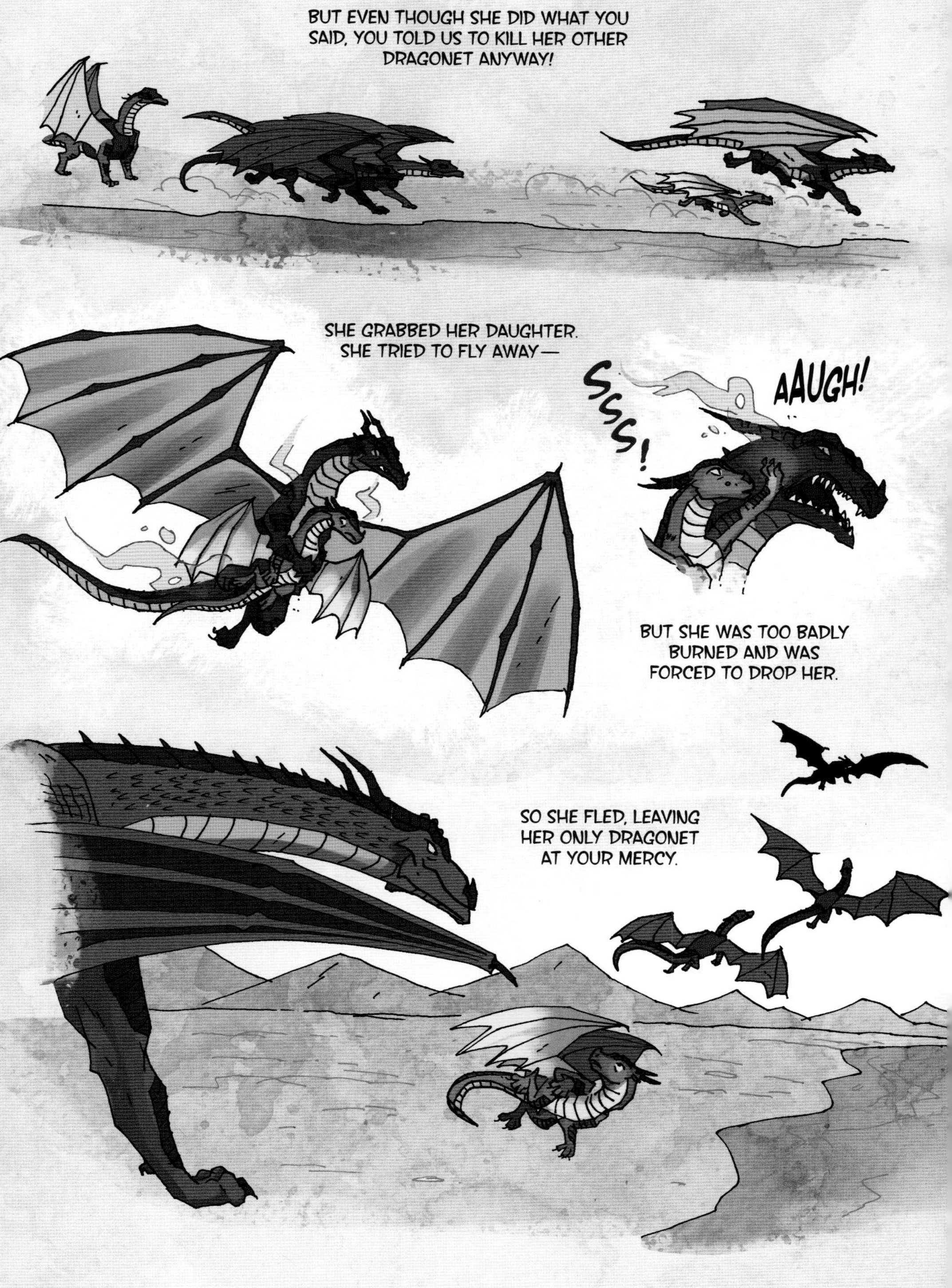
BUT EVEN THOUGH SHE DID WHAT YOU SAID, YOU TOLD US TO KILL HER OTHER DRAGONET ANYWAY!
SHE GRABBED HER DAUGHTER. SHE TRIED TO FLY AWAY—
SSS!
AAUGH!
BUT SHE WAS TOO BADLY BURNED AND WAS FORCED TO DROP HER.
SO SHE FLED, LEAVING HER ONLY DRAGONET AT YOUR MERCY.

NO! MY BROTHER DIED IN THE EGG! I KILLED HIM!

AND MY *MOTHER* TRIED TO KILL *ME!*

SCARLET IS THE ONE WHO SAVED ME!

AT LEAST, THAT'S WHAT SHE TOLD YOU.

YOU ADMIT KESTREL DISOBEYED ME. I THINK WE'RE DONE HERE.

BUT SHE *TRIED* TO OBEY YOU. YOU'RE THE ONE WHO REVERSED YOUR ORDER.

I CHANGED MY MIND. I'M THE QUEEN. I CAN DO THAT.

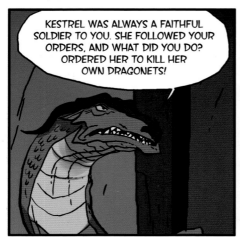

KESTREL WAS ALWAYS A FAITHFUL SOLDIER TO YOU. SHE FOLLOWED YOUR ORDERS, AND WHAT DID YOU DO? ORDERED HER TO KILL HER OWN DRAGONETS!

ENOUGH! WE'LL EXECUTE HER TOMORROW. AND WHILE WE'RE AT IT, EXECUTE HIM, TOO, FOR BORING ME.

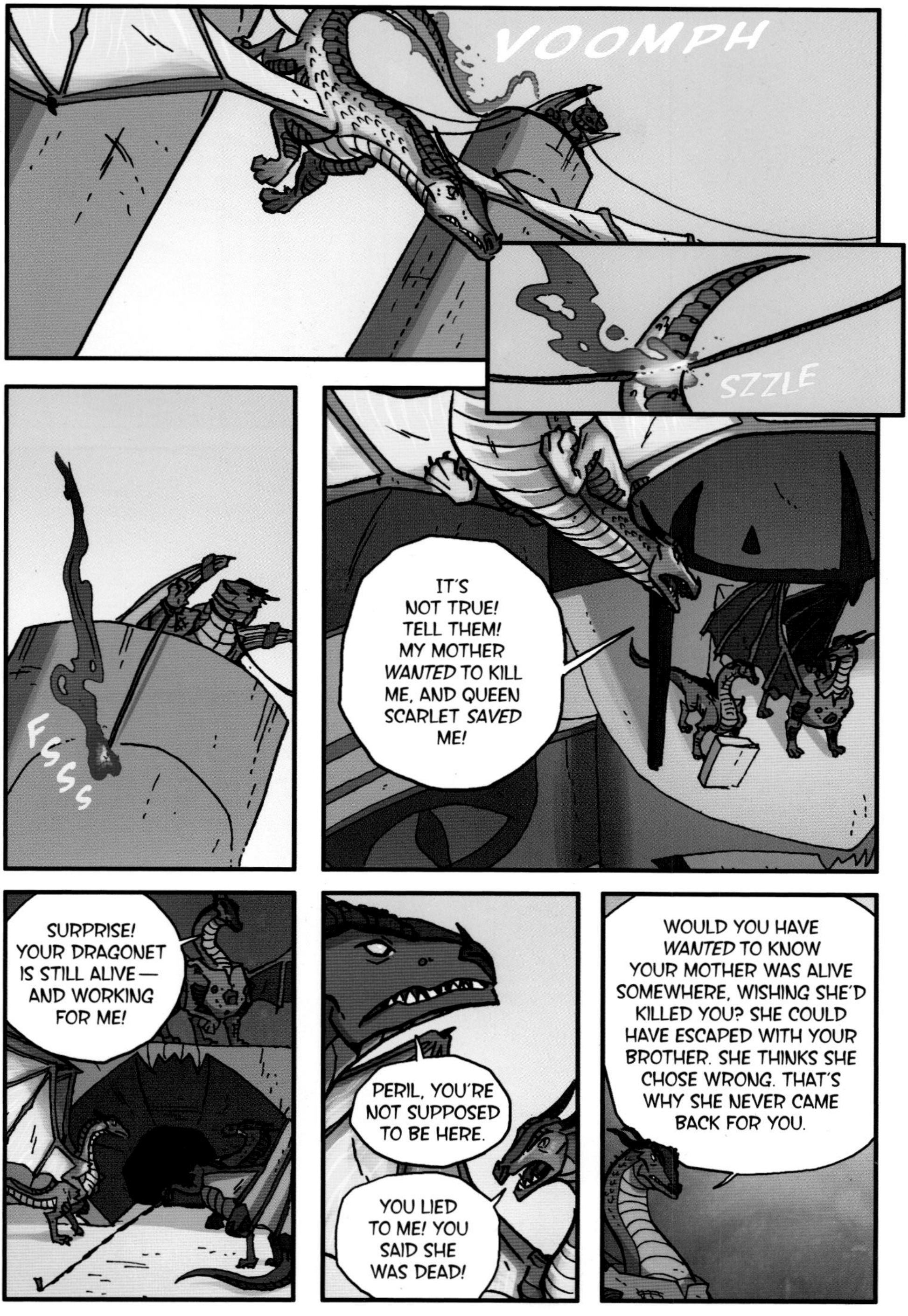
VOOMPH
SZZLE
FSSS
IT'S NOT TRUE! TELL THEM! MY MOTHER *WANTED* TO KILL ME, AND QUEEN SCARLET *SAVED* ME!
SURPRISE! YOUR DRAGONET IS STILL ALIVE— AND WORKING FOR ME!
PERIL, YOU'RE NOT SUPPOSED TO BE HERE.
YOU LIED TO ME! YOU SAID SHE WAS DEAD!
WOULD YOU HAVE *WANTED* TO KNOW YOUR MOTHER WAS ALIVE SOMEWHERE, WISHING SHE'D KILLED YOU? SHE COULD HAVE ESCAPED WITH YOUR BROTHER. SHE THINKS SHE CHOSE WRONG. THAT'S WHY SHE NEVER CAME BACK FOR YOU.

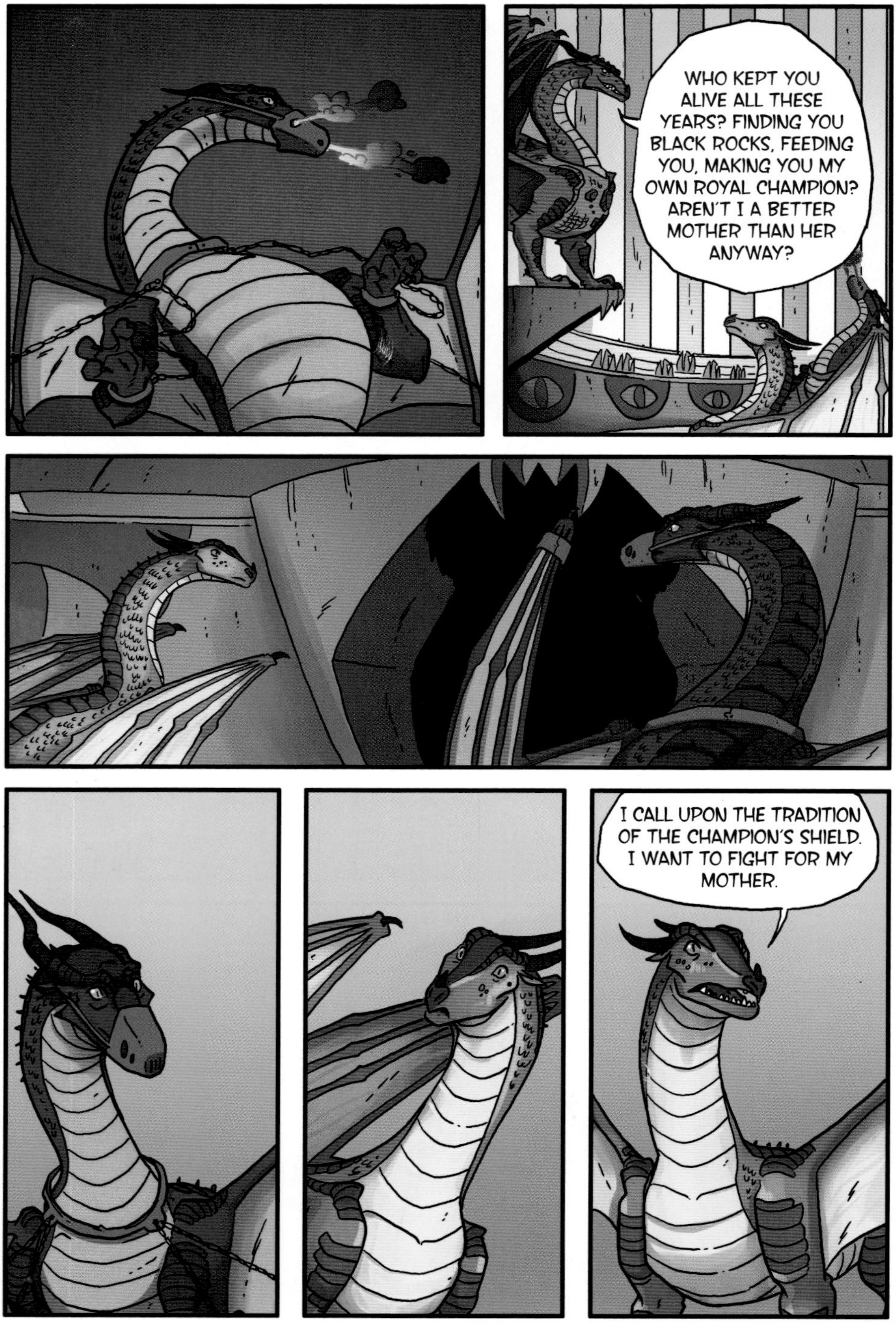
WHO KEPT YOU ALIVE ALL THESE YEARS? FINDING YOU BLACK ROCKS, FEEDING YOU, MAKING YOU MY OWN ROYAL CHAMPION? AREN'T I A BETTER MOTHER THAN HER ANYWAY?
I CALL UPON THE TRADITION OF THE CHAMPION'S SHIELD. I WANT TO FIGHT FOR MY MOTHER.

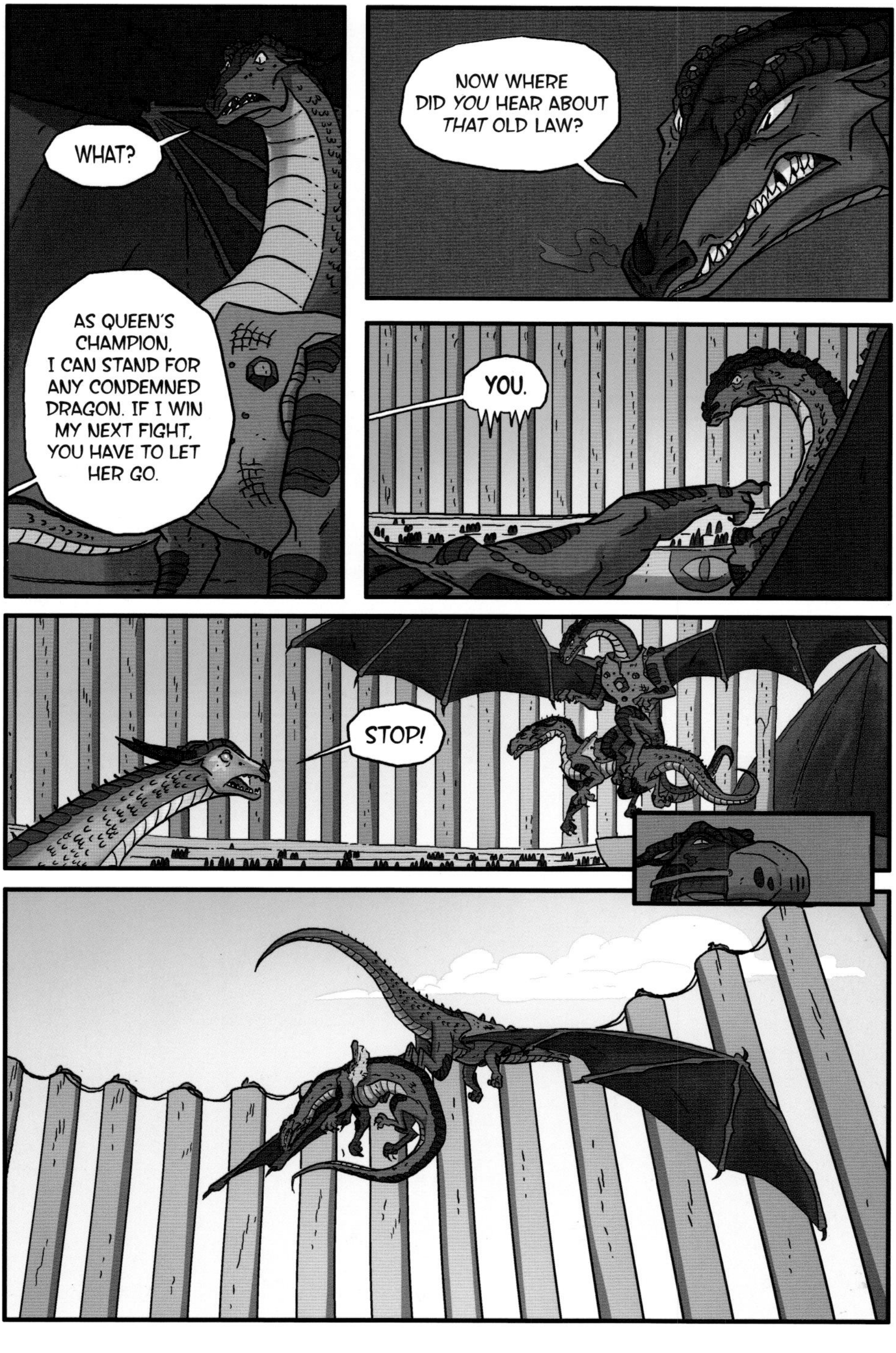
WHAT?
AS QUEEN'S CHAMPION, I CAN STAND FOR ANY CONDEMNED DRAGON. IF I WIN MY NEXT FIGHT, YOU HAVE TO LET HER GO.
NOW WHERE DID *YOU* HEAR ABOUT *THAT* OLD LAW?
YOU.
STOP!

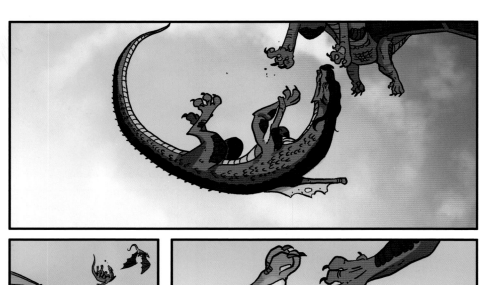

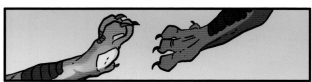

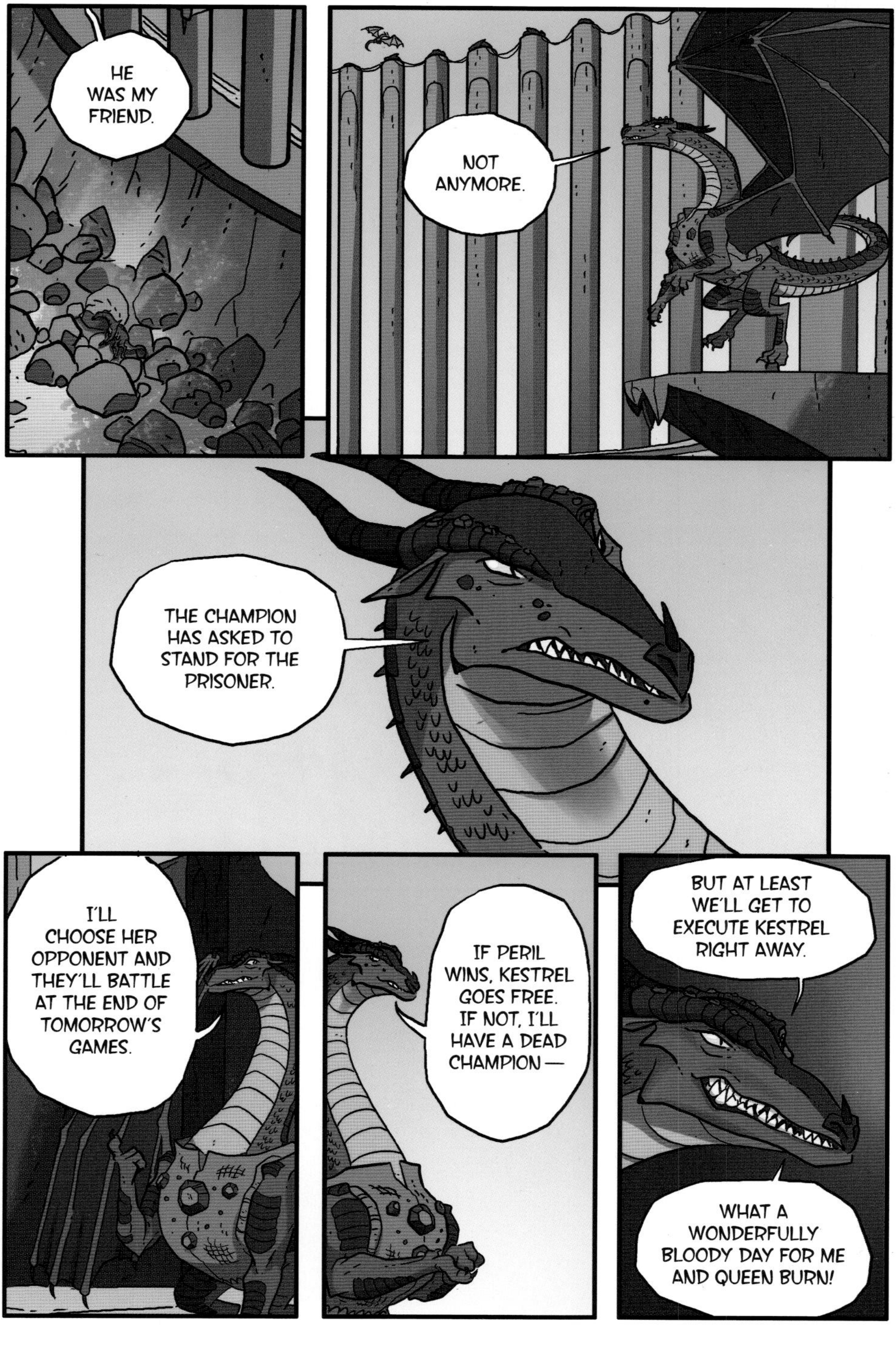
HE WAS MY FRIEND.
NOT ANYMORE.
THE CHAMPION HAS ASKED TO STAND FOR THE PRISONER.
I'LL CHOOSE HER OPPONENT AND THEY'LL BATTLE AT THE END OF TOMORROW'S GAMES.
IF PERIL WINS, KESTREL GOES FREE. IF NOT, I'LL HAVE A DEAD CHAMPION —
BUT AT LEAST WE'LL GET TO EXECUTE KESTREL RIGHT AWAY.
WHAT A WONDERFULLY BLOODY DAY FOR ME AND QUEEN BURN!

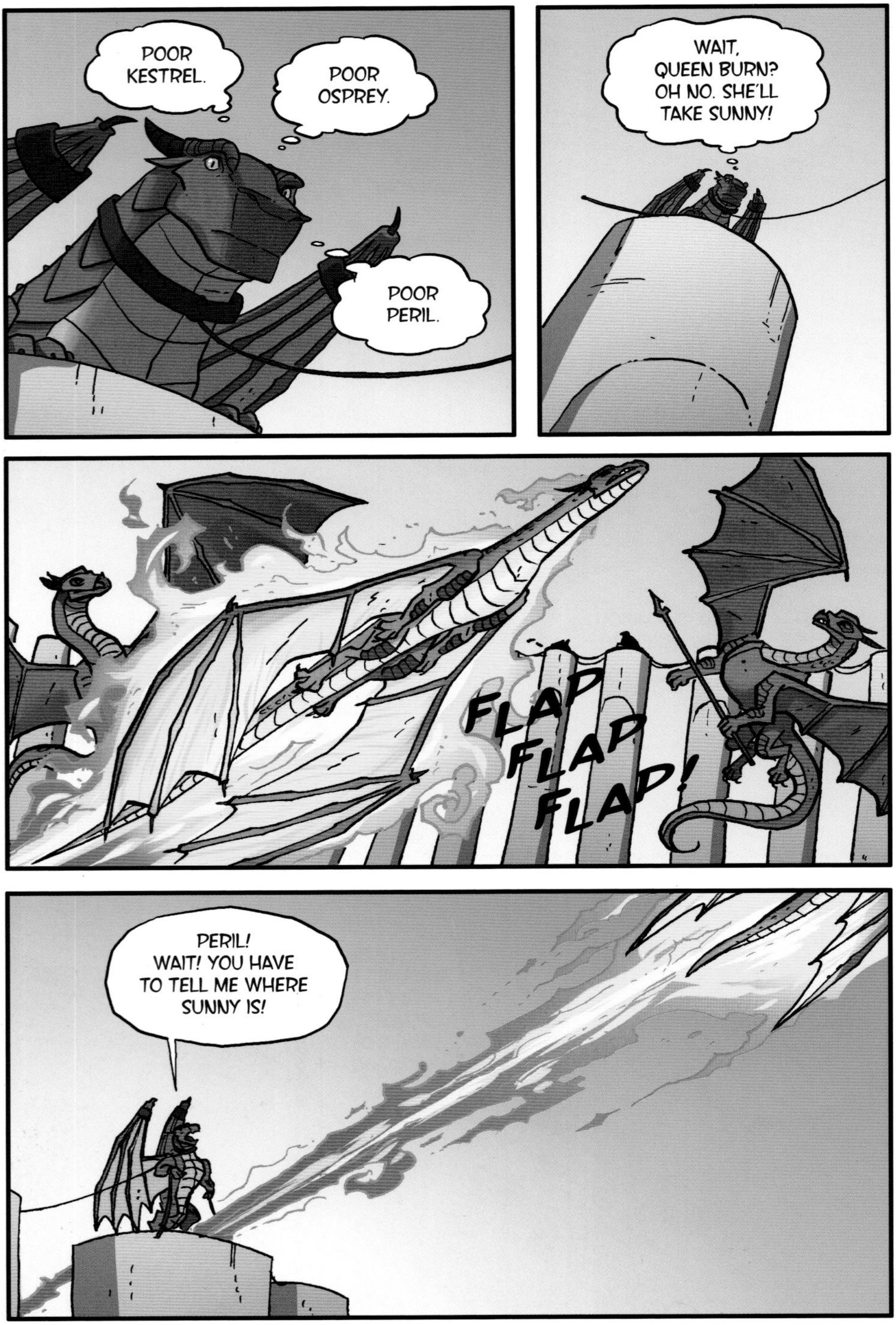
POOR KESTREL.
POOR OSPREY.
POOR PERIL.
WAIT, QUEEN BURN? OH NO. SHE'LL TAKE SUNNY!
FLAP FLAP FLAP!
PERIL! WAIT! YOU HAVE TO TELL ME WHERE SUNNY IS!

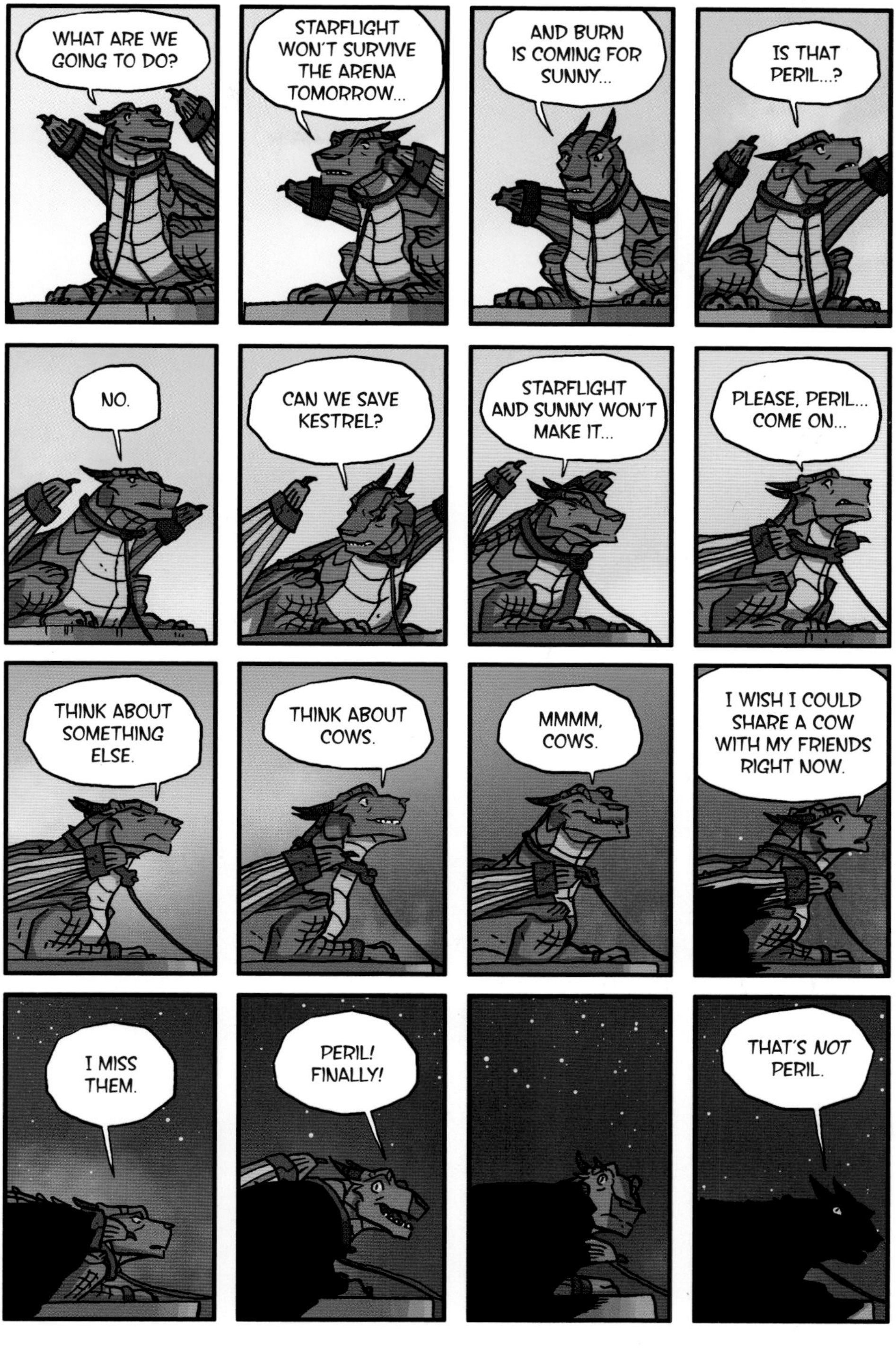
WHAT ARE WE GOING TO DO?
STARFLIGHT WON'T SURVIVE THE ARENA TOMORROW...
AND BURN IS COMING FOR SUNNY...
IS THAT PERIL...?
NO.
CAN WE SAVE KESTREL?
STARFLIGHT AND SUNNY WON'T MAKE IT...
PLEASE, PERIL... COME ON...
THINK ABOUT SOMETHING ELSE.
THINK ABOUT COWS.
MMMM, COWS.
I WISH I COULD SHARE A COW WITH MY FRIENDS RIGHT NOW.
I MISS THEM.
PERIL! FINALLY!
THAT'S *NOT* PERIL.

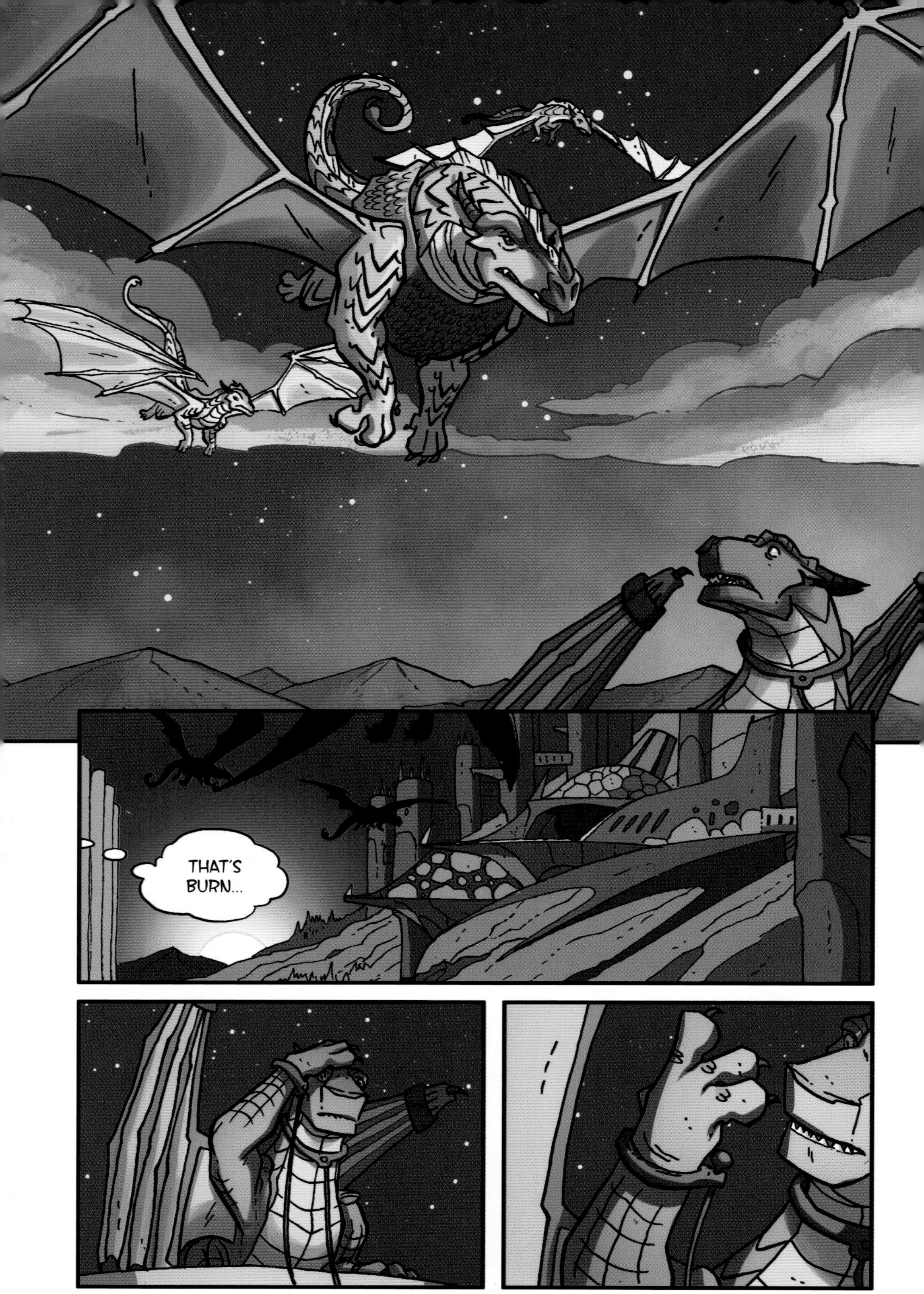
THAT'S BURN...

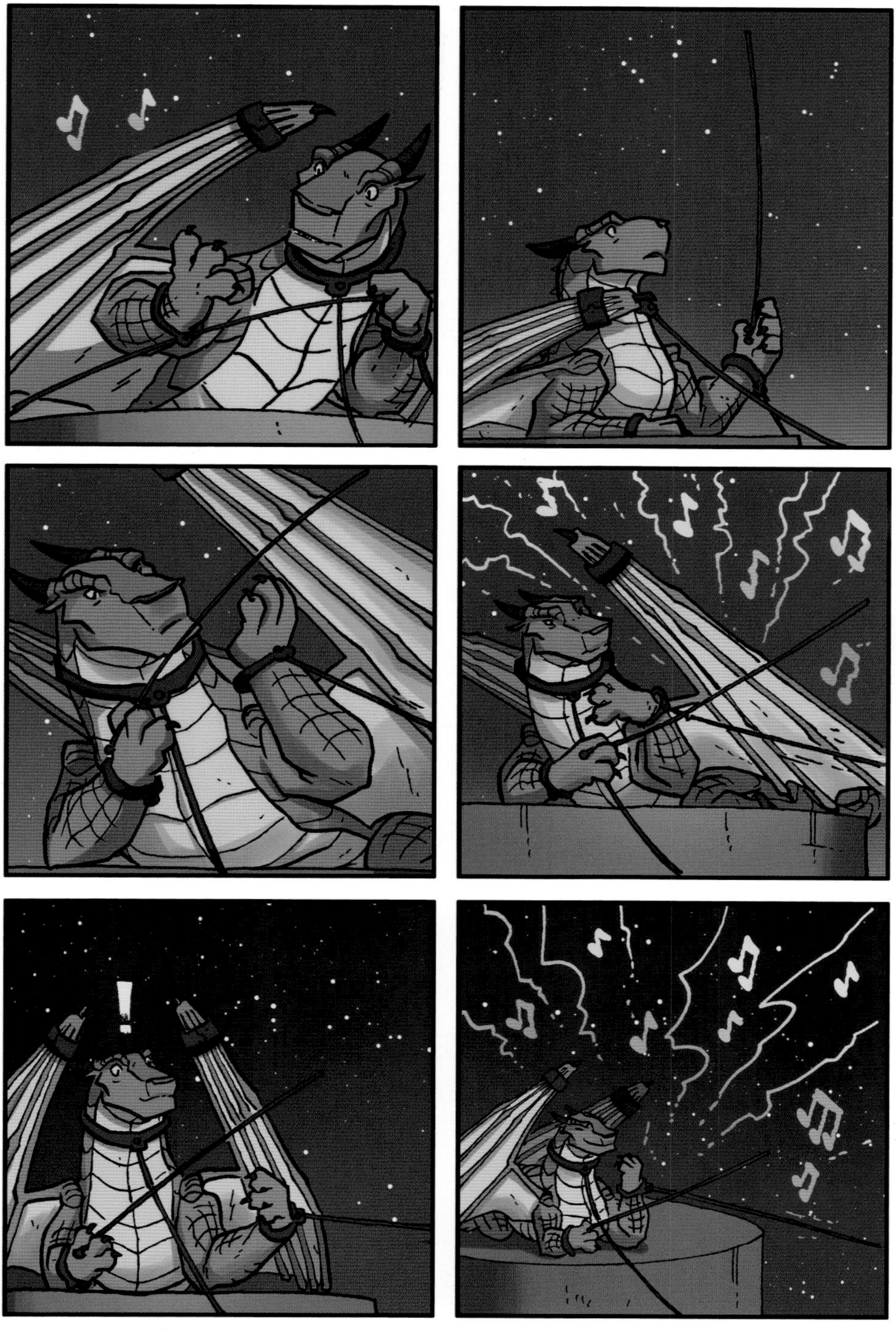
!

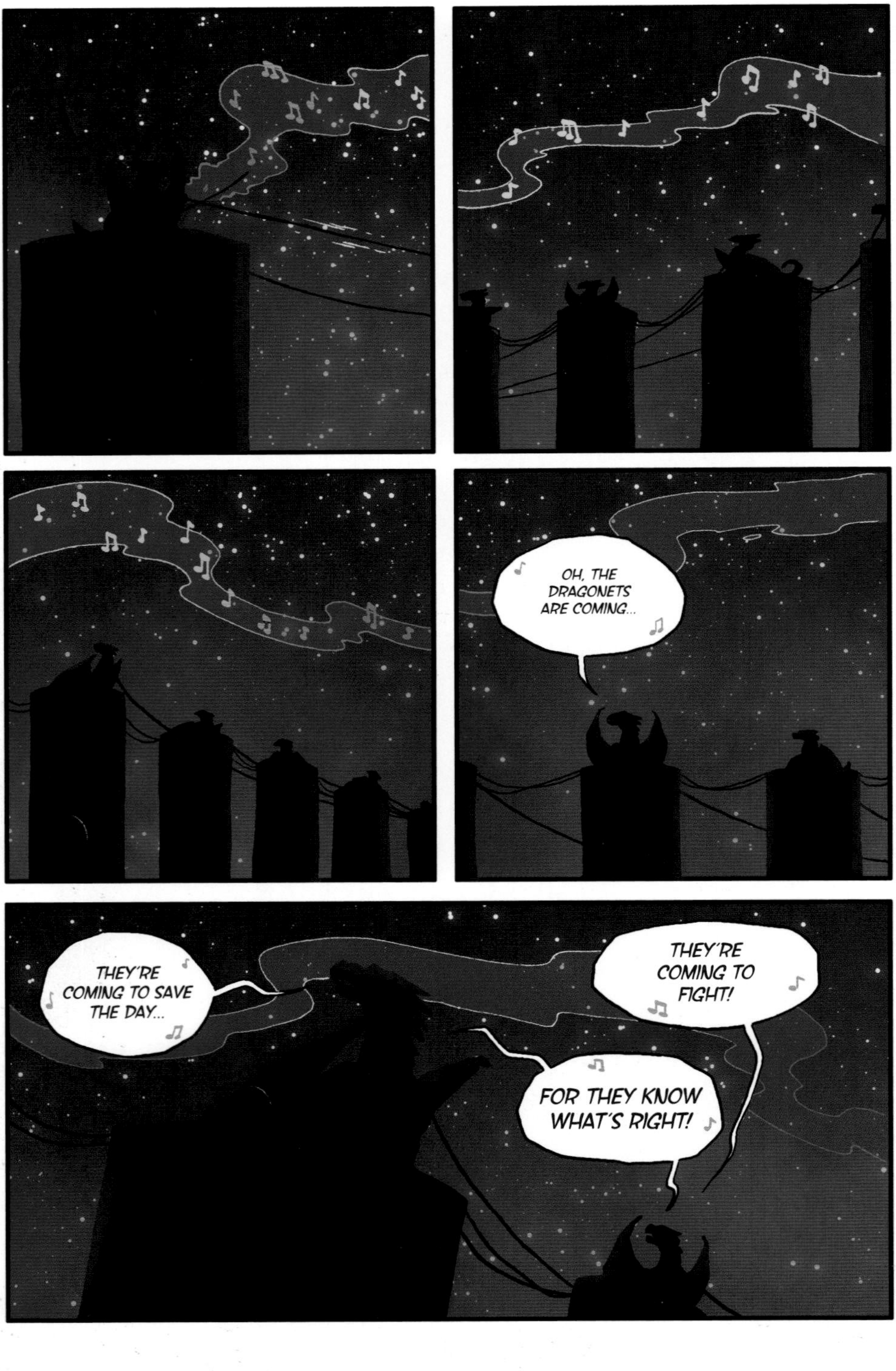
OH, THE DRAGONETS ARE COMING...
THEY'RE COMING TO SAVE THE DAY...
THEY'RE COMING TO FIGHT!
FOR THEY KNOW WHAT'S RIGHT!

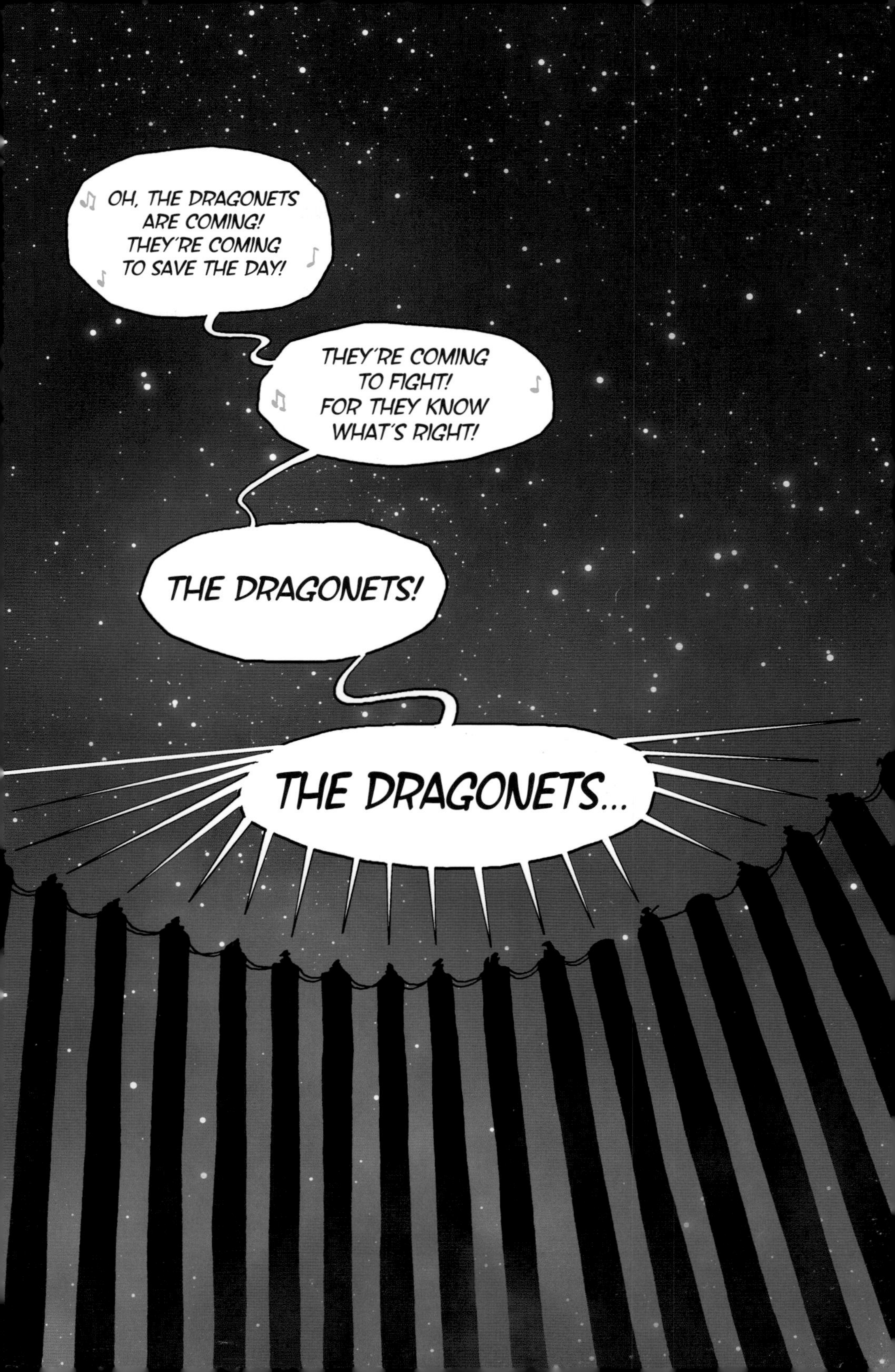
OH, THE DRAGONETS ARE COMING! THEY'RE COMING TO SAVE THE DAY!
THEY'RE COMING TO FIGHT! FOR THEY KNOW WHAT'S RIGHT!
THE DRAGONETS!
THE DRAGONETS...

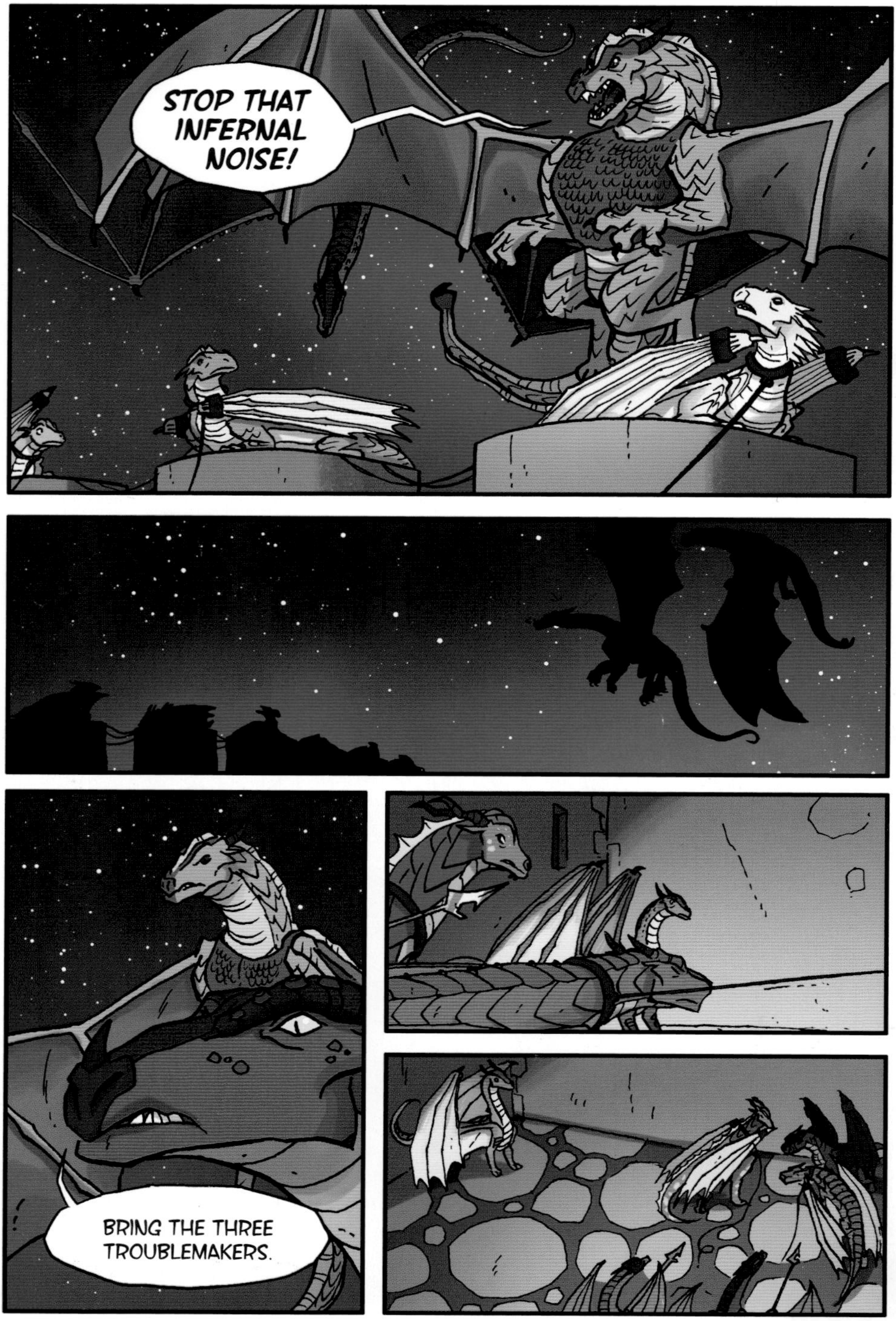
STOP THAT INFERNAL NOISE!
BRING THE THREE TROUBLEMAKERS.

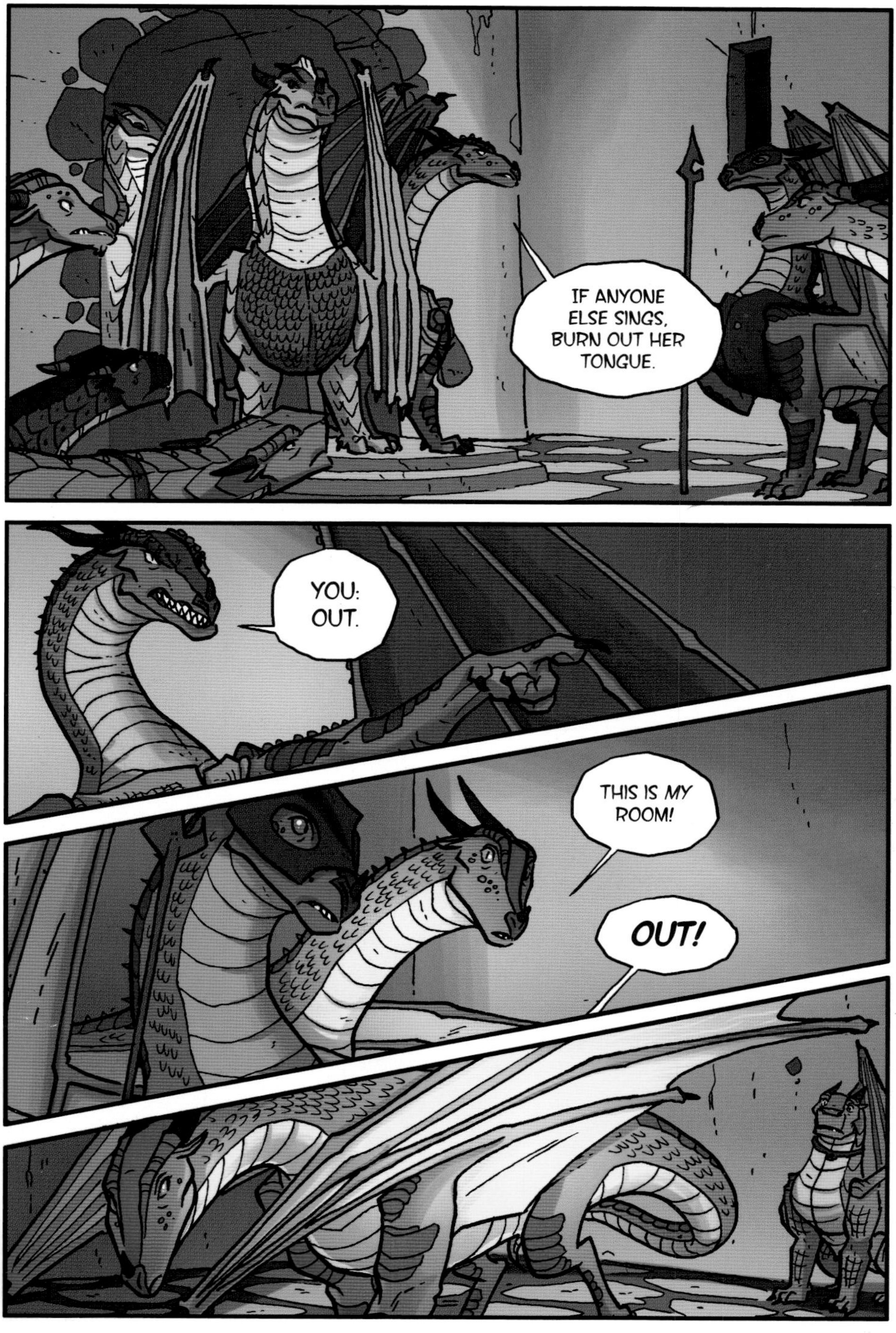
IF ANYONE ELSE SINGS, BURN OUT HER TONGUE.
YOU: OUT.
THIS IS *MY* ROOM!
OUT!

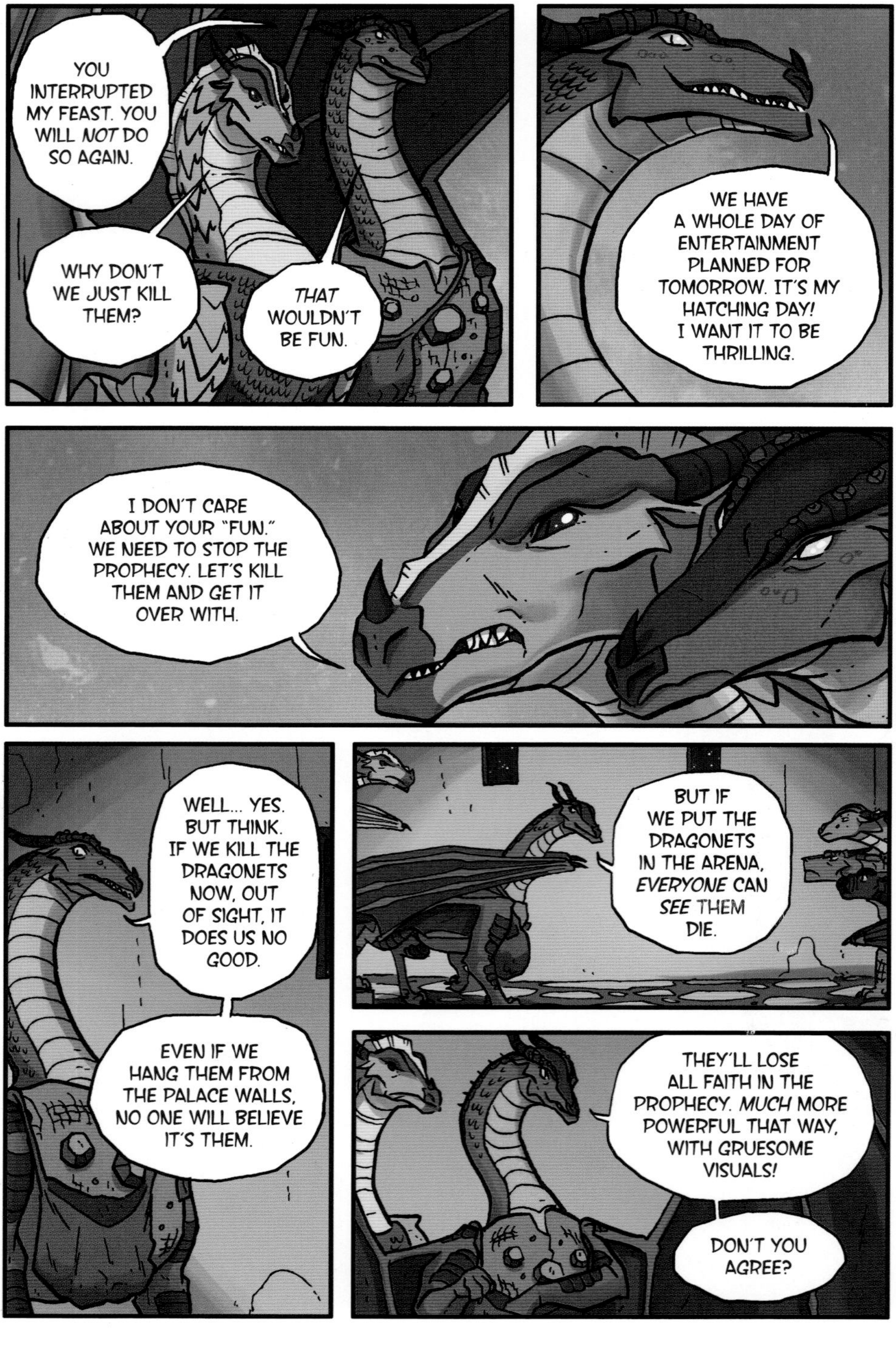
YOU INTERRUPTED MY FEAST. YOU WILL *NOT* DO SO AGAIN.
WHY DON'T WE JUST KILL THEM?
THAT WOULDN'T BE FUN.
WE HAVE A WHOLE DAY OF ENTERTAINMENT PLANNED FOR TOMORROW. IT'S MY HATCHING DAY! I WANT IT TO BE THRILLING.
I DON'T CARE ABOUT YOUR "FUN." WE NEED TO STOP THE PROPHECY. LET'S KILL THEM AND GET IT OVER WITH.
WELL... YES. BUT THINK. IF WE KILL THE DRAGONETS NOW, OUT OF SIGHT, IT DOES US NO GOOD.
EVEN IF WE HANG THEM FROM THE PALACE WALLS, NO ONE WILL BELIEVE IT'S THEM.
BUT IF WE PUT THE DRAGONETS IN THE ARENA, *EVERYONE* CAN *SEE* THEM DIE.
THEY'LL LOSE ALL FAITH IN THE PROPHECY. *MUCH* MORE POWERFUL THAT WAY, WITH GRUESOME VISUALS!
DON'T YOU AGREE?

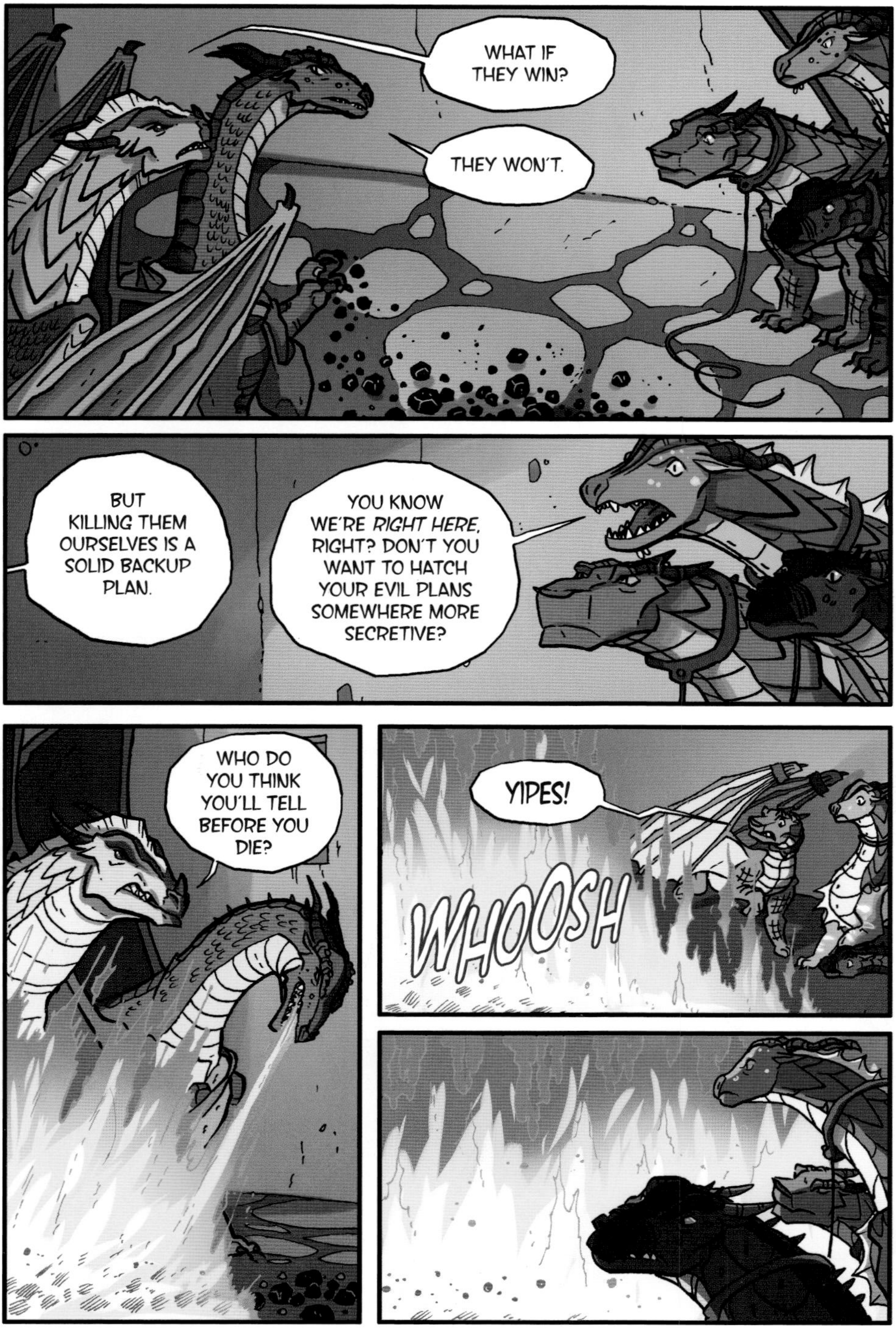
WHAT IF THEY WIN?
THEY WON'T.
BUT KILLING THEM OURSELVES IS A SOLID BACKUP PLAN.
YOU KNOW WE'RE *RIGHT HERE*, RIGHT? DON'T YOU WANT TO HATCH YOUR EVIL PLANS SOMEWHERE MORE SECRETIVE?
WHO DO YOU THINK YOU'LL TELL BEFORE YOU DIE?
YIPES!
WHOOSH

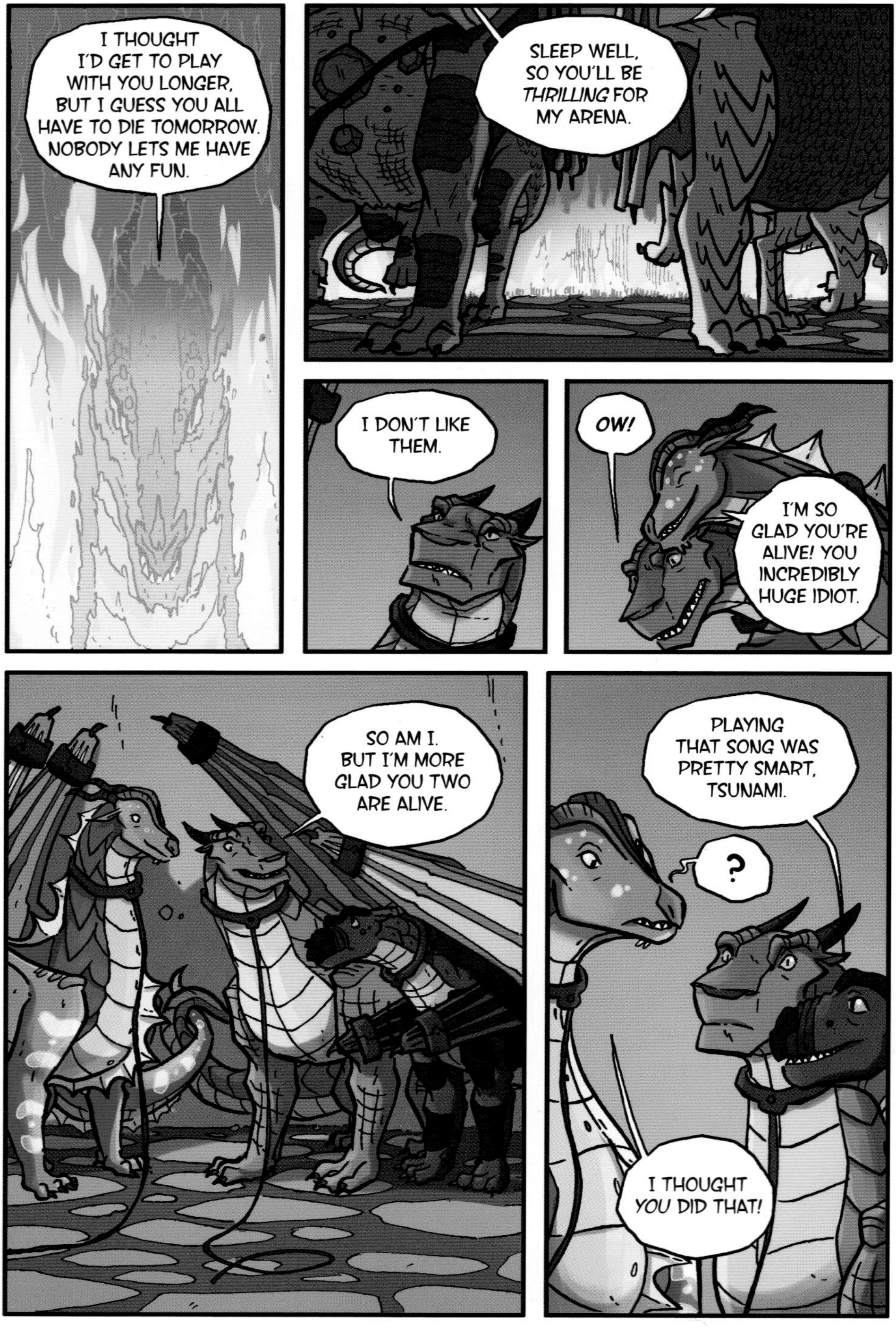
I THOUGHT I'D GET TO PLAY WITH YOU LONGER, BUT I GUESS YOU ALL HAVE TO DIE TOMORROW. NOBODY LETS ME HAVE ANY FUN.
SLEEP WELL, SO YOU'LL BE *THRILLING* FOR MY ARENA.
I DON'T LIKE THEM.
OW!
I'M SO GLAD YOU'RE ALIVE! YOU INCREDIBLY HUGE IDIOT.
SO AM I. BUT I'M MORE GLAD YOU TWO ARE ALIVE.
PLAYING THAT SONG WAS PRETTY SMART, TSUNAMI.
?
I THOUGHT *YOU* DID THAT!

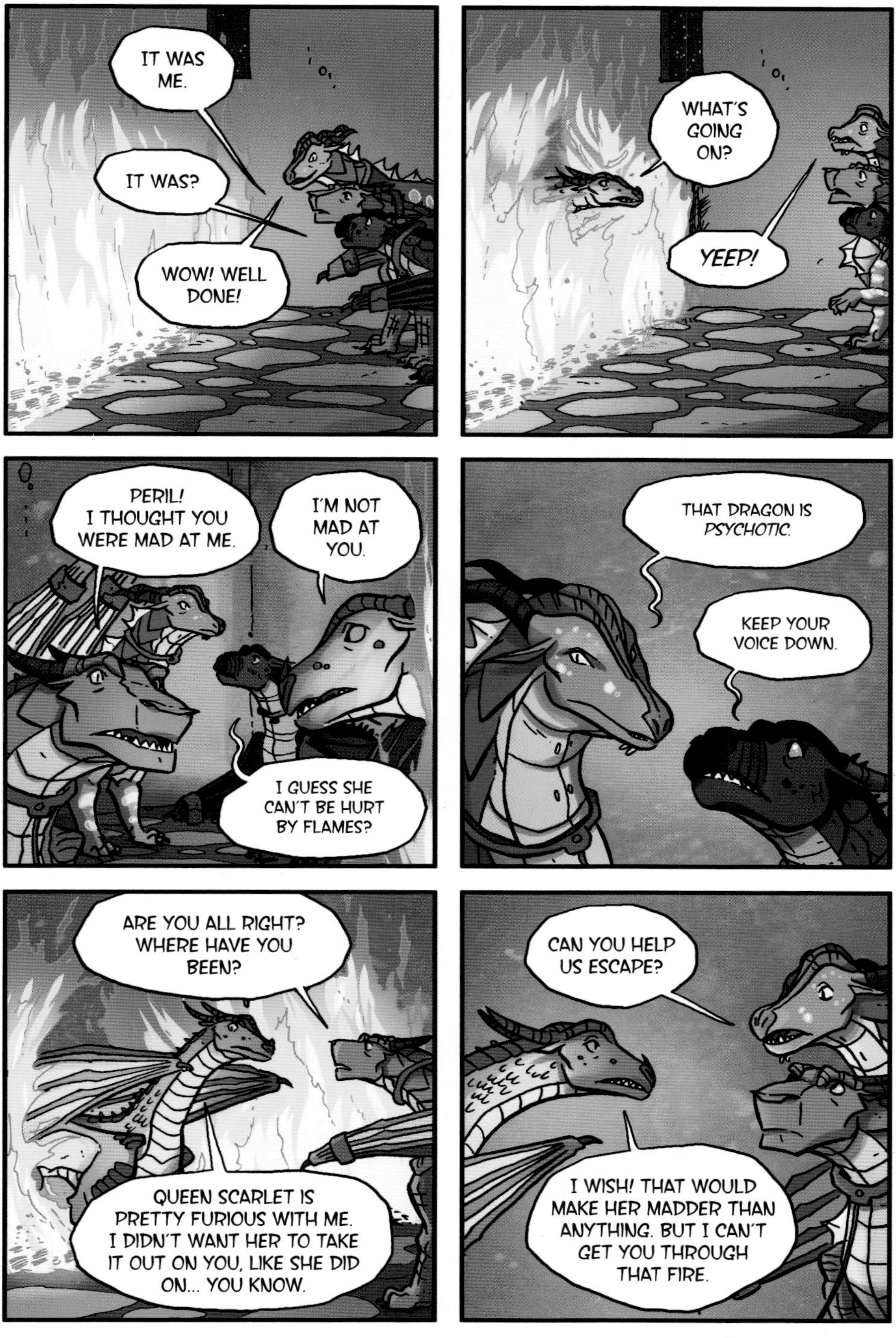
IT WAS ME.
IT WAS?
WOW! WELL DONE!
WHAT'S GOING ON?
YEEP!
PERIL! I THOUGHT YOU WERE MAD AT ME.
I'M NOT MAD AT YOU.
I GUESS SHE CAN'T BE HURT BY FLAMES?
THAT DRAGON IS *PSYCHOTIC*.
KEEP YOUR VOICE DOWN.
ARE YOU ALL RIGHT? WHERE HAVE YOU BEEN?
QUEEN SCARLET IS PRETTY FURIOUS WITH ME. I DIDN'T WANT HER TO TAKE IT OUT ON YOU, LIKE SHE DID ON... YOU KNOW.
CAN YOU HELP US ESCAPE?
I WISH! THAT WOULD MAKE HER MADDER THAN ANYTHING. BUT I CAN'T GET YOU THROUGH THAT FIRE.

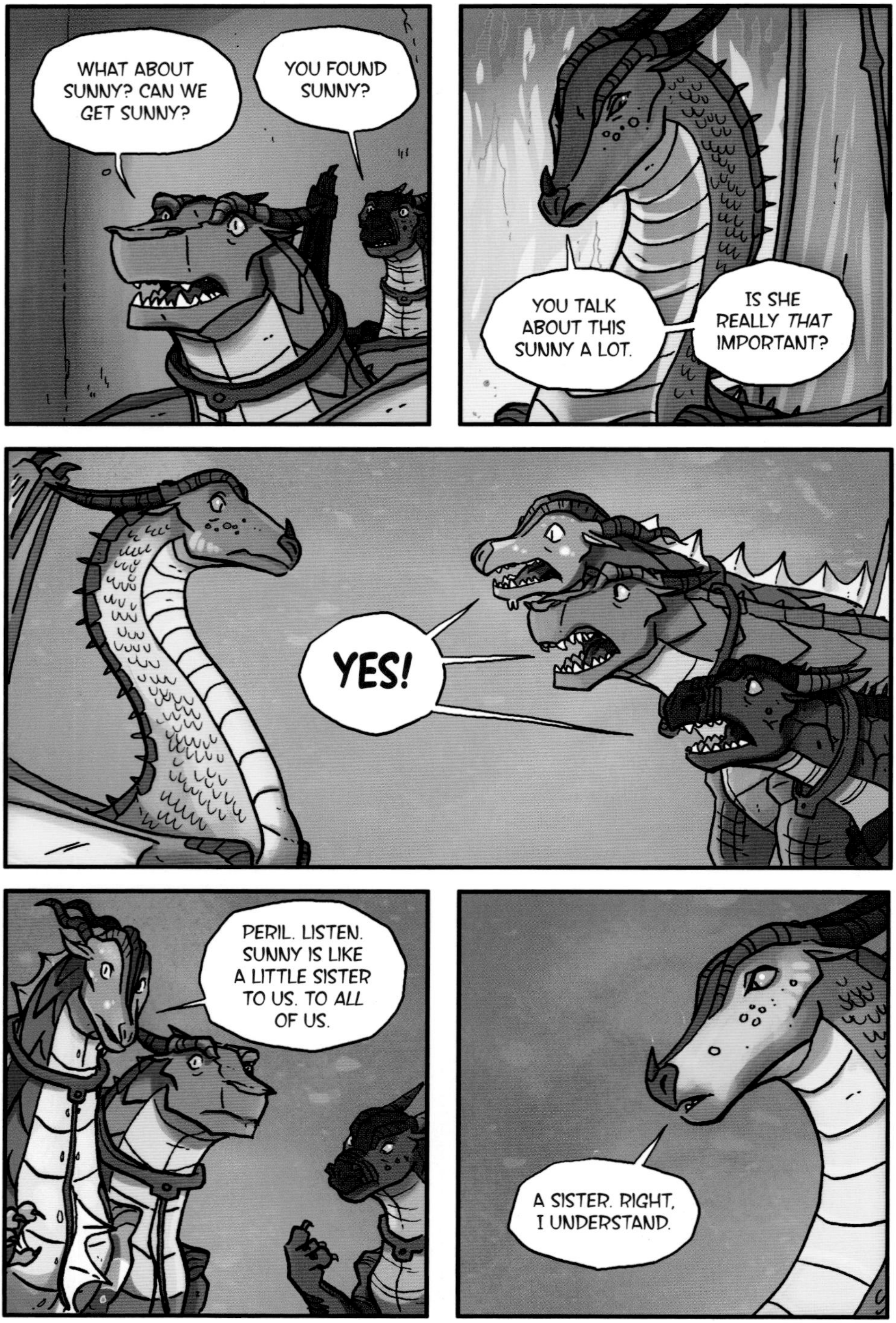
WHAT ABOUT SUNNY? CAN WE GET SUNNY?
YOU FOUND SUNNY?
YOU TALK ABOUT THIS SUNNY A LOT.
IS SHE REALLY *THAT* IMPORTANT?
YES!
PERIL. LISTEN. SUNNY IS LIKE A LITTLE SISTER TO US. TO *ALL* OF US.
A SISTER. RIGHT, I UNDERSTAND.

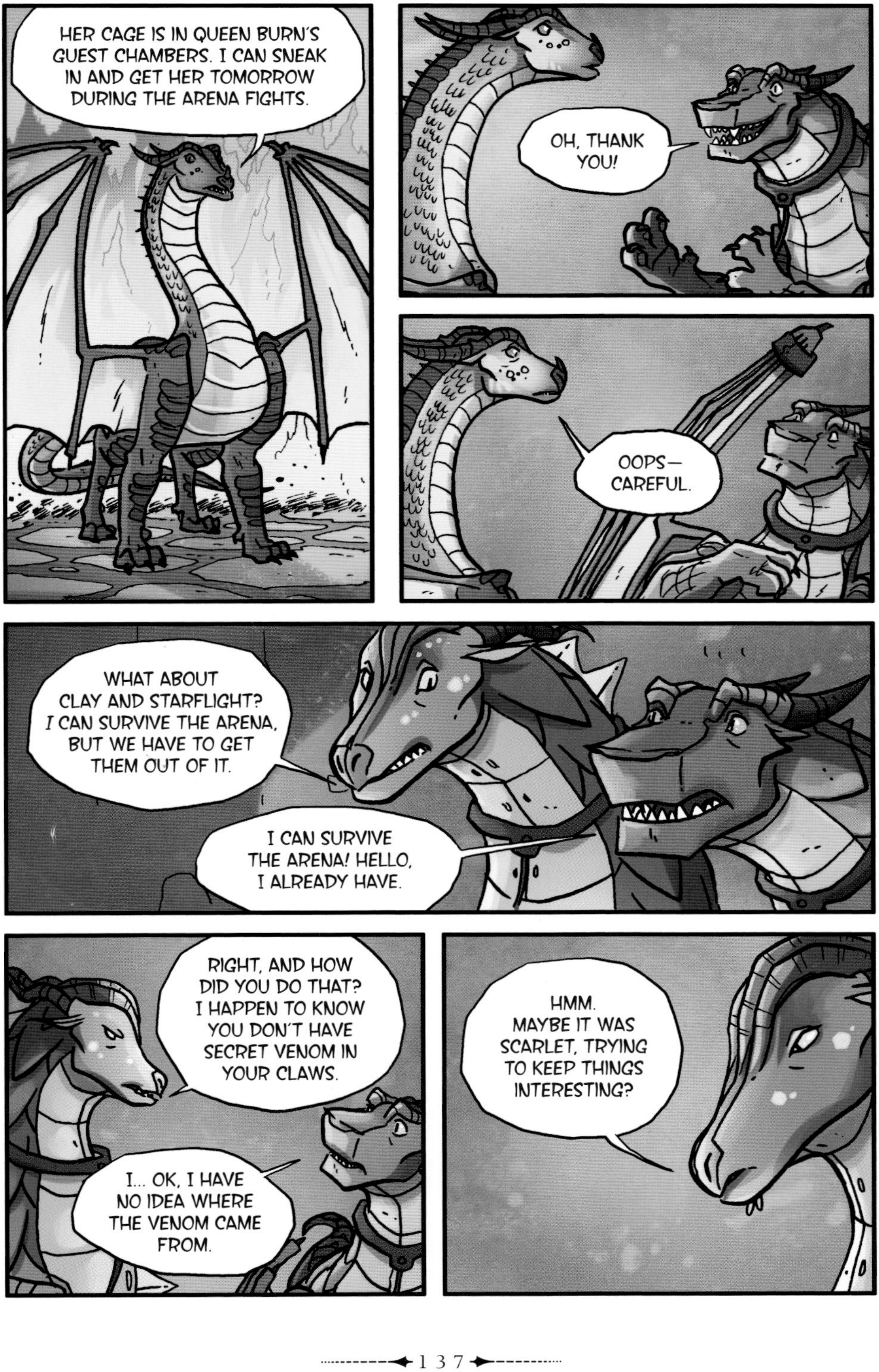
HER CAGE IS IN QUEEN BURN'S GUEST CHAMBERS. I CAN SNEAK IN AND GET HER TOMORROW DURING THE ARENA FIGHTS.
OH, THANK YOU!
OOPS— CAREFUL.
WHAT ABOUT CLAY AND STARFLIGHT? *I* CAN SURVIVE THE ARENA, BUT WE HAVE TO GET THEM OUT OF IT.
I CAN SURVIVE THE ARENA! HELLO, I ALREADY HAVE.
RIGHT, AND HOW DID YOU DO THAT? I HAPPEN TO KNOW YOU DON'T HAVE SECRET VENOM IN YOUR CLAWS.
I... OK, I HAVE NO IDEA WHERE THE VENOM CAME FROM.
HMM. MAYBE IT WAS SCARLET, TRYING TO KEEP THINGS INTERESTING?

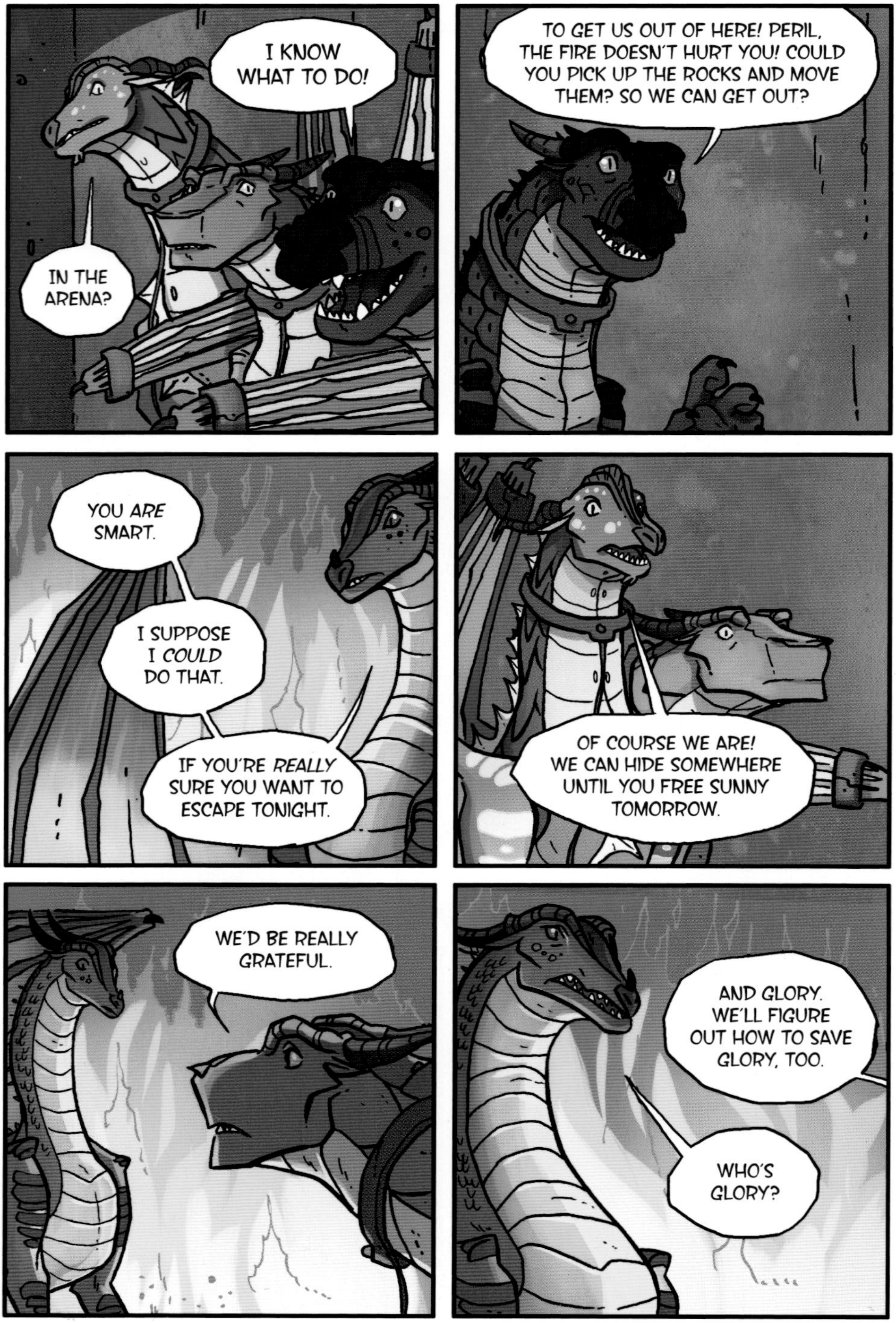
I KNOW WHAT TO DO!
IN THE ARENA?
TO GET US OUT OF HERE! PERIL, THE FIRE DOESN'T HURT YOU! COULD YOU PICK UP THE ROCKS AND MOVE THEM? SO WE CAN GET OUT?
YOU *ARE* SMART.
I SUPPOSE I *COULD* DO THAT.
IF YOU'RE *REALLY* SURE YOU WANT TO ESCAPE TONIGHT.
OF COURSE WE ARE! WE CAN HIDE SOMEWHERE UNTIL YOU FREE SUNNY TOMORROW.
WE'D BE REALLY GRATEFUL.
AND GLORY. WE'LL FIGURE OUT HOW TO SAVE GLORY, TOO.
WHO'S GLORY?

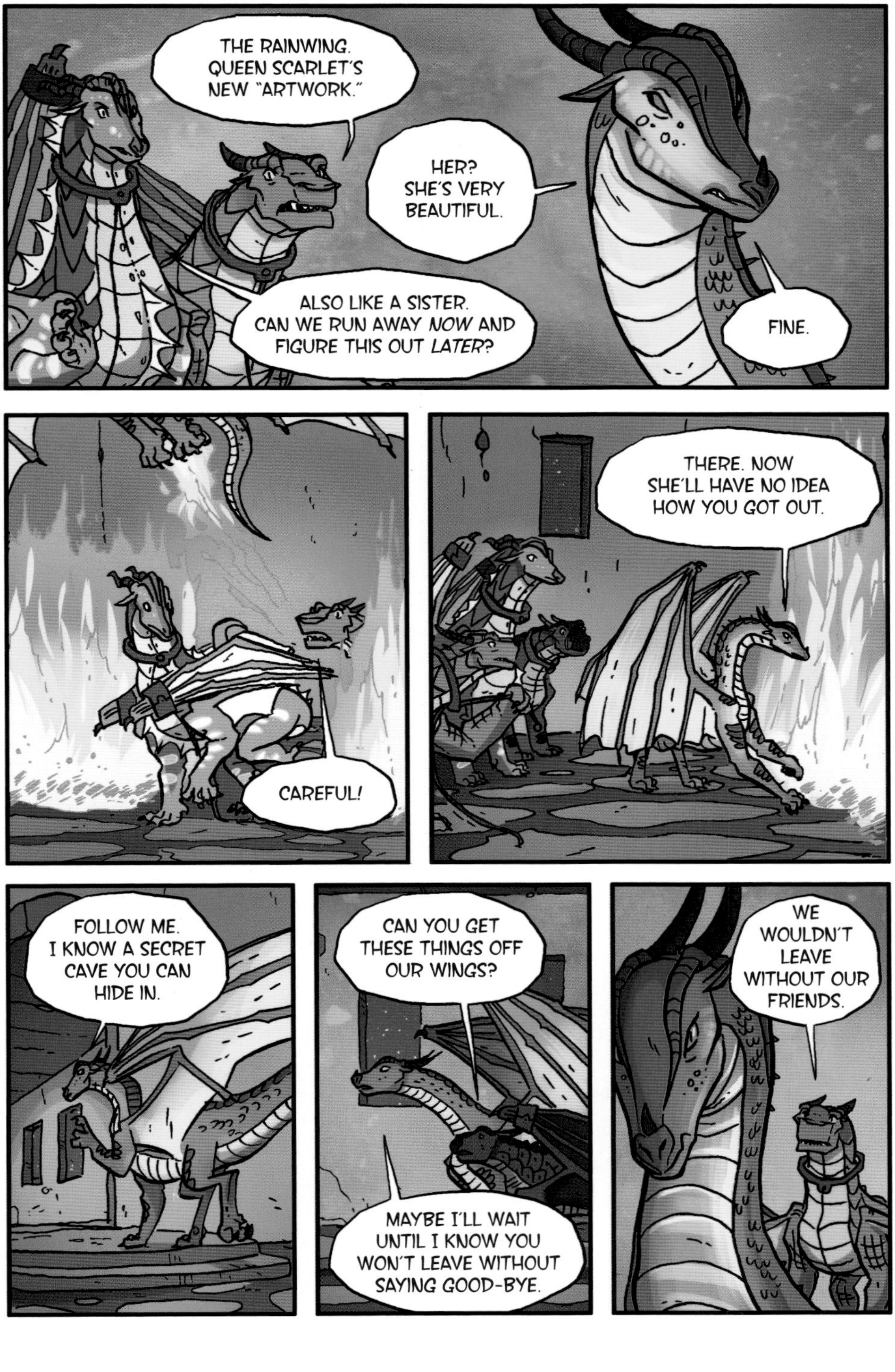
THE RAINWING. QUEEN SCARLET'S NEW "ARTWORK."
HER? SHE'S VERY BEAUTIFUL.
ALSO LIKE A SISTER. CAN WE RUN AWAY *NOW* AND FIGURE THIS OUT *LATER*?
FINE.
CAREFUL!
THERE. NOW SHE'LL HAVE NO IDEA HOW YOU GOT OUT.
FOLLOW ME. I KNOW A SECRET CAVE YOU CAN HIDE IN.
CAN YOU GET THESE THINGS OFF OUR WINGS?
MAYBE I'LL WAIT UNTIL I KNOW YOU WON'T LEAVE WITHOUT SAYING GOOD-BYE.
WE WOULDN'T LEAVE WITHOUT OUR FRIENDS.

ONCE YOU'RE FREE... WHAT ARE YOU GOING TO DO?

FIND OUR PARENTS! I'VE NEVER BEEN TO THE MUDWING KINGDOM.

YOU'RE GOING STRAIGHT THERE?

ABSOLUTELY. AS SOON AS POSS—

OW!

SINCE YOU CAN'T FLY, I'LL HAVE TO GO AROUND AND OPEN THE DOOR FROM THE OTHER SIDE. WAIT HERE.

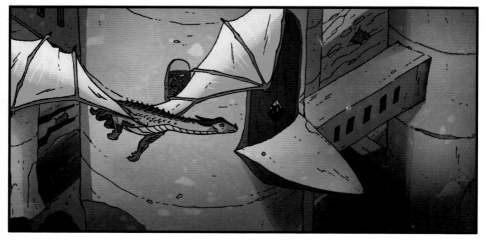

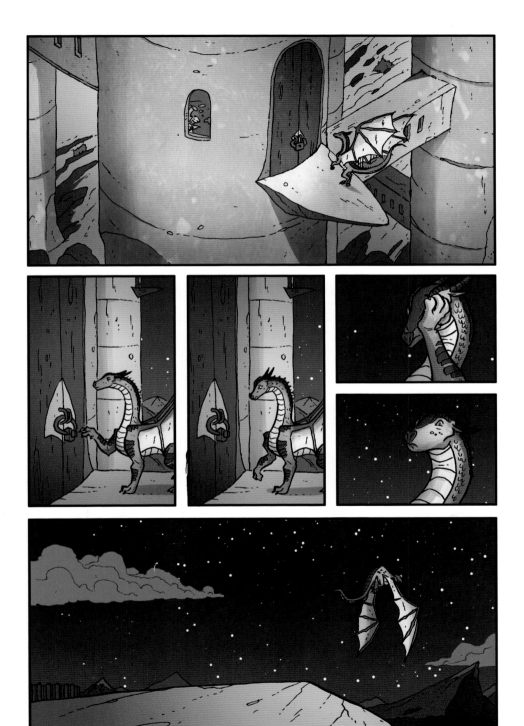

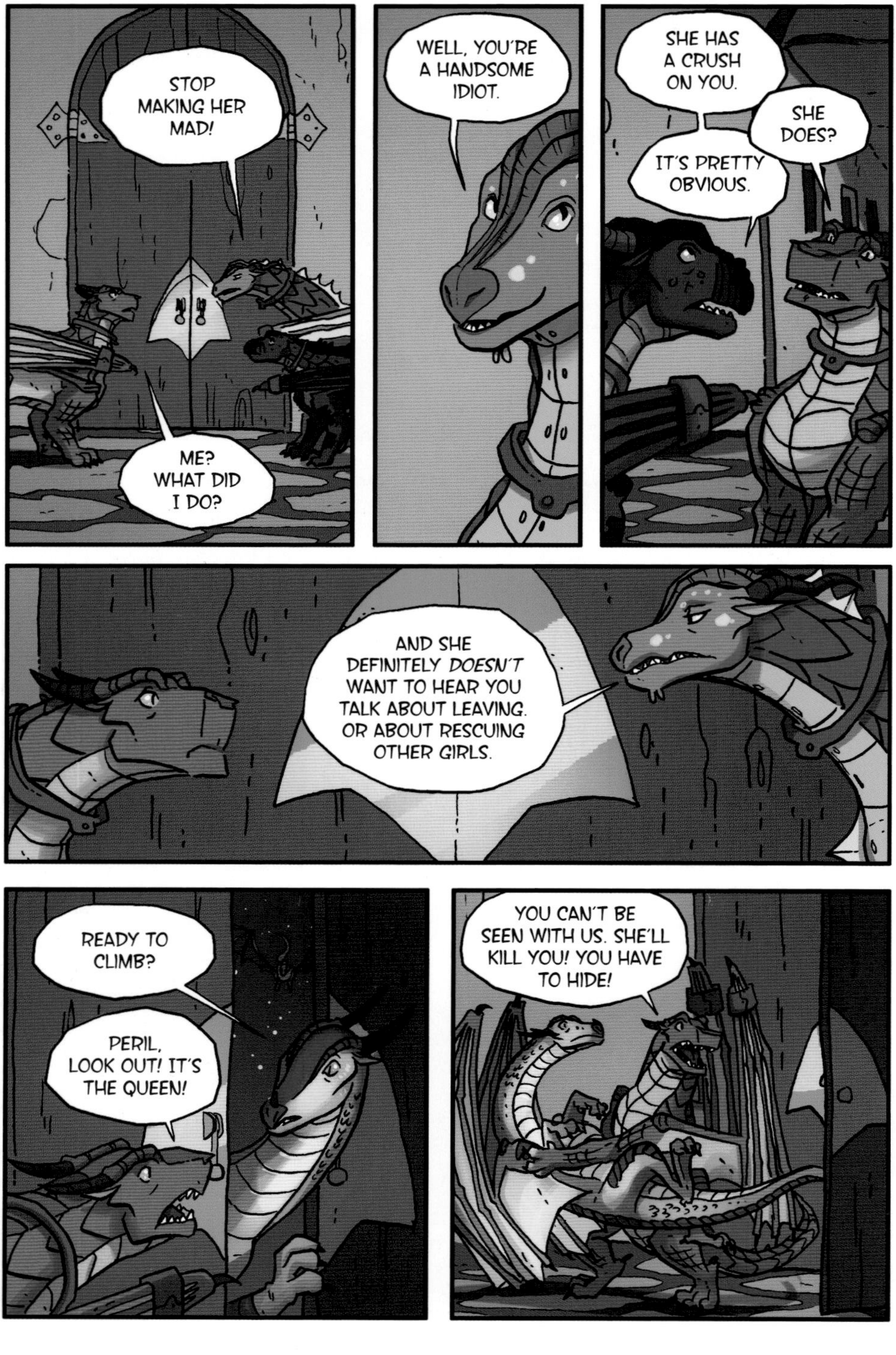
STOP MAKING HER MAD!
ME? WHAT DID I DO?
WELL, YOU'RE A HANDSOME IDIOT.
SHE HAS A CRUSH ON YOU.
IT'S PRETTY OBVIOUS.
SHE DOES?
AND SHE DEFINITELY *DOESN'T* WANT TO HEAR YOU TALK ABOUT LEAVING. OR ABOUT RESCUING OTHER GIRLS.
READY TO CLIMB?
PERIL, LOOK OUT! IT'S THE QUEEN!
YOU CAN'T BE SEEN WITH US. SHE'LL KILL YOU! YOU HAVE TO HIDE!

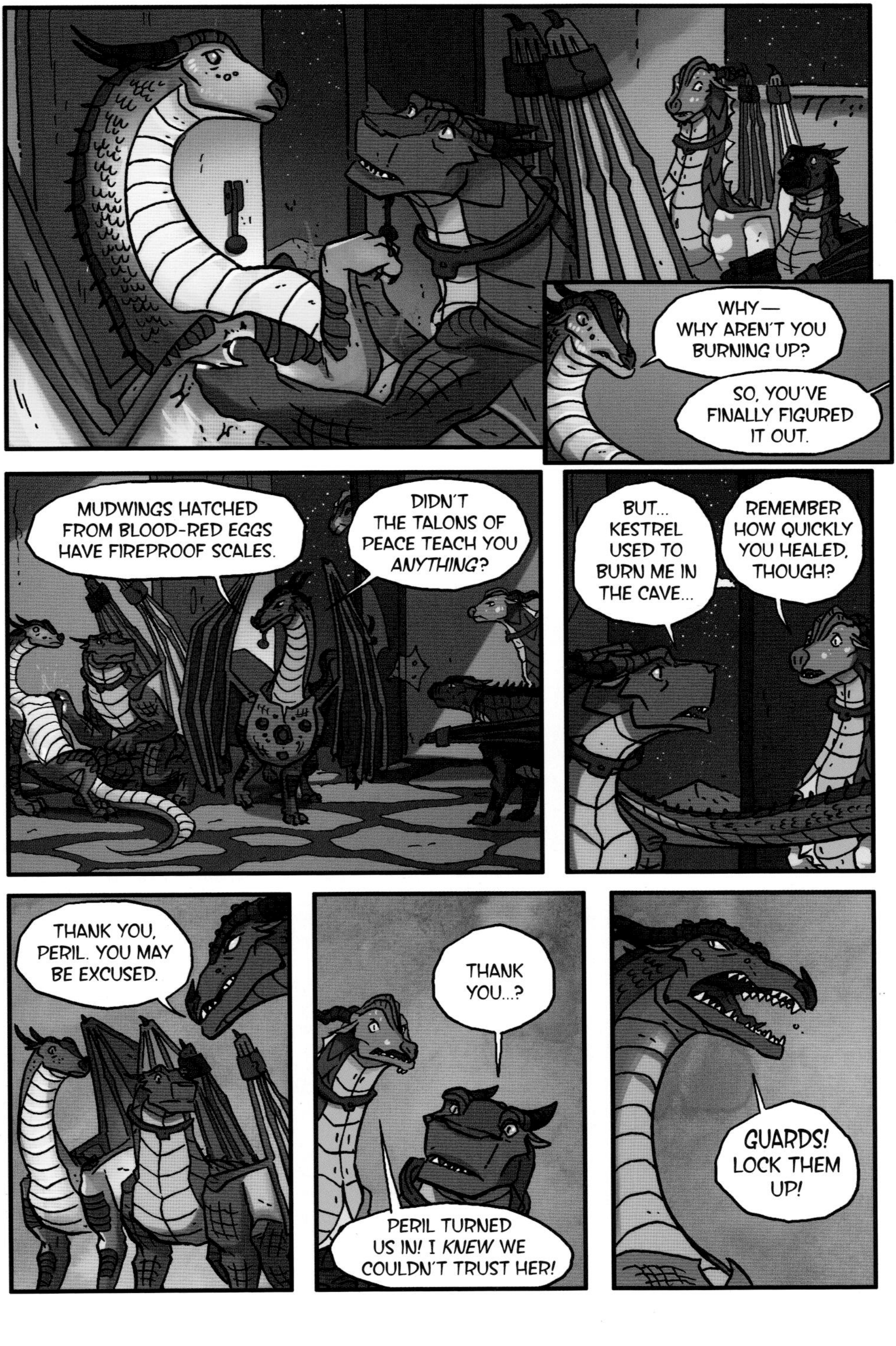
WHY—
WHY AREN'T YOU
BURNING UP?
SO, YOU'VE
FINALLY FIGURED
IT OUT.
MUDWINGS HATCHED
FROM BLOOD-RED EGGS
HAVE FIREPROOF SCALES.
DIDN'T
THE TALONS OF
PEACE TEACH YOU
ANYTHING?
BUT...
KESTREL
USED TO
BURN ME IN
THE CAVE...
REMEMBER
HOW QUICKLY
YOU HEALED,
THOUGH?
THANK YOU,
PERIL. YOU MAY
BE EXCUSED.
THANK
YOU...?
PERIL TURNED
US IN! I *KNEW* WE
COULDN'T TRUST HER!
GUARDS!
LOCK THEM
UP!

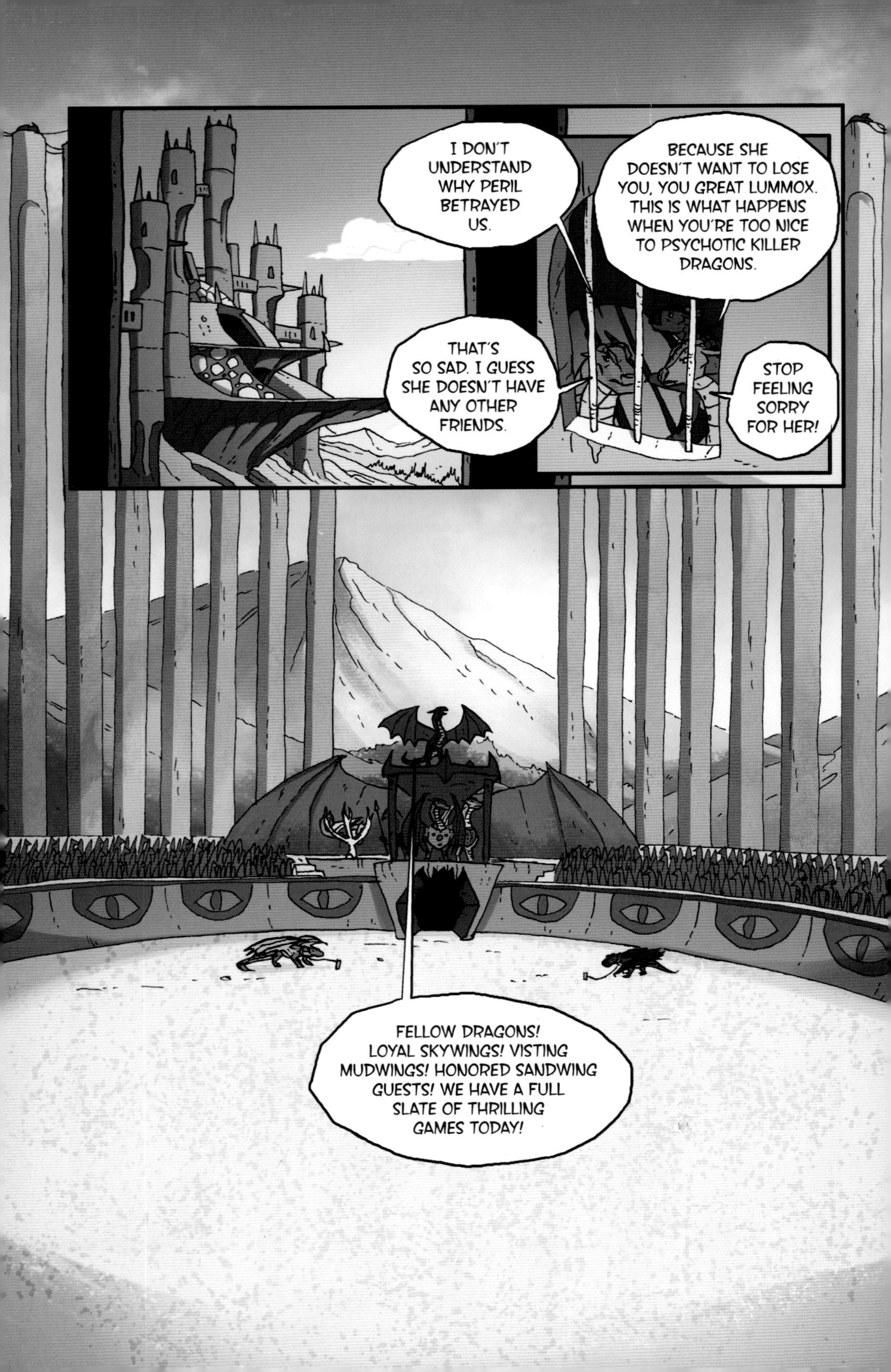

I DON'T UNDERSTAND WHY PERIL BETRAYED US.
BECAUSE SHE DOESN'T WANT TO LOSE YOU, YOU GREAT LUMMOX. THIS IS WHAT HAPPENS WHEN YOU'RE TOO NICE TO PSYCHOTIC KILLER DRAGONS.
THAT'S SO SAD. I GUESS SHE DOESN'T HAVE ANY OTHER FRIENDS.
STOP FEELING SORRY FOR HER!
FELLOW DRAGONS! LOYAL SKYWINGS! VISTING MUDWINGS! HONORED SANDWING GUESTS! WE HAVE A FULL SLATE OF THRILLING GAMES TODAY!

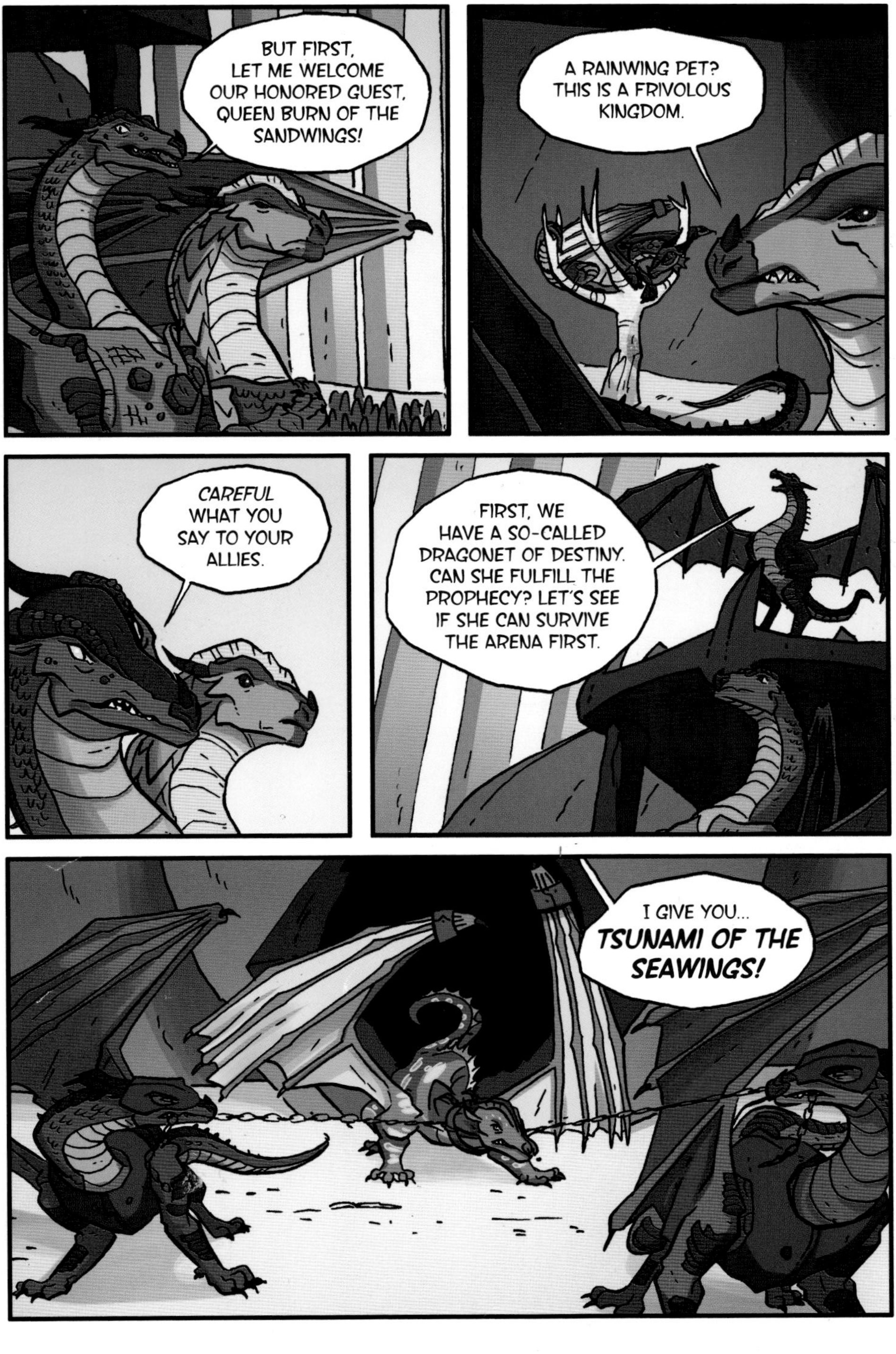
BUT FIRST, LET ME WELCOME OUR HONORED GUEST, QUEEN BURN OF THE SANDWINGS!
A RAINWING PET? THIS IS A FRIVOLOUS KINGDOM.
CAREFUL WHAT YOU SAY TO YOUR ALLIES.
FIRST, WE HAVE A SO-CALLED DRAGONET OF DESTINY. CAN SHE FULFILL THE PROPHECY? LET'S SEE IF SHE CAN SURVIVE THE ARENA FIRST.
I GIVE YOU... ***TSUNAMI OF THE SEAWINGS!***

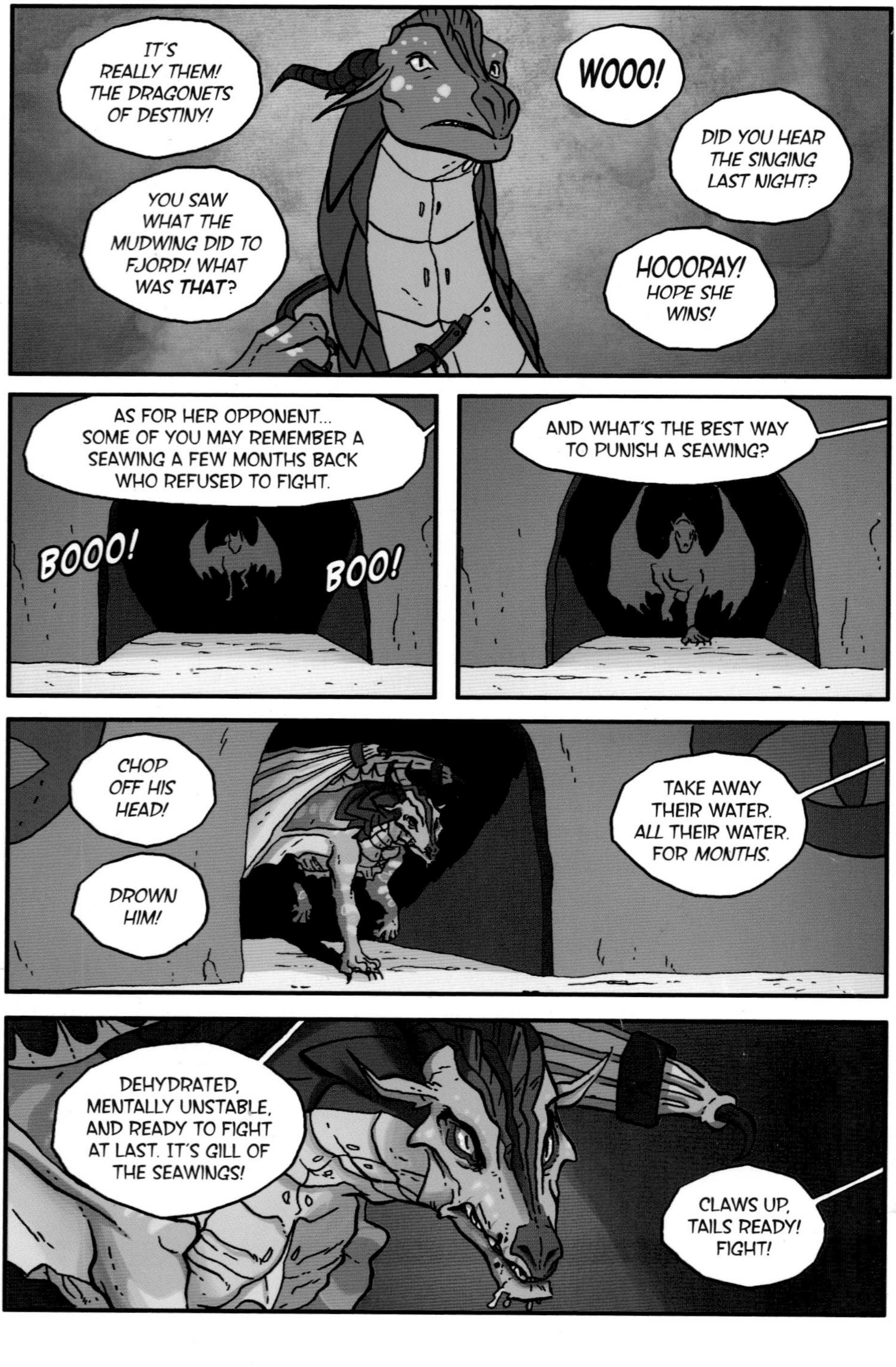
IT'S REALLY THEM! THE DRAGONETS OF DESTINY!
WOOO!
YOU SAW WHAT THE MUDWING DID TO FJORD! WHAT WAS THAT?
DID YOU HEAR THE SINGING LAST NIGHT?
HOOORAY! HOPE SHE WINS!
AS FOR HER OPPONENT... SOME OF YOU MAY REMEMBER A SEAWING A FEW MONTHS BACK WHO REFUSED TO FIGHT.
BOOO!
BOO!
AND WHAT'S THE BEST WAY TO PUNISH A SEAWING?
CHOP OFF HIS HEAD!
DROWN HIM!
TAKE AWAY THEIR WATER. ALL THEIR WATER. FOR MONTHS.
DEHYDRATED, MENTALLY UNSTABLE, AND READY TO FIGHT AT LAST. IT'S GILL OF THE SEAWINGS!
CLAWS UP, TAILS READY! FIGHT!

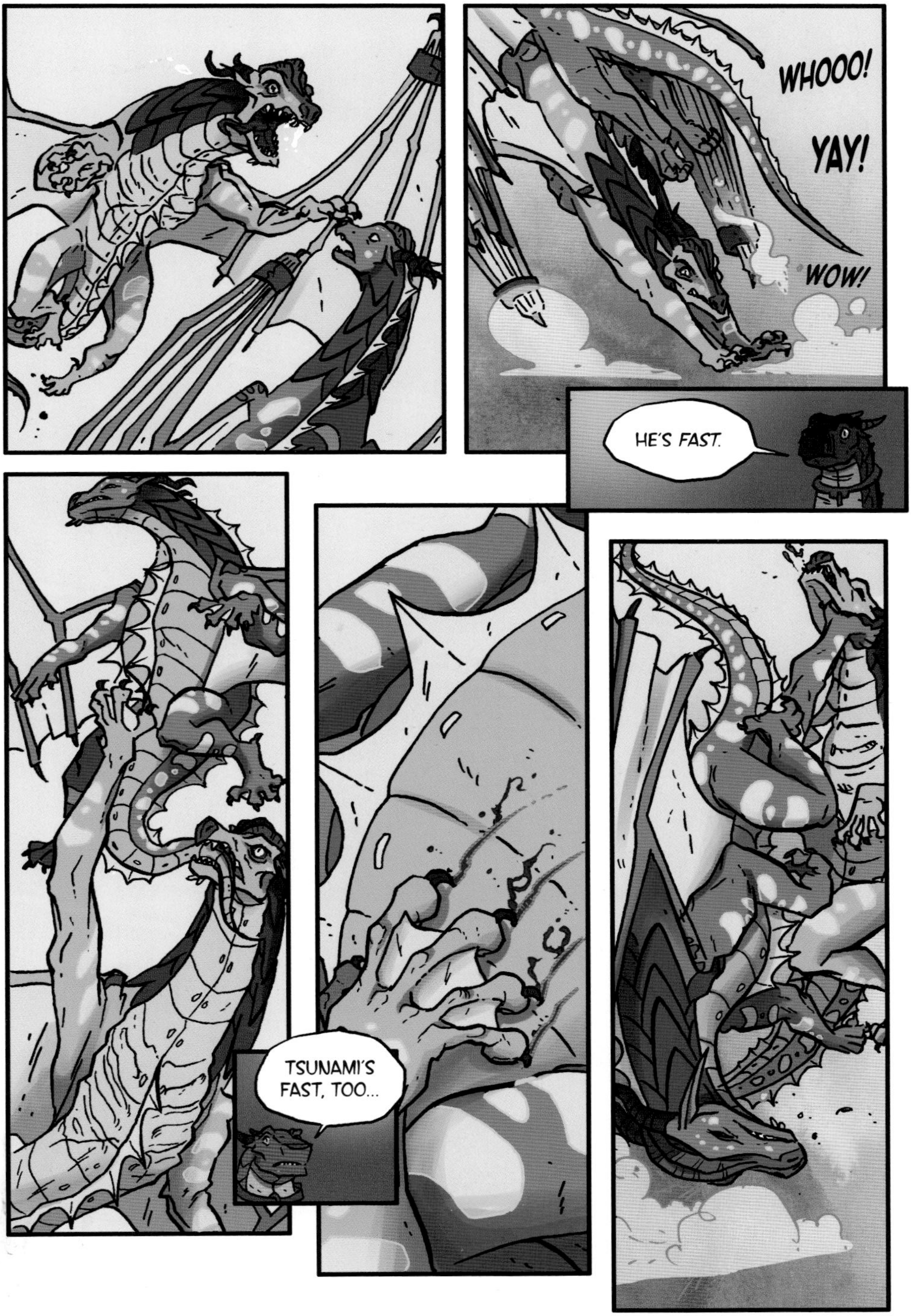
WHOOO!
YAY!
WOW!
HE'S FAST.
TSUNAMI'S FAST, TOO...

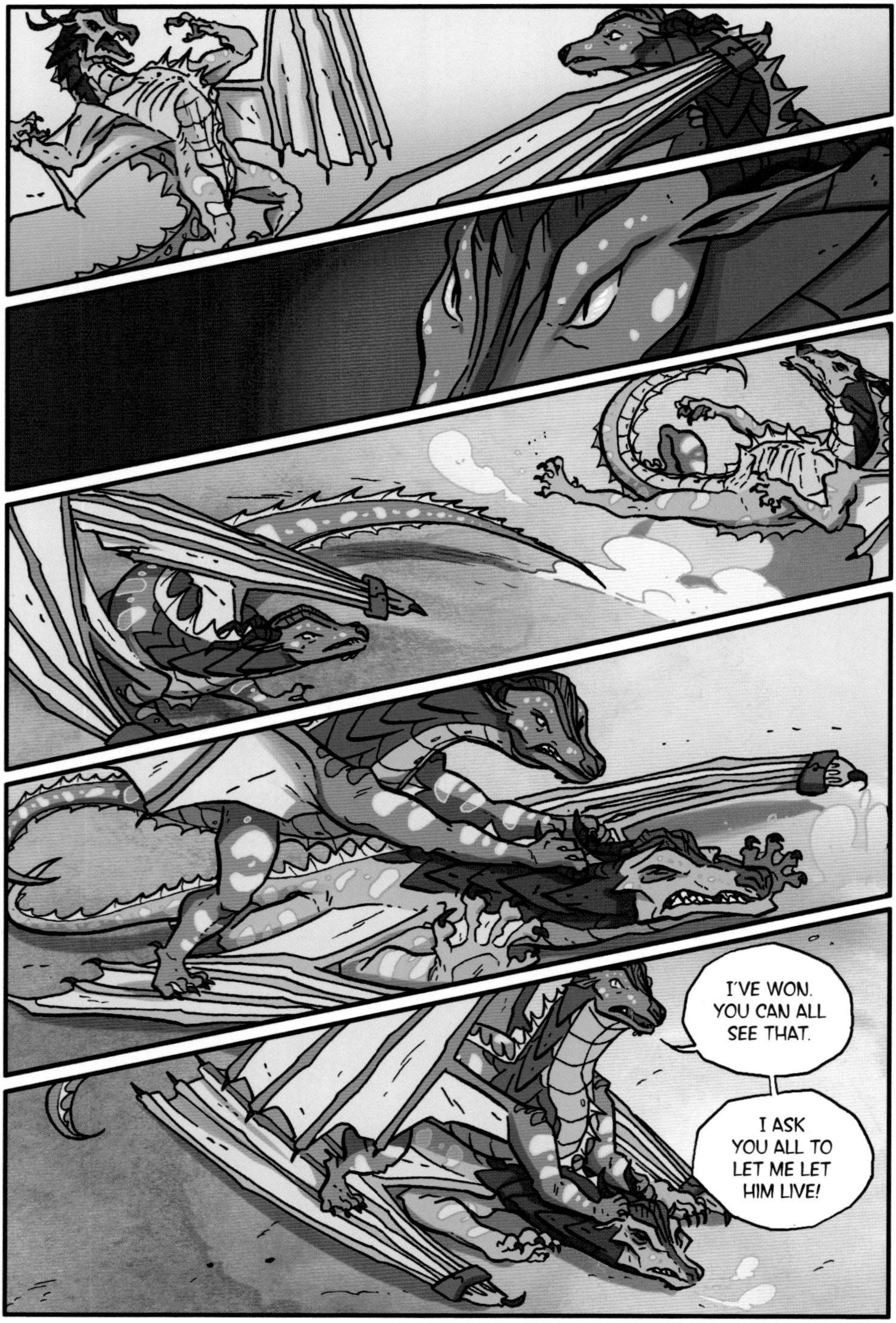
I'VE WON. YOU CAN ALL SEE THAT.
I ASK YOU ALL TO LET ME LET HIM LIVE!

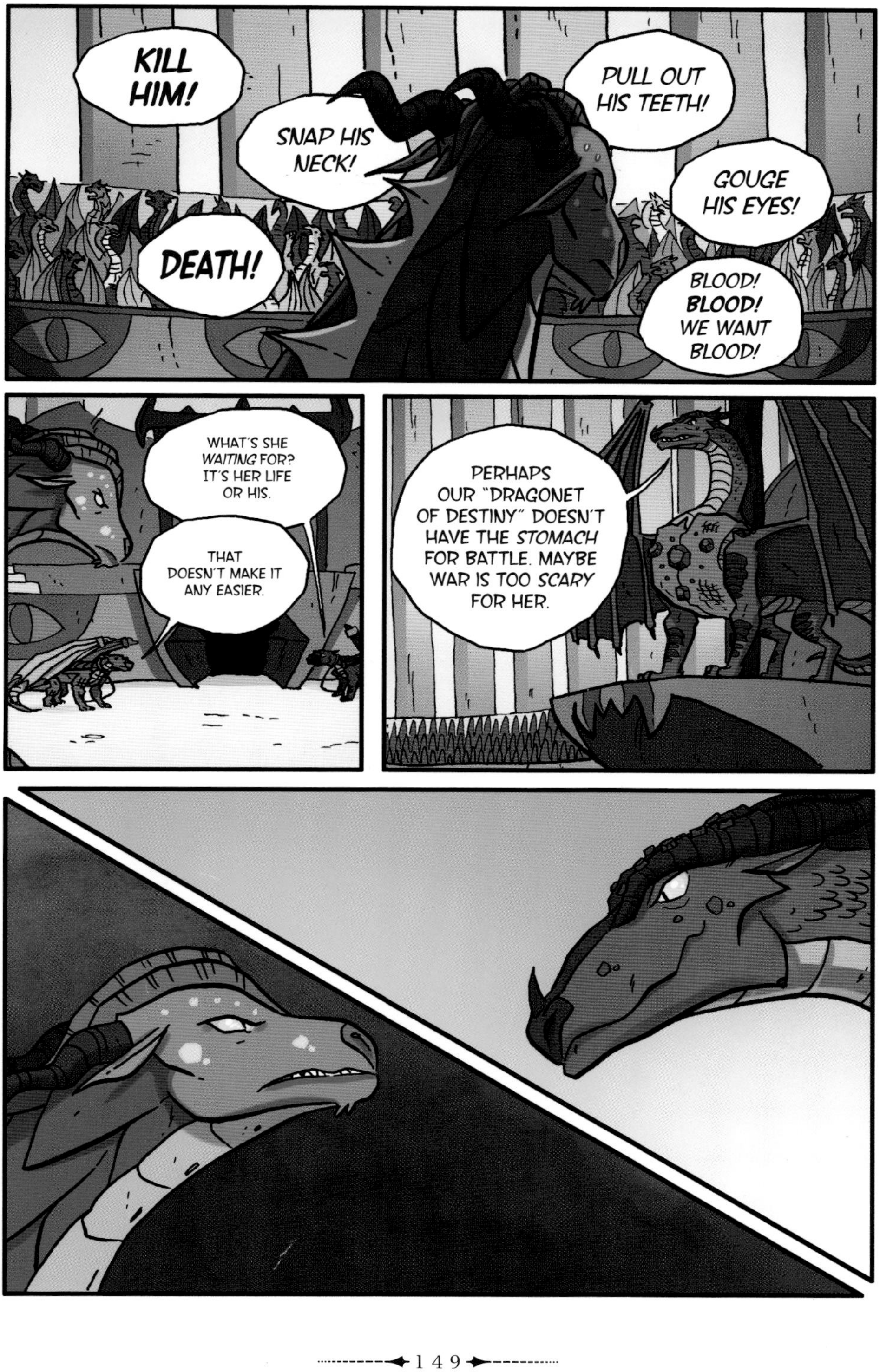
KILL HIM!
SNAP HIS NECK!
PULL OUT HIS TEETH!
GOUGE HIS EYES!
DEATH!
BLOOD! BLOOD! WE WANT BLOOD!
WHAT'S SHE *WAITING* FOR? IT'S HER LIFE OR HIS.
THAT DOESN'T MAKE IT ANY EASIER.
PERHAPS OUR "DRAGONET OF DESTINY" DOESN'T HAVE THE *STOMACH* FOR BATTLE. MAYBE WAR IS TOO *SCARY* FOR HER.

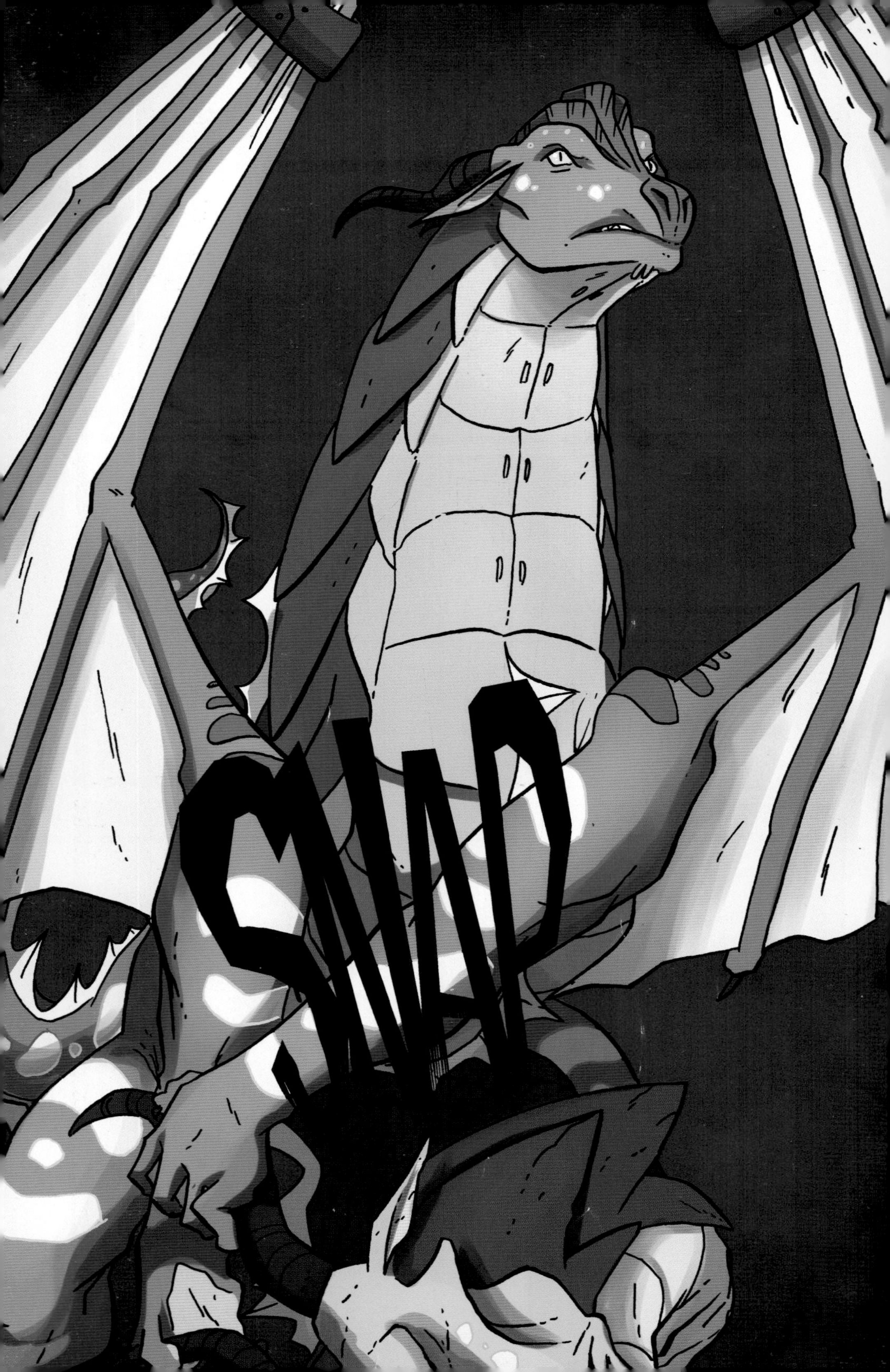
SNAP

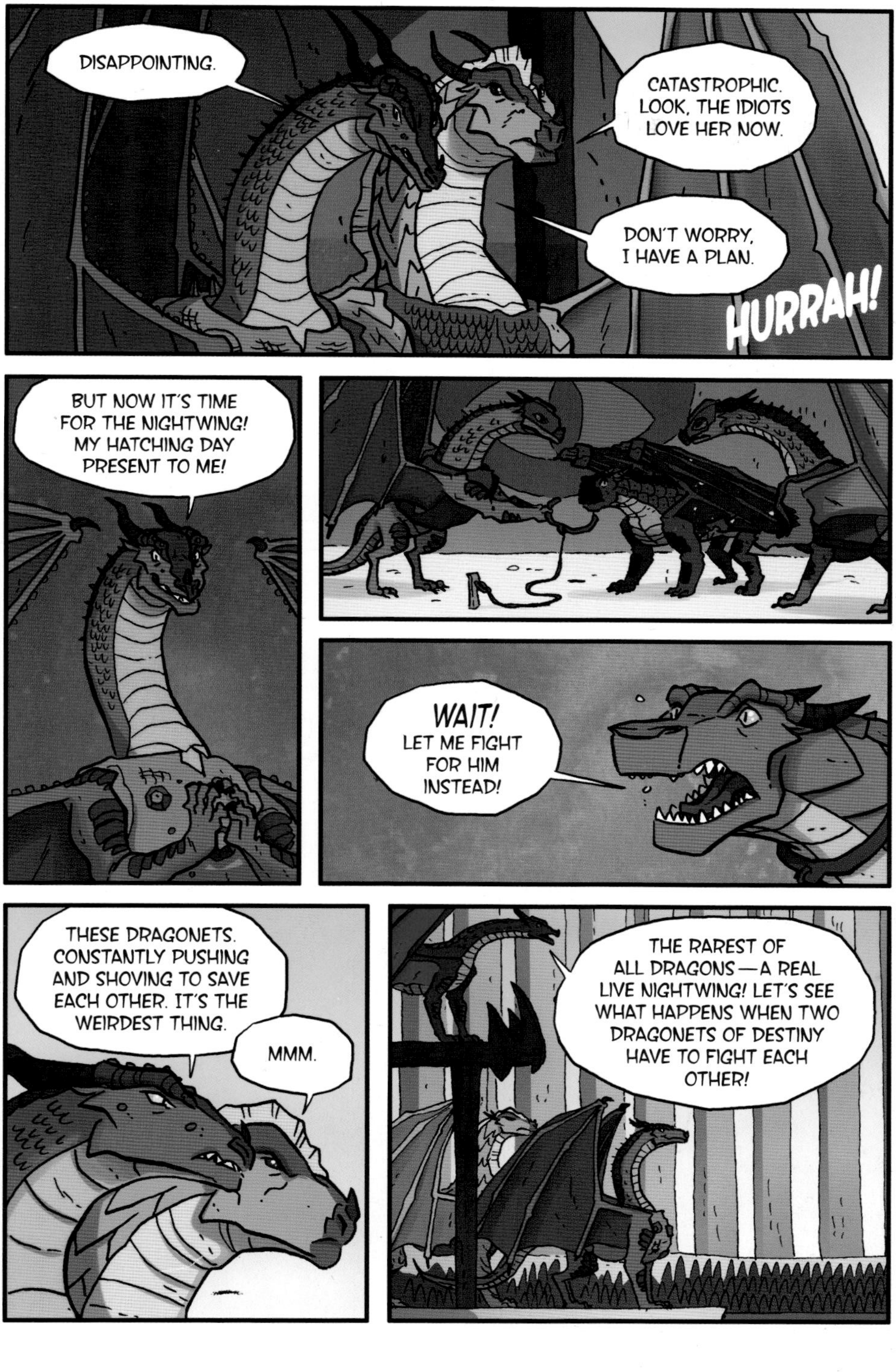
DISAPPOINTING.
CATASTROPHIC. LOOK, THE IDIOTS LOVE HER NOW.
DON'T WORRY, I HAVE A PLAN.
HURRAH!
BUT NOW IT'S TIME FOR THE NIGHTWING! MY HATCHING DAY PRESENT TO ME!
WAIT! LET ME FIGHT FOR HIM INSTEAD!
THESE DRAGONETS. CONSTANTLY PUSHING AND SHOVING TO SAVE EACH OTHER. IT'S THE WEIRDEST THING.
MMM.
THE RAREST OF ALL DRAGONS—A REAL LIVE NIGHTWING! LET'S SEE WHAT HAPPENS WHEN TWO DRAGONETS OF DESTINY HAVE TO FIGHT EACH OTHER!

TSUNAMI OF THE SEAWINGS AND STARFLIGHT OF THE NIGHTWINGS! CLAWS UP, TEETH READY! *FIGHT!*

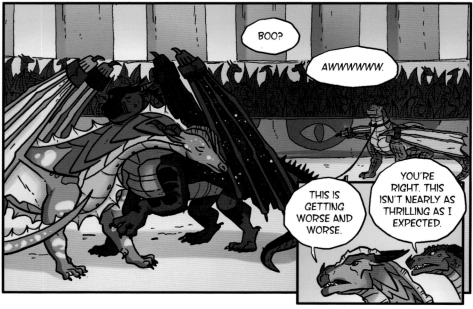

BOO?

AWWWWWW.

THIS IS GETTING WORSE AND WORSE.

YOU'RE RIGHT. THIS ISN'T NEARLY AS THRILLING AS I EXPECTED.

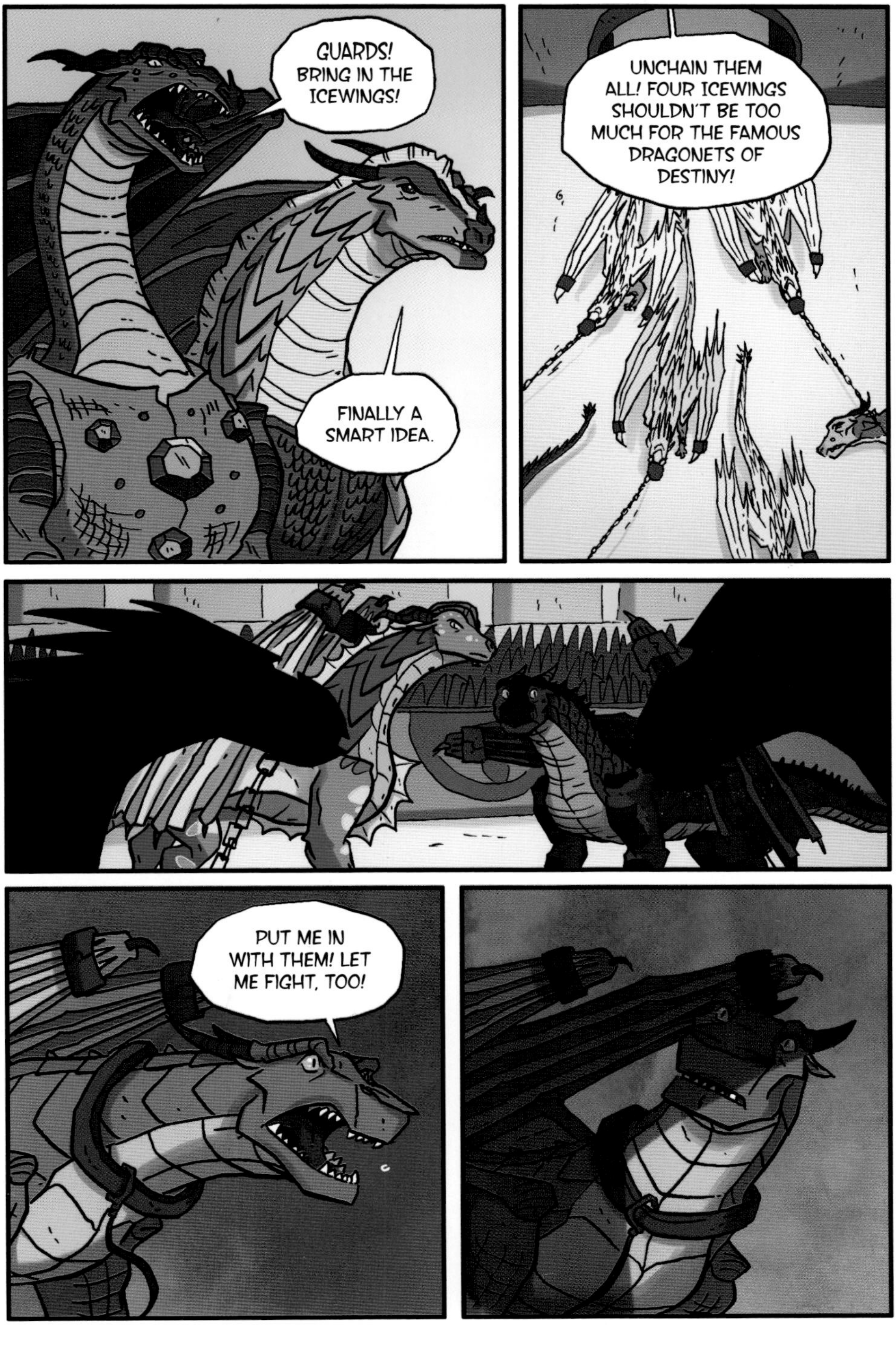
GUARDS! BRING IN THE ICEWINGS!
FINALLY A SMART IDEA.
UNCHAIN THEM ALL! FOUR ICEWINGS SHOULDN'T BE TOO MUCH FOR THE FAMOUS DRAGONETS OF DESTINY!
PUT ME IN WITH THEM! LET ME FIGHT, TOO!

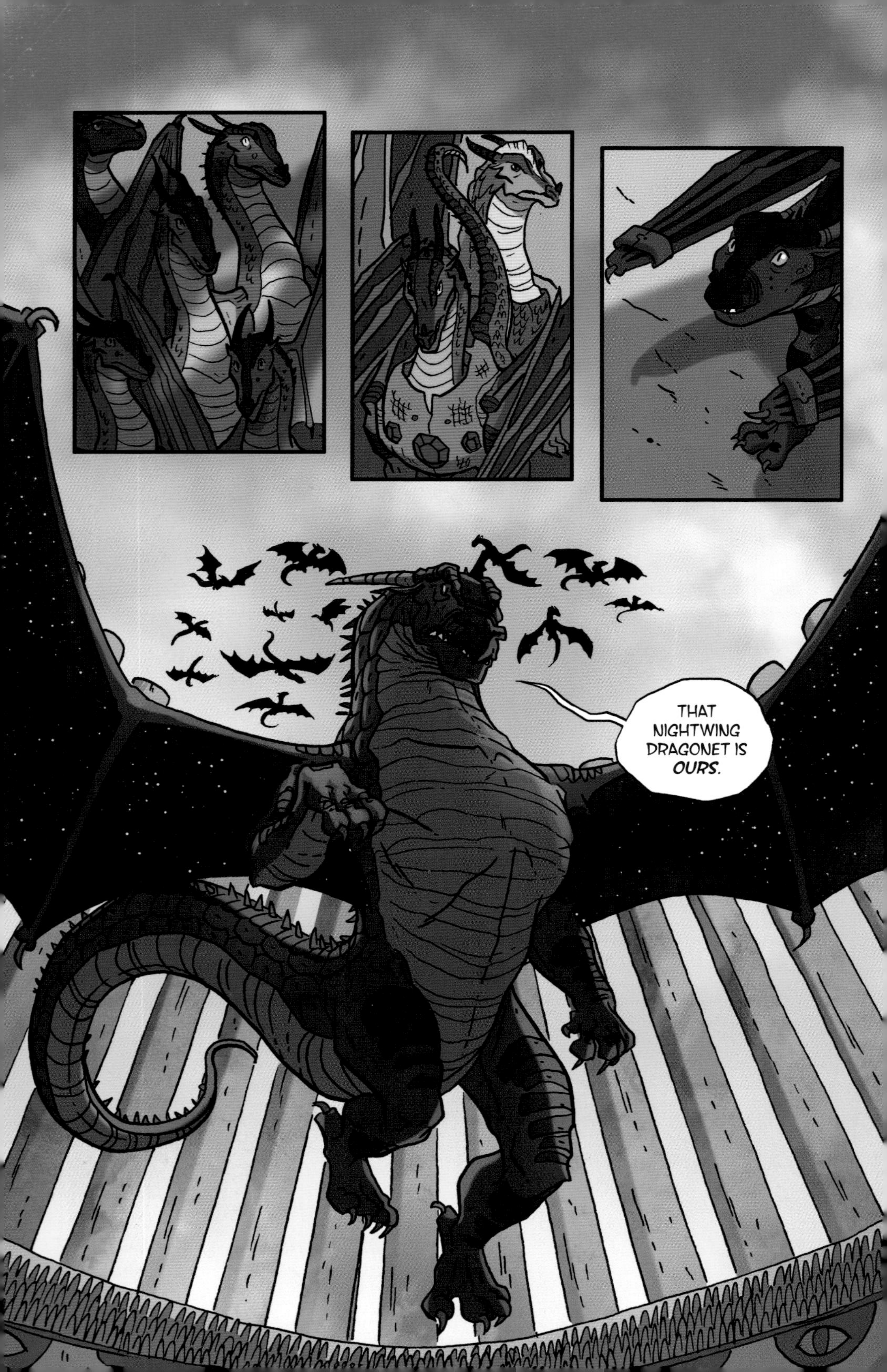
THAT NIGHTWING DRAGONET IS OURS.

WHAT ABOUT THE REST OF US?

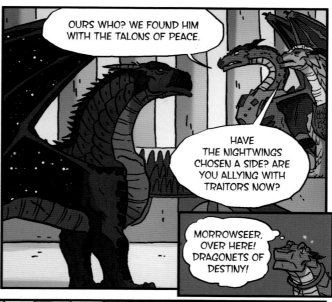

OURS WHO? WE FOUND HIM WITH THE TALONS OF PEACE.

HAVE THE NIGHTWINGS CHOSEN A SIDE? ARE YOU ALLYING WITH TRAITORS NOW?

MORROWSEER, OVER HERE! DRAGONETS OF DESTINY!

NO. I COME TO CLAIM THIS DRAGONET AS OURS. WE WILL TAKE HIM AND GO.

OH, WILL YOU?

DO NOT ANGER THE NIGHTWINGS, SKY DRAGON.

COME ON!

CAN'T YOU HEAR ME?

WE NEED HELP!

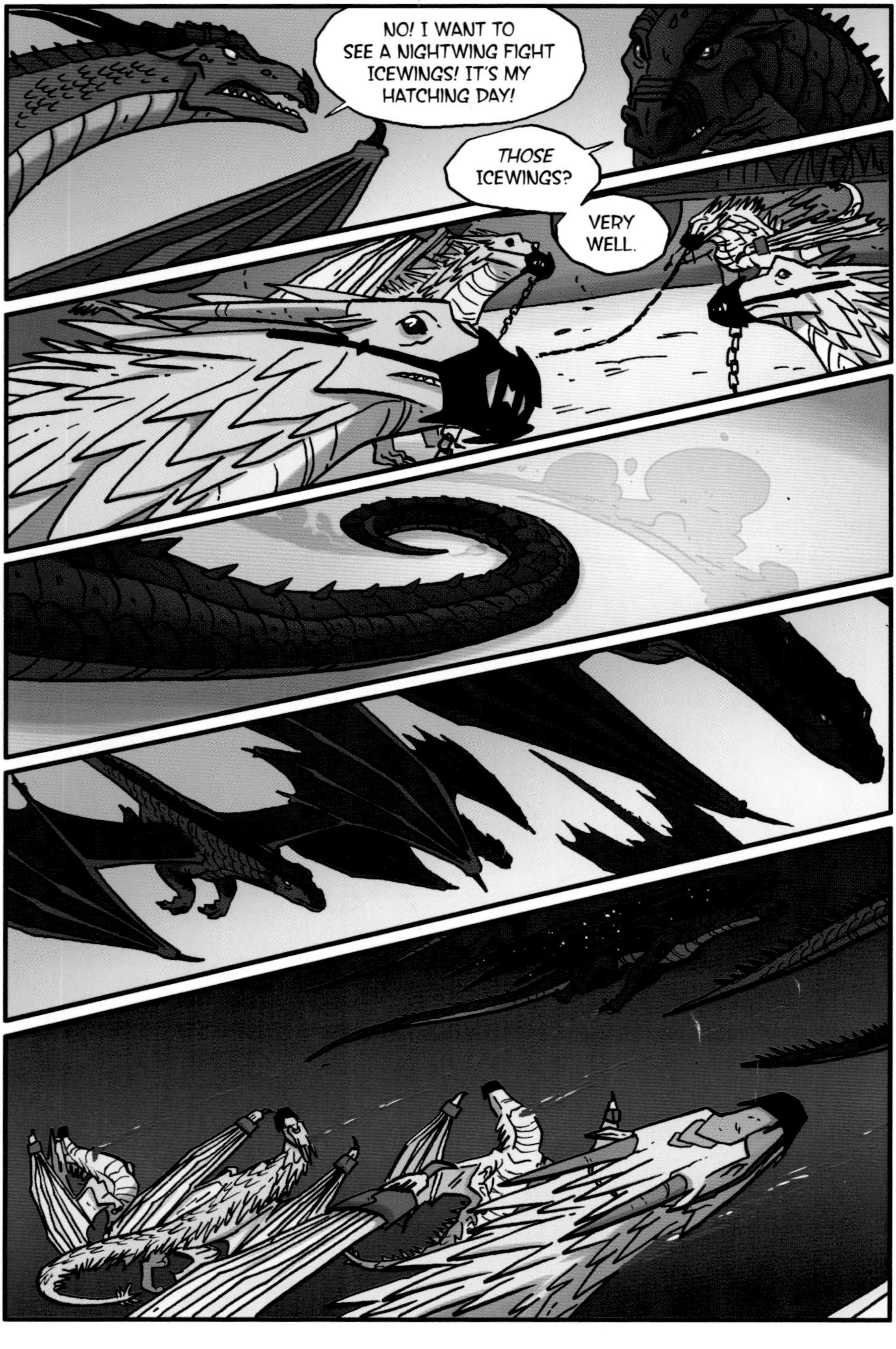
NO! I WANT TO SEE A NIGHTWING FIGHT ICEWINGS! IT'S MY HATCHING DAY!
THOSE ICEWINGS?
VERY WELL.

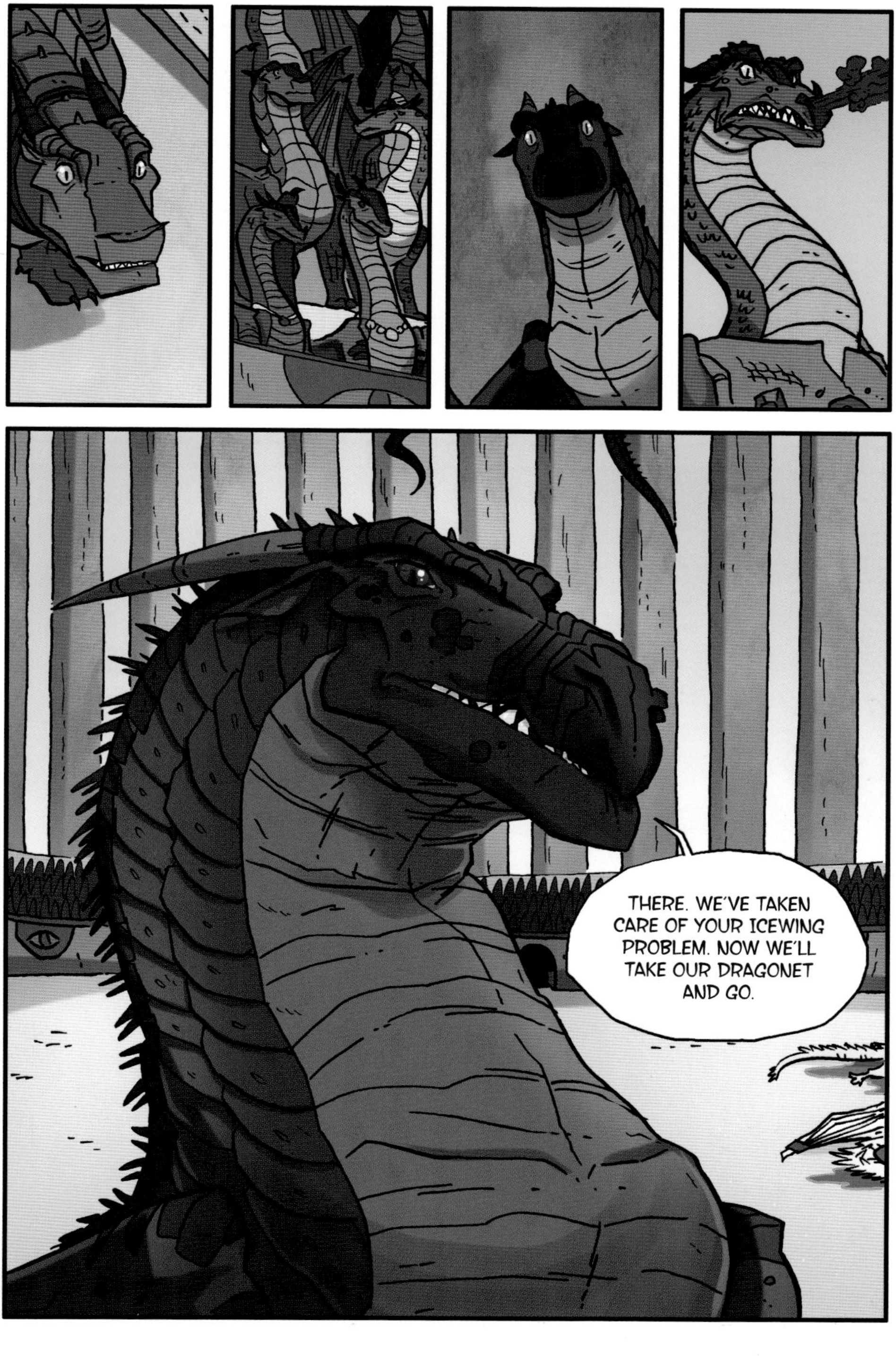
THERE. WE'VE TAKEN CARE OF YOUR ICEWING PROBLEM. NOW WE'LL TAKE OUR DRAGONET AND GO.

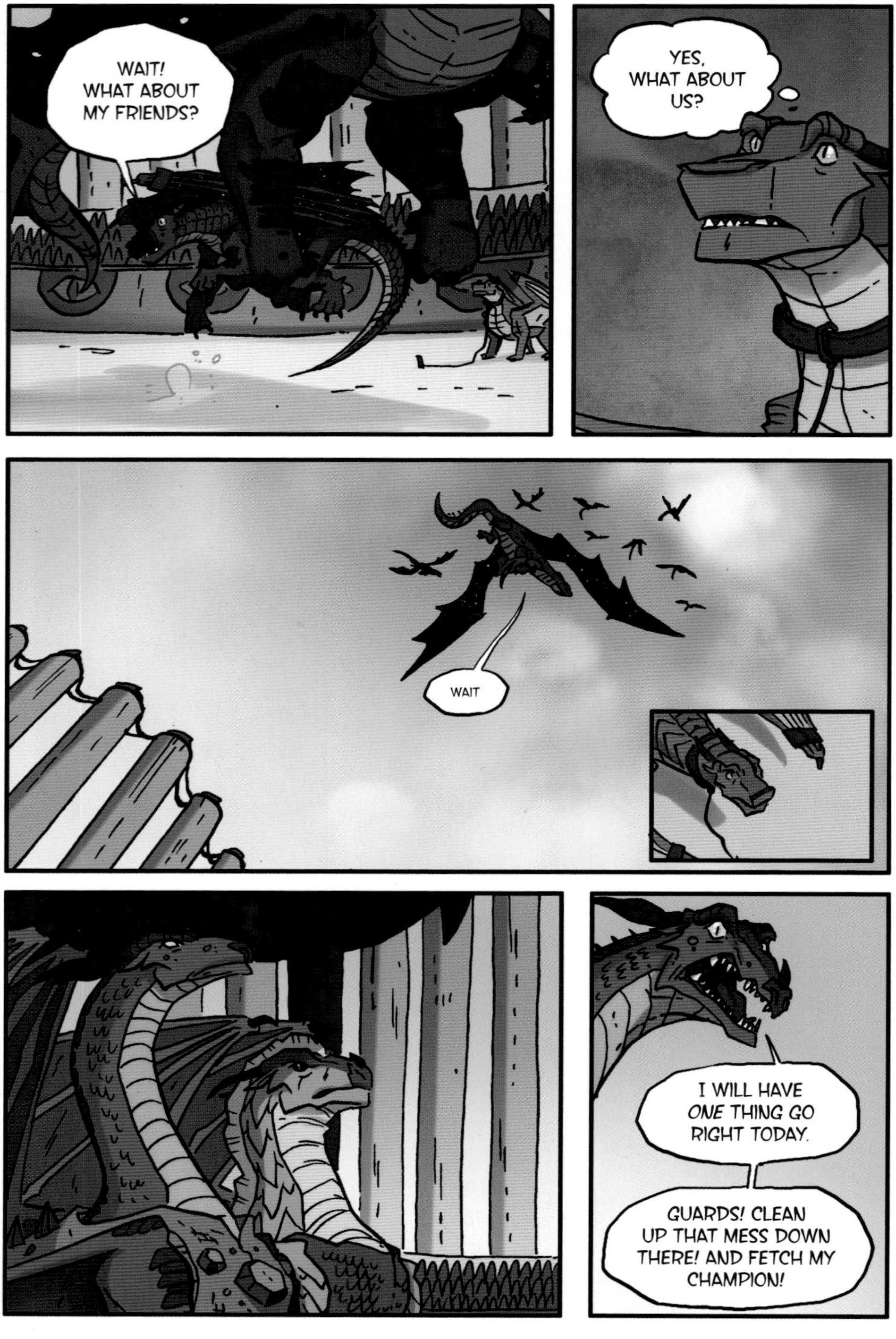
WAIT! WHAT ABOUT MY FRIENDS?
YES, WHAT ABOUT US?
WAIT
I WILL HAVE *ONE* THING GO RIGHT TODAY.
GUARDS! CLEAN UP THAT MESS DOWN THERE! AND FETCH MY CHAMPION!

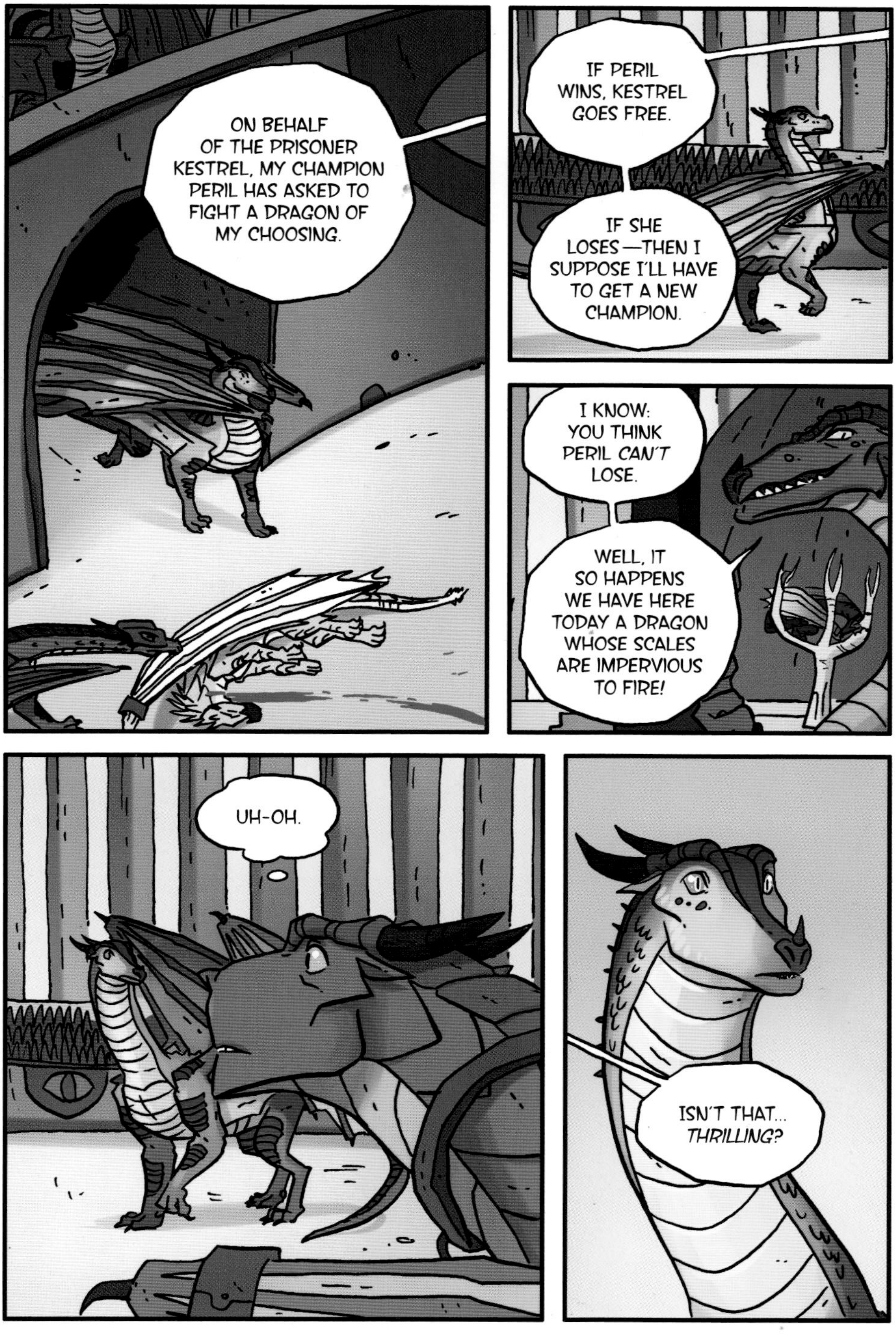
ON BEHALF OF THE PRISONER KESTREL, MY CHAMPION PERIL HAS ASKED TO FIGHT A DRAGON OF MY CHOOSING.
IF PERIL WINS, KESTREL GOES FREE.
IF SHE LOSES—THEN I SUPPOSE I'LL HAVE TO GET A NEW CHAMPION.
I KNOW: YOU THINK PERIL *CAN'T* LOSE.
WELL, IT SO HAPPENS WE HAVE HERE TODAY A DRAGON WHOSE SCALES ARE IMPERVIOUS TO FIRE!
UH-OH.
ISN'T THAT... *THRILLING?*

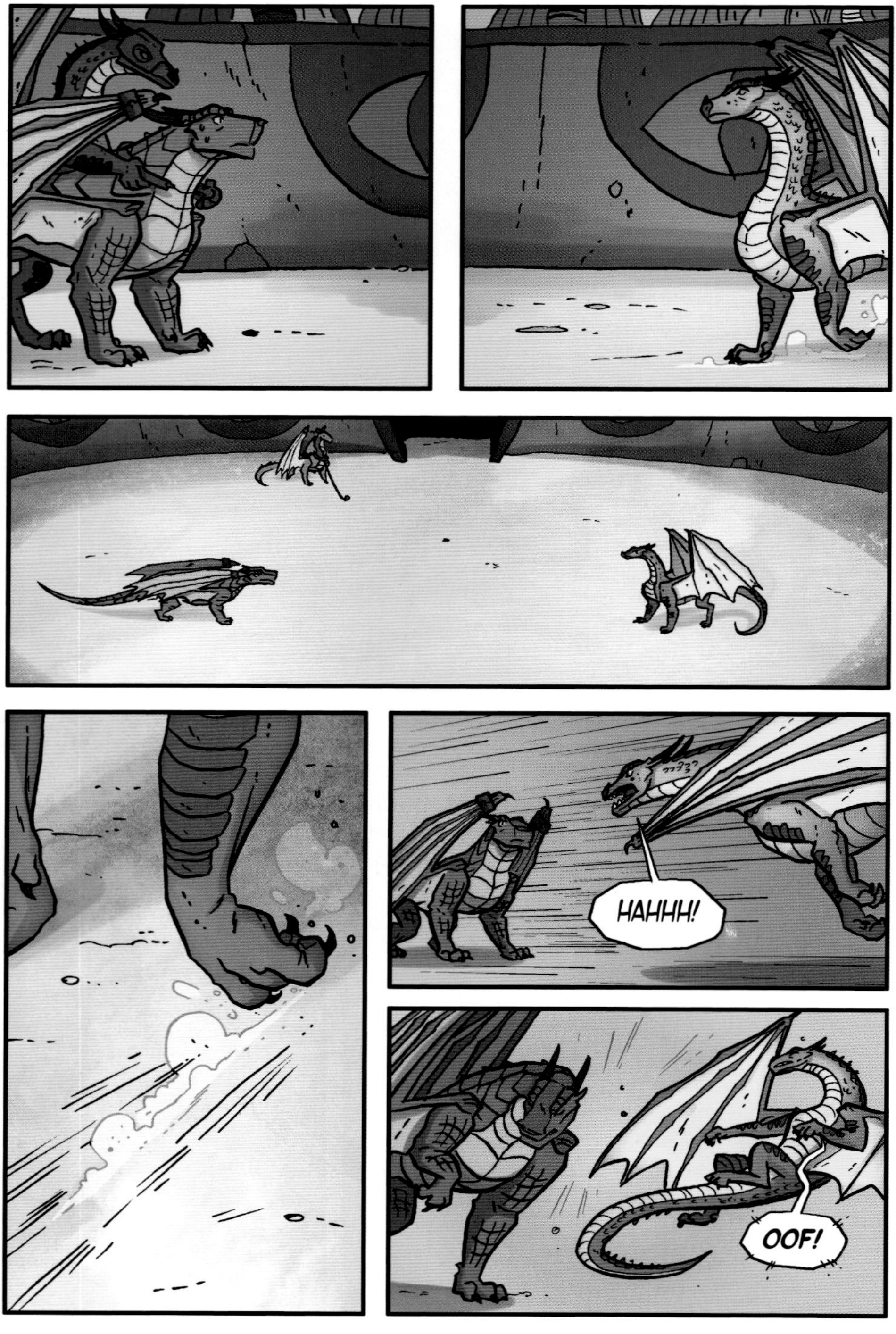
HAHHH!
OOF!

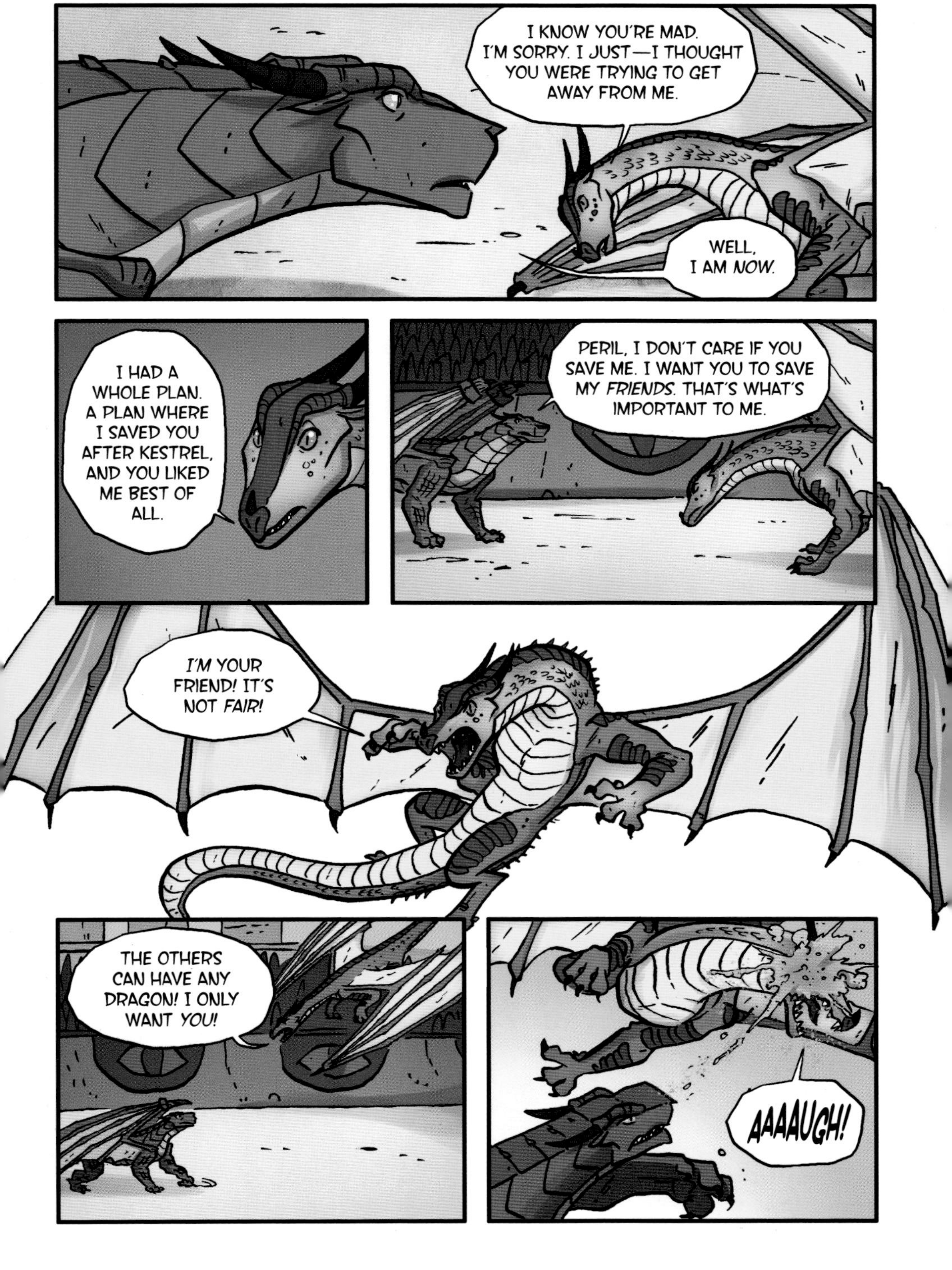
I KNOW YOU'RE MAD. I'M SORRY. I JUST—I THOUGHT YOU WERE TRYING TO GET AWAY FROM ME.
WELL, I AM *NOW*.
I HAD A WHOLE PLAN. A PLAN WHERE I SAVED YOU AFTER KESTREL, AND YOU LIKED ME BEST OF ALL.
PERIL, I DON'T CARE IF YOU SAVE ME. I WANT YOU TO SAVE MY *FRIENDS*. THAT'S WHAT'S IMPORTANT TO ME.
I'M YOUR FRIEND! IT'S NOT *FAIR*!
THE OTHERS CAN HAVE ANY DRAGON! I ONLY WANT *YOU*!
AAAAUGH!

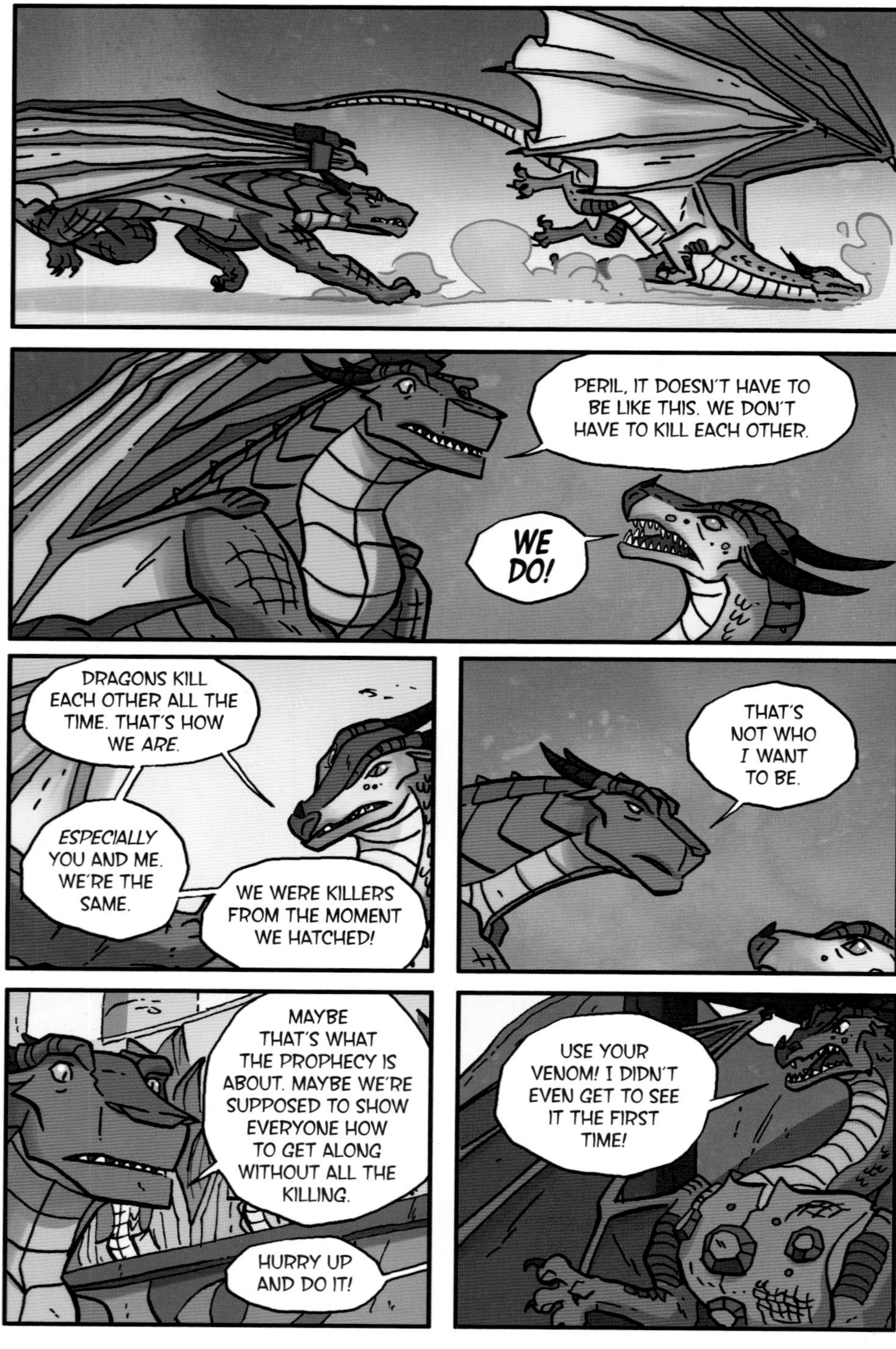
PERIL, IT DOESN'T HAVE TO BE LIKE THIS. WE DON'T HAVE TO KILL EACH OTHER.
WE DO!
DRAGONS KILL EACH OTHER ALL THE TIME. THAT'S HOW WE *ARE*.
ESPECIALLY YOU AND ME. WE'RE THE SAME.
WE WERE KILLERS FROM THE MOMENT WE HATCHED!
THAT'S NOT WHO *I* WANT TO BE.
MAYBE THAT'S WHAT THE PROPHECY IS ABOUT. MAYBE WE'RE SUPPOSED TO SHOW EVERYONE HOW TO GET ALONG WITHOUT ALL THE KILLING.
HURRY UP AND DO IT!
USE YOUR VENOM! I DIDN'T EVEN GET TO SEE IT THE FIRST TIME!

BUT I DIDN'T—

IT REALLY WASN'T YOU?

HSSSSSSS!

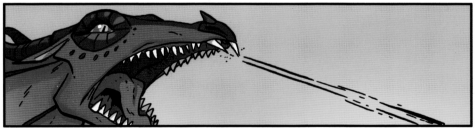

RRRAAAHHH! GAAAAAHHHH!

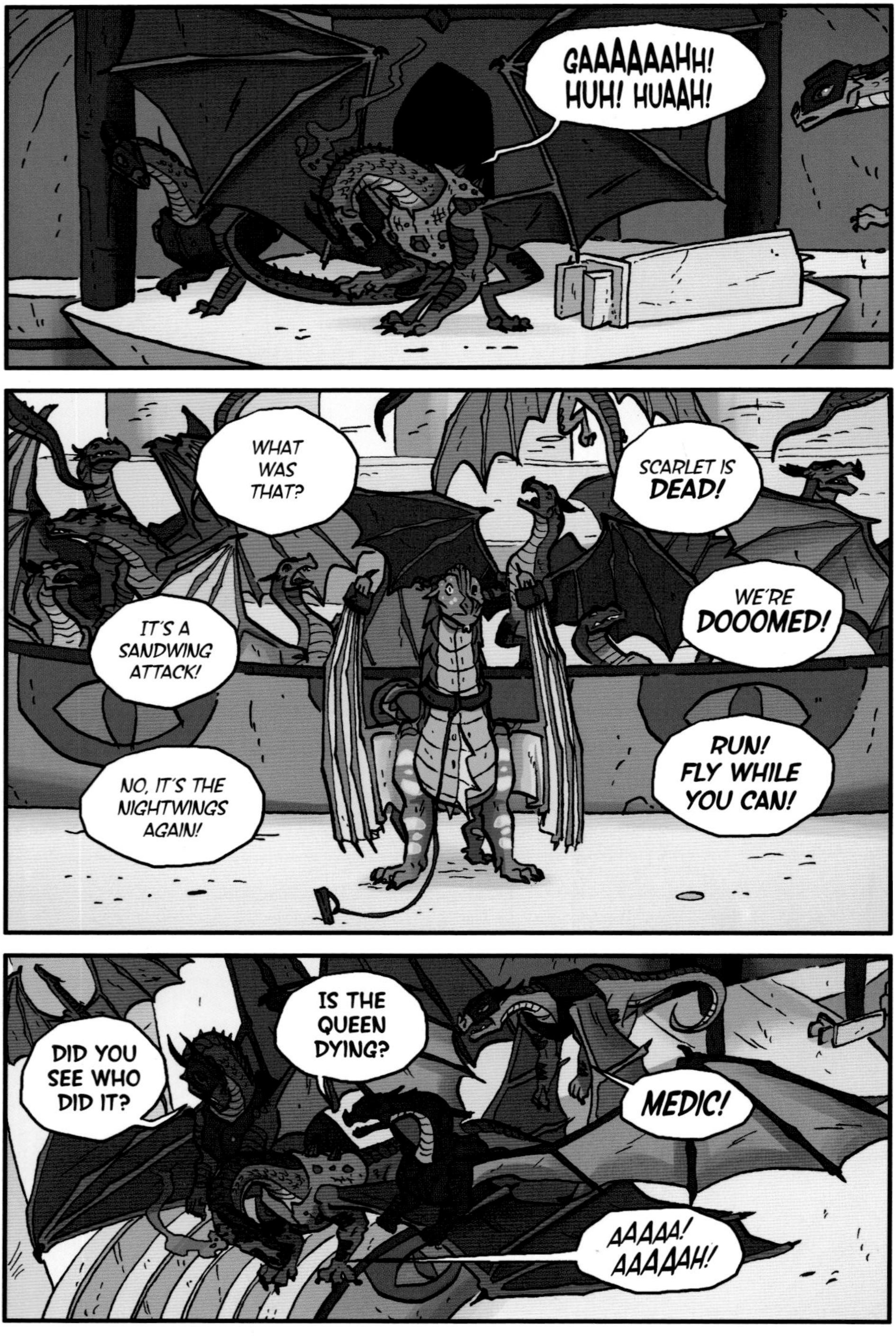
GAAAAAAHH! HUH! HUAAH!
WHAT WAS THAT?
SCARLET IS DEAD!
IT'S A SANDWING ATTACK!
WE'RE DOOOMED!
NO, IT'S THE NIGHTWINGS AGAIN!
RUN! FLY WHILE YOU CAN!
DID YOU SEE WHO DID IT?
IS THE QUEEN DYING?
MEDIC!
AAAAA! AAAAAH!

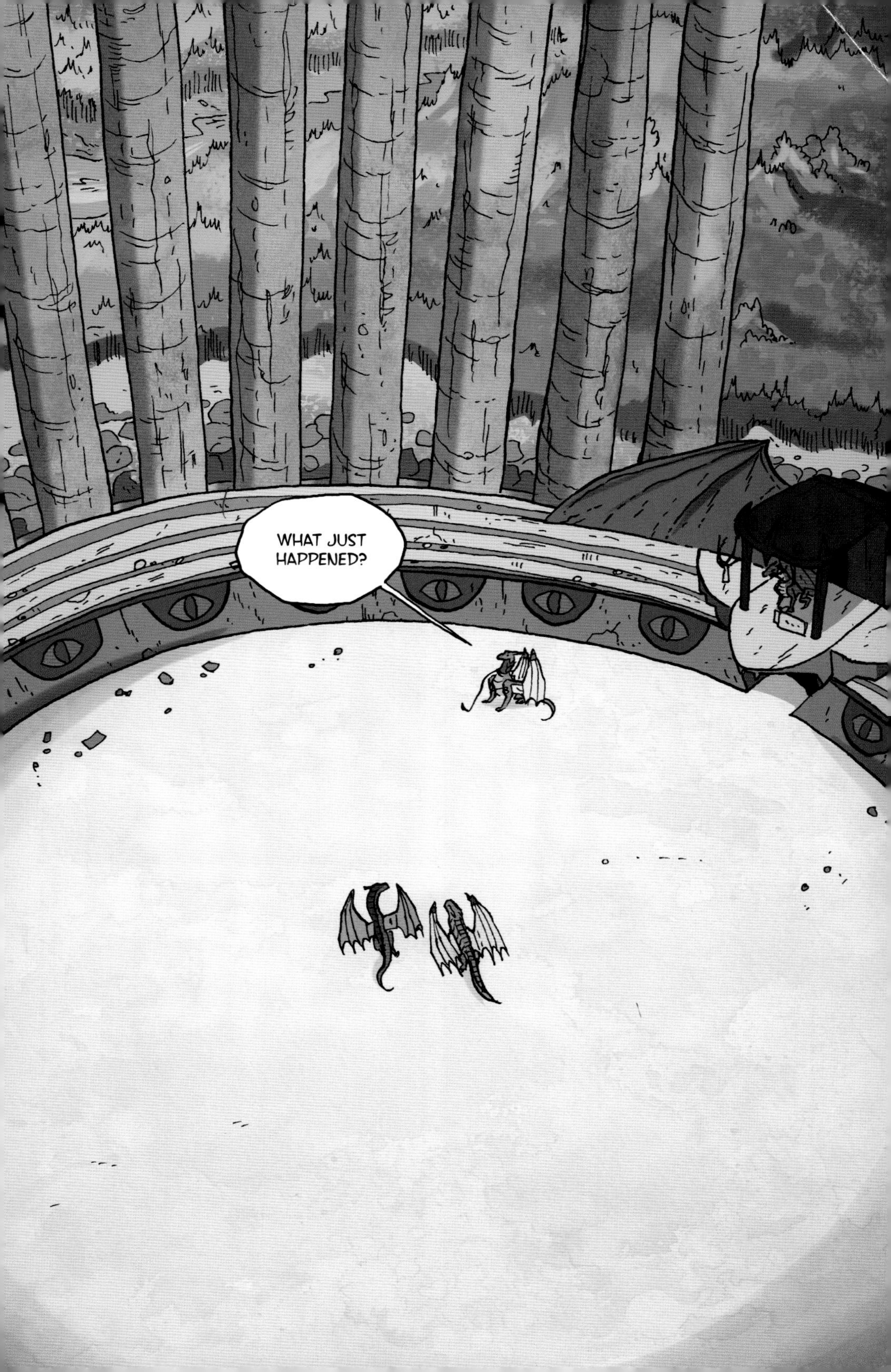
WHAT JUST HAPPENED?

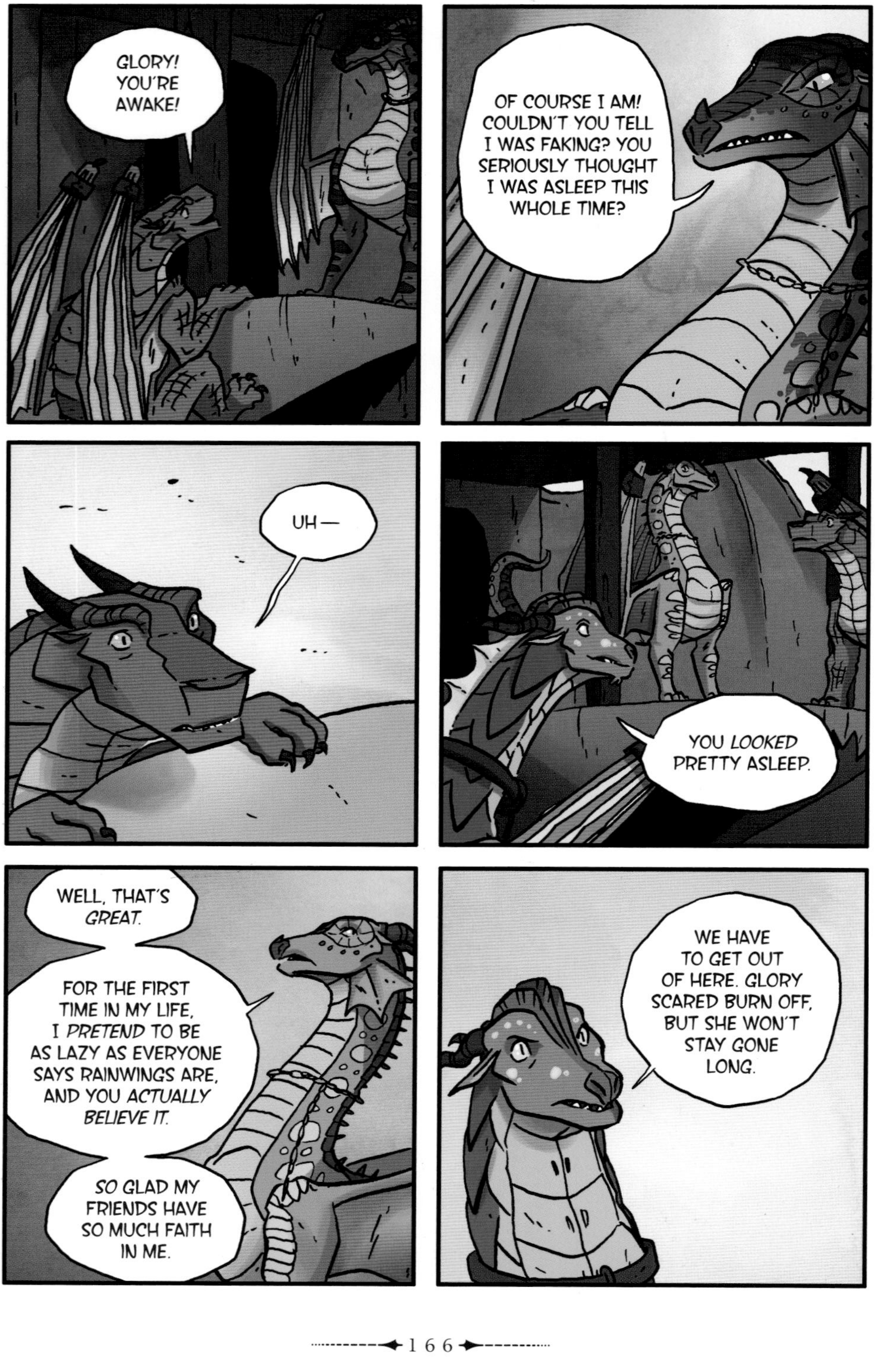
GLORY! YOU'RE AWAKE!
OF COURSE I AM! COULDN'T YOU TELL I WAS FAKING? YOU SERIOUSLY THOUGHT I WAS ASLEEP THIS WHOLE TIME?
UH—
YOU *LOOKED* PRETTY ASLEEP.
WELL, THAT'S *GREAT*.
FOR THE FIRST TIME IN MY LIFE, I *PRETEND* TO BE AS LAZY AS EVERYONE SAYS RAINWINGS ARE, AND YOU *ACTUALLY BELIEVE IT*.
SO GLAD MY FRIENDS HAVE SO MUCH FAITH IN ME.
WE HAVE TO GET OUT OF HERE. GLORY SCARED BURN OFF, BUT SHE WON'T STAY GONE LONG.

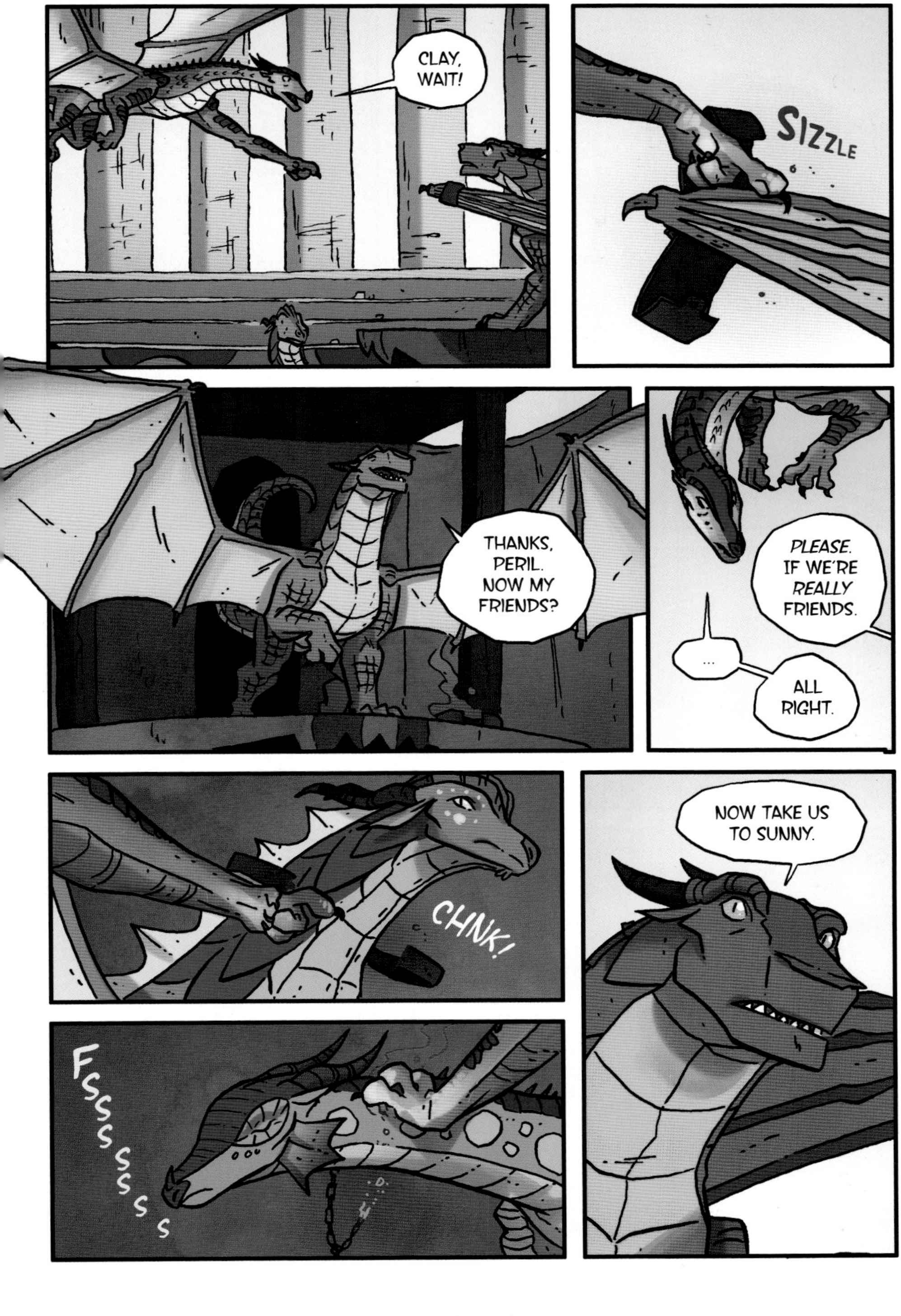
CLAY, WAIT!
SIZZLE
THANKS, PERIL. NOW MY FRIENDS?
PLEASE. IF WE'RE *REALLY* FRIENDS.
...
ALL RIGHT.
CHNK!
FSSSSSSS
NOW TAKE US TO SUNNY.

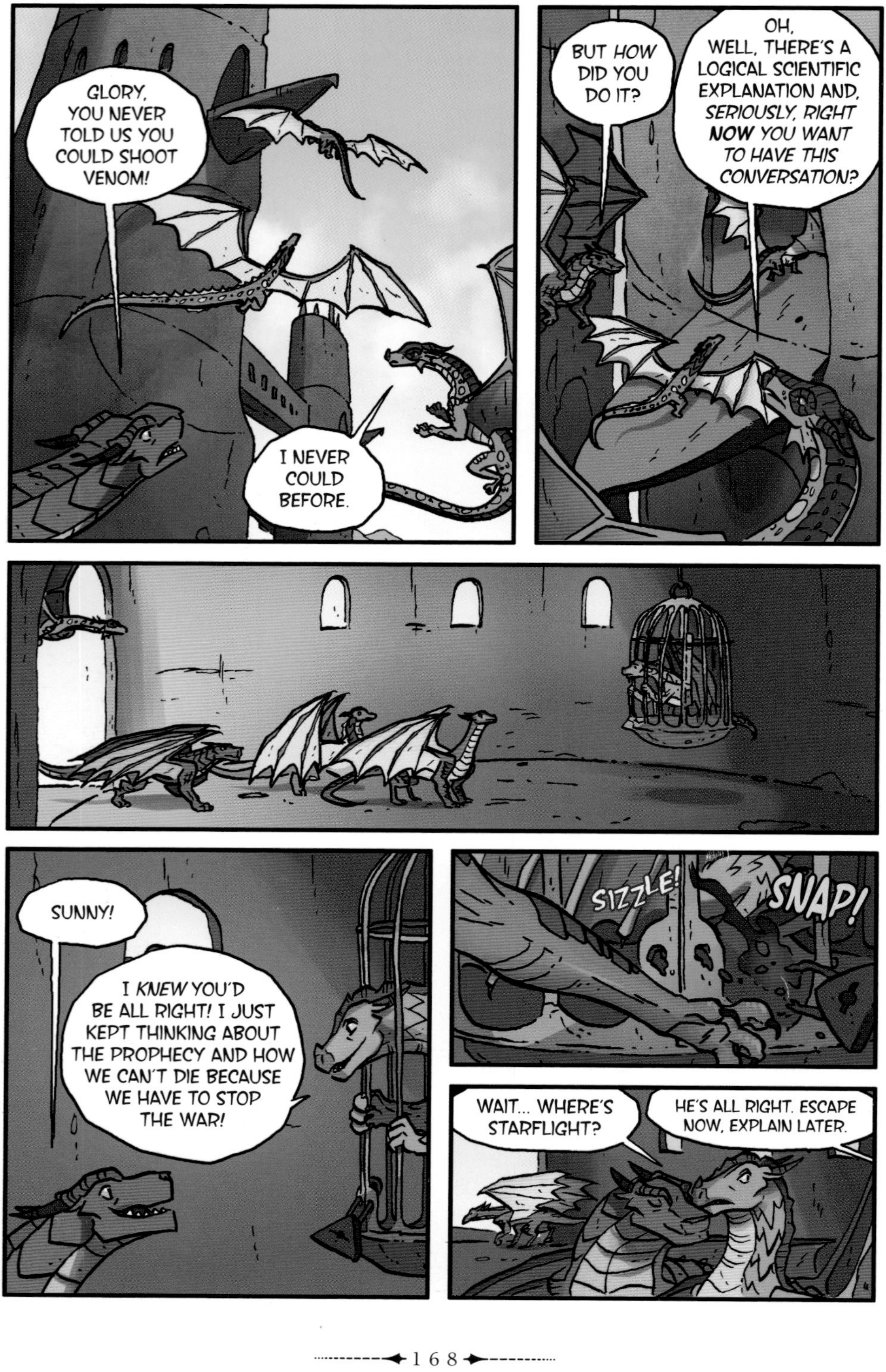
GLORY, YOU NEVER TOLD US YOU COULD SHOOT VENOM!
I NEVER COULD BEFORE.
BUT *HOW* DID YOU DO IT?
OH, WELL, THERE'S A LOGICAL SCIENTIFIC EXPLANATION AND, *SERIOUSLY, RIGHT* **NOW** *YOU WANT TO HAVE THIS CONVERSATION?*
SUNNY!
I *KNEW* YOU'D BE ALL RIGHT! I JUST KEPT THINKING ABOUT THE PROPHECY AND HOW WE CAN'T DIE BECAUSE WE HAVE TO STOP THE WAR!
SIZZLE!
SNAP!
WAIT... WHERE'S STARFLIGHT?
HE'S ALL RIGHT. ESCAPE NOW, EXPLAIN LATER.

CLAY, WAIT. MY MOTHER! IF QUEEN SCARLET ISN'T DEAD, SHE'LL KILL HER.

YOU'RE RIGHT. WE HAVE TO GET KESTREL OUT.

WHY? WHAT DO WE CARE?

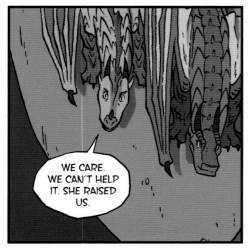

WE CARE. WE CAN'T HELP IT. SHE RAISED US.

I DON'T. SHE WAS GOING TO KILL ME.

SHE DIDN'T RAISE US TO CARE ABOUT HER. SHE RAISED US TO STAY ALIVE.

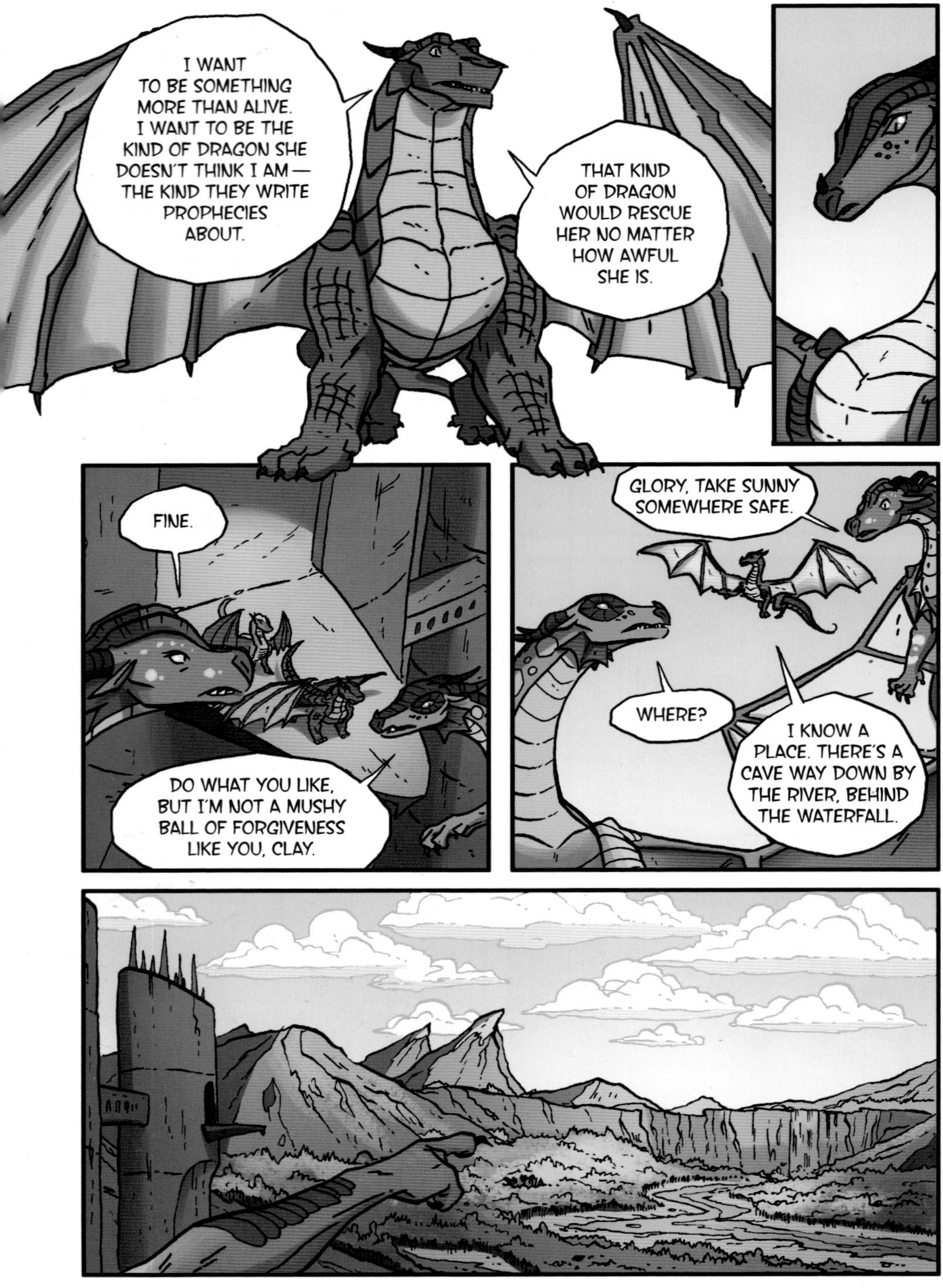
I WANT TO BE SOMETHING MORE THAN ALIVE. I WANT TO BE THE KIND OF DRAGON SHE DOESN'T THINK I AM — THE KIND THEY WRITE PROPHECIES ABOUT.
THAT KIND OF DRAGON WOULD RESCUE HER NO MATTER HOW AWFUL SHE IS.
FINE.
DO WHAT YOU LIKE, BUT I'M NOT A MUSHY BALL OF FORGIVENESS LIKE YOU, CLAY.
GLORY, TAKE SUNNY SOMEWHERE SAFE.
WHERE?
I KNOW A PLACE. THERE'S A CAVE WAY DOWN BY THE RIVER, BEHIND THE WATERFALL.

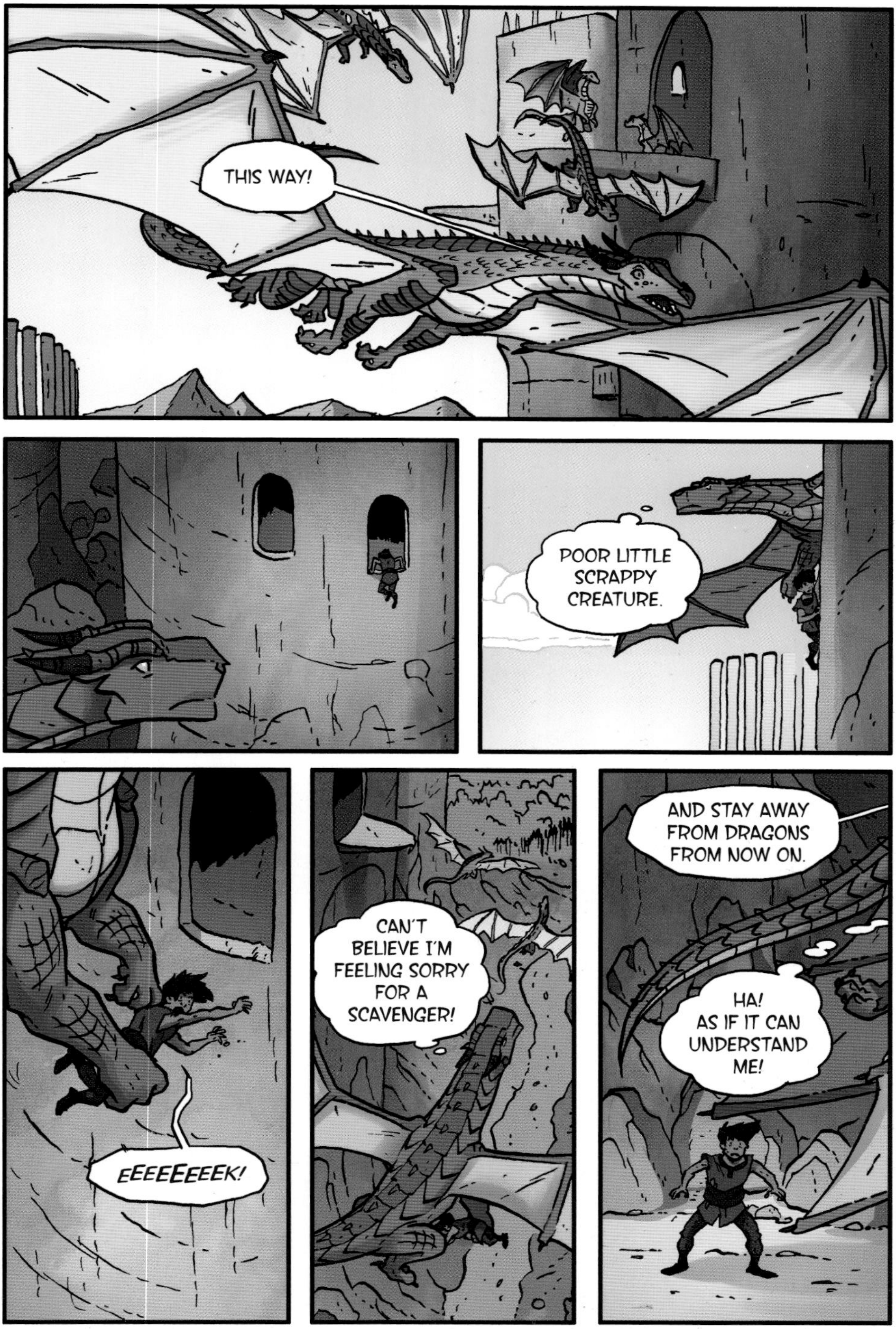
THIS WAY!
POOR LITTLE SCRAPPY CREATURE.
EEEEEEEEK!
CAN'T BELIEVE I'M FEELING SORRY FOR A SCAVENGER!
AND STAY AWAY FROM DRAGONS FROM NOW ON.
HA! AS IF IT CAN UNDERSTAND ME!

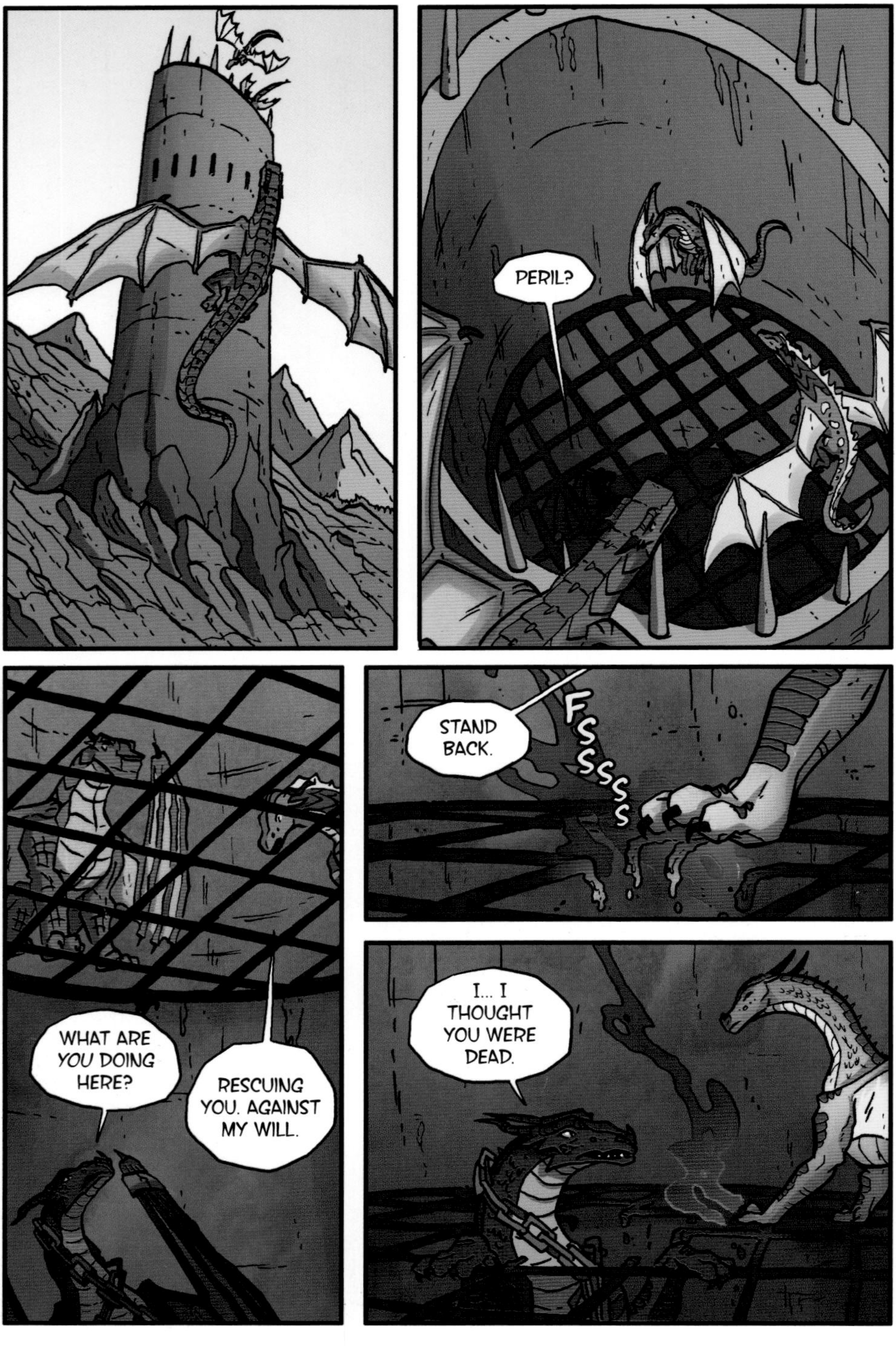
PERIL?
STAND BACK.
FSSSSS
WHAT ARE YOU DOING HERE?
RESCUING YOU. AGAINST MY WILL.
I... I THOUGHT YOU WERE DEAD.

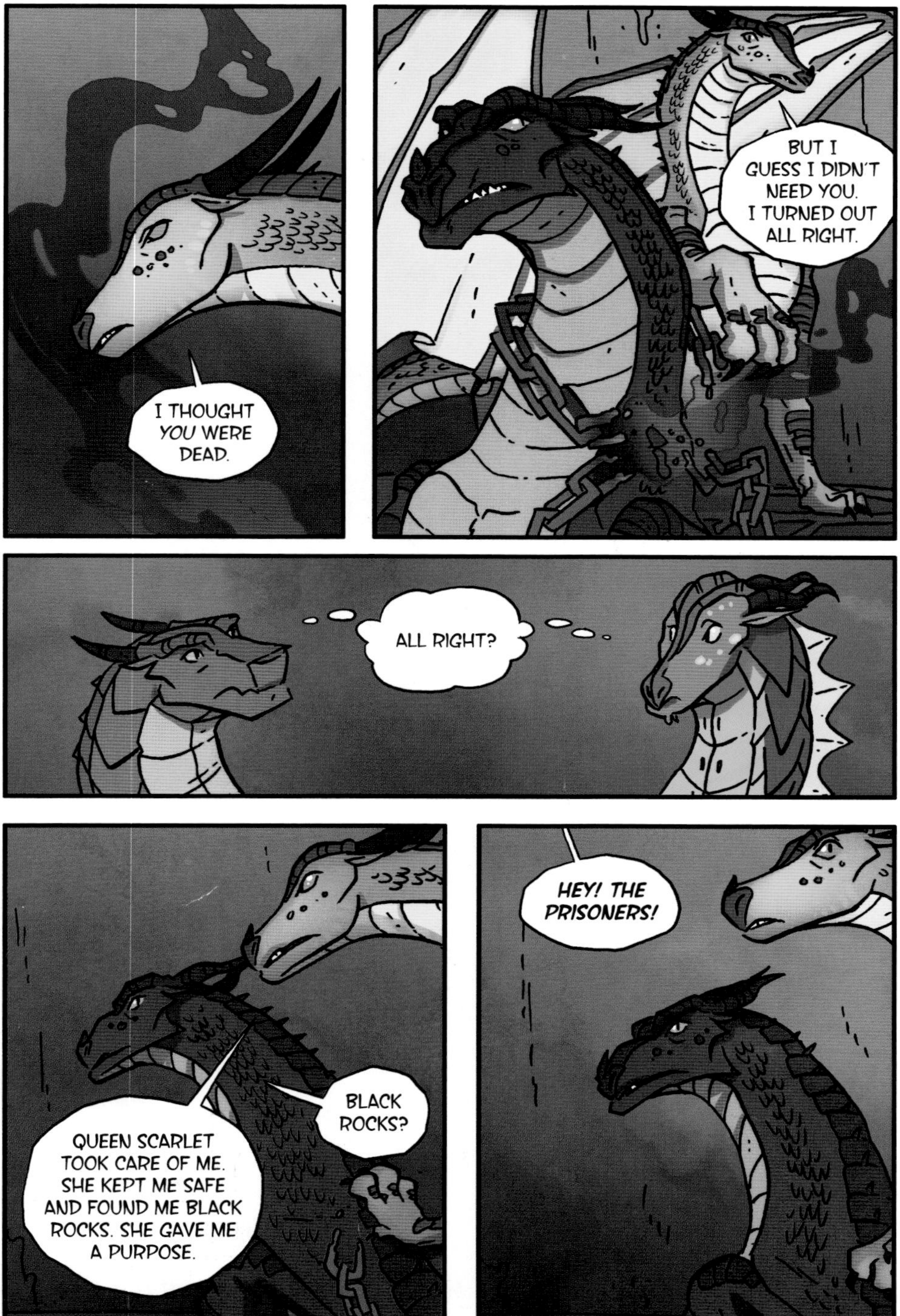
I THOUGHT *YOU* WERE DEAD.
BUT I GUESS I DIDN'T NEED YOU. I TURNED OUT ALL RIGHT.
ALL RIGHT?
QUEEN SCARLET TOOK CARE OF ME. SHE KEPT ME SAFE AND FOUND ME BLACK ROCKS. SHE GAVE ME A PURPOSE.
BLACK ROCKS?
HEY! THE PRISONERS!

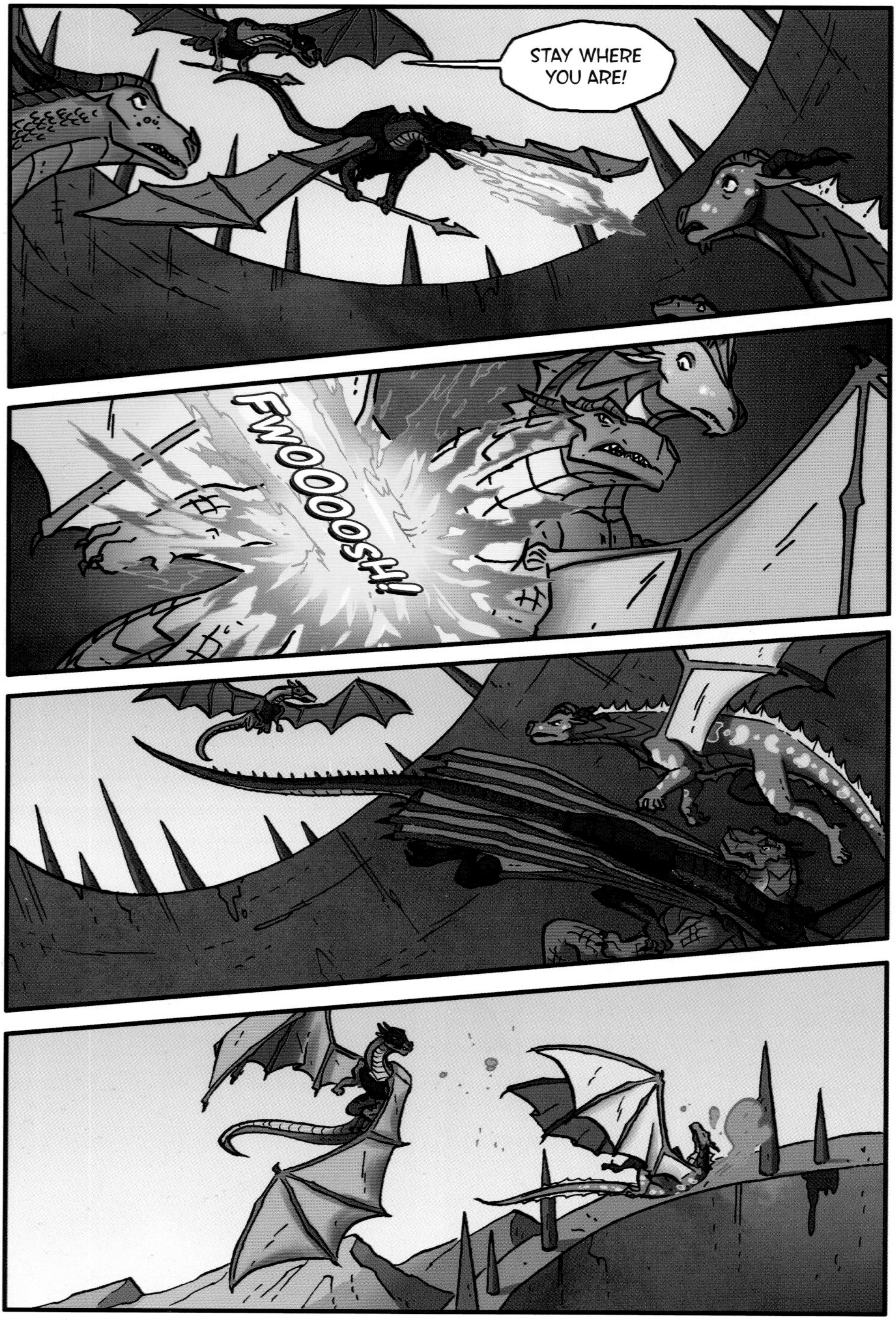
STAY WHERE YOU ARE!
FWOOOOSH!

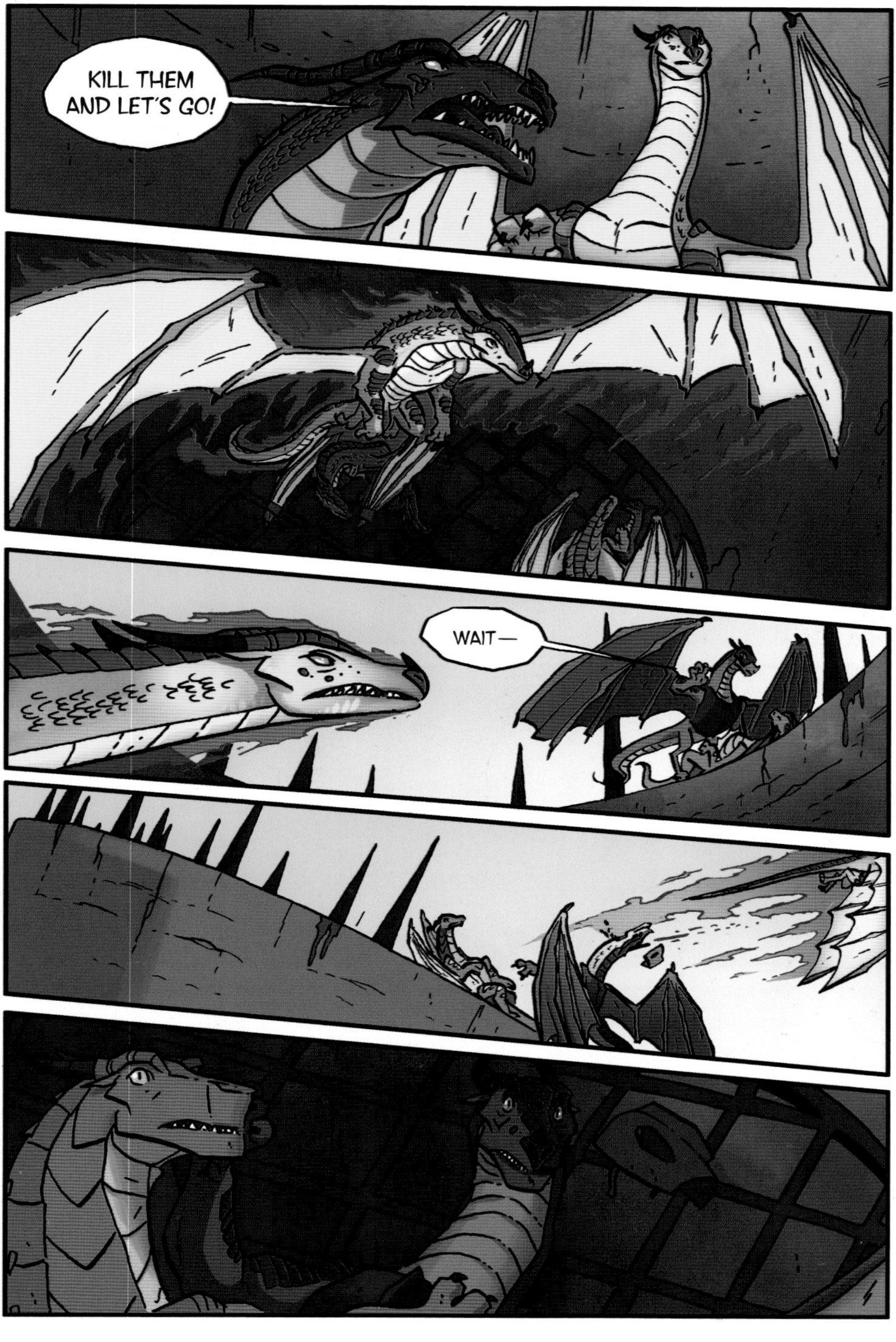
KILL THEM AND LET'S GO!
WAIT—

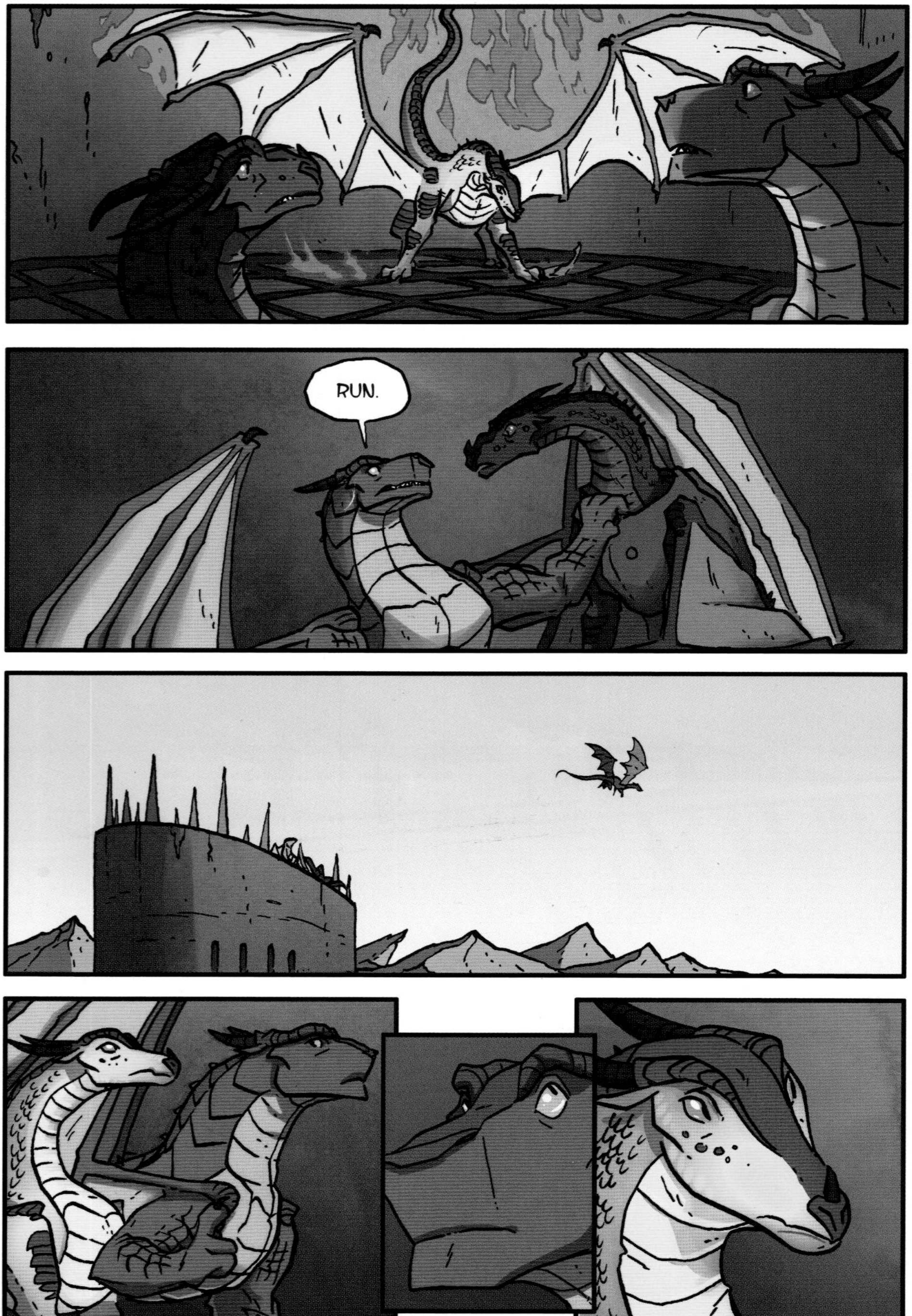
RUN.

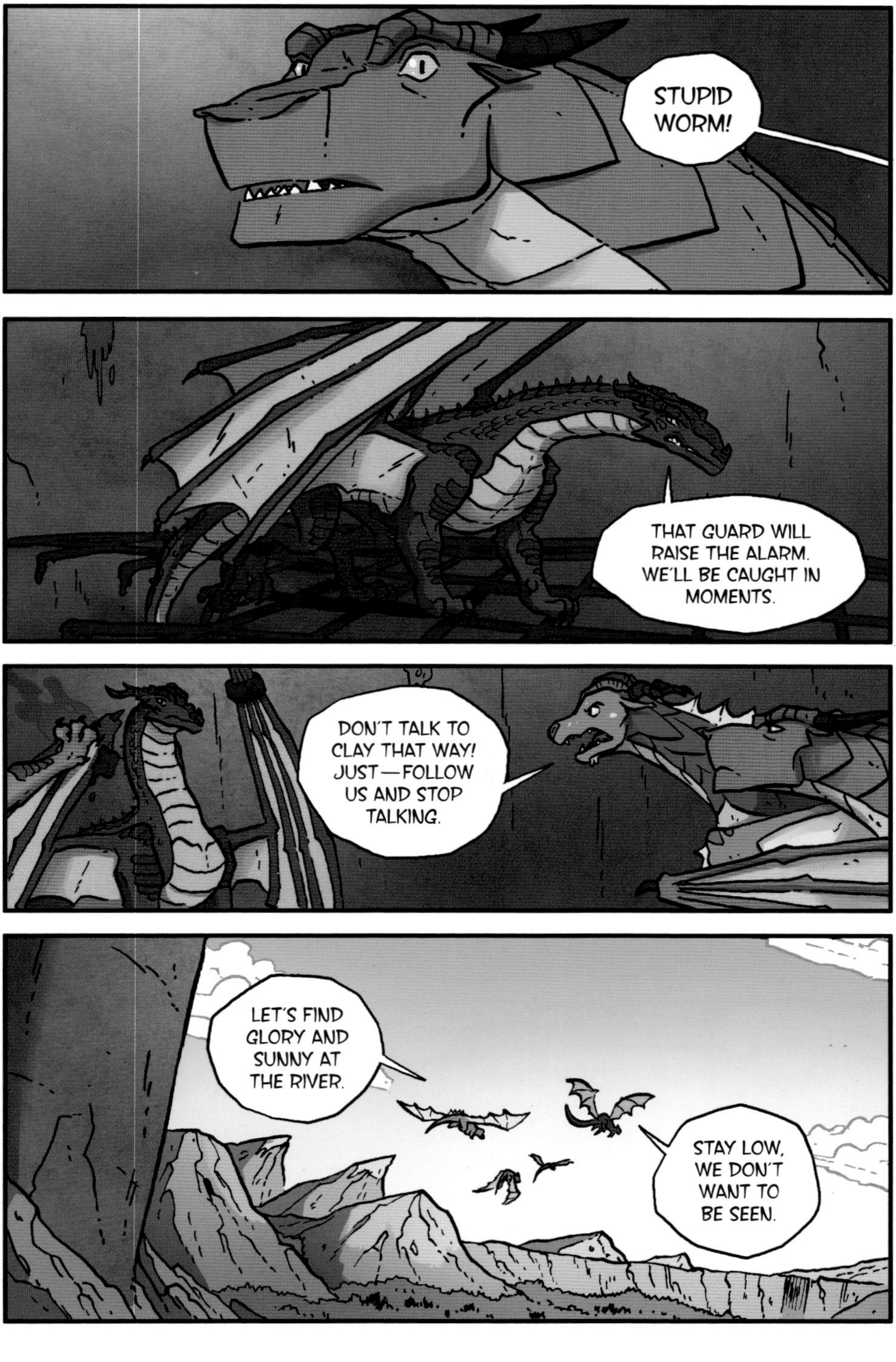
STUPID WORM!
THAT GUARD WILL RAISE THE ALARM. WE'LL BE CAUGHT IN MOMENTS.
DON'T TALK TO CLAY THAT WAY! JUST—FOLLOW US AND STOP TALKING.
LET'S FIND GLORY AND SUNNY AT THE RIVER.
STAY LOW, WE DON'T WANT TO BE SEEN.

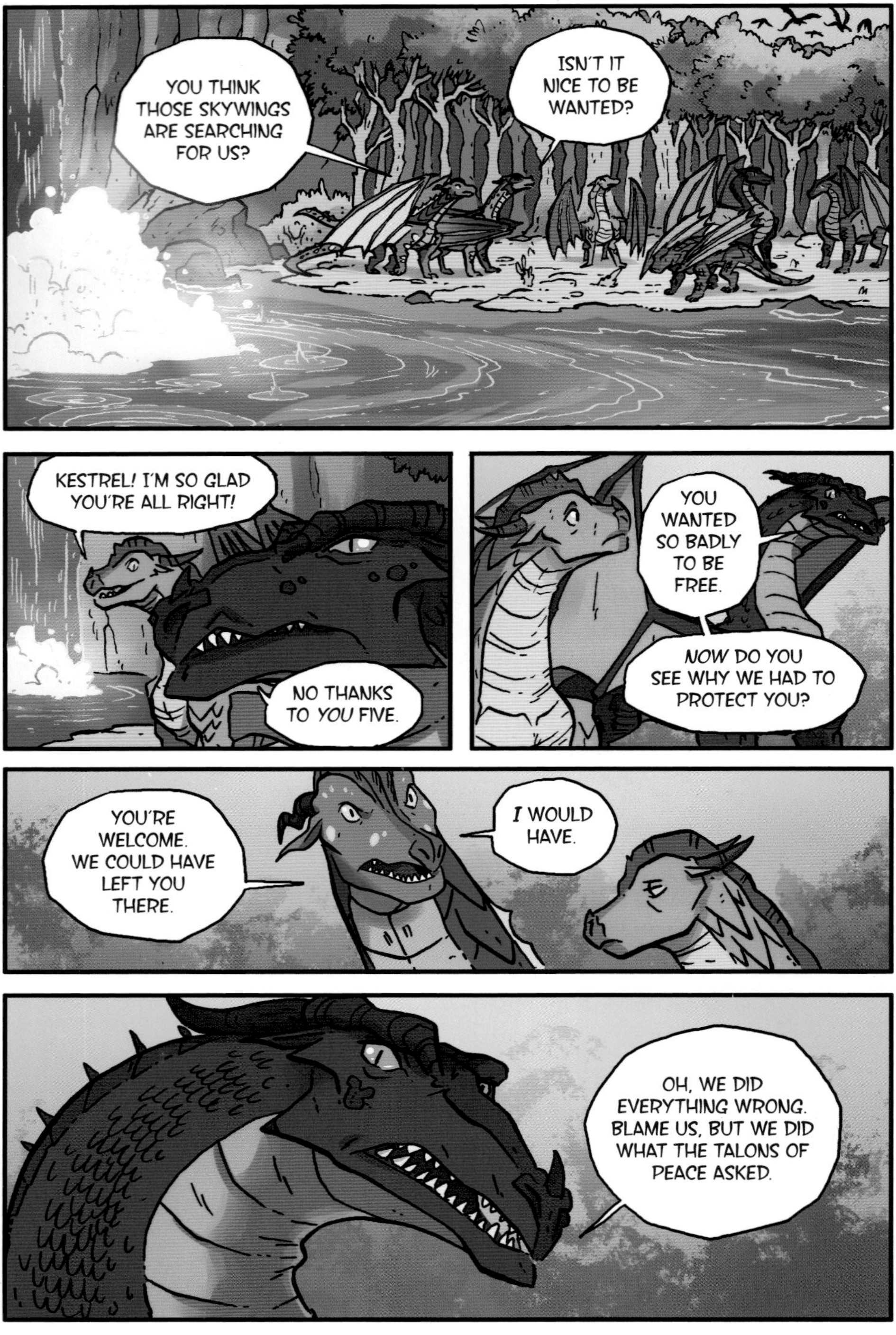
YOU THINK THOSE SKYWINGS ARE SEARCHING FOR US?
ISN'T IT NICE TO BE WANTED?
KESTREL! I'M SO GLAD YOU'RE ALL RIGHT!
NO THANKS TO *YOU* FIVE.
YOU WANTED SO BADLY TO BE FREE.
NOW DO YOU SEE WHY WE HAD TO PROTECT YOU?
YOU'RE WELCOME. WE COULD HAVE LEFT YOU THERE.
I WOULD HAVE.
OH, WE DID EVERYTHING WRONG. BLAME US, BUT WE DID WHAT THE TALONS OF PEACE ASKED.

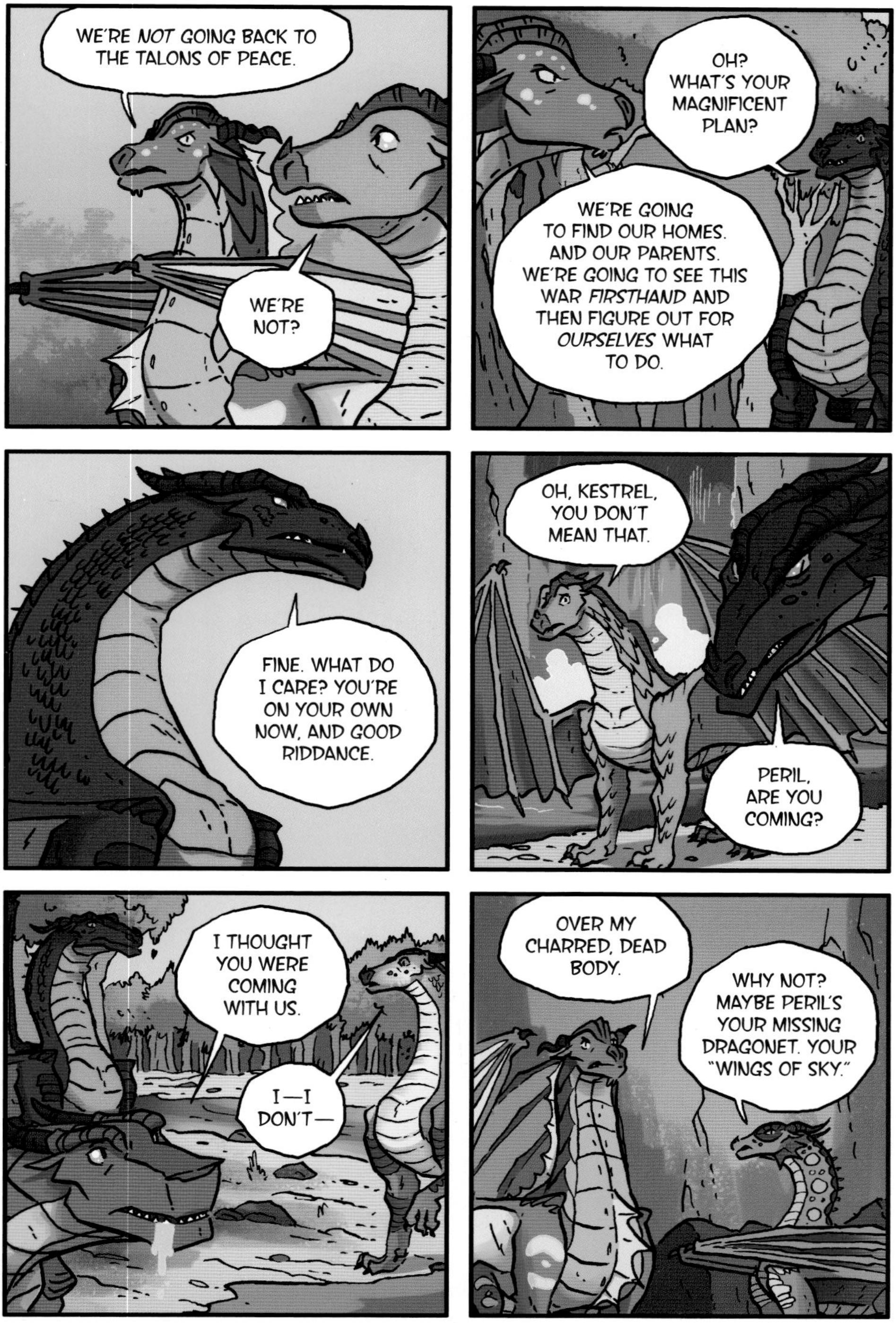
WE'RE *NOT* GOING BACK TO THE TALONS OF PEACE.
WE'RE NOT?
OH? WHAT'S YOUR MAGNIFICENT PLAN?
WE'RE GOING TO FIND OUR HOMES. AND OUR PARENTS. WE'RE GOING TO SEE THIS WAR *FIRSTHAND* AND THEN FIGURE OUT FOR *OURSELVES* WHAT TO DO.
FINE. WHAT DO I CARE? YOU'RE ON YOUR OWN NOW, AND GOOD RIDDANCE.
OH, KESTREL, YOU DON'T MEAN THAT.
PERIL, ARE YOU COMING?
I THOUGHT YOU WERE COMING WITH US.
I—I DON'T—
OVER MY CHARRED, DEAD BODY.
WHY NOT? MAYBE PERIL'S YOUR MISSING DRAGONET. YOUR "WINGS OF SKY."

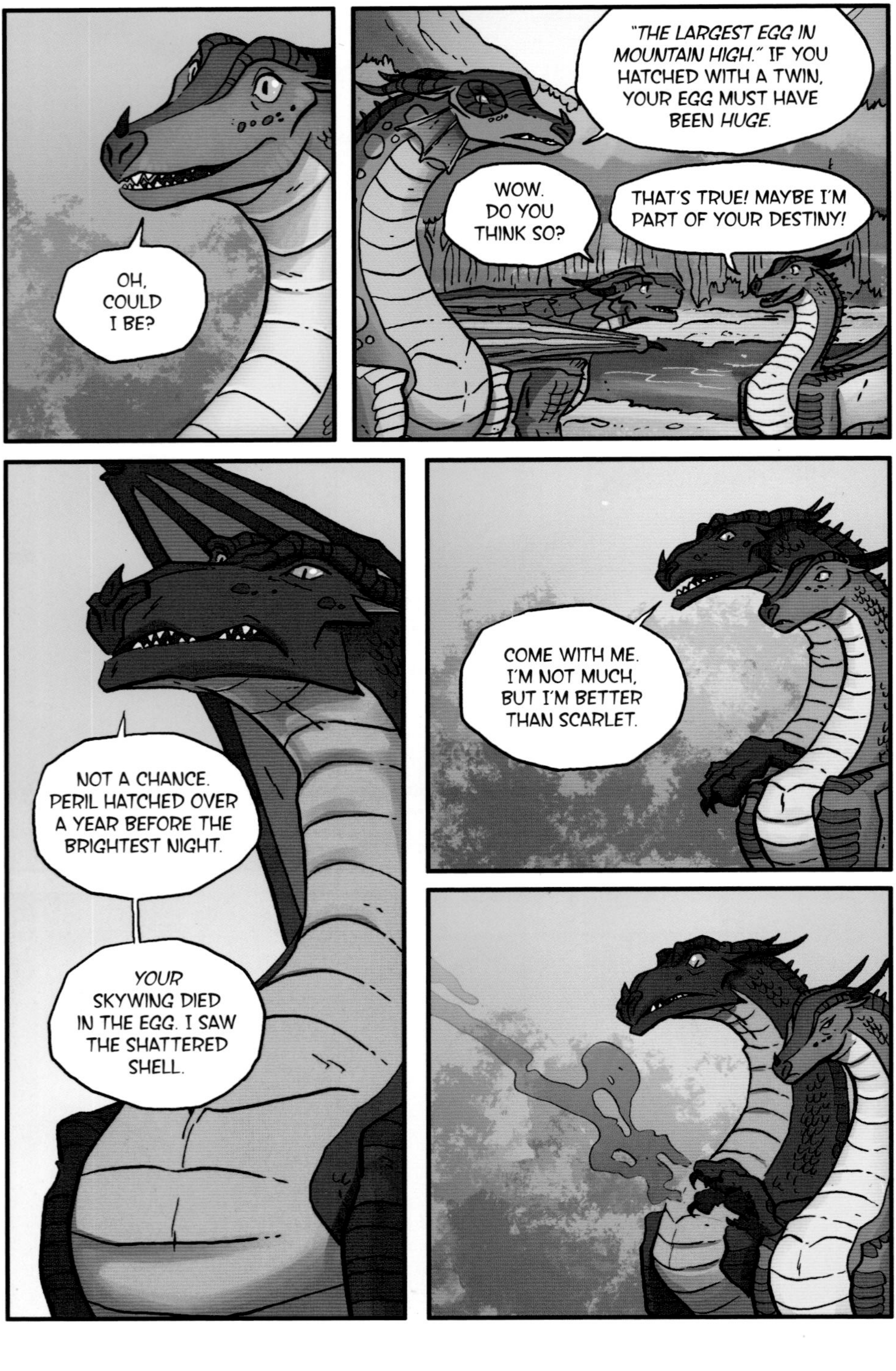
OH, COULD I BE?
"THE LARGEST EGG IN MOUNTAIN HIGH." IF YOU HATCHED WITH A TWIN, YOUR EGG MUST HAVE BEEN *HUGE*.
WOW. DO YOU THINK SO?
THAT'S TRUE! MAYBE I'M PART OF YOUR DESTINY!
NOT A CHANCE. PERIL HATCHED OVER A YEAR BEFORE THE BRIGHTEST NIGHT.
YOUR SKYWING DIED IN THE EGG. I SAW THE SHATTERED SHELL.
COME WITH ME. I'M NOT MUCH, BUT I'M BETTER THAN SCARLET.

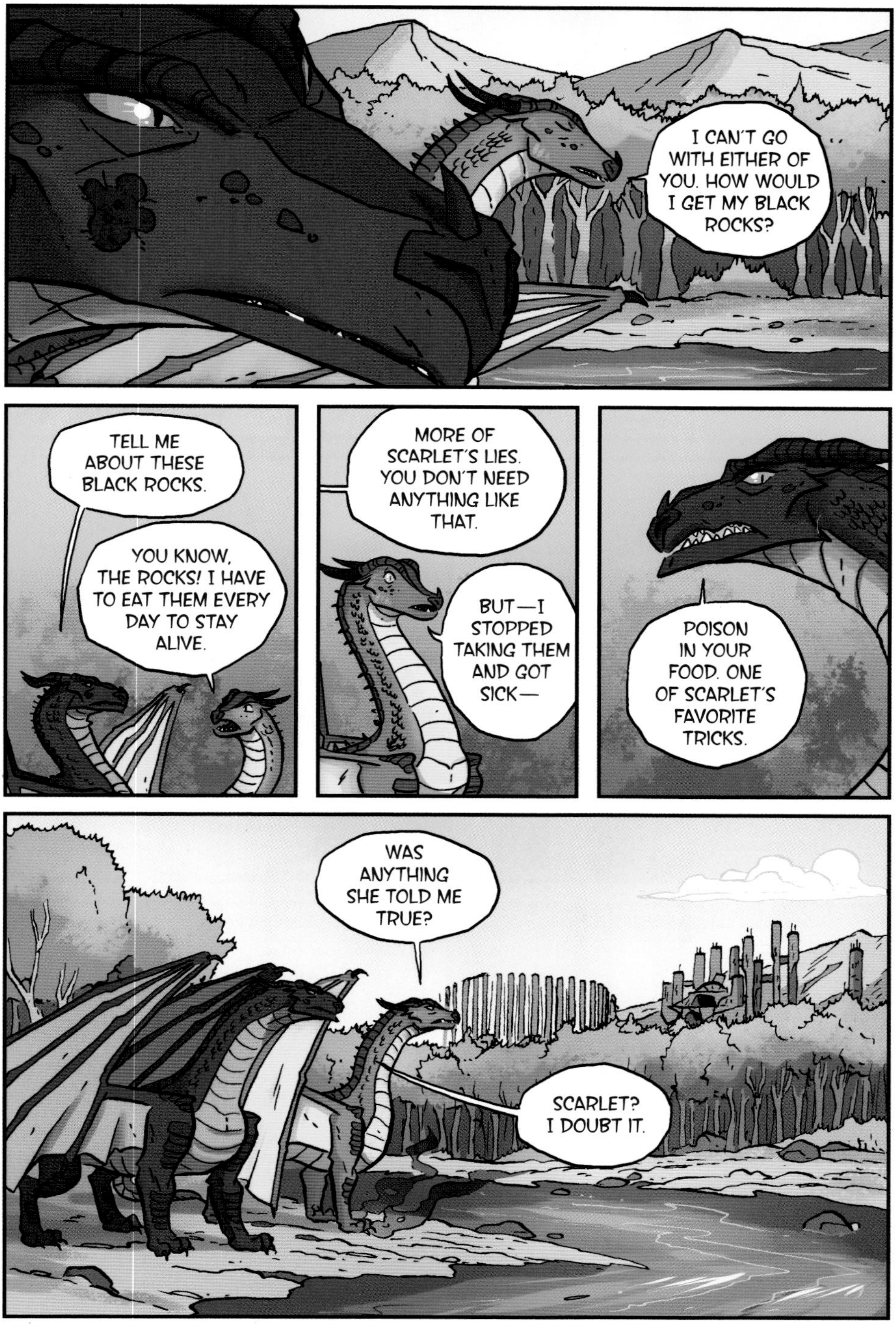
I CAN'T GO WITH EITHER OF YOU. HOW WOULD I GET MY BLACK ROCKS?
TELL ME ABOUT THESE BLACK ROCKS.
YOU KNOW, THE ROCKS! I HAVE TO EAT THEM EVERY DAY TO STAY ALIVE.
MORE OF SCARLET'S LIES. YOU DON'T NEED ANYTHING LIKE THAT.
BUT—I STOPPED TAKING THEM AND GOT SICK—
POISON IN YOUR FOOD. ONE OF SCARLET'S FAVORITE TRICKS.
WAS ANYTHING SHE TOLD ME TRUE?
SCARLET? I DOUBT IT.

BEFORE YOU GO, TELL US WHAT YOU KNOW ABOUT OUR EGGS. WE DESERVE TO KNOW WHERE WE CAME FROM.

NO SURPRISES WITH YOU. WEBS STOLE YOUR EGG FROM THE SEAWING QUEEN'S HATCHERY.

TSUNAMI! YOU REALLY *ARE* ROYALTY!

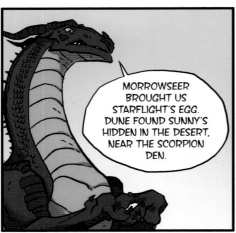

MORROWSEER BROUGHT US STARFLIGHT'S EGG. DUNE FOUND SUNNY'S HIDDEN IN THE DESERT, NEAR THE SCORPION DEN.

AND BEFORE SHE DIED, A MUDWING NAMED ASHA BROUGHT US YOUR BIG, STRONG HERO FROM THE DIAMOND SPRAY DELTA, WHERE THE *LOWEST-* BORN MUDWINGS LIVE.

THE DIAMOND SPRAY DELTA! I BET THAT'S NOT FAR FROM HERE.

WHAT ABOUT ME?

WEBS SCROUNGED YOU UP WHEN WE LOST THE SKYWING EGG. I NEVER ASKED HIM WHERE. I KNEW *YOU* WEREN'T IMPORTANT.

OH, GO AWAY! YOU'RE JUST MEAN *ALL THE TIME.*

EVERYTHING I SAY IS TRUE.

I NEVER IMAGINED YOU LIKE THIS.

I'M THE WAY LIFE MADE ME. TAKE IT OR LEAVE IT.

SHE'S NOT THE KINDEST DRAGON, BUT SHE DID TRY TO SAVE YOU.

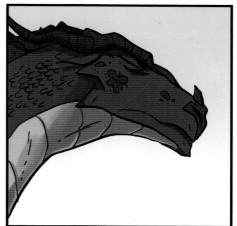

NO. NOT NOW. MAYBE—

MAYBE SOMEDAY.

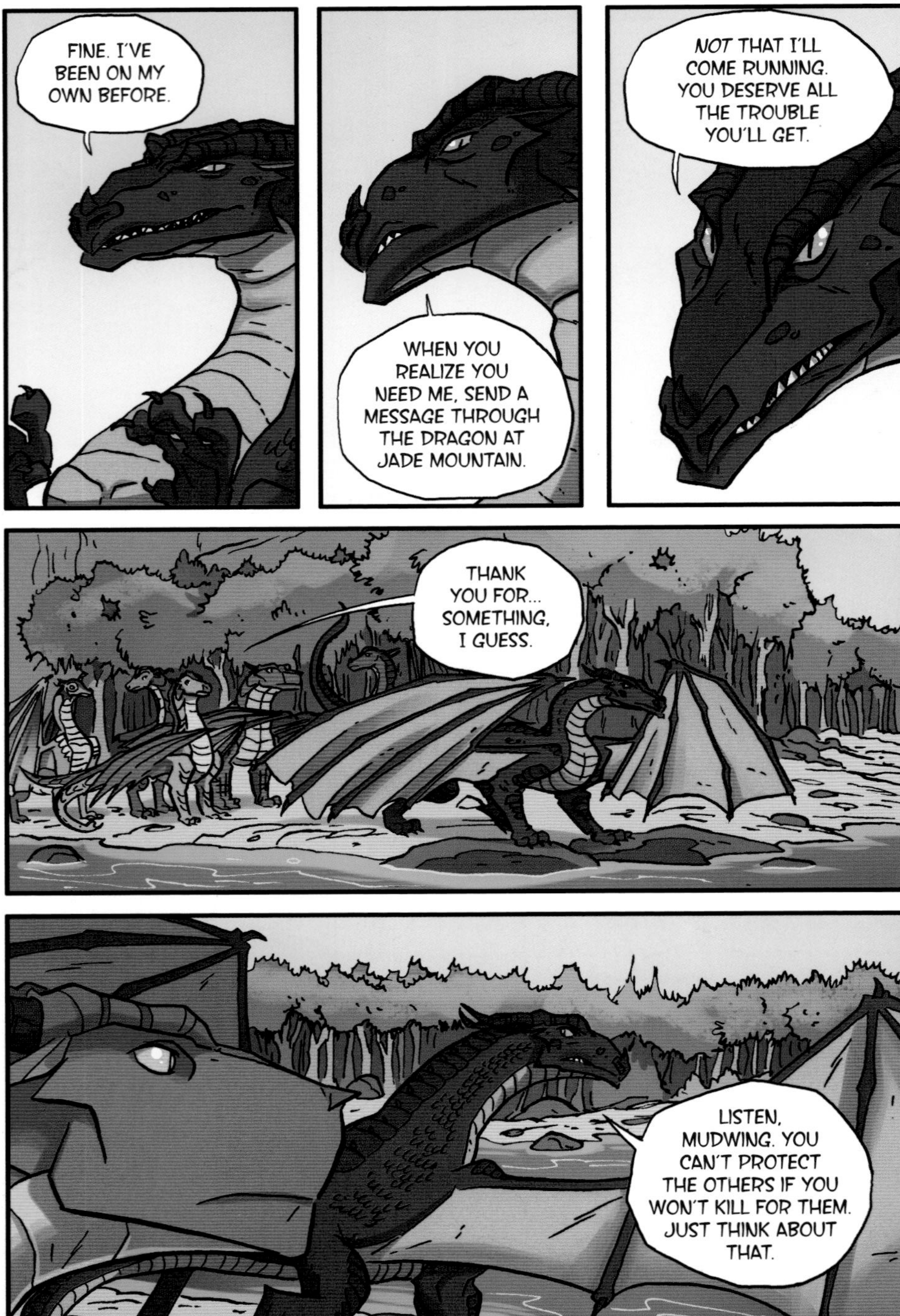
FINE. I'VE BEEN ON MY OWN BEFORE.
WHEN YOU REALIZE YOU NEED ME, SEND A MESSAGE THROUGH THE DRAGON AT JADE MOUNTAIN.
NOT THAT I'LL COME RUNNING. YOU DESERVE ALL THE TROUBLE YOU'LL GET.
THANK YOU FOR... SOMETHING, I GUESS.
LISTEN, MUDWING. YOU CAN'T PROTECT THE OTHERS IF YOU WON'T KILL FOR THEM. JUST THINK ABOUT THAT.

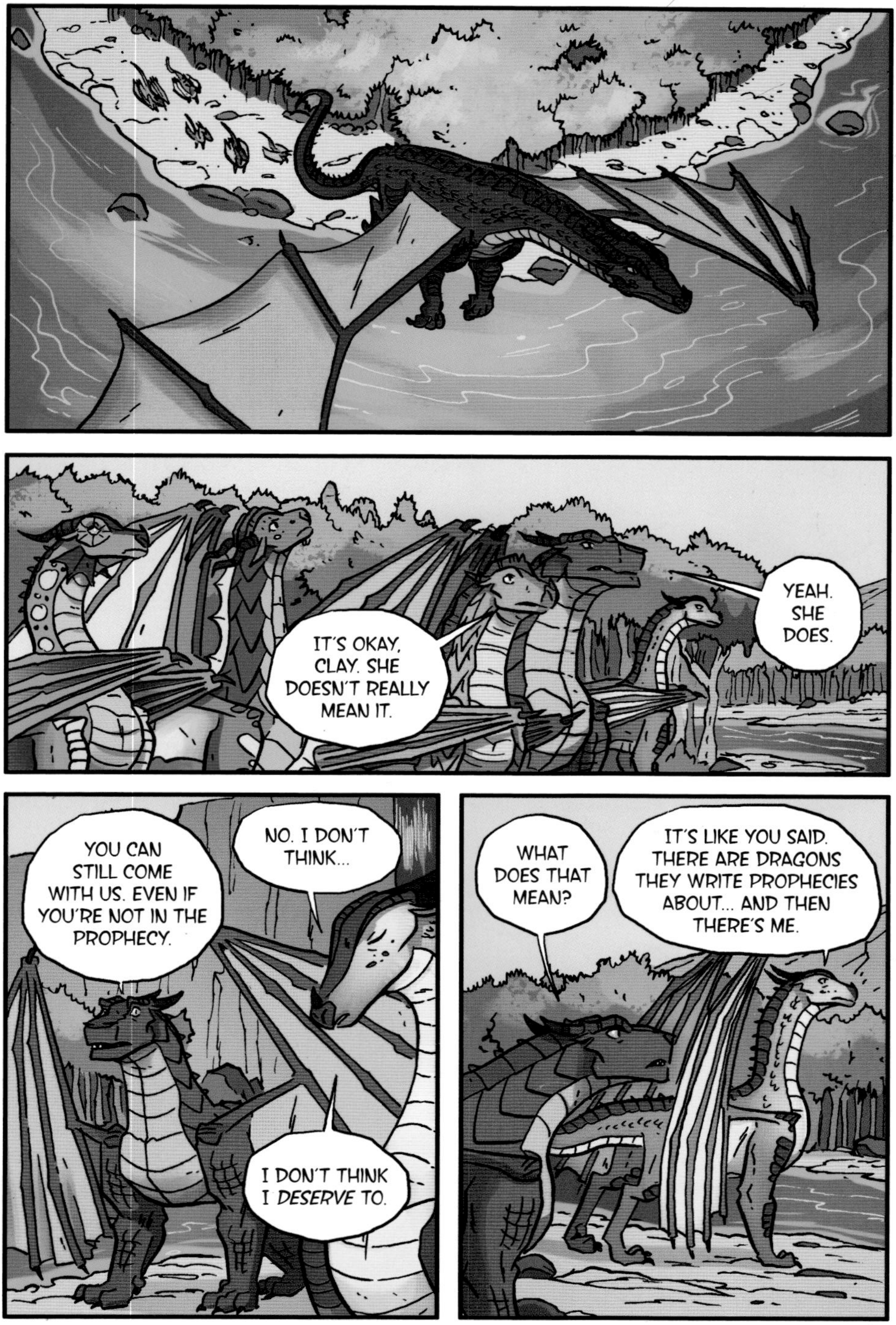
IT'S OKAY, CLAY. SHE DOESN'T REALLY MEAN IT.
YEAH. SHE DOES.
YOU CAN STILL COME WITH US. EVEN IF YOU'RE NOT IN THE PROPHECY.
NO. I DON'T THINK...
I DON'T THINK I *DESERVE* TO.
WHAT DOES THAT MEAN?
IT'S LIKE YOU SAID. THERE ARE DRAGONS THEY WRITE PROPHECIES ABOUT... AND THEN THERE'S ME.

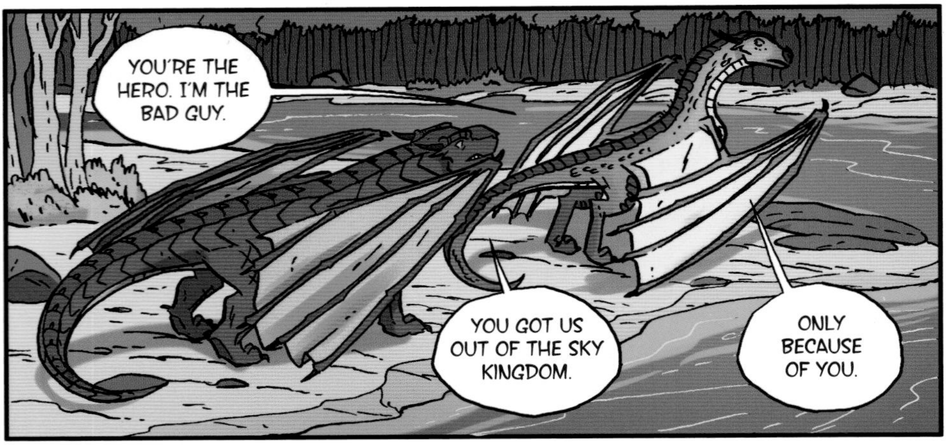
YOU'RE THE HERO. I'M THE BAD GUY.
YOU GOT US OUT OF THE SKY KINGDOM.
ONLY BECAUSE OF YOU.

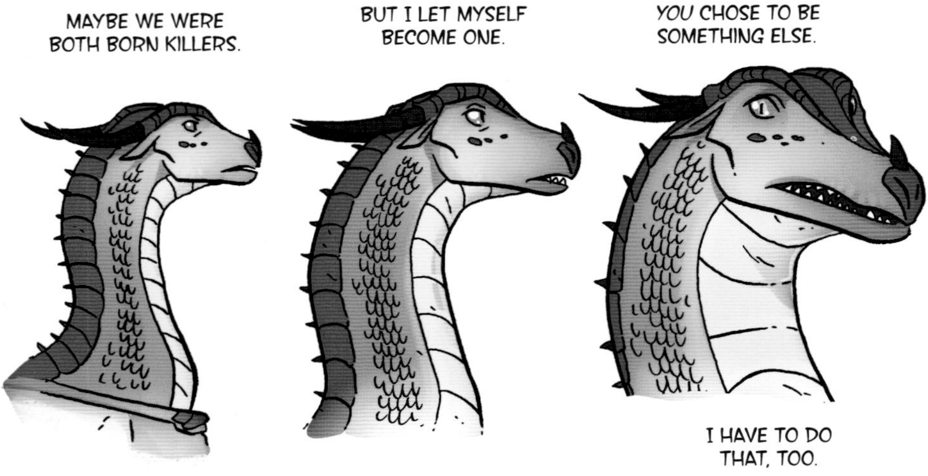
MAYBE WE WERE BOTH BORN KILLERS.
BUT I LET MYSELF BECOME ONE.
YOU CHOSE TO BE SOMETHING ELSE.
I HAVE TO DO THAT, TOO.

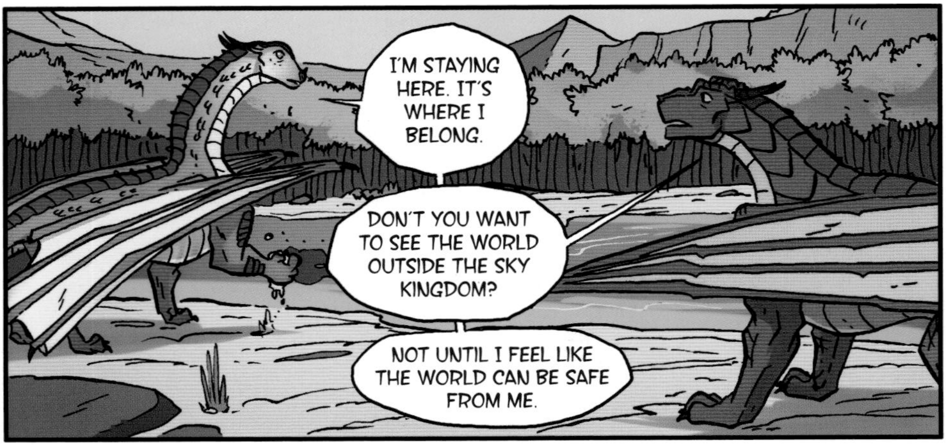
I'M STAYING HERE. IT'S WHERE I BELONG.
DON'T YOU WANT TO SEE THE WORLD OUTSIDE THE SKY KINGDOM?
NOT UNTIL I FEEL LIKE THE WORLD CAN BE SAFE FROM ME.

CAN WE GET GOING? BEFORE WE ATTRACT COMPANY?

I'LL WAIT TILL YOU'RE GONE, THEN FLY IN A DIFFERENT DIRECTION. MAYBE I CAN LEAD THEM AWAY.

ARE YOU SURE? WHAT IF BURN TRIES TO PUNISH YOU?

THERE'S ONLY ONE GOOD THING ABOUT ME. NO DRAGON CAN HURT ME.

EXCEPT YOU.

THAT'S NOT THE ONLY GOOD THING ABOUT YOU, PERIL.

YOU MAKE ME HOPE THAT'S TRUE.

CLAY. WE *HAVE* TO GO.

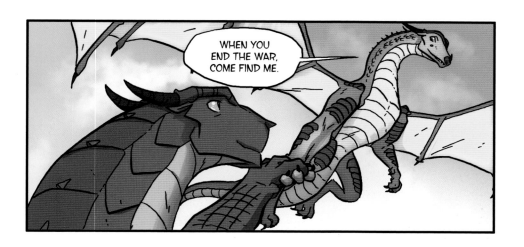

WHEN YOU END THE WAR, COME FIND ME.

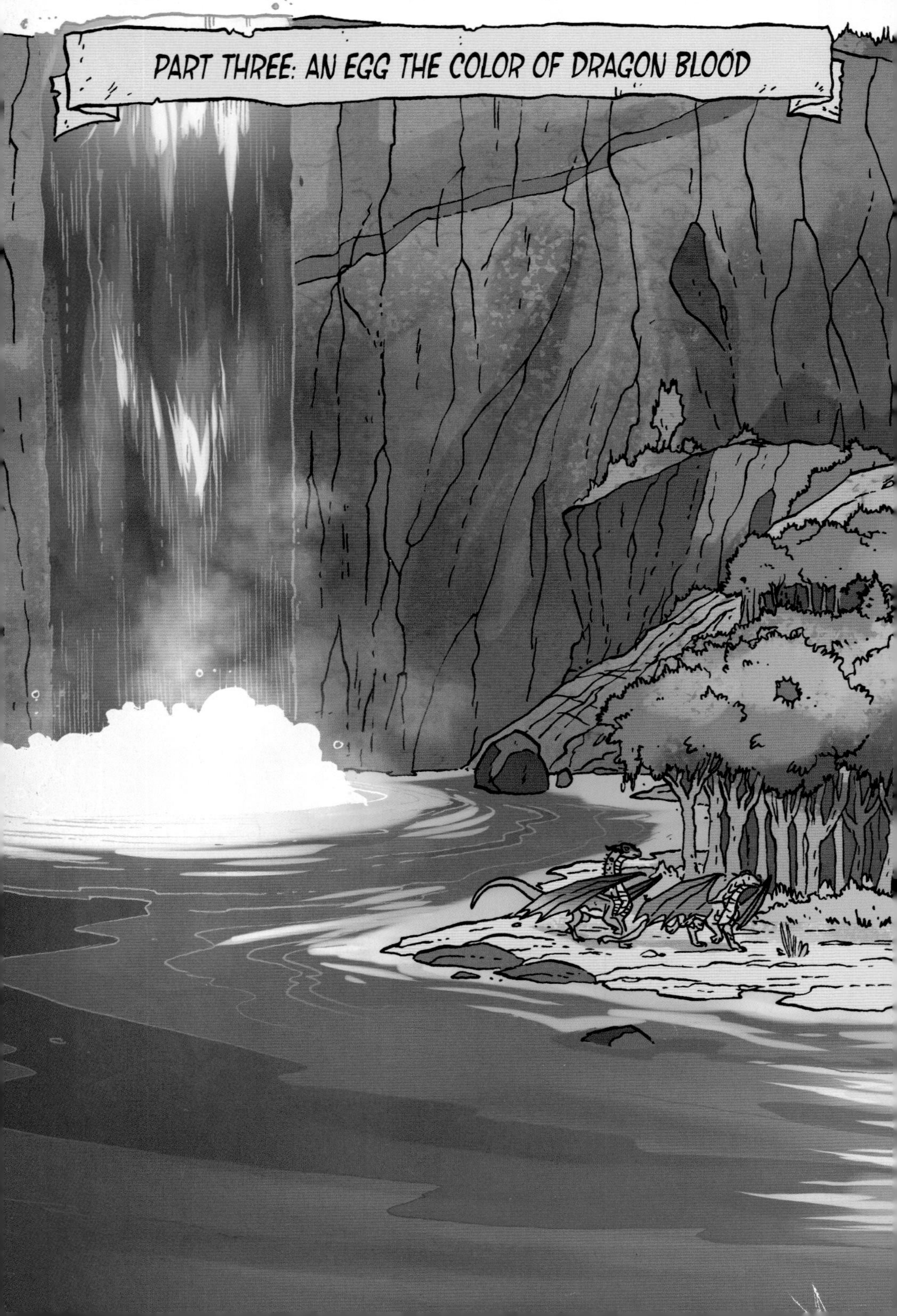
PART THREE: AN EGG THE COLOR OF DRAGON BLOOD

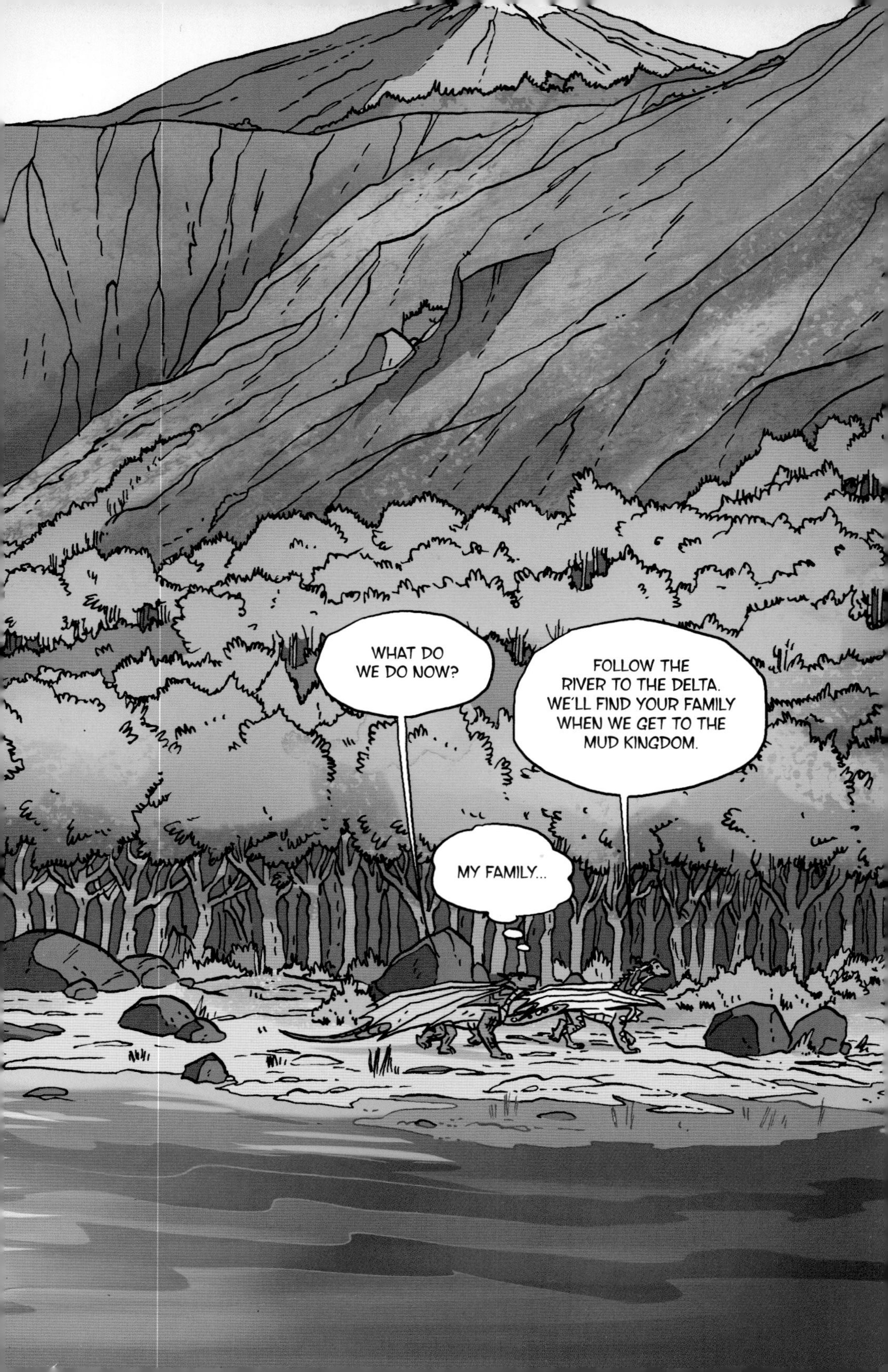
WHAT DO WE DO NOW?
FOLLOW THE RIVER TO THE DELTA. WE'LL FIND YOUR FAMILY WHEN WE GET TO THE MUD KINGDOM.
MY FAMILY...

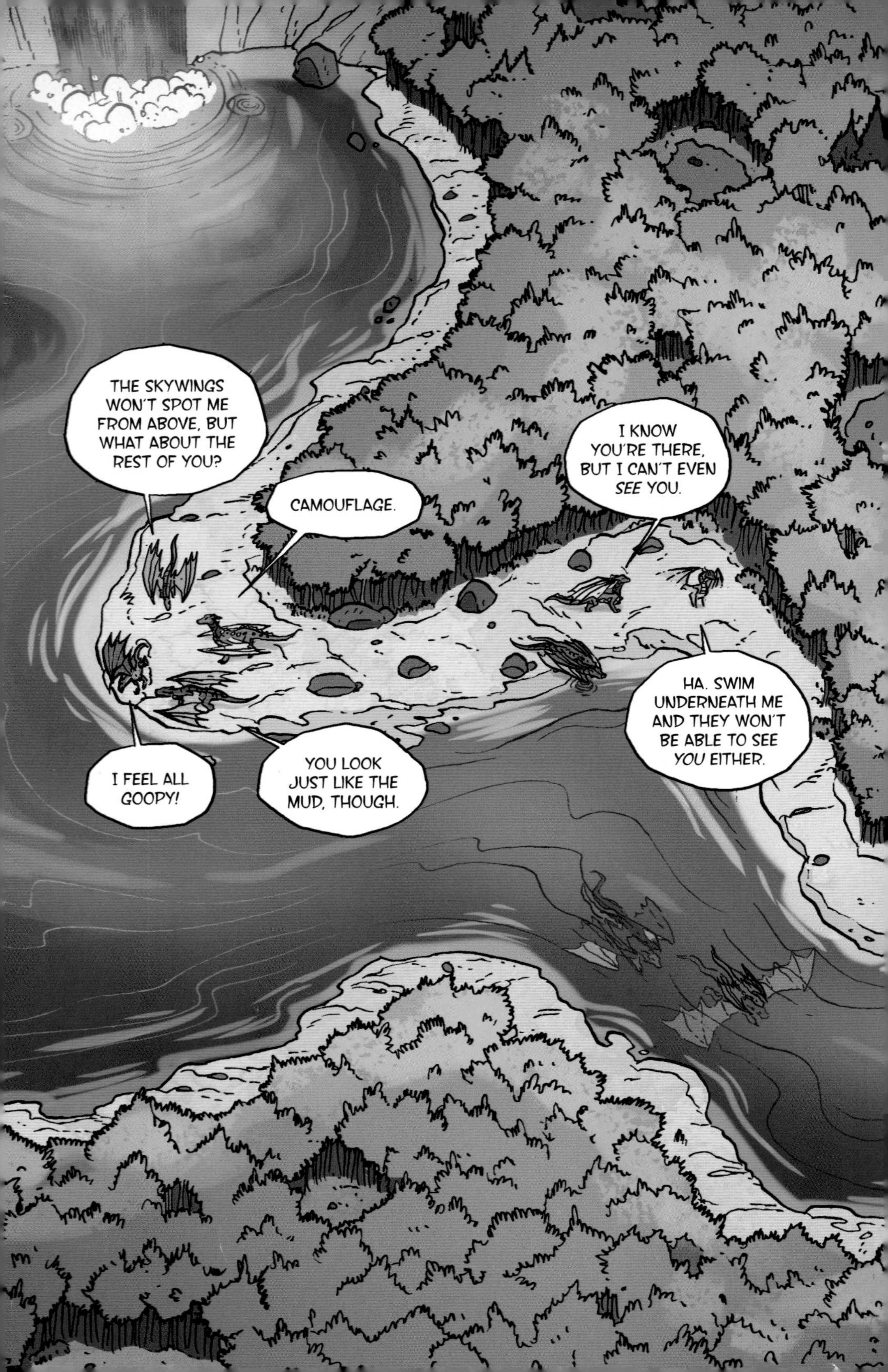
THE SKYWINGS WON'T SPOT ME FROM ABOVE, BUT WHAT ABOUT THE REST OF YOU?
CAMOUFLAGE.
I FEEL ALL GOOPY!
YOU LOOK JUST LIKE THE MUD, THOUGH.
I KNOW YOU'RE THERE, BUT I CAN'T EVEN *SEE* YOU.
HA. SWIM UNDERNEATH ME AND THEY WON'T BE ABLE TO SEE *YOU* EITHER.

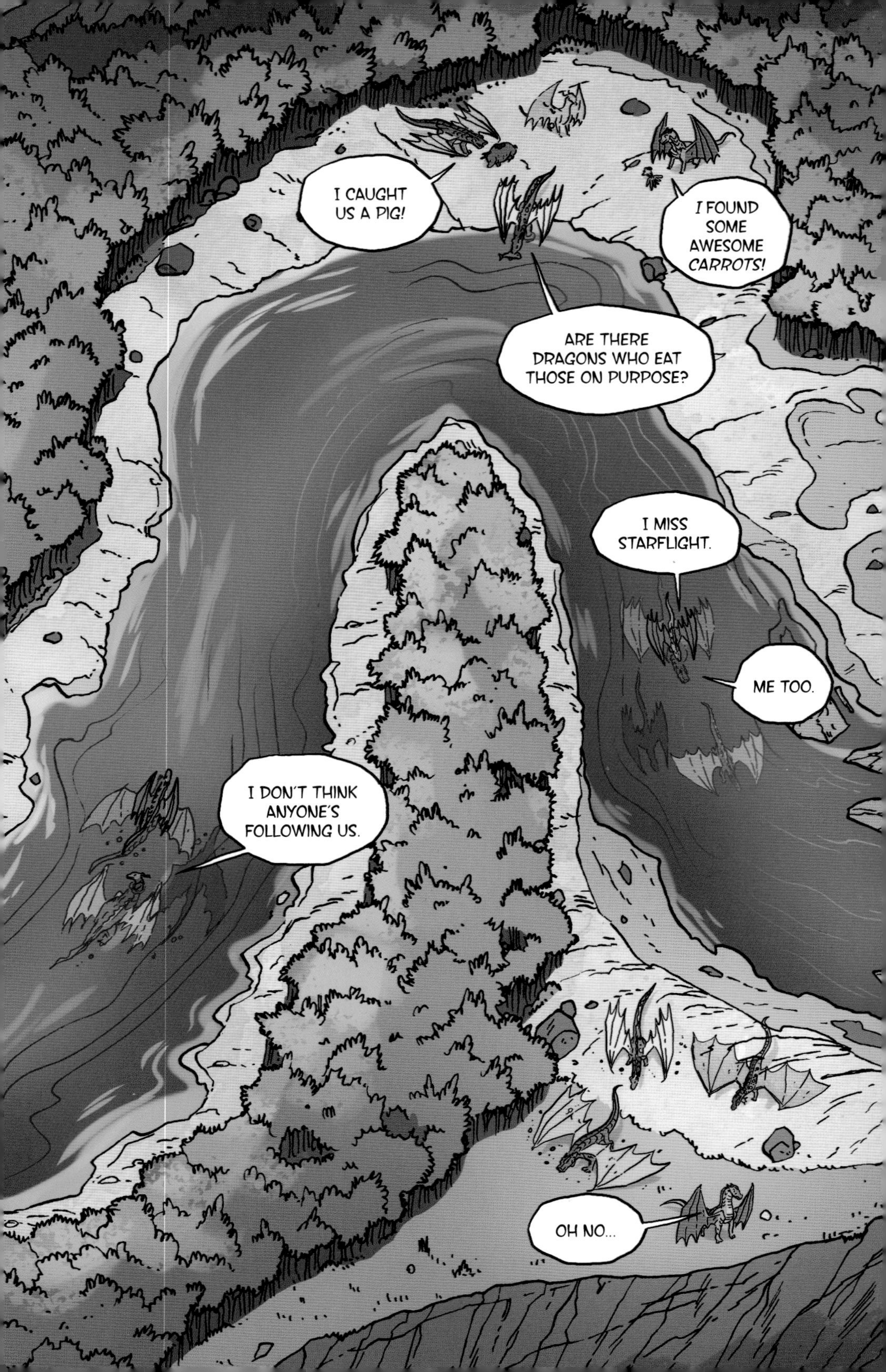
I CAUGHT US A PIG!
I FOUND SOME AWESOME *CARROTS!*
ARE THERE DRAGONS WHO EAT THOSE ON PURPOSE?
I MISS STARFLIGHT.
ME TOO.
I DON'T THINK ANYONE'S FOLLOWING US.
OH NO...

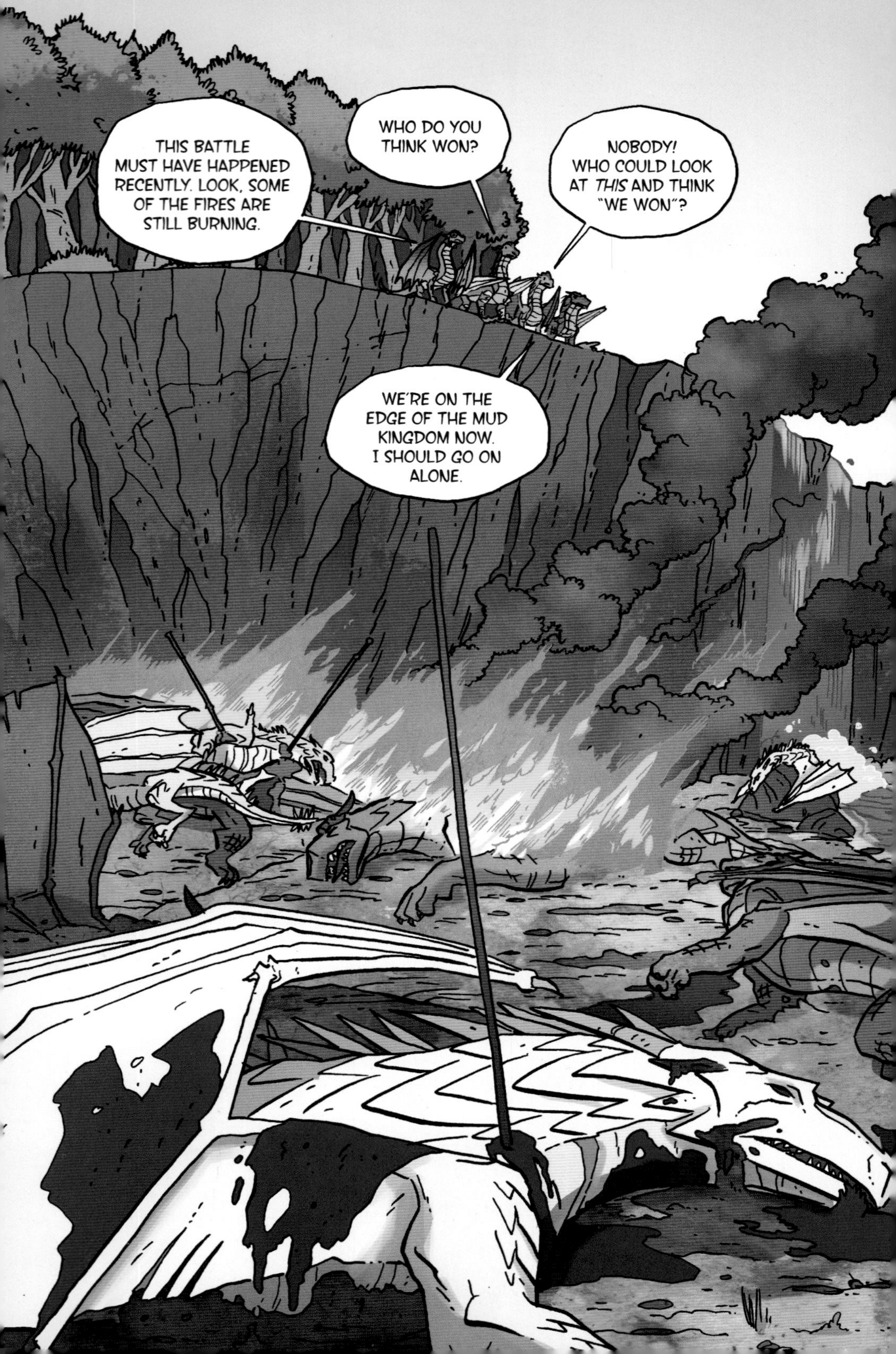
THIS BATTLE MUST HAVE HAPPENED RECENTLY. LOOK, SOME OF THE FIRES ARE STILL BURNING.
WHO DO YOU THINK WON?
NOBODY! WHO COULD LOOK AT *THIS* AND THINK "WE WON"?
WE'RE ON THE EDGE OF THE MUD KINGDOM NOW. I SHOULD GO ON ALONE.

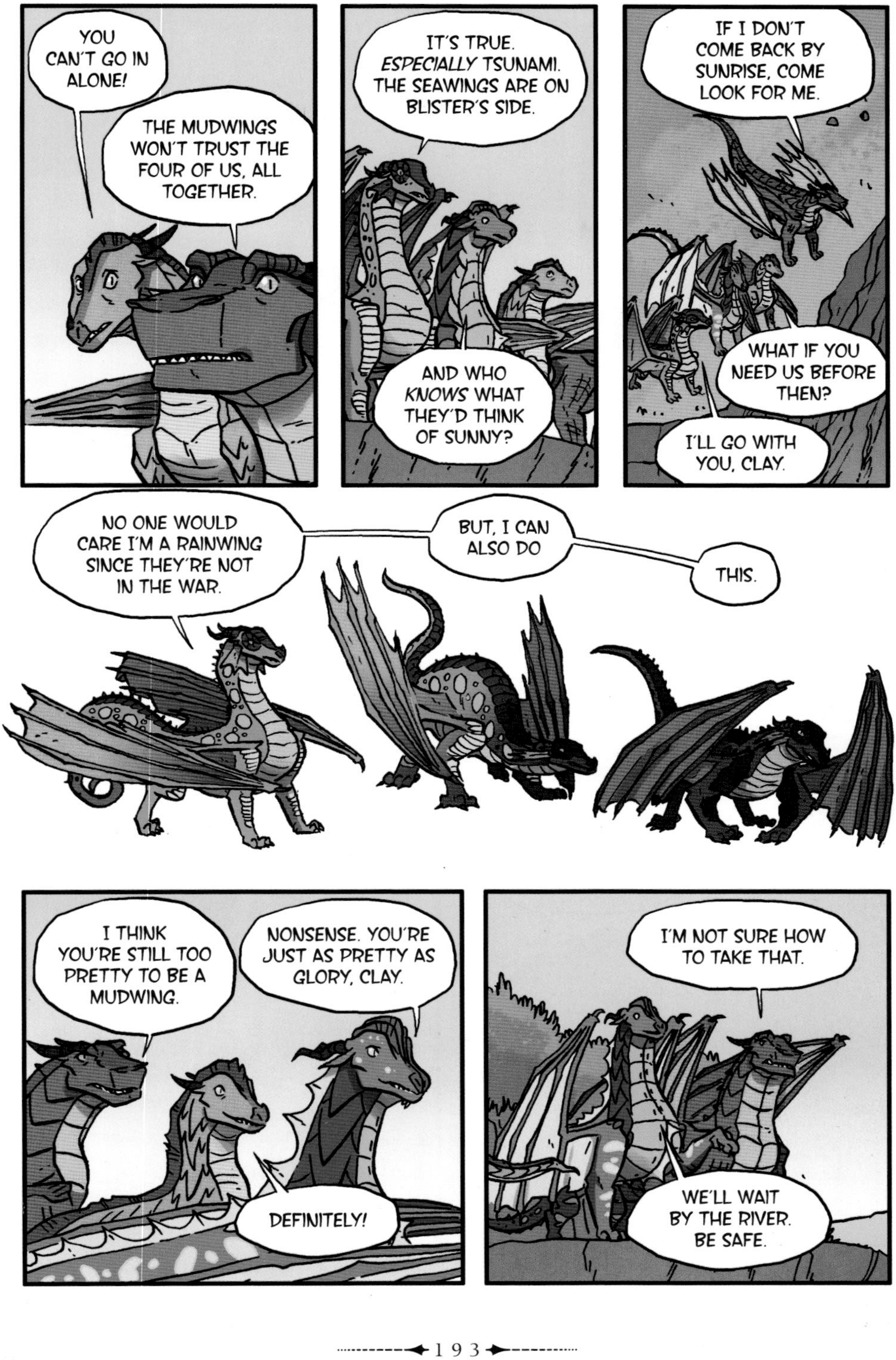
YOU CAN'T GO IN ALONE!
THE MUDWINGS WON'T TRUST THE FOUR OF US, ALL TOGETHER.
IT'S TRUE. *ESPECIALLY* TSUNAMI. THE SEAWINGS ARE ON BLISTER'S SIDE.
AND WHO *KNOWS* WHAT THEY'D THINK OF SUNNY?
IF I DON'T COME BACK BY SUNRISE, COME LOOK FOR ME.
WHAT IF YOU NEED US BEFORE THEN?
I'LL GO WITH YOU, CLAY.
NO ONE WOULD CARE I'M A RAINWING SINCE THEY'RE NOT IN THE WAR.
BUT, I CAN ALSO DO
THIS.
I THINK YOU'RE STILL TOO PRETTY TO BE A MUDWING.
NONSENSE. YOU'RE JUST AS PRETTY AS GLORY, CLAY.
DEFINITELY!
I'M NOT SURE HOW TO TAKE THAT.
WE'LL WAIT BY THE RIVER. BE SAFE.

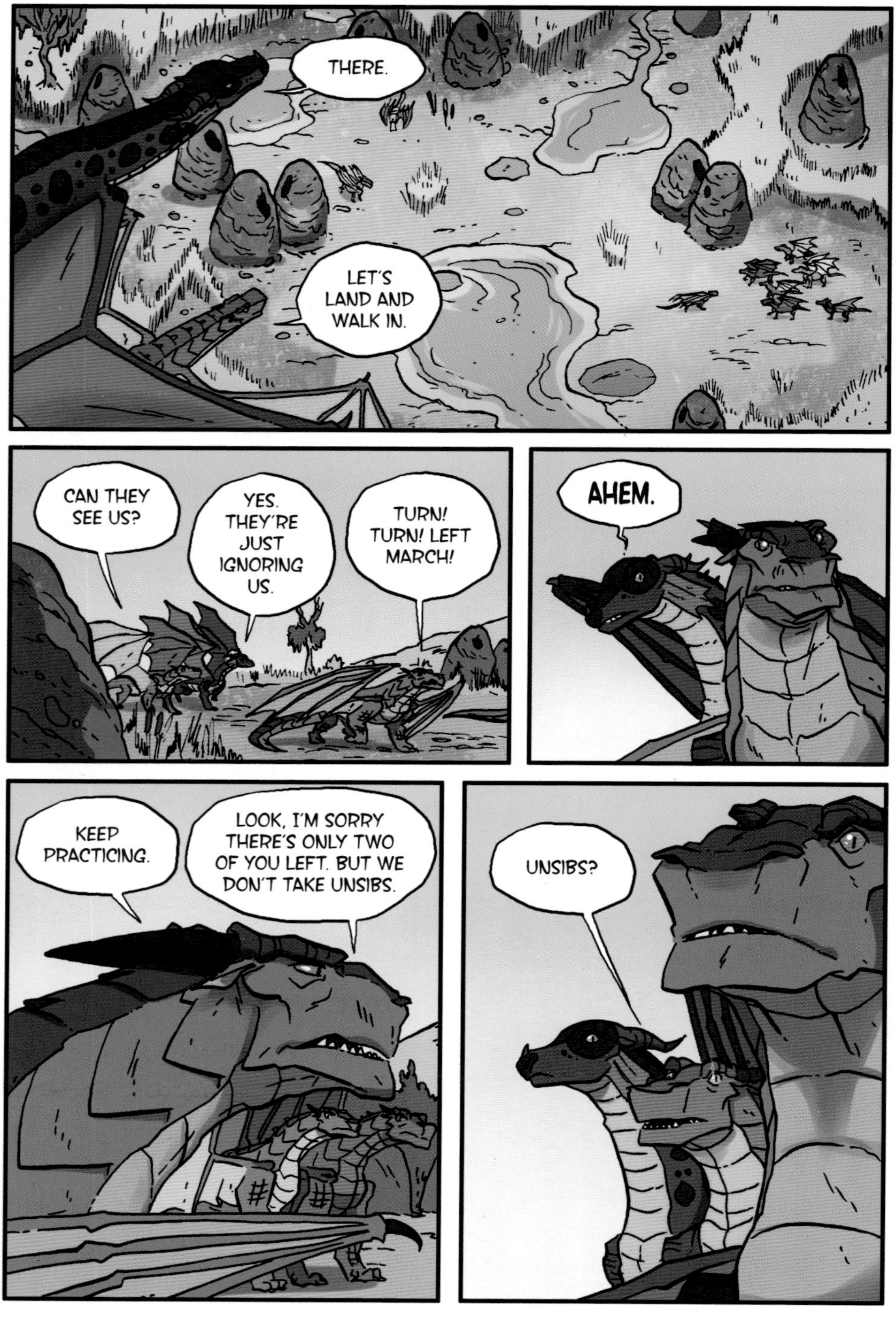

THERE.
LET'S LAND AND WALK IN.
CAN THEY SEE US?
YES. THEY'RE JUST IGNORING US.
TURN! TURN! LEFT MARCH!
AHEM.
KEEP PRACTICING.
LOOK, I'M SORRY THERE'S ONLY TWO OF YOU LEFT. BUT WE DON'T TAKE UNSIBS.
UNSIBS?

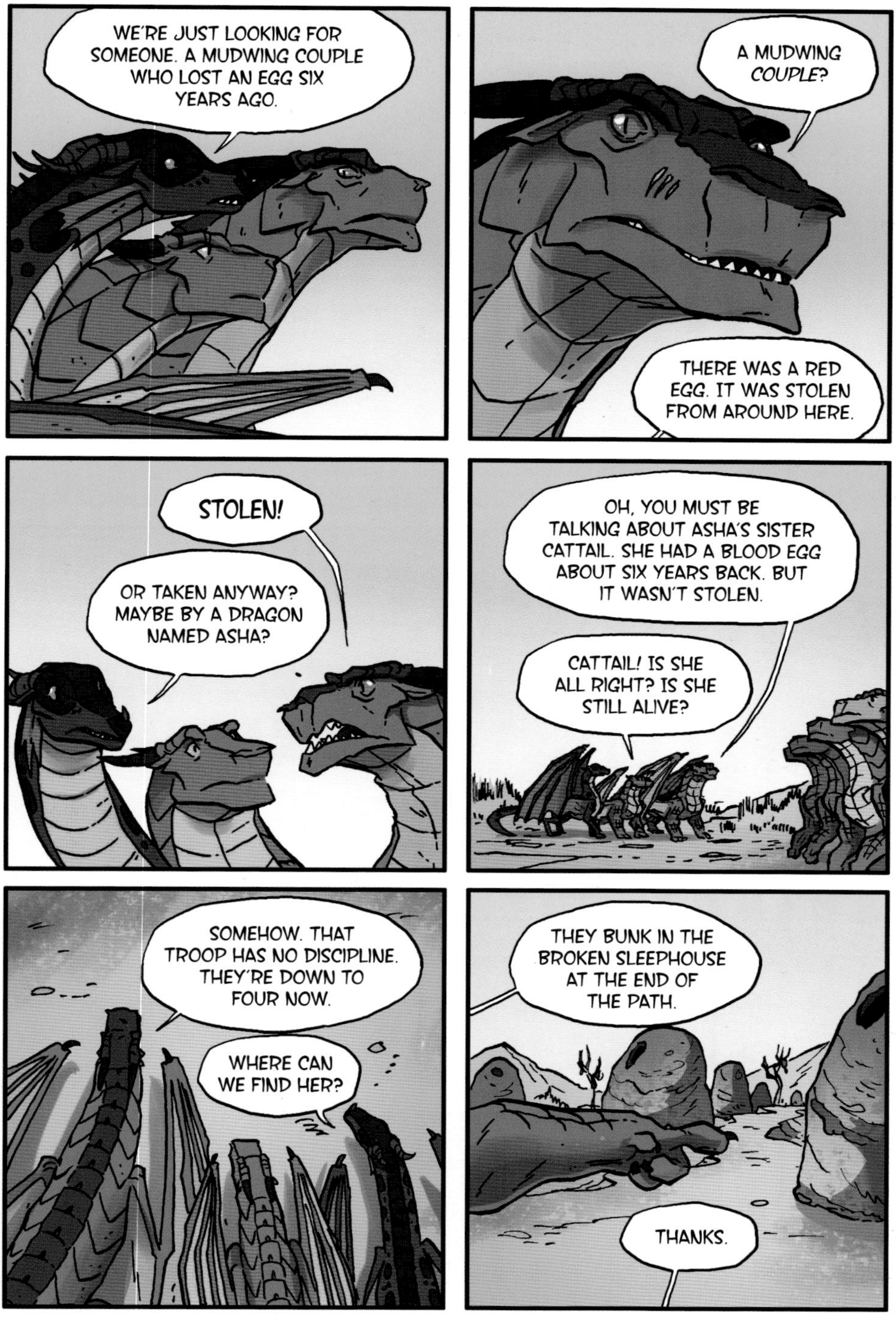
WE'RE JUST LOOKING FOR SOMEONE. A MUDWING COUPLE WHO LOST AN EGG SIX YEARS AGO.
A MUDWING COUPLE?
THERE WAS A RED EGG. IT WAS STOLEN FROM AROUND HERE.
STOLEN!
OR TAKEN ANYWAY? MAYBE BY A DRAGON NAMED ASHA?
OH, YOU MUST BE TALKING ABOUT ASHA'S SISTER CATTAIL. SHE HAD A BLOOD EGG ABOUT SIX YEARS BACK. BUT IT WASN'T STOLEN.
CATTAIL! IS SHE ALL RIGHT? IS SHE STILL ALIVE?
SOMEHOW. THAT TROOP HAS NO DISCIPLINE. THEY'RE DOWN TO FOUR NOW.
WHERE CAN WE FIND HER?
THEY BUNK IN THE BROKEN SLEEPHOUSE AT THE END OF THE PATH.
THANKS.

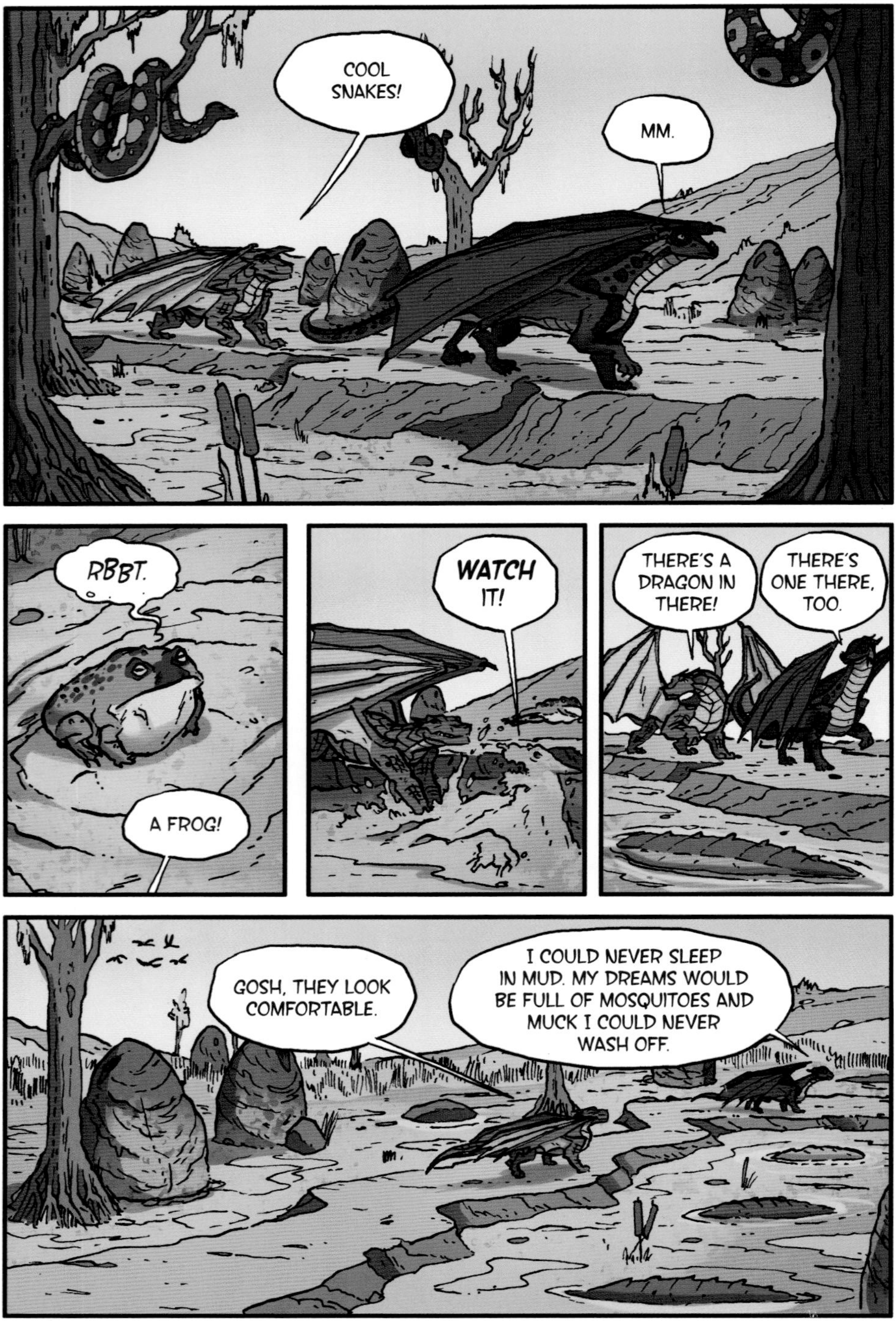
COOL SNAKES!
MM.
RBBT.
A FROG!
WATCH IT!
THERE'S A DRAGON IN THERE!
THERE'S ONE THERE, TOO.
GOSH, THEY LOOK COMFORTABLE.
I COULD NEVER SLEEP IN MUD. MY DREAMS WOULD BE FULL OF MOSQUITOES AND MUCK I COULD NEVER WASH OFF.

HAVE YOU NOTICED NO ONE'S PAYING ATTENTION TO US?

I HAVE A THEORY ABOUT THAT.

THE SCROLLS WE HAD ON THE MUDWINGS WERE NEVER ANY GOOD. BUT YOU SEE THESE GROUPS OF DRAGONS FLYING AROUND?

MAYBE THEY'RE LIKE ARMY TROOPS.

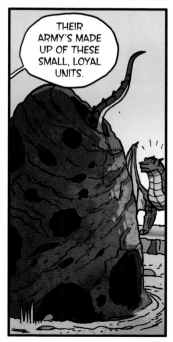

THEIR ARMY'S MADE UP OF THESE SMALL, LOYAL UNITS.

MAYBE THAT'S WHAT MAKES THEM SUCH GOOD FIGHTERS.

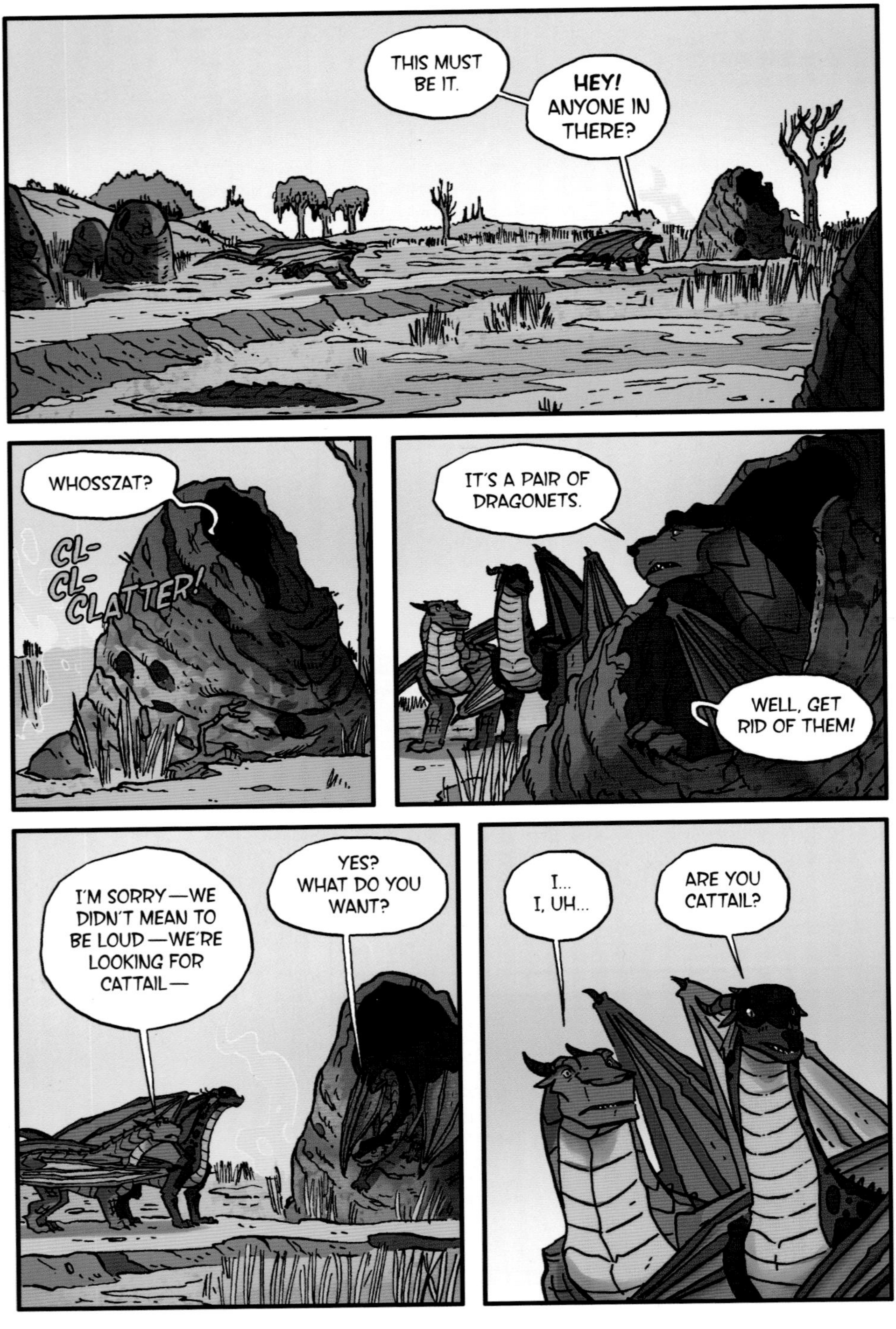
THIS MUST BE IT.
HEY! ANYONE IN THERE?
WHOSSZAT?
CL-CL-CLATTER!
IT'S A PAIR OF DRAGONETS.
WELL, GET RID OF THEM!
I'M SORRY—WE DIDN'T MEAN TO BE LOUD—WE'RE LOOKING FOR CATTAIL—
YES? WHAT DO YOU WANT?
ARE YOU CATTAIL?
I... I, UH...

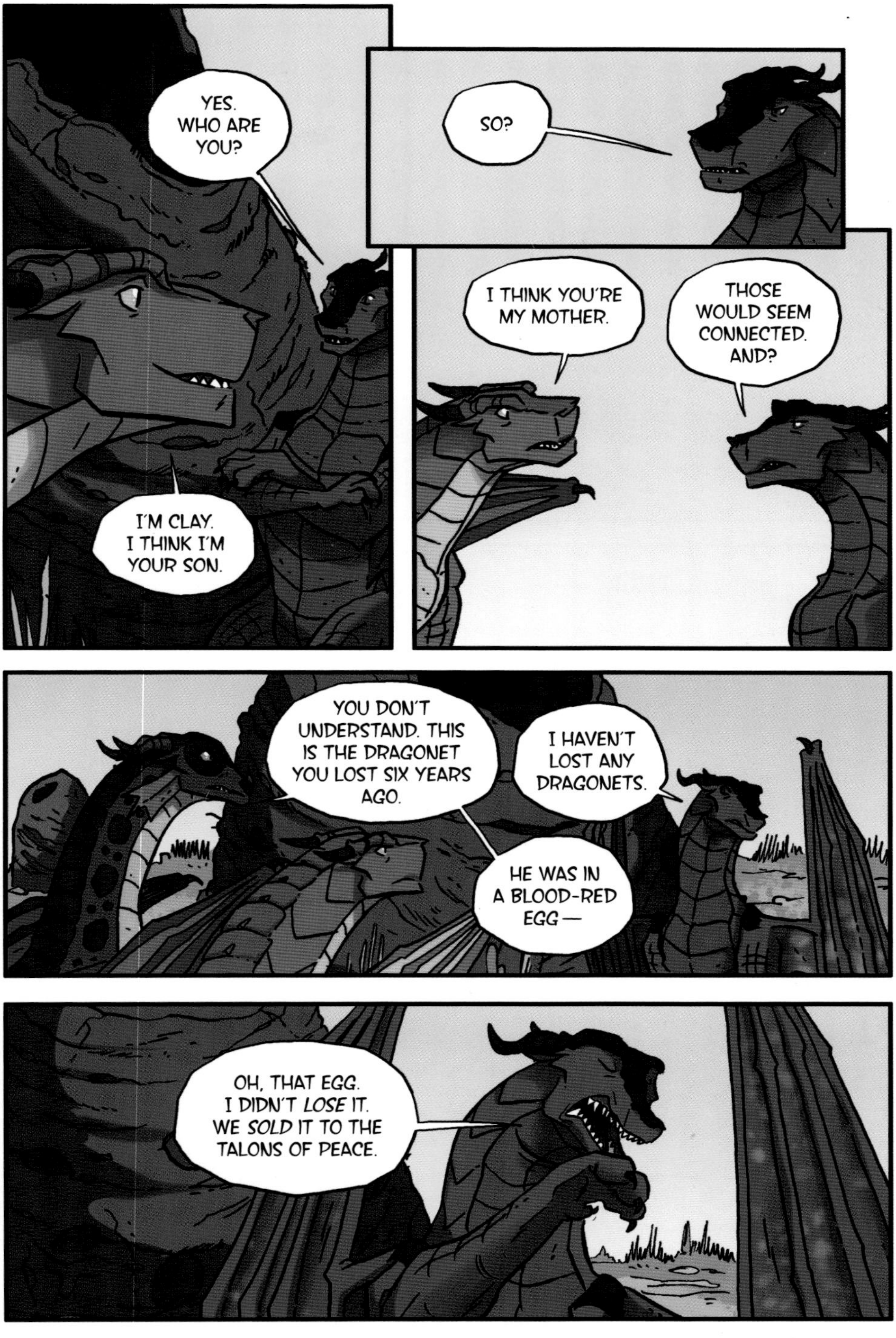
YES. WHO ARE YOU?
I'M CLAY. I THINK I'M YOUR SON.
SO?
I THINK YOU'RE MY MOTHER.
THOSE WOULD SEEM CONNECTED. AND?
YOU DON'T UNDERSTAND. THIS IS THE DRAGONET YOU LOST SIX YEARS AGO.
HE WAS IN A BLOOD-RED EGG —
I HAVEN'T LOST ANY DRAGONETS.
OH, THAT EGG. I DIDN'T *LOSE* IT. WE *SOLD* IT TO THE TALONS OF PEACE.

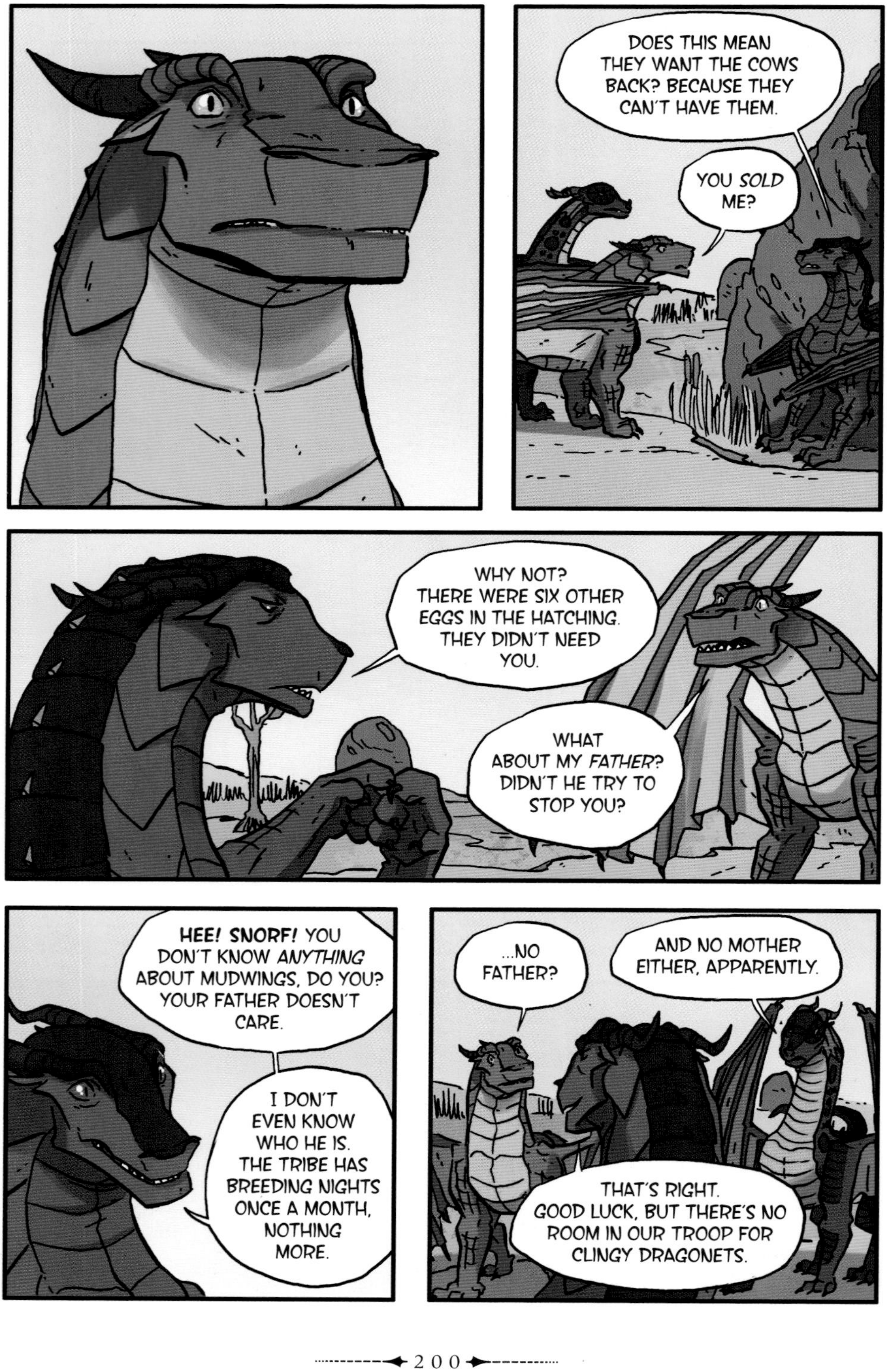
DOES THIS MEAN THEY WANT THE COWS BACK? BECAUSE THEY CAN'T HAVE THEM.
YOU *SOLD* ME?
WHY NOT? THERE WERE SIX OTHER EGGS IN THE HATCHING. THEY DIDN'T NEED YOU.
WHAT ABOUT MY *FATHER*? DIDN'T HE TRY TO STOP YOU?
HEE! SNORF! YOU DON'T KNOW *ANYTHING* ABOUT MUDWINGS, DO YOU? YOUR FATHER DOESN'T CARE.
I DON'T EVEN KNOW WHO HE IS. THE TRIBE HAS BREEDING NIGHTS ONCE A MONTH, NOTHING MORE.
...NO FATHER?
AND NO MOTHER EITHER, APPARENTLY.
THAT'S RIGHT. GOOD LUCK, BUT THERE'S NO ROOM IN OUR TROOP FOR CLINGY DRAGONETS.

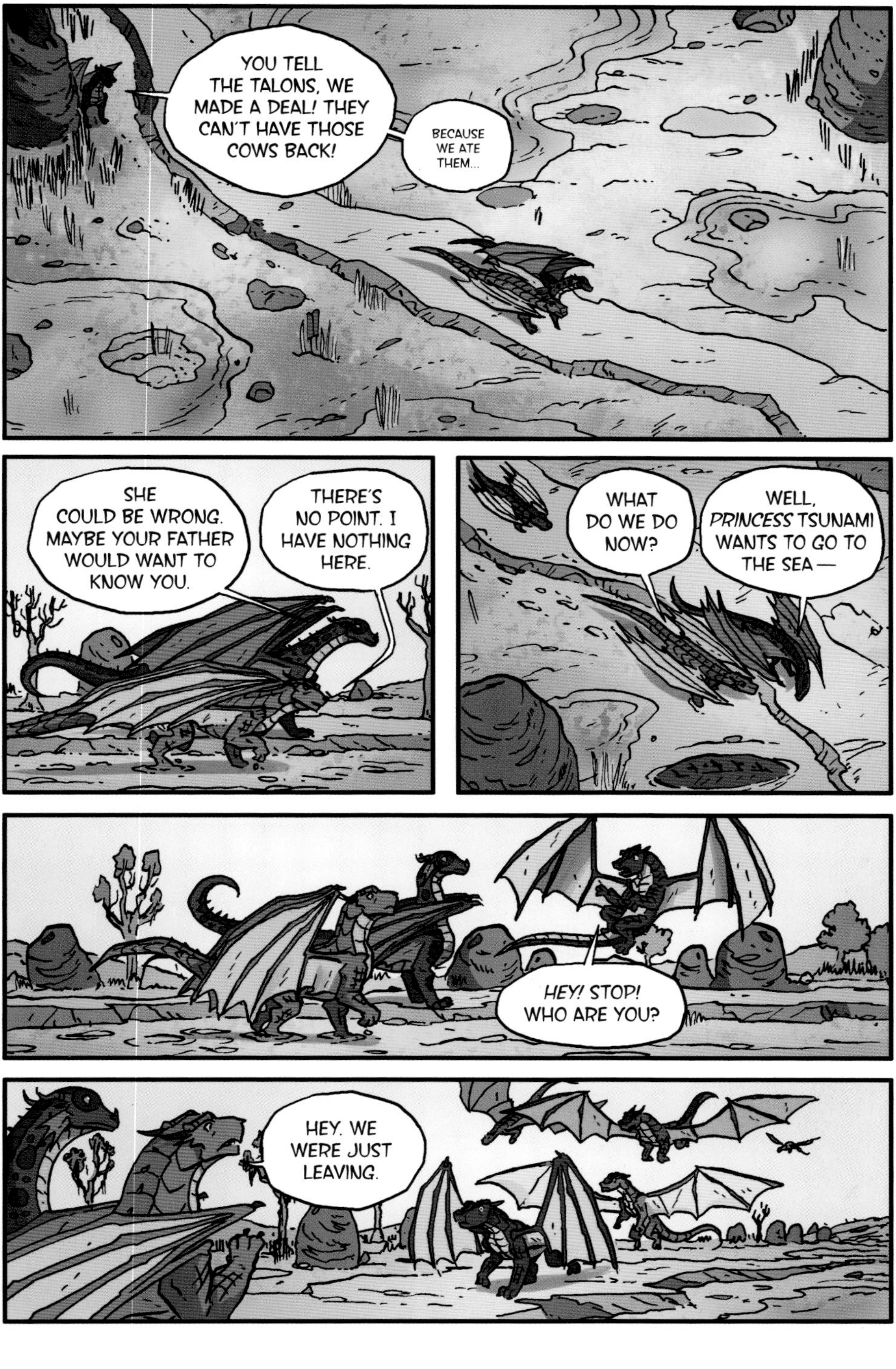
YOU TELL THE TALONS, WE MADE A DEAL! THEY CAN'T HAVE THOSE COWS BACK!
BECAUSE WE ATE THEM...
SHE COULD BE WRONG. MAYBE YOUR FATHER WOULD WANT TO KNOW YOU.
THERE'S NO POINT. I HAVE NOTHING HERE.
WHAT DO WE DO NOW?
WELL, *PRINCESS* TSUNAMI WANTS TO GO TO THE SEA —
HEY! STOP! WHO ARE YOU?
HEY. WE WERE JUST LEAVING.

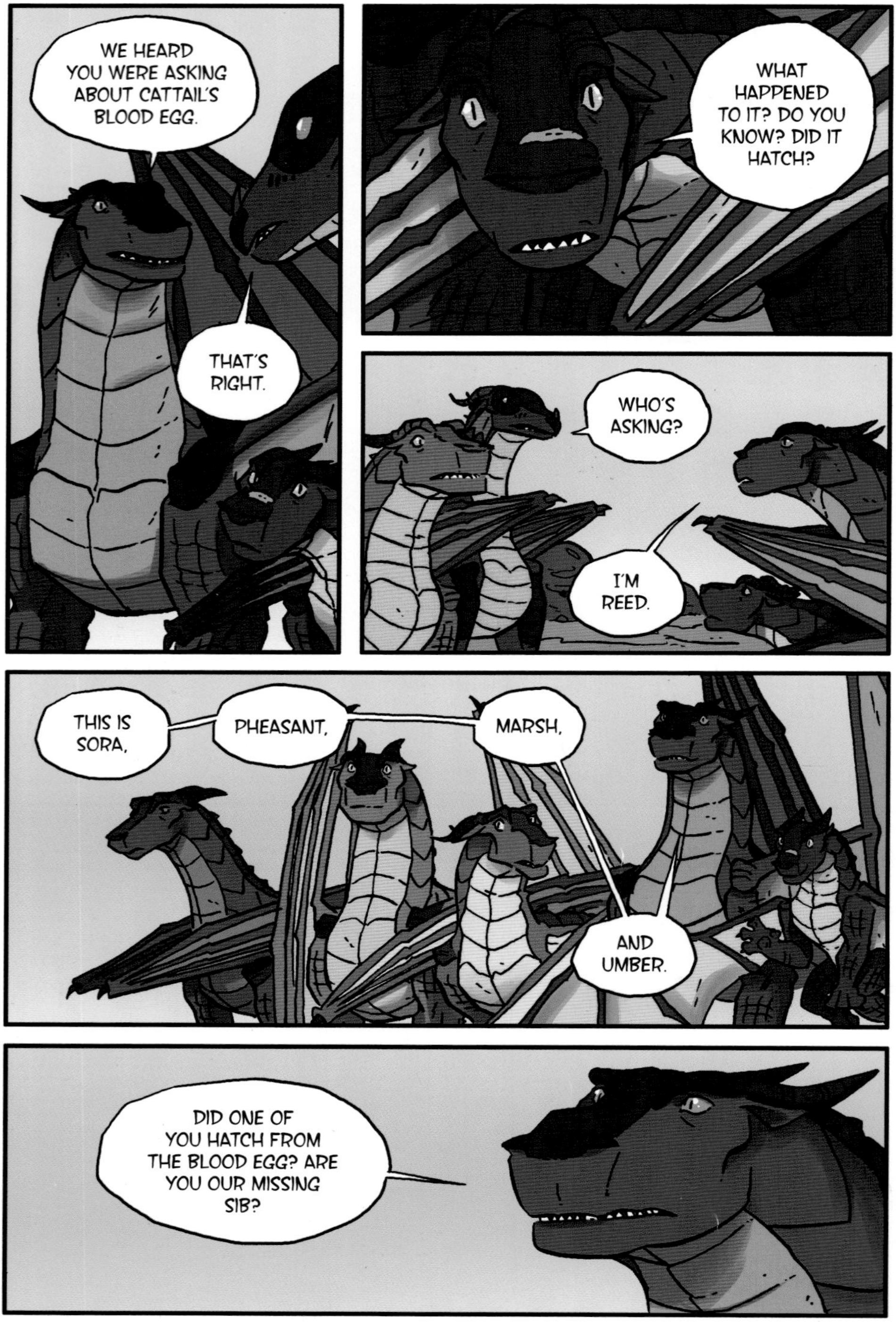
WE HEARD YOU WERE ASKING ABOUT CATTAIL'S BLOOD EGG.
THAT'S RIGHT.
WHAT HAPPENED TO IT? DO YOU KNOW? DID IT HATCH?
WHO'S ASKING?
I'M REED.
THIS IS SORA,
PHEASANT,
MARSH,
AND UMBER.
DID ONE OF YOU HATCH FROM THE BLOOD EGG? ARE YOU OUR MISSING SIB?

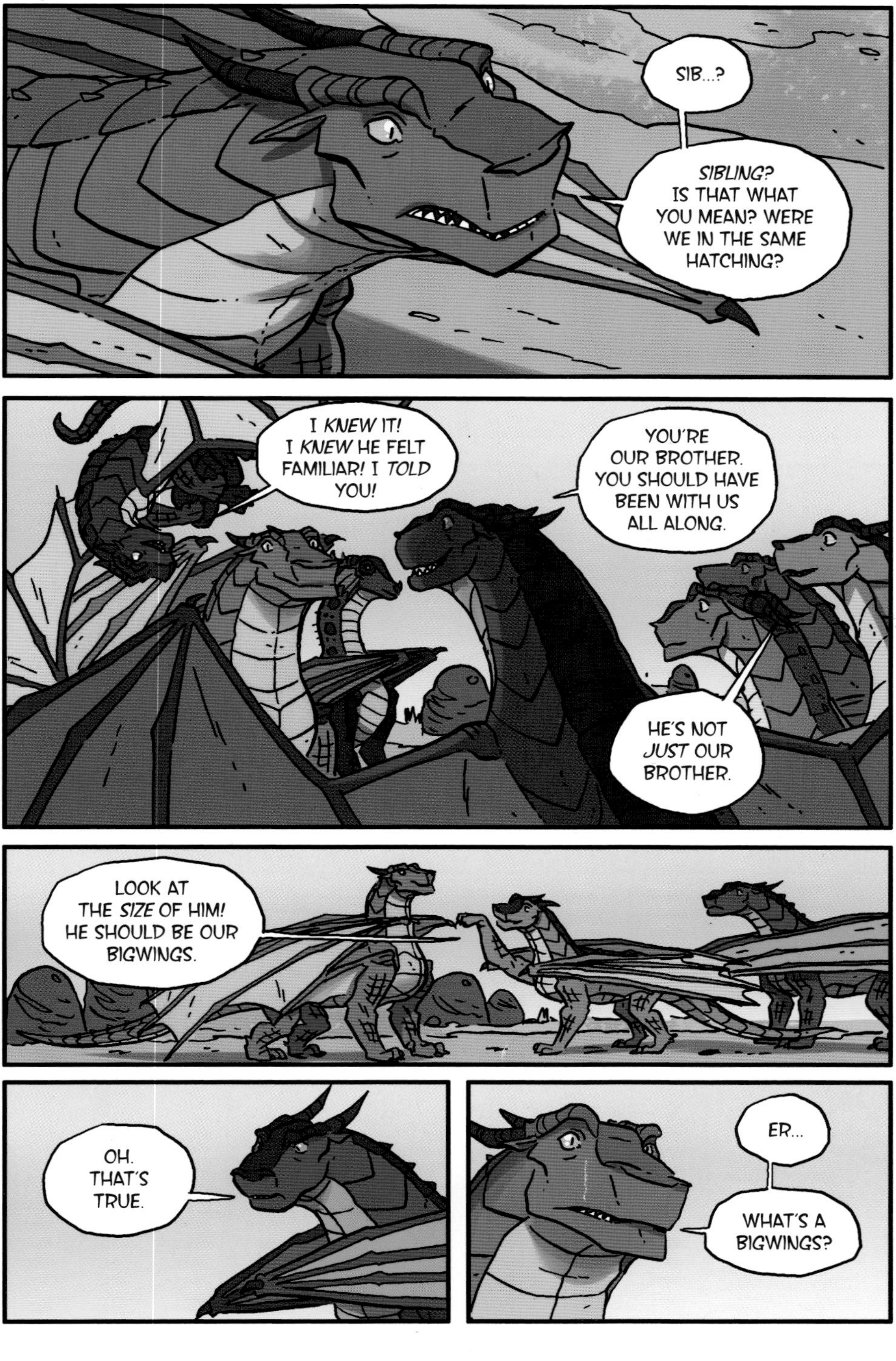
SIB...?
SIBLING? IS THAT WHAT YOU MEAN? WERE WE IN THE SAME HATCHING?
I *KNEW* IT! I *KNEW* HE FELT FAMILIAR! I *TOLD* YOU!
YOU'RE OUR BROTHER. YOU SHOULD HAVE BEEN WITH US ALL ALONG.
HE'S NOT *JUST* OUR BROTHER.
LOOK AT THE *SIZE* OF HIM! HE SHOULD BE OUR BIGWINGS.
OH. THAT'S TRUE.
ER...
WHAT'S A BIGWINGS?

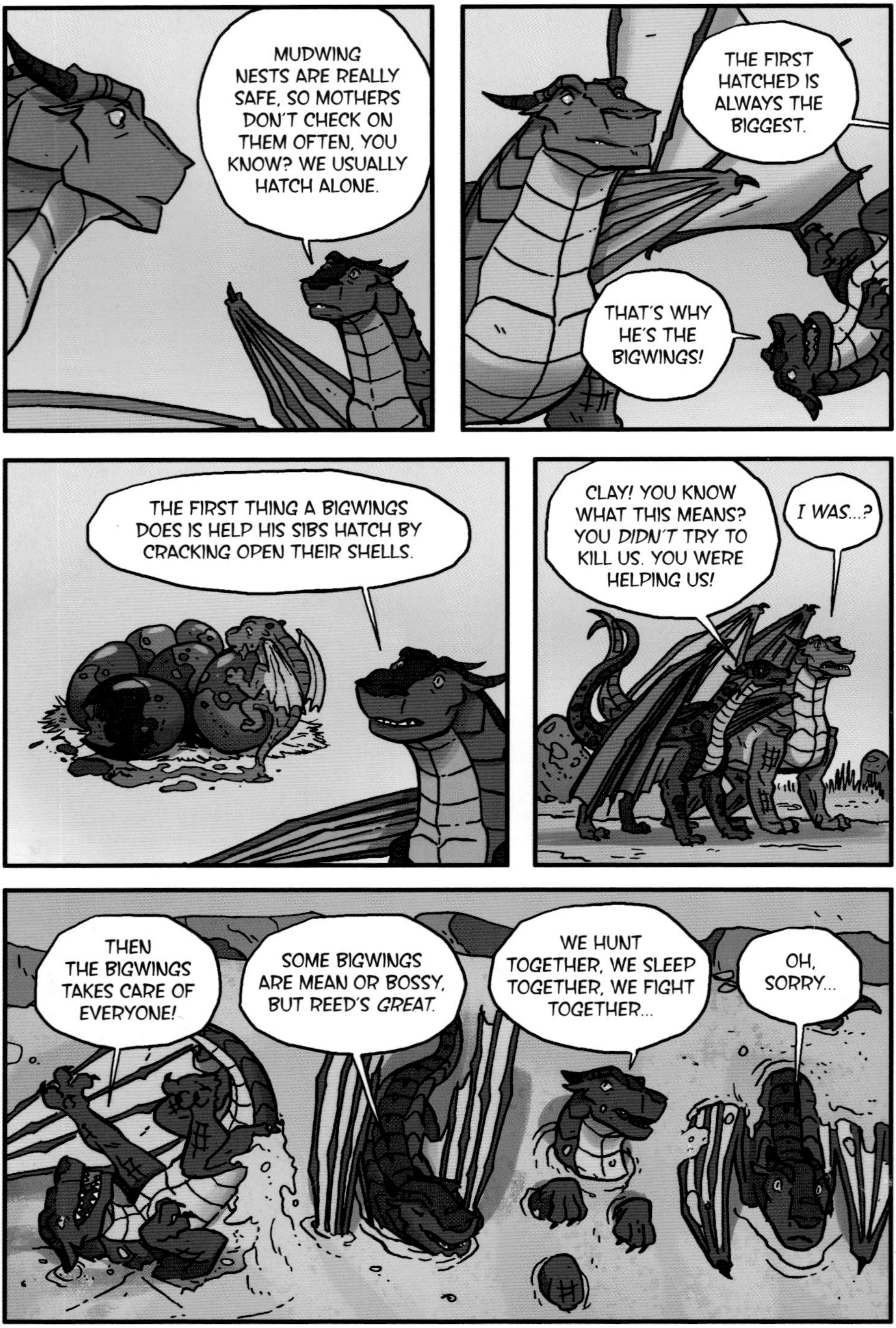
MUDWING NESTS ARE REALLY SAFE, SO MOTHERS DON'T CHECK ON THEM OFTEN, YOU KNOW? WE USUALLY HATCH ALONE.
THE FIRST HATCHED IS ALWAYS THE BIGGEST.
THAT'S WHY HE'S THE BIGWINGS!
THE FIRST THING A BIGWINGS DOES IS HELP HIS SIBS HATCH BY CRACKING OPEN THEIR SHELLS.
CLAY! YOU KNOW WHAT THIS MEANS? YOU *DIDN'T* TRY TO KILL US. YOU WERE HELPING US!
I WAS...?
THEN THE BIGWINGS TAKES CARE OF EVERYONE!
SOME BIGWINGS ARE MEAN OR BOSSY, BUT REED'S *GREAT*.
WE HUNT TOGETHER, WE SLEEP TOGETHER, WE FIGHT TOGETHER...
OH, SORRY...

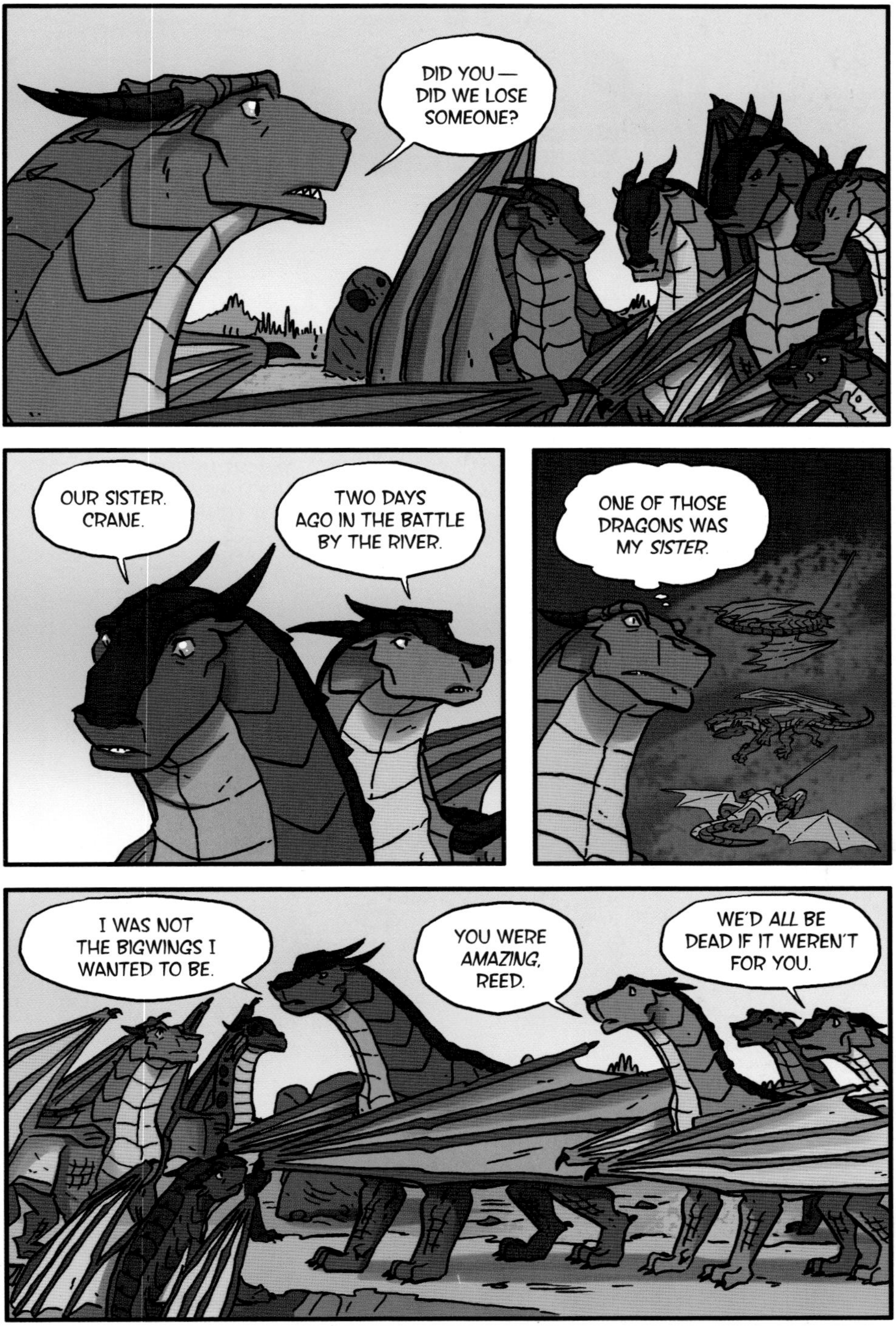
DID YOU — DID WE LOSE SOMEONE?
OUR SISTER. CRANE.
TWO DAYS AGO IN THE BATTLE BY THE RIVER.
ONE OF THOSE DRAGONS WAS MY *SISTER.*
I WAS NOT THE BIGWINGS I WANTED TO BE.
YOU WERE *AMAZING,* REED.
WE'D *ALL* BE DEAD IF IT WEREN'T FOR YOU.

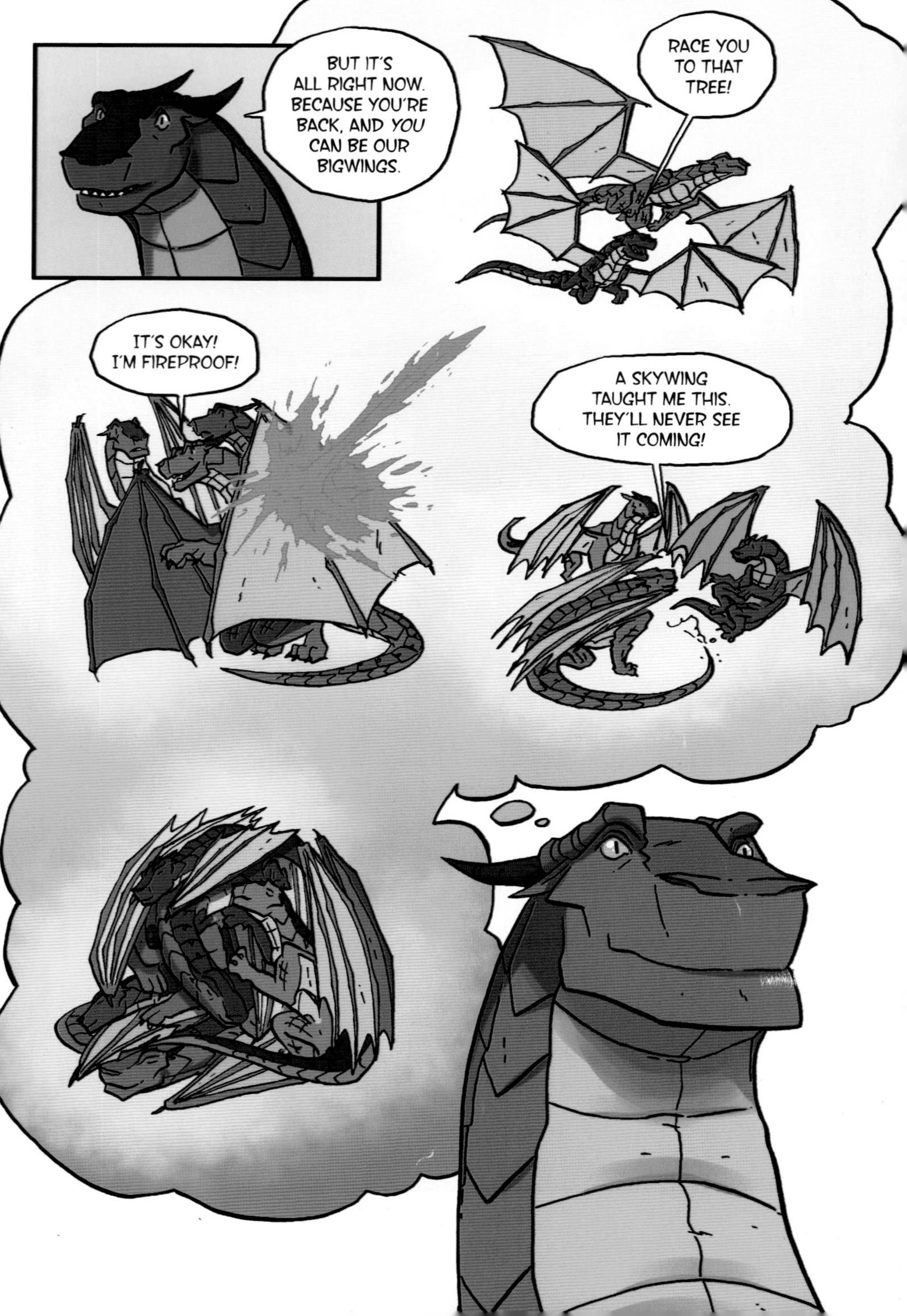
BUT IT'S ALL RIGHT NOW. BECAUSE YOU'RE BACK, AND *YOU* CAN BE OUR BIGWINGS.
RACE YOU TO THAT TREE!
IT'S OKAY! I'M FIREPROOF!
A SKYWING TAUGHT ME THIS. THEY'LL NEVER SEE IT COMING!

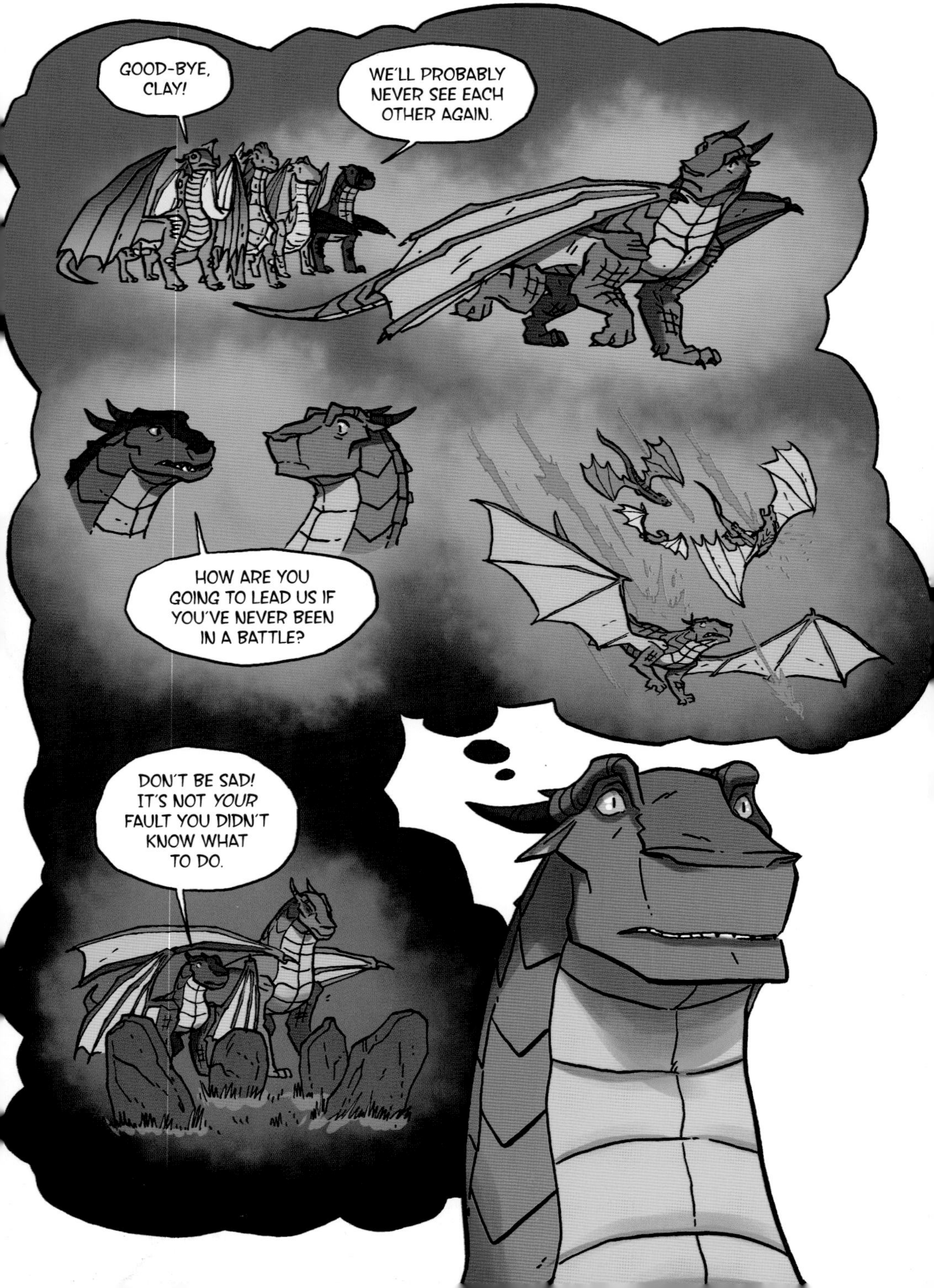
GOOD-BYE, CLAY!
WE'LL PROBABLY NEVER SEE EACH OTHER AGAIN.
HOW ARE YOU GOING TO LEAD US IF YOU'VE NEVER BEEN IN A BATTLE?
DON'T BE SAD! IT'S NOT *YOUR* FAULT YOU DIDN'T KNOW WHAT TO DO.

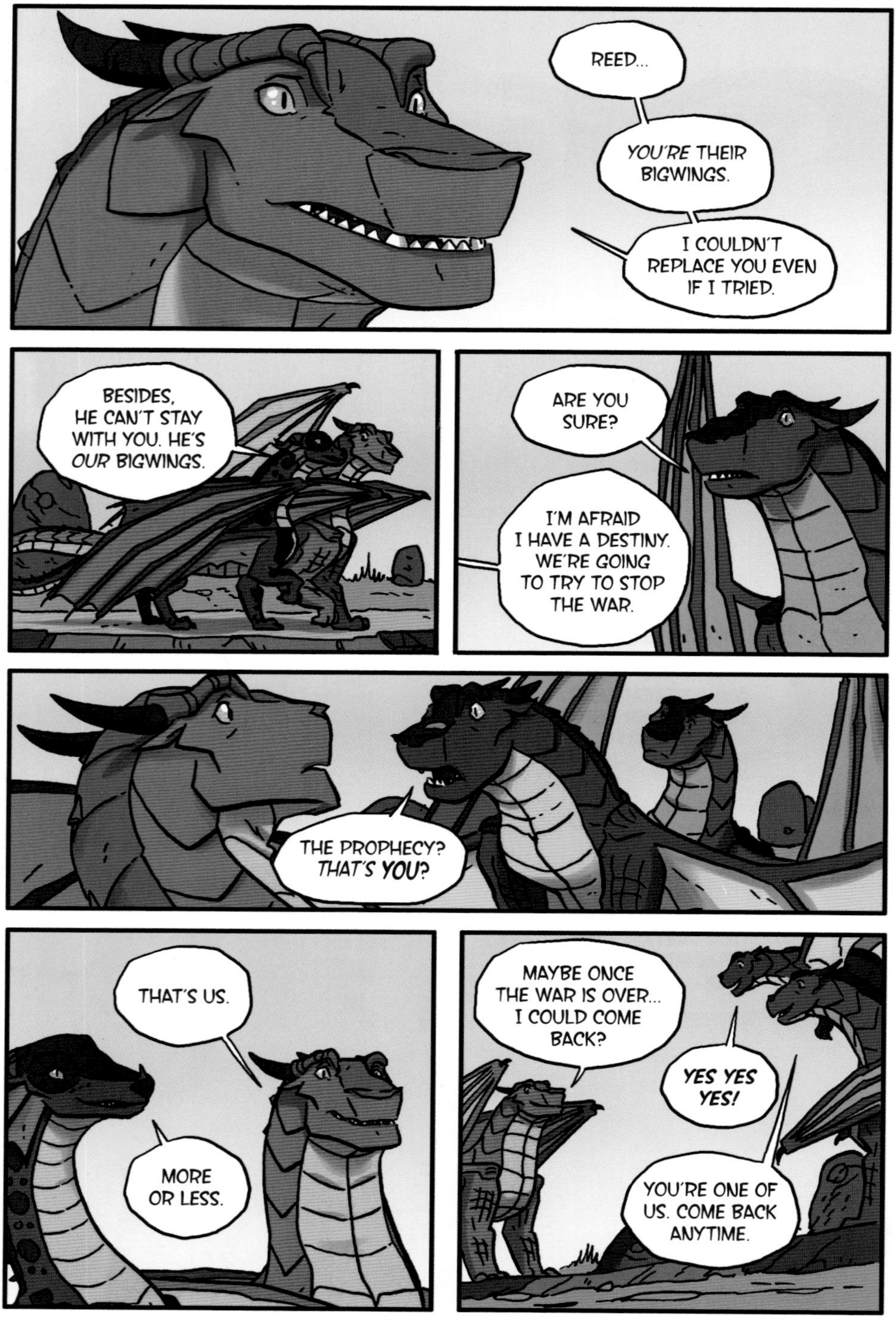
REED...
YOU'RE THEIR BIGWINGS.
I COULDN'T REPLACE YOU EVEN IF I TRIED.
BESIDES, HE CAN'T STAY WITH YOU. HE'S *OUR* BIGWINGS.
ARE YOU SURE?
I'M AFRAID I HAVE A DESTINY. WE'RE GOING TO TRY TO STOP THE WAR.
THE PROPHECY? *THAT'S* **YOU**?
THAT'S US.
MORE OR LESS.
MAYBE ONCE THE WAR IS OVER... I COULD COME BACK?
YES YES YES!
YOU'RE ONE OF US. COME BACK ANYTIME.

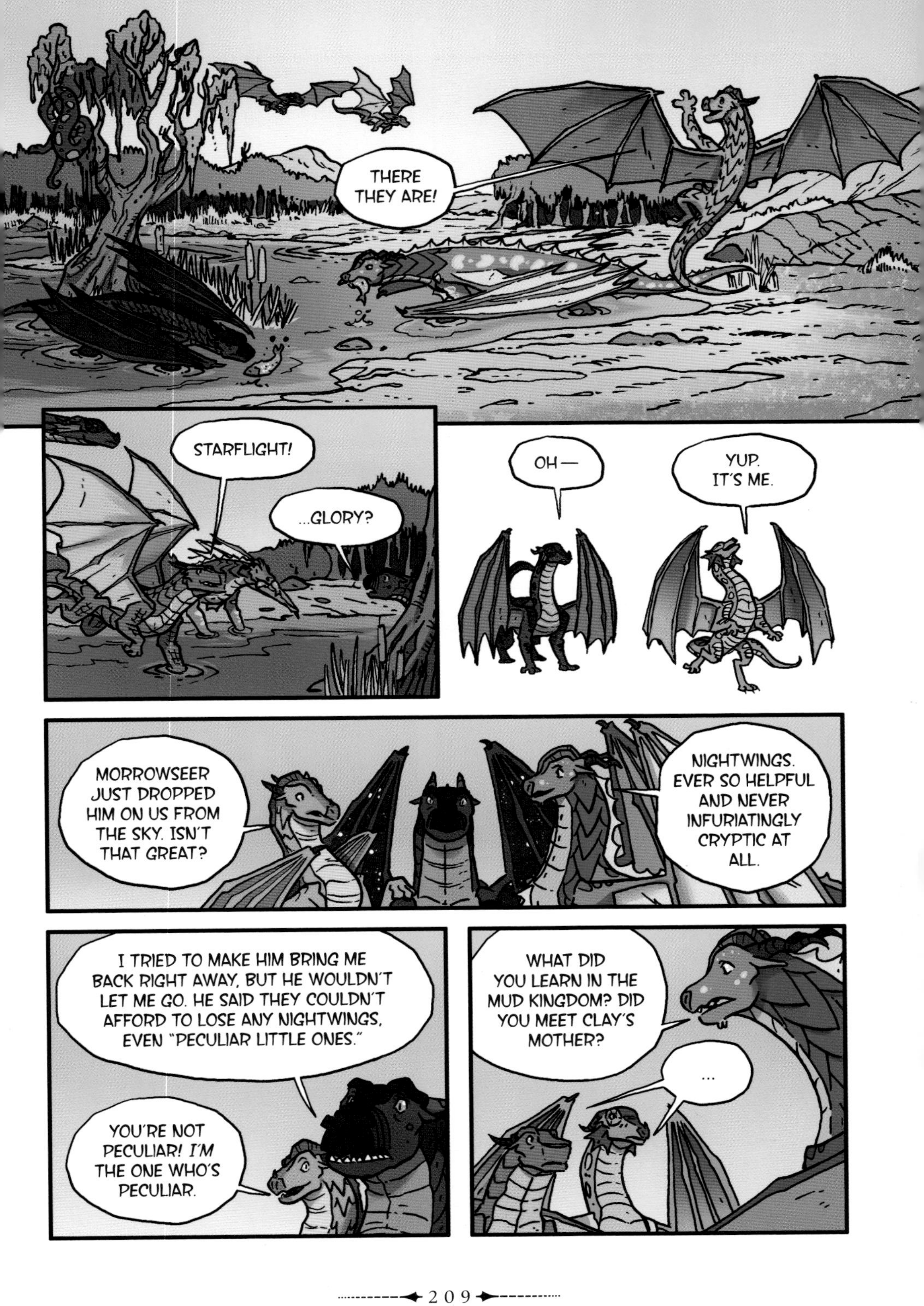
THERE THEY ARE!
STARFLIGHT!
...GLORY?
OH—
YUP. IT'S ME.
MORROWSEER JUST DROPPED HIM ON US FROM THE SKY. ISN'T THAT GREAT?
NIGHTWINGS. EVER SO HELPFUL AND NEVER INFURIATINGLY CRYPTIC AT ALL.
I TRIED TO MAKE HIM BRING ME BACK RIGHT AWAY, BUT HE WOULDN'T LET ME GO. HE SAID THEY COULDN'T AFFORD TO LOSE ANY NIGHTWINGS, EVEN "PECULIAR LITTLE ONES."
YOU'RE NOT PECULIAR! *I'M* THE ONE WHO'S PECULIAR.
WHAT DID YOU LEARN IN THE MUD KINGDOM? DID YOU MEET CLAY'S MOTHER?
...

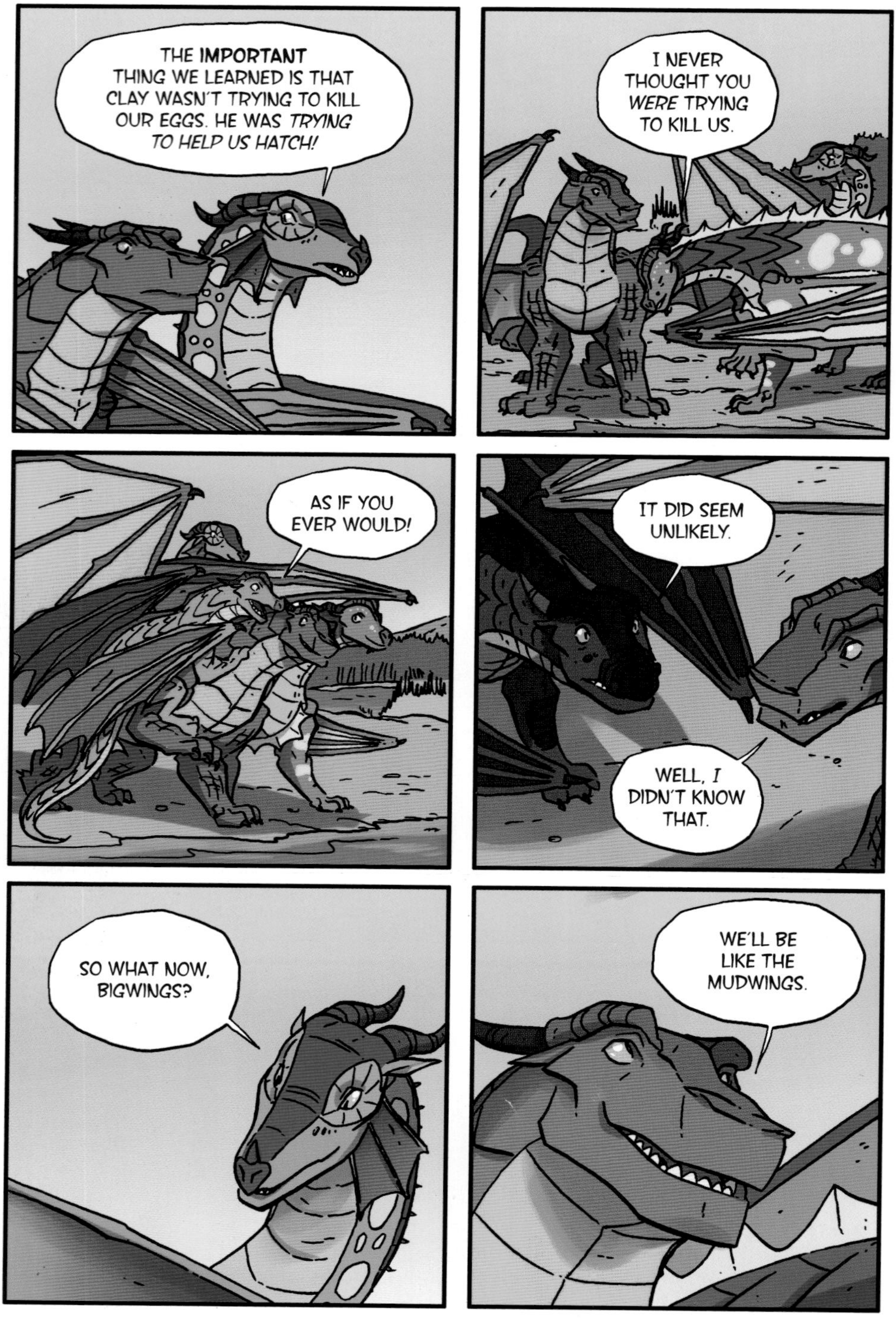
THE **IMPORTANT** THING WE LEARNED IS THAT CLAY WASN'T TRYING TO KILL OUR EGGS. HE WAS *TRYING* TO HELP US HATCH!
I NEVER THOUGHT YOU *WERE* TRYING TO KILL US.
AS IF YOU EVER WOULD!
IT DID SEEM UNLIKELY.
WELL, *I* DIDN'T KNOW THAT.
SO WHAT NOW, BIGWINGS?
WE'LL BE LIKE THE MUDWINGS.

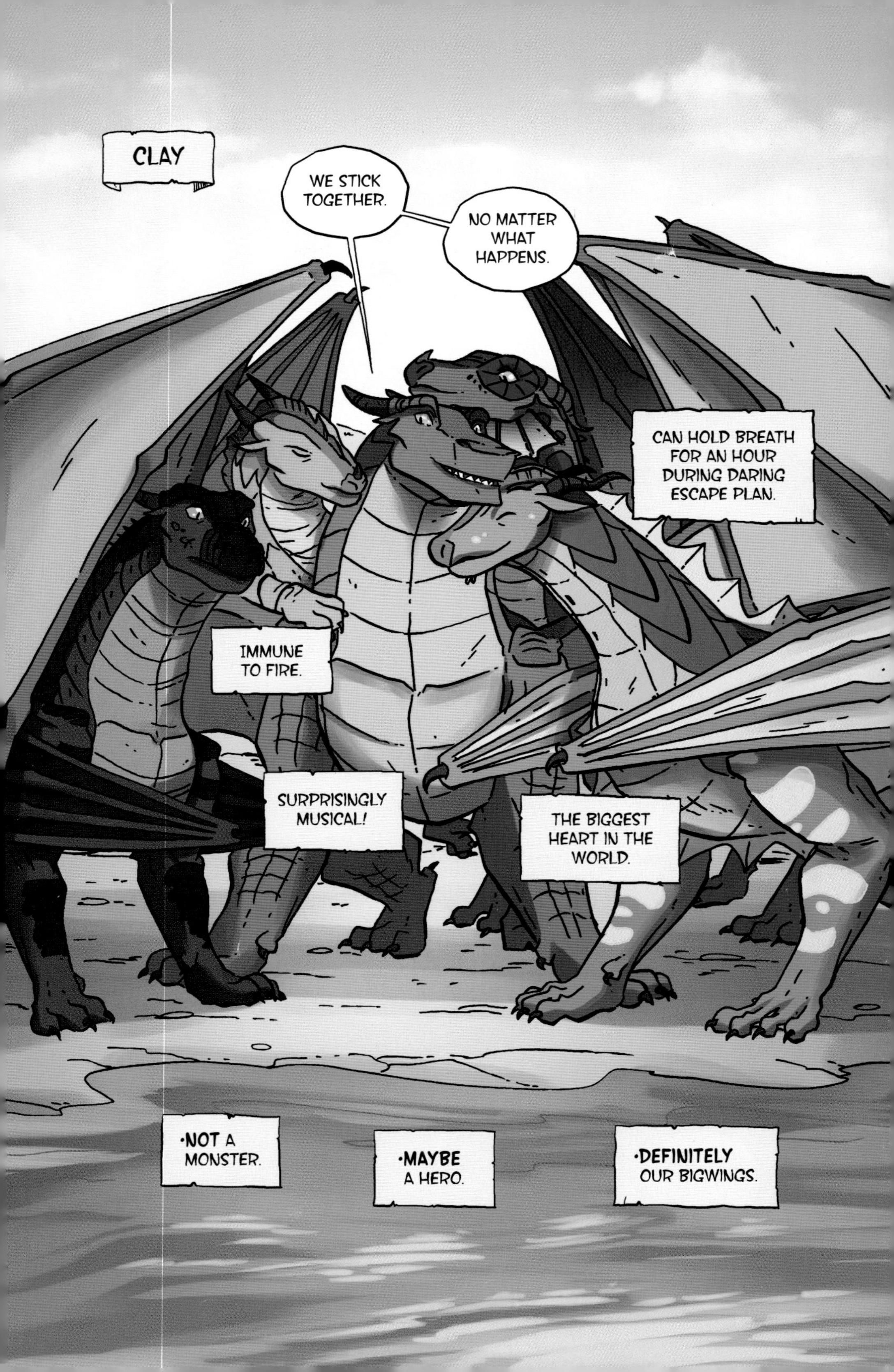
CLAY
WE STICK TOGETHER.
NO MATTER WHAT HAPPENS.
CAN HOLD BREATH FOR AN HOUR DURING DARING ESCAPE PLAN.
IMMUNE TO FIRE.
SURPRISINGLY MUSICAL!
THE BIGGEST HEART IN THE WORLD.
•NOT A MONSTER.
•MAYBE A HERO.
•DEFINITELY OUR BIGWINGS.

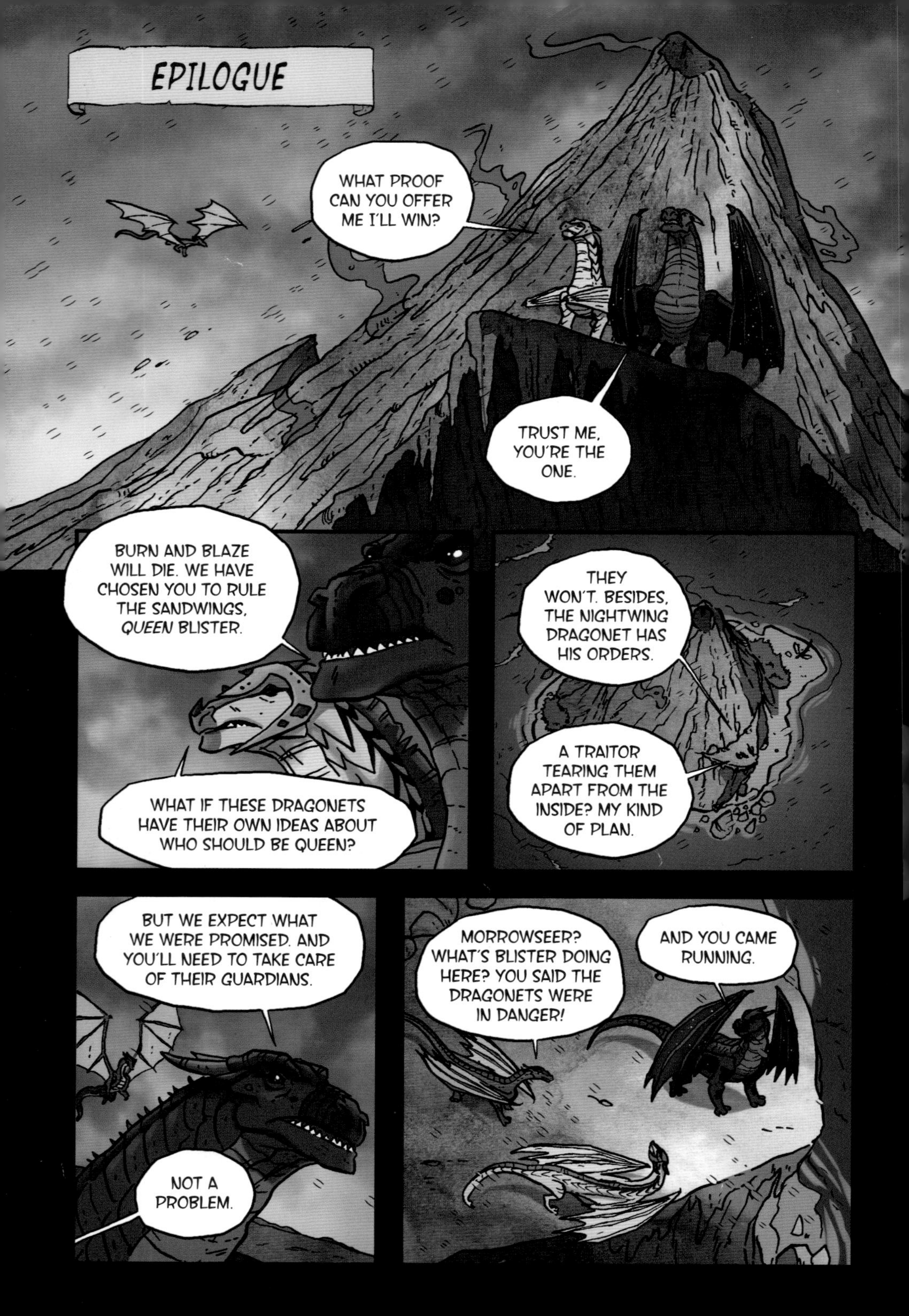
EPILOGUE
WHAT PROOF CAN YOU OFFER ME I'LL WIN?
TRUST ME, YOU'RE THE ONE.
BURN AND BLAZE WILL DIE. WE HAVE CHOSEN YOU TO RULE THE SANDWINGS, *QUEEN* BLISTER.
WHAT IF THESE DRAGONETS HAVE THEIR OWN IDEAS ABOUT WHO SHOULD BE QUEEN?
THEY WON'T. BESIDES, THE NIGHTWING DRAGONET HAS HIS ORDERS.
A TRAITOR TEARING THEM APART FROM THE INSIDE? MY KIND OF PLAN.
BUT WE EXPECT WHAT WE WERE PROMISED. AND YOU'LL NEED TO TAKE CARE OF THEIR GUARDIANS.
NOT A PROBLEM.
MORROWSEER? WHAT'S BLISTER DOING HERE? YOU SAID THE DRAGONETS WERE IN DANGER!
AND YOU CAME RUNNING.

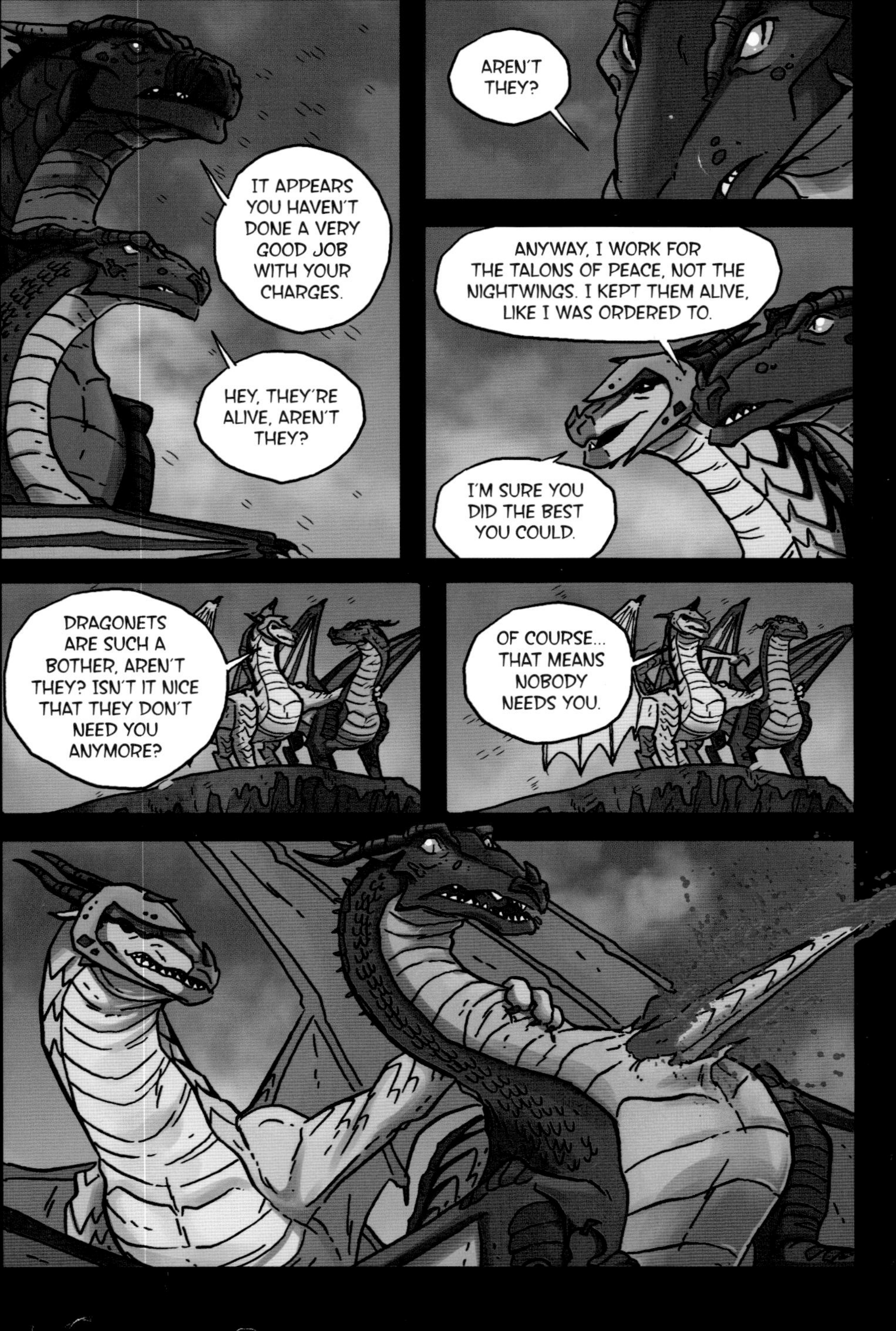

IT APPEARS YOU HAVEN'T DONE A VERY GOOD JOB WITH YOUR CHARGES.
HEY, THEY'RE ALIVE, AREN'T THEY?
AREN'T THEY?
ANYWAY, I WORK FOR THE TALONS OF PEACE, NOT THE NIGHTWINGS. I KEPT THEM ALIVE, LIKE I WAS ORDERED TO.
I'M SURE YOU DID THE BEST YOU COULD.
DRAGONETS ARE SUCH A BOTHER, AREN'T THEY? ISN'T IT NICE THAT THEY DON'T NEED YOU ANYMORE?
OF COURSE... THAT MEANS NOBODY NEEDS YOU.

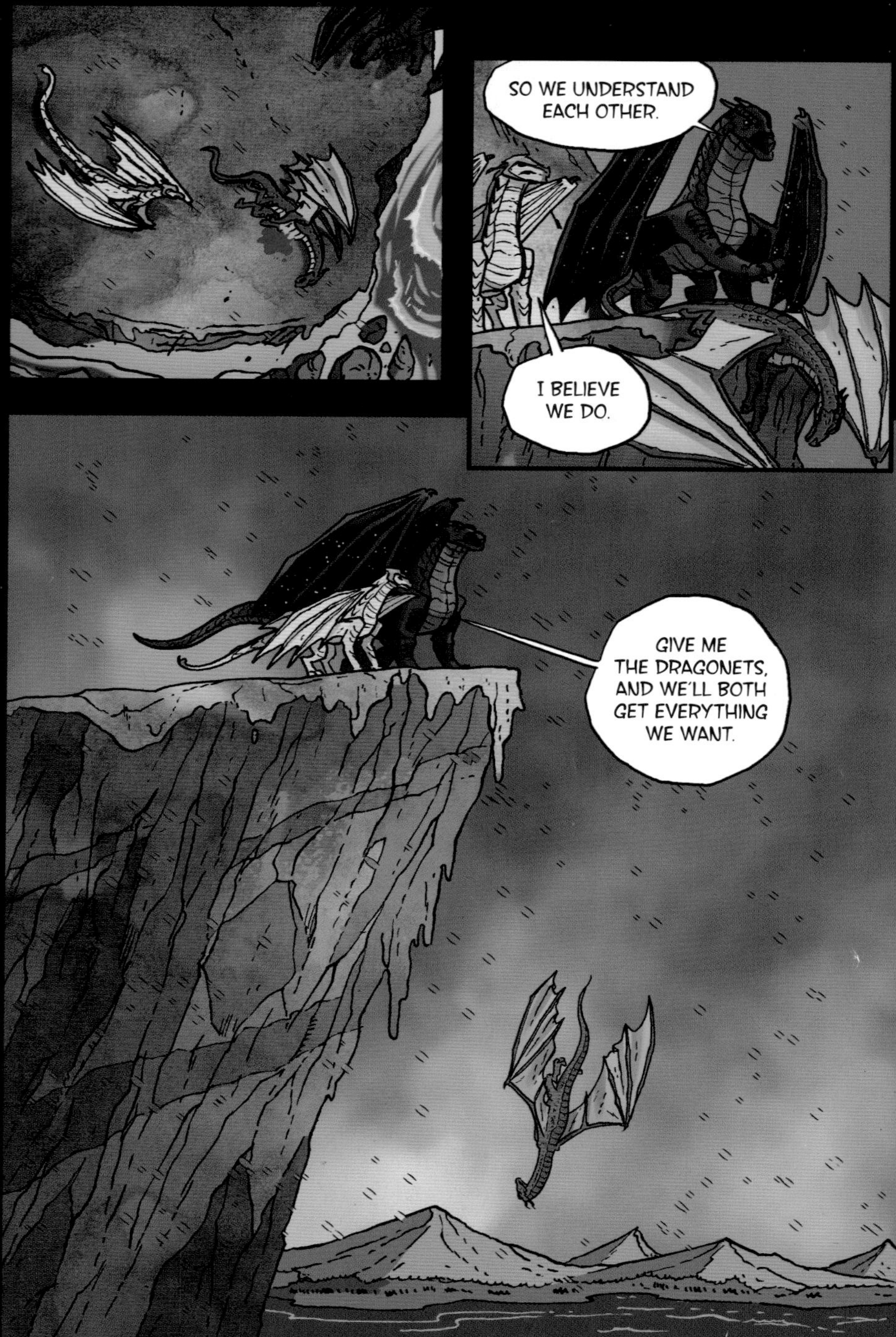
SO WE UNDERSTAND EACH OTHER.
I BELIEVE WE DO.
GIVE ME THE DRAGONETS, AND WE'LL BOTH GET EVERYTHING WE WANT.

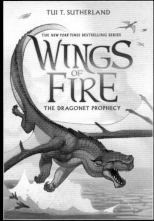

DISCOVER
THE EPIC
SERIES
WHERE
IT ALL
BEGAN!

PREQUEL

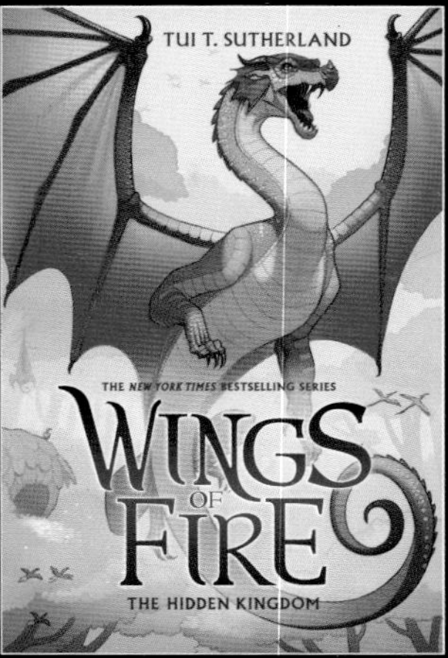
TUI T. SUTHERLAND
THE NEW YORK TIMES BESTSELLING SERIES
WINGS OF FIRE
THE HIDDEN KINGDOM

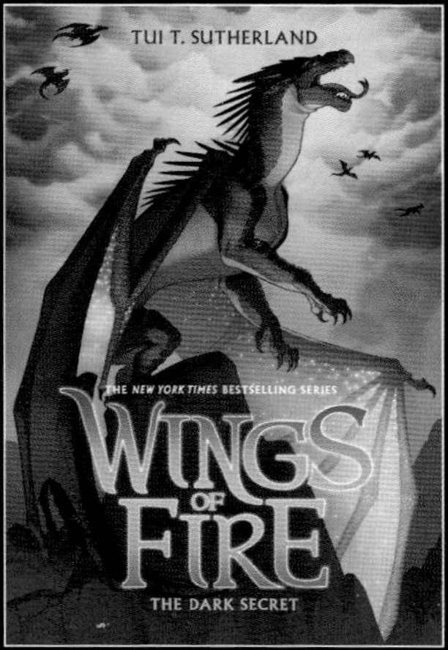
TUI T. SUTHERLAND
THE NEW YORK TIMES BESTSELLING SERIES
WINGS OF FIRE
THE DARK SECRET

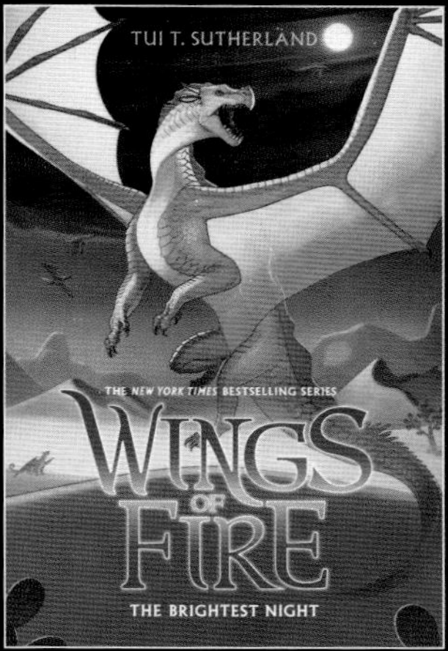
TUI T. SUTHERLAND
THE NEW YORK TIMES BESTSELLING SERIES
WINGS OF FIRE
THE BRIGHTEST NIGHT

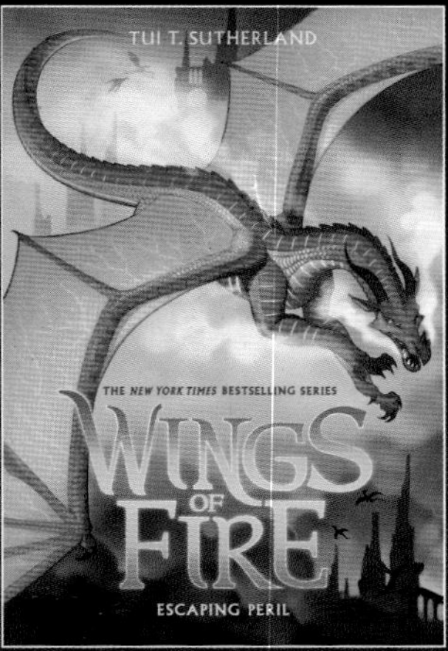
TUI T. SUTHERLAND
THE NEW YORK TIMES BESTSELLING SERIES
WINGS OF FIRE
ESCAPING PERIL

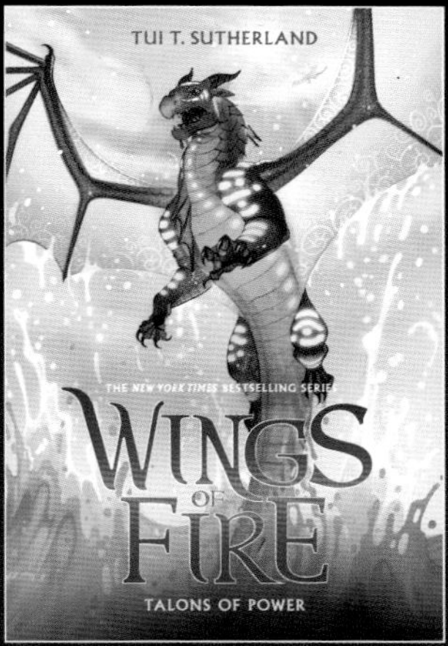
TUI T. SUTHERLAND
THE NEW YORK TIMES BESTSELLING SERIES
WINGS OF FIRE
TALONS OF POWER

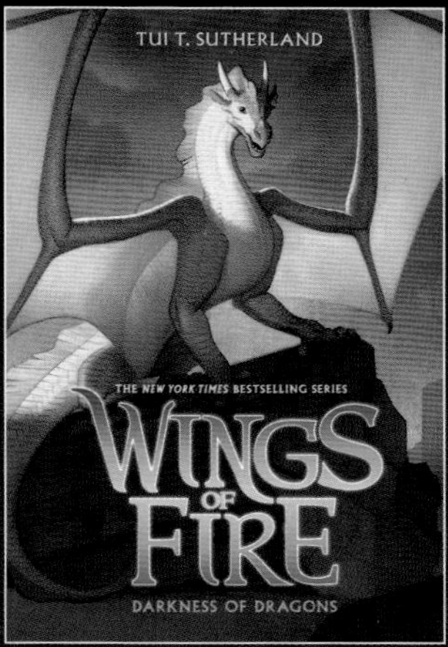
TUI T. SUTHERLAND
THE NEW YORK TIMES BESTSELLING SERIES
WINGS OF FIRE
DARKNESS OF DRAGONS

EBOOK ORIGINALS

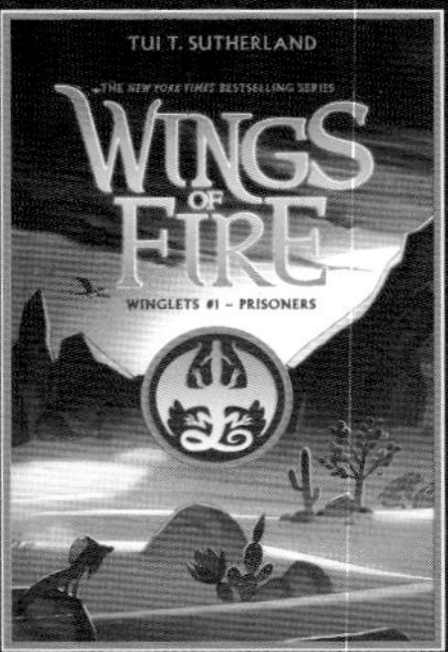
TUI T. SUTHERLAND
THE NEW YORK TIMES BESTSELLING SERIES
WINGS OF FIRE
WINGLETS #1 – PRISONERS

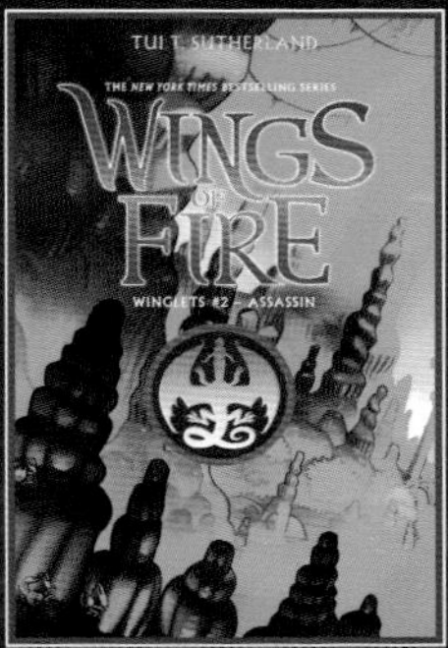
TUI T. SUTHERLAND
THE NEW YORK TIMES BESTSELLING SERIES
WINGS OF FIRE
WINGLETS #2 – ASSASSIN

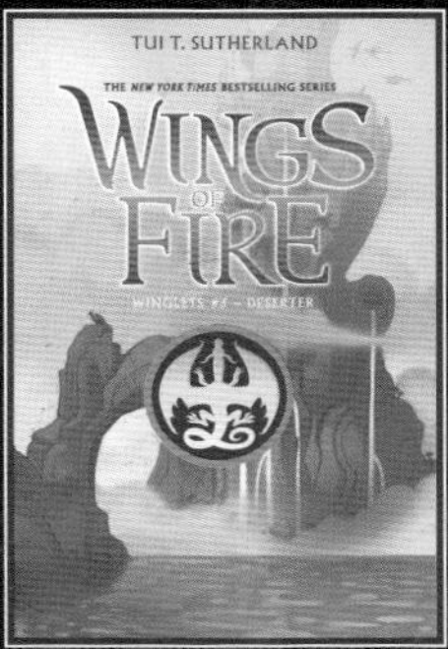
TUI T. SUTHERLAND
THE NEW YORK TIMES BESTSELLING SERIES
WINGS OF FIRE

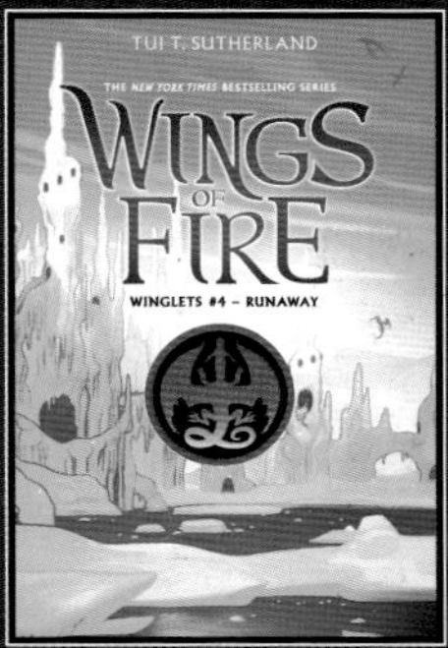
TUI T. SUTHERLAND
THE NEW YORK TIMES BESTSELLING SERIES
WINGS OF FIRE
WINGLETS #4 – RUNAWAY

the Menagerie trilogy, and the Pet Trouble series, as well as a contributing author to the bestselling Spirit Animals and Seekers series (as part of the Erin Hunter team). In 2009, she was a two-day champion on *Jeopardy!* She lives in Massachusetts with her wonderful husband, two adorable sons, and two very patient dogs. To learn more about Tui's books, visit her online at www.tuibooks.com.

BARRY DEUTSCH is an award-winning cartoonist and the creator of the Hereville series of graphic novels, about yet another troll-fighting 11-year-old Orthodox Jewish girl. He lives in Portland, Oregon, with a variable number of cats and fish.

MIKE HOLMES has drawn for the comics series Bravest Warriors and Adventure Time and is the creator of the art project *Mikenesses*. His books include *Secret Coders* (written by Gene Luen Yang), *Animal Crackers: Circus Mayhem* (written by Scott Christian Sava), and the *True Story* collection. He lives in Philadelphia with his wife, Meredith; Heidi the dog; and Ella the cat.

MAARTA LAIHO spends her days and nights as a comic colorist, where her work includes the comics series Lumberjanes, Adventure Time, and The Mighty Zodiac. When she's not doing that, she can be found hoarding houseplants and talking to her cat. She lives in the woods of Maine.